THE CELL & OTHER
TRANSMORPHIC TALES

THE CELL &
OTHER
TRANSMORPHIC
TALES

DAVID CASE

Edited with an Introduction by
STEPHEN JONES

Afterword by
KIM NEWMAN

VALANCOURT BOOKS

Published by Valancourt Books, Richmond, Virginia
http://www.valancourtbooks.com

ISBN 978-1-943910-06-9
Also available as an electronic book.

All Valancourt Books publications are printed on acid free paper that meets all ANSI standards for archival quality paper.

Set in Dante MT

Contents

Introduction

I FIRST MET DAVID CASE in October 1979. I was attending the Fifth World Fantasy Convention in Providence, Rhode Island. It was my fourth successive World Fantasy, and I was still overawed by both the convention and just how different America was from Britain in the 1970s.

And so it was that I found myself on the Saturday afternoon sitting with a group of authors in the bar of the Biltmore Plaza Hotel and experiencing with fellow Brit Peter Tremayne (Peter Berresford Ellis) the previously unknown delights of free hot food and copious cuts of cheese served during the "Happy Hour". (Back in those days, Peter was a well-known horror writer, long before he became world-famous as the author of the popular "Sister Fidelma" mysteries.)

Anyway, we were enjoying a few beers and good conversation when Ramsey Campbell returned from the bar with a man I had never seen before wearing a fisherman's cap. A big man. An outdoors-type of man.

"Do you know who *this* is?" Ramsey asked me, almost in awe, indicating his impressive-looking companion. "Er . . . no," I replied. Everyone around the table held equally blank looks.

"This is *David Case*," he said. I could tell by the note of awe in Ramsey's voice that this was someone I should take notice of. But, to tell the truth, I was still none the wiser.

While Ramsey introduced David and his English wife, Valerie, around the table, I wracked my brains trying to remember where I had come across his name before.

It turned out that David and his wife had come into town to buy some supplies and had stopped into one of his favorite bars for a drink. He had no idea that the World Fantasy Convention was being held in the same hotel that weekend or that, even more bizarrely, his current editor—the late, great James Turner of Arkham House—was also in attendance.

While all these pleasantries were going on, I was desperately sifting through my beer-impaired memory for where I had heard of David before—and then I had it! Herbert van Thal's legendary, if not to say infamous, *The Pan Book of Horror Stories*.

During the early 1970s I had read a number of David's stories in that annual anthology series. Not only did some of them take up more pages in the book than almost all the other contributions combined, but the quality of the writing was noticeably superior to much of the misogynistic and sadistic dross that van Thal was using in the series around that time. What I did not know at the time was that a number of these stories and novellas had been culled from David's first two collections of horror stories.

Following our very pleasant meeting in the Biltmore bar in Providence, I kept an eye out for more of David's work and was rewarded a couple of years later by his Egyptian novel, *The Third Grave* (1981), published by the venerable Arkham House imprint with illustrations by Stephen E. Fabian.

In fact, David was busy writing in various genres, and he has reputedly produced more than three hundred books, ranging from softcore porn to popular westerns, under at least seventeen pseudonyms. His 1975 western, *Plumb Drillin'*, was optioned as a movie project for Steve McQueen before the actor's untimely death in 1980, and David's work has been adapted for film twice.

Since my first meeting with him back in Providence, I had heard that David had been travelling around Europe, spending much of his time in Greece and Spain. I was therefore surprised to learn from Ramsey Campbell (there's that man again!) that David had settled in London, less than half-an-hour's journey from where I lived.

We eventually renewed our acquaintance, and over the next couple of decades I was able to publish a number of his stories in my anthologies, bringing several of his classic tales back into print for a whole new generation of readers.

David Case has always been interested in the theme of lycanthropy since his first collection, the now-fabulously rare (and expensive!) *The Cell: Three Tales of Horror*, published by Hill & Wang (US) and Macdonald & Co. (UK) in 1969. The title novella is a modern masterpiece of psychological horror that recalls the work of Edgar

Allan Poe and stands as one of the most powerful werewolf stories ever written.

The author continued to explore the theme of transformation in "Strange Roots" and "Among the Wolves", both of which originally appeared in his second collection, *Fengriffen and Other Stories* (1971), but were not included in the American edition which was simply titled *Fengriffen: A Chilling Tale*, while "A Cross to Bear" was an infrequent original story which was published in *The 22nd Pan Book of Horror Stories* (1981).

"The Hunter", another masterful novella, also originally appeared in *The Cell* and prefigured the psychological horror fiction of authors such as David Morrell. In 1974 renowned fantasy author Richard Matheson adapted the story for director Dan Curtis, who turned it into an ABC-TV movie entitled *Scream of the Wolf*. Peter Graves and Clint Walker played two macho friends, one of whom was a werewolf. Unfortunately, the talky drama did not do justice to its source material.

David's Canadian werewolf murder mystery *Wolf Tracks* was published in paperback by Belmont Tower in 1980 with a cover depicting Lon Chaney, Jr.'s classic movie Wolf Man. He went on to explore the origin of the werewolf myth in his short prehistoric novel "The Cave", which appeared in the collection *Pelican Cay & Other Disquieting Tales* that I put together in 2010 for PS Publishing to celebrate the author's stint at being a Guest of Honour that year at the World Horror Convention held in Brighton, England. The collection took its title from the author's powerful zombie novella, which was nominated for a World Fantasy Award in 2001.

Meanwhile, Centipede Press has recently produced a major retrospective of David Case's fiction in its "Masters of the Weird Tale" series, edited by S.T. Joshi, and now Valancourt Books is issuing new compilations of his work in attractive, affordable editions.

David's meticulous attention to detail has always set his writing apart from much of the literature labeled as "horror", which can only be applauded in a genre that all too often sacrifices both substance and style for cheap effect.

David Case is a true original and, as with his previous collections, this present volume showcases that individuality in every story. These transmorphic tales combine the psychological with the super-

natural to dazzle the reader with their author's precise command of
language, setting, and character.

Stephen Jones
London
September 2015

The Cell

WHEN MY OLD AUNT HELEN DIED I inherited her house. I was the only relative. I wasn't sad about her death because I hardly knew her, and I wasn't overjoyed about the house because it was an ancient thing, ugly and dilapidated and unpleasant. I suppose that it had been a decent enough house in its day, but Aunt Helen had lived there all alone for many years, ever since her husband disappeared. She was slightly crazy and never left the house. The house and the old woman sort of fell apart together. Sometimes she could be seen rocking on the front porch, cackling or laughing or moaning. It was a singular sound and rather hard to define. No one knew just how crazy she was, and no one cared. She seemed to be harmless enough and they left her alone and in the end she died quite peaceably of old age. So the house was mine.

I went there one miserable afternoon to look it over and see if there was anything that I wanted to keep before putting it up for auction. There was nothing. I would have left after the first ten minutes if the rain had not increased. But it increased. It came down very heavily and I had only a light coat with me. I decided to wait and see if it would let up presently. There was nothing else to do so I continued to poke around those damp and dirty rooms. Nothing seemed of the slightest value on the ground floor. I opened the basement door, thinking there might be something stored down there, but a gust of foul air belched out and I shut the door again. I was certain there would be nothing worth going down for. Instead, I went upstairs and looked through the bedrooms. They were all just skeletons of rooms, except the one that Aunt Helen must have used. There was some furniture there but it was broken and worthless. I was ready to leave and it was only some whim of chance that made me open one of the bureau drawers. That was where I found the book.

It was moldy with age. It had been torn and then repaired with tape. When I opened it the binding groaned stiffly and the pages crackled. They were dry and stained and creased, but I could still read the writing on them. It was in a man's hand, small and precise and neat and careful. The hand of a boring person, I thought. It appeared to be a diary or journal of some sort. I read a line or two, started to toss it back in the drawer, read another line. I opened it towards the middle and read a few more words. Then I closed the book and took it downstairs and sat in the front room, by the window. The light was dull and the pages brittle, but I began to read that extraordinary journal. I didn't stop ... I didn't pause ... until I had read it all. I couldn't. I was glued to the chair. My spine seemed fixed and my flesh fluid and creeping around it. The light grew dimmer but my eyes would not leave those pages. Beside my chair the rain was drumming against the glass, the sky was dark with clouds unbroken, and the wind rushed across the unkempt lawn. It was the right day to read such a book.

This is the book:

May 4
God! It was horrible last night.

Last night it was the worst that it has been to date. I wish that I could remember the other times more clearly. I should have started keeping a record earlier, I know that now. But it took a great effort to begin this book that will show what I am, and I could not bring myself to do it before. At any rate, I am sure that last night was much worse than ever before. Perhaps that is why I feel that I must start this record now. Perhaps I must drain my feelings off in some way. It makes me wonder if I will be able to force myself to go down to my cell again next month ...

But of course I must. There can be no doubt of that, and I must never attempt to rationalize about it. No excuse will do. What I must do is to go down earlier next month. I can never leave it too late, or who knows what might happen? I suppose I could control it, but ... I left it just a bit too long last night, I think. I didn't mean to, but it is so difficult to tell. When I know that the thing is going to begin soon I get nervous and anticipate the first signs, and it is often impossible to tell the anticipation from the beginnings. The change starts with a certain nervous feeling and when I am already nervous it can begin before I realize it. That frightens me. I shall have to be more careful in the future.

I am in my room now. I am trying to remember all the details. This record will be useless if it is not completely accurate. It will be of no value to me, or to anyone else. I have not yet decided if anyone else will ever see it. Under the circumstances that is a terrible decision to be forced to make. I know that if I ever offer this record, I must also offer proof. That is the terrible part. I don't want anyone to think I am mad . . .

Last night my wife began to get agitated just after dinner. We were in the front room. She kept looking at her wristwatch and then glancing sideways at me. I didn't like the way she let her eyes slide towards me without moving her head. I can't blame her, of course, and I pretended not to notice. I dreaded the thought of going down, and wanted to put it off as long as possible. It wasn't really very late and the sky was still light. I was sitting beside the window where I would be able to know when it was time. I pretended to be absorbed in the evening paper, but I was much too restless to read. I just saw the print as a blur. But I don't think that was a symptom. All the lights were on in the room and I was careful not to let Helen see me looking out of the window. I didn't want to make her any more troubled than she already was, poor thing. But, at the same time, I can remember feeling a strange sense of pleasure as I noticed the frightened look in her eyes. It was almost a sexual pleasure, I think. I don't know. Perhaps it was a preliminary sign of my disease, or perhaps it is a reaction normal to men. I can't tell, because I am not like other men. Still, I felt disgusted with myself as soon as I recognized that feeling, and so I knew that nothing had really started to take effect.

The bad part at that time was the contrast. Sitting there in that comfortable living room with the bright lights and the leather chairs and the new carpet and, at the time, knowing what was coming in an hour or so . . . it was grotesque. Leading a completely normal life most of the time, and trying to pretend that it was normal, made the change so much more repulsive. It made me almost hate myself, even though I fully understand that it is a sickness and no fault of my own. Perhaps no fault of anyone's, possibly the fault of a distant ancestor, I don't know. But certainly I am not to blame. If I were I would kill myself, I think . . .

I kept stealing glances at the gilt-framed mirror on the wall and expecting to see some sign, although I knew that it was too early. It had to be too early, or else it would have been too late. Even if I were able to control myself in the first stages it would have been too horrible for my wife. I doubt that I could have borne it myself, if I saw it begin. If I looked in that normal, gilt-framed mirror, and actually saw it . . .

That is why there is no mirror in the cell.

At nine o'clock I stood up. The sky was darkening outside the window. The window was bordered by pretty lace curtains. My wife looked quickly at me, then looked away. I carefully folded the newspaper and put it down in the chair. I looked normal and calm.

"Well, it's time," I said.

"Yes, I suppose so," she said, and I could hear the struggle to keep relief out of her voice.

We went into the hallway and down the dark stairs to the basement. My wife went down first. They are old wooden stairs with the clammy basement wall on one side and a handrail on the other. This is an old house and although I have kept the upstairs in good repair the basement is ancient and gloomy. I cannot seem to force myself to go down there at normal times. But that is understandable enough, under the circumstances. And, in a way, it seems proper that it should be dank and unkempt. It at least lessens the contrast at the last minute.

The stairs groaned underfoot. The dead air seemed to climb the steps to meet us, and suddenly I felt dizzy. I put one hand against the moldy wall for support. My foot slipped and I had to clutch at the handrail. I caught myself, but my foot passed one step and banged down on the next. My wife turned at the noise. Her face was terrible. Her eyes were white and wide. Her mouth was open. For a long instant she could not control that expression. I have seldom seen more fear and horror in a face. Never without cause certainly. And certainly she had no cause. She must know that I would never hurt her. Still, I cannot blame her for being afraid. It was the horror that hurt me. I hated to see the horror that I could inspire in one I loved. And then the expression vanished and she smiled, a little lip-biting smile. I think that she was ashamed that she had shown her fear. I smiled back at her, and that was when I realized that I had left it to the very last moment. My mouth was stiff and my teeth felt too large. I knew that my control was going.

The cell is at the far end of the basement. I went ahead of her and opened the door myself. She stood back a bit, I walked in and looked out of the door and smiled again. Her face was very pale, almost illuminated, in the dark basement. She moved forward and it was as if her face were floating, disembodied. Her throat was the whitest part of all, and I could see the veins in her neck. I looked away from the veins in her neck. She tried her best to look as though she regretted having to close the door. I suppose she did, in a way. Then she closed it and I heard the key turn in the lock and the heavy bar slide into place. I listened behind the door and for a few moments there was no sound. I knew that she was waiting outside. I could picture her standing there, looking at the barred door with a mixture of relief and regret on that phosphorescent face. And then I heard her footsteps very faintly as she went back to the stairs, I heard the upstairs door close. I felt sorry for both of us.

I sat down in the bare corner and buried my face in my hands. It was still my face. But it was very stiff. I could tell that it would not be long. It seems to be getting quicker and easier for the change to come each month. It is not as painful. I wonder if that is a good sign or a bad sign?

But I can't really talk about that yet. It would be too hard to write about the details. It would be almost as hard as it is for me to go into that cell, knowing the agonies to come . . .

When my wife knocked at the door in the morning I was still very weak. But I was all right. I was surprised that it was morning already. There is no way to tell time inside the cell, of course. I do not take my watch with me.

Helen did not hear me answer the first time, and knocked again before she opened the door. She opened it a crack and I saw one big eye peering in. Then she saw that everything was all right, and she opened the door wide. I am glad that she is cautious, of course, but still it hurts me. Damn this disease!

She didn't ask how I was. She knows that I can't talk about it. I wonder if she is curious? I suppose she must be. She doesn't know that I am keeping this journal. I am going to keep it locked in the desk in my study. I'm sitting at the desk now, looking out of the window at the trees. Everything is very peaceful today, and last night is more nightmare than memory. If it only were! It is strange the way that the memories come through to me, after I have become myself again. I must think about that and try to describe it later. I don't know why, though. I don't know why I feel compelled to keep this record. It must be some form of release. I feel more relaxed now, at any rate. I am going to rest now. My body suffers the damage that the other thing inflicts on itself. We share the same body and I am exhausted. I will write later.

May 6

I have been thinking about the disease. I thought about it all day yesterday. It is hard to do this clearly, because when I am . . . not myself . . . I seem to have no thoughts. Or, if I do, I don't remember them after I have become myself again. I suppose that, at those times, my mind must work much as an animal's does. I am left with only a vague, general impression of how I felt. How it felt. I do not know if I and it are the same, but we share the same body. Anyway, there is certainly no reasoning involved when I am changed. It must be purely instinct that motivates the thing, and instinct does not fit well into the pattern of the human brain. Or does my brain also change? The impressions are very strong. I can recall the impressions, almost to the point of summoning them up again. But this is simply a matter of remembering what the other thing was feeling at that time, not what it was doing, or what it looked like. It is a matter of recalling an emotion without the circumstances that caused it. But what a powerful emotion! It is always hard to express a feeling in words, and this is a very complex feeling.

I think it was need, most of all. Need and frustration. But there is all that violence and hatred and lust mingled with it. I don't suppose any normal man could ever feel it in quite the same way. Perhaps emotion is always stronger when it is instinctive and when there is no rational force working on it. It all came from within and seemed to have nothing to do with the actual physical action. It burned like an inferno within the thing. That was what drove it to its wild ferocity. That was what it felt at the time.

As far as what actually happens . . . I see that objectively, divorced from the emotion and impressions, as though I were a separate person who had been in the cell and had witnessed the whole thing. (God help any person who ever had! It would surely drive him mad ... although I doubt that there would be time for madness, locked in that cell with the thing that I became.)

I can clearly see the scene within that cell. It flings itself at those padded walls, tearing at them with talons and ripping with terrible fangs. It drops to the floor, crouches for a moment, snarling, then springs at the walls again. It is driven by that rage within, again and again, in a frenzied passion. It pauses only to summon renewed rage, and then springs again, more savagely than before, until at last its energy is spent and it grovels, panting and waiting. Last night it attempted to batter the door down, but the door is too strong.

I wonder if my wife can hear the sounds that it makes as it attacks the walls? Or worse, far worse, the sounds that come from its snarling lips? That would be ghastly. They are very revolting sounds.

At dinner yesterday I noticed the way that she looked at me as I ate. We had steak. I have always liked my steak rare. But she looked at me as though she expected I would tear at the meat like some wild beast. Perhaps she does hear ... Thank heavens that she can never see it! It takes her several days to recover as it is ... to become normal again.

I am quite normal now, of course.

May 7
I am completely sane.

It occurs to me that I have not yet stated that, and it is necessary. If anyone ever reads this, they must understand that I am not crazy. It is not a disease of the mind, it is a disease of the body. It is purely physical. It must be, to cause the physical change that it does. I haven't yet written about the change. That will be very hard, although I can see it objectively. I can see my hands and body, and feel my face. I cannot see my face, of course, because there is no mirror. I don't know if I could bear it if I had a memory of what my face must become. And I don't know if I can describe it honestly, or honestly describe it. Perhaps some night I shall bring this book into my cell with me and write as long as I can — describe the changes as they occur in my body, until my mind can no longer cope with the effort ... until it is no longer my body.

The question that plagues me most in this is whether any other human being has ever suffered from the same disease. Somehow I think it would be easier to bear up to it, if I knew that I was not the only one. It is not a case of misery enjoying company; it is just that I want the reassurance that it is not peculiar to me, that it is in no way my fault that I suffer with it. I can be patient under this trial only so long as I know that it could not have been prevented.

I have tried to find a case similar to mine. I have done a great deal of research . . . enough to make the librarian suspicious, if she were of a superstitious nature. But she is not. She is an old maid and she is fat. I believe she thinks that lycanthropy is the study of butterflies. But the research has turned up nothing. The moldy old volumes and the big, leather-bound psychological books record legends and myths on the one hand, and madness on the other. There are cases that are similar in the recorded details, but in each of these the subject was mentally ill. There were no physical changes, although sometimes the poor madman thought that there were. And yet . . . there must be a basis for the legends. All legends have some anchor in the truth. I cling to that belief. I must cling to something.

My grandfather on my father's side came from the Balkans. Somewhere in the Transylvanian Alps. I don't know if that has any relevance, but most of the legends seem to have begun in that area. It is surely a diseased area. And, too, I feel sure that it must be an inherited disease. It is nothing that I could have caught. I have always been a temperate and clean-living man. I practice moderation in all things. I neither drink nor smoke nor womanize, and my health has always been good. So I am certain that the disease was congenital. I suffer for the sins of my forebears through some jest of fate — some terrible jest of a wicked fate that punishes the innocent for the crimes of the guilty.

The disease must be carried in the blood or, more likely, in the genes. I suppose that it is passed on to one's children in a recessive state, waiting, lurking latently in man after man down through the generations until, once every century . . . once every thousand years perhaps . . . there is the proper combination to turn it into a dominant trait. And then it becomes a malignant, raging disease, growing stronger as the victim grows older, gaining strength from the body that it shares, and tries to destroy . . .

I must believe this, and I do.

I must not think that I am unique, or that I could be in any way, no matter how indirectly and innocently, responsible for it. I must know that it was a curse born with me as surely as my brown hair or greenish eyes, and that it was predestined from the time—who knows how many generations ago?—when my ancestor committed some vile act that brought him into contact with the germs of the sickness. I hate my ancestors for this, but I am grateful that it is their sin and not my own. If I thought that any action of my life had brought about this affliction the thought would surely drive me mad. It would destroy my mind. I have a great fear of that. It is a rational fear. This thing that I suffer from is enough to drive anyone to insanity . . .

June 2

Last week I thought seriously about going to a doctor. It is out of the question. I knew that all along, of course, but the fact that I even considered it shows how desperate I have become. I am ready to clutch at straws; to take any risk that has the slightest chance of saving me. But I know that I must cure myself; any salvation must come from within.

It was my wife who put the idea into my head; indirectly, of course. She mentioned something about psychiatrists—something that she had read in the newspaper, I think—just some vague statement so that she could use the term while talking with me, and suggest it without saying so. Well, her plan worked, because I did think about it, but it is quite impossible.

I was hurt that she mentioned a psychiatrist instead of a medical doctor. She knows as well as I that it is a physical affliction. I have told her that often enough. Still, she has a point. No doctor would believe me. They would think me insane, and refer me to a psychiatrist anyway. And the psychiatrist would be useless because he would try to cure a nonexistent concept. The only way that I could prove that the disease is physical would be to have them actually witness the change, and that must never be.

That thought gave me the first laugh that I have had for a long, long time. I can picture myself in the psychiatrist's office. It is at night. The night. I am lying on my back on his leather couch and he is sitting in a chair beside me. I have just finished telling him all about my illness while he listened patiently, nodding from time to time. When I finish explaining he begins to talk in his low, confident tones. He is a very professional type with a bald head and gold-rimmed spectacles. He sits with his legs crossed, his notebook on his knee. He is not looking at me while he speaks, he is looking down at his notes. And I am not looking at him. I am looking at the window. I see the whole scene so clearly. I can even see his degrees framed on the wall. They are on the wall opposite the window, where the moonlight glitters on the gold seals. There are rows of huge and heavy books and a large desk. I see everything and then I look at the window again. The change always comes much more quickly and smoothly when I can see the moon than when I am in the cell. I feel it begin. The doctor talks on, softly. Perhaps he tells me that it is all nonsense, that it is impossible; that it is merely a figment of my imagination, a delusion of a sick mind. He turns towards me to impress his point. He looks into my eyes. And his face ... this is what makes me laugh ... his face would break and shatter. That cold, scientific, intelligent face would plunge down through all the long aeons of time, and become the primitive and superstitious and terrified face of his ancestors. And then ...

I don't suppose that it is really so funny, but it is pleasant to laugh again.

June 3

Tonight I must go to the cell.

I dread it. So does my wife. Yesterday I detected signs of nervousness in her. She is getting worse. She hinted again that I should get help. Help! What help is there for me? But she doesn't seem to understand. Perhaps she is blocking the terrible truth from her mind. Perhaps she would prefer it if I were mad. But it is her sanity I worry about at these times, not my own. For myself I can only hope that it does not get worse, and that I shall be able to live my life out this way, normal but for that one night each month ... But how I dread that night, that cell! Even when I am no longer myself, I am still me to the extent that we share the same body, and that the emotions and the impressions remain with me and hurt me. Even now, a month later, I can still recall the feeling, not objectively the way that I can remember the way that the thing moved and acted, but deep inside me as one recalls a great pain from the past. It is unbearable to think of a future like this. I can bear the present, but not the thought of the future. And if it should get worse . . .

But perhaps it may get better. That is possible. Diseases can cure themselves, bodies can develop tolerances and antibodies and immunity. I can only hope for that as I face the future — hope that someday the month will pass and it will not happen and I will know that I am on the way to recovery.

I must never have children, of course. Even if I recover there can be no children. The disease must never be passed on. My wife is sorry about this. She wants children. She doesn't seem to understand why it is impossible, why it would be a monstrous act. I think that she truly might prefer it if I were insane. Sometimes I even think that she doubts me . . . that she thinks that I am not quite right. Well, of course I am not all right. But I mean . . . sometimes she seems to think that I am insane. There! I have stated that for this record. But perhaps I am being overly sensitive.

I have a right to be.

I have neglected this record during the past month. I meant to write every day, but I found it too oppressive to write about it when it was not imminent. I prefer to forget it as long and as often as I can. Thinking about it only reminds me that the night must come again. This night I intend to bring this notebook into the cell with me. I want to record as much as I can . . . perhaps the record will prove valuable. Perhaps it will only be disgusting. But I must try, I must gain all the possible knowledge that I can. It is my only hope that I may find a cure.

I must rest now. Tonight will be exhausting. It is a lovely clear day and I know that the sky will be sparkling. It will be an effort to go to the cell.

June 3 (Night)

Well, the door is locked and barred. I listened until her footsteps went up the stairs, and the door closed at the top. Now I am alone in the cell. I feel all right. I came down earlier tonight. I was afraid to wait any longer. It was a good idea to bring this book with me. It is something to do, something to occupy myself with while I wait. Anything is better than just sitting here and waiting for it to happen.

I keep watching my hands as I write; my fingernails. They are all right. Nothing has begun. My fingers are long and straight and my nails are clipped. I must watch carefully so that I can detect the very first signs. I want to be able to describe everything in complete detail.

There is no furniture here in the cell. Furniture would only be destroyed. I am sitting in one corner with my knees drawn up and the notebook on them. The pages look slightly tinted, I should have thought to put a brighter bulb in the light. The light is in a recess in the ceiling and covered by a wire netting. The netting is a little twisted, but I don't remember doing that. I wouldn't, probably. It is light enough to observe the cell, anyway. I have never really noticed it before. I suppose that I was always too concerned with myself to notice my surroundings. But it is earlier tonight . . .

The cell is concrete. The walls are thick and the door is metal with large bolts. The walls are heavily padded on the inside. Helen and I did the padding ourselves, of course. It might have been difficult to explain to the contractor why we wanted a padded cell in our basement. I think that we told him the concrete structure was for our dog. He didn't seem curious about it. We don't really have a dog. Dogs don't like me. I frighten them. I suppose that they can sense my affliction even when I am normal. That is further proof that it is a physical disease. I killed a dog once, but it was a vicious dog and I had to.

The smell is stifling and musty, I expect that the walls are damp under the pads, and the stuffing has begun to molder. We shall have to replace the padding soon. I must try to make the cell as bearable as possible. The pads are ripped in places and the stuffing is running out and curling to the floor. The cover of the padding is tough and thick and smooth, so I know that my . . . its . . . talons must be very powerful and sharp. They must be able to slice through those pads like a knife through butter. I wonder if I have ever broken a nail tearing at the walls? I should look in the ripped places to see. It would be evidence of an actual change. I will look later; it seems likely that I will find something. I know the terrible rage that drives the thing at those walls, the unbelievable strength that it possesses, and it seems that even those heavy nails would be splintered by the force that is behind them.

Those wicked claws! I shudder when I think of them, moving at the ends of constricted and hooked fingers. The way that they can rend and tear those heavy pads . . . think what they could do to the softness of flesh! Think what they would do to a man's throat! It makes me tremble all over to imagine it. I can almost feel what it would be like and the feeling sickens me. But it persists. It wants to be recognized. I can see how those fingers would close, drawing the white skin up in little trails until the skin parted and the fingers sank into the bubbling, pulsing throat. I can see the talons disappear, the fingers themselves gouge in, feel the heat of the blood as it comes spurting out into my face. Taste the hot, salty blood, smell it until my head reels and everything fades away and there is only the stricken face beneath me. I can see that face change and hear the death that would gurgle in his throat as my fangs . . . as I bring myself . . . soft throat as my fangs . . . close . . . soft, hot flesh and they sink in . . . and . . . tear . . .

June 4

I have just finished patching this book together. I had to use tape where it was torn. I must have ripped it last night, during the sickness. I don't remember doing it. I don't think that it was deliberate, it is just that anything within reach is destroyed in the blind fury. The book was not methodically torn in half or quarters, but just mutilated at random. The front cover was torn to shreds, but the pages are all still readable. My fountain pen had been snapped in two, like a twig. It is hard to imagine such unleashed energy and power. I have always been a strong man, and I have always kept myself in perfect fitness through exercise and moderation, but the strength that comes with the change is beyond comprehension. It seems that the very muscles and sinews of my body must change, that it must be internal as well as external. Perhaps we do not share the same body, but the same small part of the brain that remembers. That would be encouraging, to be able to think of the thing as a different entity. And yet my own body bears the bruises and the marks of the tortured flesh. The two bodies cannot exist at the same time. It is very confusing, it is beyond my powers of reasoning, and I am as rational as any man and more so than most. How many other men could face this thing that I struggle with and retain their sanity? I am proud of that. I am not a vain man, but of that strength of mind I am proud.

I didn't write about the change. I remember feeling it start, and it seems that I was writing, but somehow it is not recorded. The last few lines of what I wrote are scribbled and blurred and do not look at all like my handwriting, and I suppose that was a symptom. I was writing about how strong the thing's hands were and then it just seems to come to an end, in the middle of a sentence. I imagine that my fingers had started to contract while I wrote, and that would account for the different style. But there is nothing there about the change.

The change seemed different last night. Not greater, but different somehow. I think that I have reached a new stage in the disease, and that the disease is changing . . . perhaps modifying.

The thing is beginning to think more. Or else I am beginning to remember more. Whichever it is, I can distinctly recall certain thoughts along with the impressions this time. I remember all that frustration and need and hatred, but I also remember snatches of vague thought. Not my thoughts. Its thoughts. They are closer to the human than I imagined they would be. It is hard to envisage human thoughts in that monstrous body. Disturbing. I do not want to share my mind with it. But I remember that it was reasoning, trying to figure some way to get out of the cell. I remember a pause in the violence while it crouched and rolled its white eyes around, seeking some weak point in the walls, the door. Perhaps it was seeking some deception to get Helen to open the door. There was no escape, of course. We have taken all necessary precautions. Even if it were able to reason as well as I, it could figure no way to get out of the cell.

But that is the change in the disease, that reasoning power. It is possible that the thing is becoming more normal, more human. It is possible that the person I am and the thing that I become are drawing closer together. But it is impossible to say which of us is moving towards that closer relationship, whether the disease is conquering me, or I am beginning to cure myself, I cannot decide if this new development is a good thing or a bad thing. It makes me tremble. I am sweating profusely and my stomach is knotted with fright.

I am calmer now. I lay down for a few minutes. I can still taste the blood and foam on my lips, although I have brushed my teeth several times. I bit my lip last night. It is swollen and painful. I cannot get the taste from my mouth—I suppose that it is all in my mind. It was nauseating to awaken this morning and swallow and know that I could not brush my teeth and rinse my mouth until Helen came and let me out. It seemed as if I waited a very long time, but there was no way to tell. Time seems to stand still when it is enclosed in that cell. Time is surely a concrete dimension, and relative to the other dimensions. Perhaps it is affected by my disease. It would be interesting if there were some way to measure it.

I am sure that it lasted longer last night. It certainly seemed to. It may be that it seemed longer because there were more impressions and memories, but my wife said that when she knocked at the usual time this morning there was no answer from the cell. I always call out that everything is all right before she opens the door, and this morning I did not call at the usual hour. She said that she heard . . . certain sounds . . . but that there was no answer. She did not say what the sounds were like.

So she went back upstairs and waited another hour. I can imagine how frightened and worried she must have been during that time, wondering what had happened. Poor woman. She loves me so, and she cannot really understand. She did not know about the illness when she married me, and it was a terrible shock. I am grateful that she has stood up under the strain so well. She must worry and suffer as much as I, in a different, woman's way.

After another hour had elapsed she came down and knocked at the cell door again. I answered this time, and she opened the door. She opened it very slowly, and I could hear her intake of breath when she first looked in. She must have been half mad with fear for me. I don't think she would be afraid of me.

I don't remember her knocking the first time. I was surprised when she told me. I do have an indistinct impression of crouching beside the door with my thighs tensed and taut and my hands open in front of me, as though I were waiting for something to open that door. But it is very vague. It could have been at any time. I know that I would never wait that way for my wife.

June 6
I have been very worried, thinking about how it lasted longer than usual this month. Longer than it ever did before, I think. I am trying to get the history of my illness in context, from the beginning, so that I can follow the progress and the process. I feel that there is definitely a change coming, and pray that it may be the first step towards recovery. Up until now it has merely become worse time after time. It would seem that since it lasted longer the last time it is just another step in the same direction, but there was also the fact that I remembered the thing's thoughts this time. That has never happened before, not since I really began to change. That is much closer to how it was when it first began. It may be the first sign that I am on the way back, that a cure has begun. It may have taken longer this time because it was less intense. I don't really see how it can get any worse than it is now . . .

Thinking back on my life, I find that I cannot tell when it first began. It must have been very gradual. I surely would remember if it came on me suddenly, all at once. A weaker mind might block the memory out to save itself from the knowledge, but I am sure that I would have faced it.

Had I only known the truth in those days there might have been some way to prevent it. I doubt it, but there might have been. But how was I to know? I was never a superstitious child. I did not even believe in . . . the thing that I become. I did not believe in Santa Claus, or fairies, or witches, or the elves that leave money under a pillow and take away the baby teeth. My parents would have none of that nonsense, and told me the truth from the first. So how was I to believe in the existence of . . . I will not write the word. I know what I am doing, that I have a block about admitting what I know to be true, as though the admission would condemn me more than the fact. But I cannot help that, and it is not the mental block of a weak man whose mind denies the truth, it is just that I rebel at putting the word on paper. I know the word. I think it. It dances in my thoughts, and I am strong enough to recognize it there, and make no effort to deny it. I live with the knowledge as best I can. I know that, all along, through all my life, the inherited sickness was there inside my blood, being carried to every capillary of my body, taking hold and growing stronger as I myself grew, waiting, lurking . . . I know that now, but how could anyone have predicted it? It was no fault of mine.

I was always a rather tempestuous child. I used to get angry, to throw tantrums. But many children do. It is common enough. There was never any physical change in me. No warnings. And yet . . . my bursts of violence, when I would fight with other children or break my favorite playthings . . . those outbursts did not seem to stem from any recognizable fact. They were not the result of something that angered or frustrated me; they seemed to come on for no reason, at any time, whether I was happy or unhappy at the moment they began. I can remember one time when a neighbour, a boy my own age but smaller, threw a rock and hit me over the eye. It hurt awfully. It broke the skin and a trickle of blood ran down the side of my face. The boy was frightened then, because he had hit me for no reason, and because I was much stronger and could have easily punished him. But I did not. I did not even get angry, which amazed him, because he knew my reputation for flaring up. I simply looked at him with the blood running down and I felt no anger at all. I can remember licking the blood from the corner of my mouth where it had gathered. I felt a bit dizzy, from the blow I suppose, and I just stood there and licked the blood away and did nothing. The other boy must have thought that I was afraid of him because I did not retaliate, because after that he persecuted me. He would wait for me after school and throw stones at me and push me. And sometimes he would hit me with his fist. I never became angry with him. I never wanted to punish him or hurt him and I took his abuse without any resentment. He used to boast about how I was terrorized and all the other children used to make fun of me about this, but I didn't care. I have never cared what other people thought. This was an example of how my temper was not aroused at times when it would have been fully justified.

And at other times . . . for no apparent reason . . . I can recall one evening, towards dusk, when I was playing with my favorite toy, a clockwork train. I had been playing with it for some time and was quite happy. And then, suddenly, I picked it up from the tracks and smashed it against the floor until it was broken to pieces. I continued to smash it, over and over again. My mother came into my room and was very angry that I had broken it, and threatened never to buy me another toy, but I didn't seem to care. Even later, the next day, I did not regret the loss of my train. When I thought of it I merely felt as though it had been a good thing to break it. I felt glad that I had done it. It seemed satisfying.

It was inconsistencies like those two that made me different from other temperamental children. I realize, now, that the outbursts must have followed the same cycle as the illness follows now, but at that time I had no reason to think about any regularity, or detect any rhythm. Neither did my parents. They must have supposed it was merely the storms of adolescence, and I don't think that it worried them unduly.

I don't remember very much about my mother. I suppose that she was overshadowed by my father. He was a big man, straight and broad shouldered and strict. He was religious and very moral, and I have him to thank for the fact that I was brought up right, and that I have always avoided all vices and corruption. Many a time he lectured me, in his deep voice, one forefinger pointing towards my heart, giving me the benefit of his age and experience and, more vital, of the experiences that he had avoided. I was overawed by him, by his knowledge and his goodness and his strength, and I always tried to live a life of which he would have been proud. And I believe that I have done that, except for the disease. It is almost impossible to realize that my father himself must have carried the disease in his blood—that that good and strict man had passed the curse on, unknowingly, to his son. It is further proof that it is no fault of my own, that even such a fine man as my father did not know, that he could have been the one whom it affected as it does me.

Only once can I remember my father being unjust and unreasonable. It was the only time that he was ever angry with me. That was when I had to kill the neighbours' dog, and I have never been able to understand why my father did not see that it was necessary.

The dog belonged to my enemy, the boy who constantly persecuted me. I do not remember his name. He was an insignificant creature and hardly worth remembering. But I remember his dog. It was a large and vicious brute, a mongrel with a great deal of Alsatian in it. It was often with the boy when he tormented me, and it added its snarls to its master's jibes. It would watch with its yellow eyes while the boy plagued me. Its tongue hung out and its muzzle twitched as though it were very satisfied that I was being tormented. I never paid any attention to the dog at those times. I ignored it and its master, but of the two I believe I hated the dog more. I know it a fallacy to believe that dog is man's best friend. It is a stupid statement made by sentimental and ignorant people who have been deceived by the brutes. And this dog was a particularly foul beast, with a filthy mottled hide and yellow teeth. It had never attacked me, but I could tell that it would have liked to.

One evening I was coming home from town rather late. Our house was in the country, a few miles from the town. I forget what I was doing out at that hour, but at any rate it was dark as I walked towards our house. It must have been a moonlit night, because everything was very clear. It was necessary to pass our neighbours' house on the way to my own, for we lived on the same road. To avoid passing their house I would have had to go through the woods, and I saw no reason for this.

Well, I was passing their house, minding my own business, when my enemy suddenly appeared. He began to throw stones at me as usual, and I ignored him. I walked on. He hit me in the back with one stone, and it hurt. I knew that it would leave a bruise. I walked on a little way and then I must have sat down beside the road. I know that I thought about the boy, and wondered why he hated me so, and after a while I began to hate him. I had never felt that way towards him before, and it must have been the sum total of all his injustices and attacks that finally added up to the whole of hatred. The longer I sat there the more I hated him. I remembered everything that he had done to me. I remembered the first time, when he had cut my head and I had tasted my own blood. For some reason the taste of that blood came back to me more strongly then than it had seemed when it happened. I knew that he would torment me forever, unless I put a stop to it, and I got up and walked back towards his house.

He was in the yard, by the woodshed. He saw me coming and picked up a stone and began to yell tauntingly, calling me unmentionable names. It enraged me to hear him use those foul words, and I knew for the first time how truly evil he was. I didn't understand why I had tolerated him before, how I could have let such a wicked person annoy me. I wanted to punish him for annoying me but, more strongly, I wanted to punish him for being a deplorable creature, a foul-mouthed and evil-minded creature. He had to be taught a lesson.

I walked right up to him. He continued to taunt me until I was quite close, and then he must have realized with his slow, dim mind that this was not the same as the other times, because he began to back away. I went after him, walking slowly. When he threw the stone it struck me in the face, but I hardly felt it. He ran backwards to the woodshed and I moved between him and the house. I remember how his eyes darted around as he looked for help, for a path to escape. I was much bigger and stronger than him—I was bigger than anyone else of my age at school—and he became very frightened. His fear did not satisfy me; for some reason it made me all the more anxious to punish him . . . I felt he realized that he must be punished, that he knew he was evil and, if he were not punished, he would think that it was all right to do as he did. I would not have that. I went at him and he tried to run, but I am very fast and nimble even now, and in those days I could move like a cat. I caught him with both hands. I caught him by the neck and threw him down on the ground. He tried to kick me but I brushed his feet aside and fell over him. He hit me in the face with his small fists but it was less than an insect sting. I got my hands very firmly around his neck and began to punish him. I intended to punish him greatly, in proportion to his sins. I squeezed, and his eyes got very large and that made me feel satisfied. Or almost satisfied—as if satisfaction were on the way, and the harder I squeezed the more rapidly it came. It seemed to run up from my fingertips to my shoulders, and then diffuse throughout my body. He stopped hitting me. His small hands were wrapped around my wrists, but they could do nothing. I put all my weight into my arms and pressed.

It was then that the savage brute attacked me.

I had not seen it sneak up behind me. It was sly and vicious and the first that I was aware of it was when it pounced at me. I had to release the boy, and the dog and I rolled over. It was a powerful creature, but it was no match for me in an equal struggle. I got over it and got my hands under its collar and twisted. I turned the collar right round, choking the brute. It had torn my forearm with its teeth and the blood ran down my arm and splattered over the dog. The sight of the blood drove me into a frenzy. I realized then how dangerous that animal was, and how necessary it was that it should be destroyed. I twisted the collar around again and it bit into the hairy throat. The tongue slid from its muzzle and I banged its head against the ground so that its own teeth buried themselves in that laughing tongue that was no longer laughing so slyly. The look in the creature's eyes was delightful! It knew that it was going to die then. It knew that it was going to pay for its viciousness, and the eyes rolled and bulged out like two yellowish hard-boiled eggs. It made me laugh to see that, but I did not laugh so much that I had to release my grip. I did not let the dog go until it was very dead.

When I stood up finally I saw that the boy had recovered and run away. He must have gone into his house. I would have followed him, but for some reason I no longer hated him. Perhaps I felt that he had been punished enough. I was sure that he would torment me no more. The dog was like a limp and oil-stained rag in the moonlight and I felt very good. A good job well done. I felt warm and satisfied and I turned and walked home. My arm did not begin to hurt until later.

In the morning the boy's father came to our house and talked with my father. After he had gone my father spoke to me. He seemed angry. I explained to him that it had been self-defence, and that the beast had tried to kill me, but he had the strange idea that I had attacked the boy first, and that the dog had died protecting its master. Even my father was fooled by that common lie about dogs being faithful and true, and I could not make him understand. I showed him the slash in my forearm, but it made no difference. He seemed to really believe that I had tried to kill the boy, ridiculous though it seems. But that was the only time that my father was ever unjust, and he forgot about it after a while.

And no one ever taunted me or threw rocks at me again.

June 7

I am up early today and intend to work on this journal until lunch-time. I read what I wrote yesterday, about the dog. I don't think that it is really relevant to the disease. I was, after all, forced into kill-ing it to save myself, and any man would have done the same. But it does show a bit of the violence of which I am capable, and also the tolerant attitude that I take at normal times, so I will leave it in the record, for what it is worth, and continue with my efforts to get the beginnings of the illness sorted out clearly in my mind, in sequence and intensity, so that they can help me to foresee what the next change will be.

My strongest impression of those early years concerns the woods. We lived in a large old house in the country and the woods were behind it. The house was drafty, and chilly and damp, and I did not like it, but I was always happy in the woods — except when those feelings took possession of me. I liked to go into the woods alone. I always felt safer when there were no other people about. I can still picture just how it looked there. I always seem to picture it in the moonlight, however. The impression of it in the day is not strong. But this may be because there were more distractions in the day-light, and fixed memories yielded to immediate sensations. But at night! Is it one night that I remember, or many nights so similar that they have blended into the same memory?

I was standing in a small clearing with the tall pine trees on every side. It was on a slight hill, and at the bottom of the hill our house nestled in the shadows. I could just see the top of the roof and the chimney against the sky because the land rose a little to the far side as well. It was dark in the clearing but the tops of the trees were white in the moonlight; silver needles under the wind. It was very quiet. A few fluffy cotton clouds avoided the moon. Standing in this place I felt a great yearning, a vague and indistinct need. It was very much the same as spring fever when one had to sit in school and could look out of the window at the flowers and grass, but it was much, much stronger. I had to do something, and there was nothing to do. I suppose that I thought it was a sexual need, at the time. That must have been why I took my clothing off. I took every-thing off, even my shoes and socks, and stood there completely

naked in the trees. It wasn't cold, but I was shivering. One shaft of
light penetrated straight down the side of a tree, and it seemed to
give off a cold glow that turned me to ice. And I just stood there,
with my head thrown back and my mouth wide open, staring up
at the sky and trembling as though every vein and every nerve of
my body had become charged with electric current. I don't know
how long I stood like that. It must have been some time because
the heavens had shifted position. And then, suddenly, it was over.
Suddenly the need had left me, and I realized that I was shouting.
Not shouting . . . it was more like a howl, a bay. I stopped. Everything was silent and dark and I felt very strange, very naked, and
very much alone and slightly ashamed at what I had done. I still
supposed that it had been sexual, I imagine. But I also felt a great
relief. I dressed and walked back to the house and everything was
all right for the rest of that month. Everything was fine. I was very
much at peace. As I say, I don't know if this was a single memory or
a combination of many months and many nights. I must have been
quite young . . .

I have been pondering for a while over what I have just written. I
think that it must have happened more than once. I have glimpses
of myself running through the woods naked, and crouching and
hiding behind trees and rocks. These are very objective memories.
They come back to me in the same way as the actions of the thing
in the cell, as opposed to the impressions and emotions. I don't
think that I was running from anyone, or hiding from anyone, however. I am sure that I was all alone in the woods. I am also sure that
there was no physical change. Quite sure. And, strangely enough,
I cannot remember the first time that I did change, or the first time
that I became aware of changing. It must have come very gradually,
so that there was no shock that would remain in my memory.

   The first recollection that I have of changing took place in my
own bedroom, not in the woods. This must have been later. I was
sitting on my bed, bent over and watching my hands. The bed
was beside the window and the moon was right there so that the
bedroom was all black and white. My hands were in my lap, and
a shaft of light passed over them. I was naked. My backbone felt
more naked than the rest of me, as though even the skin had been

peeled away. I watched my hands. This couldn't have been the first time, because I seemed to know exactly what I was looking for. And I remember how my fingernails began to grow, and my hands trembled and drew up . . .

I don't remember what I did after that.

June 8
Helen is a good wife.

Few women would have put up with what she has. I must be honest, she is not a good-looking woman. Perhaps she married me as a last resort, but I don't think so. I believe that she loves me. Sometimes it annoys me when she cannot seem to understand about my sickness, but apart from that she is a good wife. And she must know that I would never hurt her. I don't think that I would ever hurt anyone. I go out of my way not to hurt anyone. I am basically a shy and gentle person, and that is what makes the contrast so hard to imagine when one doesn't realize that it is a physical disease, and that I actually become something different, something dangerous. But I have managed to control it, and so I have never hurt anyone.

I have promised Helen that I will take her out for dinner this evening. She is very happy about it. We do not go out much, I do not care for a frivolous social life and prefer to stay at home, but once in a while it does no harm. Helen enjoys it, although she agrees that I am right in limiting such evenings to two or three times a year. She is dressing now. I may write more when we get home, if it is not too late.

Well, what a fiasco this night has been!

We have just returned and Helen has gone directly to her room. She appears to be annoyed with me. I should have known better than to go out, than to cater to the whims of a woman. Women do not understand much of life.

To begin with, to start the evening off on the wrong foot, Helen put on a dress that she knows I hate. It is an immodest dress that leaves her shoulders bare and makes her look like a tart. I tried to be pleasant about it, but she got annoyed when I told her the simple truth. Why do women get annoyed at the truth and not at deceptions? It is beyond me. Surely her own mirror would have told her the same thing that I did. She can't really think, after all this time, that I am a man who can be flattering without reason, or that I would care to have my wife dress like a tramp? But she put the dress on and we had a little argument even before we left the house. I finally let her wear it, but I should have known better; I should have known what an ill temper I would be in all night because of it.

When we got to the restaurant and got a table I could see several of the other patrons looking at Helen. She didn't seem to be aware of it. She sat smiling happily and looking around the room. I'm sure that everyone thought that she was looking for someone to flirt with. What else would they think, the way she was dressed? I was mortified. I could just imagine their thoughts. She looked like some strumpet that I had just picked up off the street. She had too much lipstick on, and her knees were uncovered when she was seated. I would have got up and walked out right then if I had not been too embarrassed to leave my seat. I determined to destroy that dress as soon as we were home, so it would never disgrace me again. And, unbelievably, poor Helen seemed to have no idea what a stir she was causing. She is so innocent and inexperienced. She looked around as though she were really enjoying herself and I tried to pretend I did not notice anyone else. I did, though. Some of the other women in the room were dressed as bad, or worse, than my wife, and I realized then that it was not the proper place for us to be. We had never eaten there before, and it had a good reputation, and so I had been deceived. It was one of those gaudy places with plush walls and candles that pretend to be European and overcharge their customers for bad food. I hate any place or any person that pretends to be something other than they are.

When the waiter came he leaned over the table a little, from behind Helen. I'm sure that he was attempting to look down the front of her dress! It enrages me, even now, as I recall that greasy smile. He had a little mustache and wavy hair and he was some sort of foreigner, an Italian perhaps. He had an accent, or affected one. I was angry and miserable and it is little wonder that I lost my temper when he brought me the wrong order.

I hate fancy, foreign foods. I had ordered a plain steak with boiled potatoes and no salad. When my order arrived the steak was ruined with some slimy sauce and there were creamed potatoes and an oily salad. It was revolting. On top of all the other annoyances it was simply too much to take. Perhaps I should have controlled my temper, even though it was justified. Perhaps, as Helen says, I should not have thrown the plate at the waiter. But I don't regret it. These foreigners have to learn that they can't push everyone around. I acted on the spur of the moment, before I even thought about what I was doing. I lifted the plate on one open hand. The waiter was leaning towards me with that nasty smile, and I hurled the plate, food first, directly into his face. I believe that I was as gentlemanly as possible under the circumstances. I did not shout or cause a scene or speak to him. I simply threw it in his face.

Well, we left after that. We weren't asked to leave, and I suppose that I was respected for sticking up for my rights, but we left anyway. Helen cried as we walked out and I kept my head up and looked about and saw that everyone in the place was looking at us. Or, more precisely, they were looking at that lewd dress that she wore. Some of them were snickering and some looked angry. But I didn't let it bother me. I kept my dignity through the whole affair.

Helen doesn't seem to realize that it was all her fault, and she has gone directly to her room and locked the door. I heard her lock it. She made sure of that. It was just a bit of feminine dramatics, of course. I never go to her room.

Anyway, perhaps this evening will serve one good cause. It may convince my wife that it is not a good thing to go out so often.

June 9
Helen was still angry this morning. For a while she did not speak to me. That was all right with me, I was still thinking about the wasted evening and that horrible restaurant that charged far too much and brought the wrong food. But then she mentioned how I had flared up for no reason! For no reason! She even suggested that it had been a symptom of my sickness! In the middle of the month! It shows that she still has no idea what it is. I had to grip the edge of the table to keep from shouting at her and I must have looked very angry because she went away without another word. She looked rather chastened.

I shall try to be more tolerant of her stupidity. It is, after all, a hard thing for a normal person to comprehend. And it was such a shock to her when I had to tell her about it. I often wonder if the shock did not unbalance her slightly? Not much, but enough to account for some of the things that she does that aren't reasonable ... such as thinking that harlot's dress that she wore last night was attractive, and wanting to go out in the evenings like a teenager, and mistaking genuine and justified anger for a symptom of my disease. Yes, I must be more tolerant of her, poor thing.

It wasn't really bad when we were first married. It wasn't until afterwards that it got really bad, and the increase was slow enough so that I could see it coming and make plans to prevent any accidents. I didn't have the cell then—I didn't need it. There was plenty of time to have it made when I saw the need.

Oh, I changed. I changed, all right, but not nearly as much as now. Never completely. I still looked human. I remember how I looked in those early stages, before I was afraid to look in a mirror. My face looked unshaven, nothing more. As if I had gone a week without a shave. My teeth were long, but I was able to keep them covered with my lips so that they looked as though they protruded. It was the eyes that were the worst. They were definitely animal eyes; at least they were definitely not human eyes. But there was nothing that was really out of the ordinary to the extent that anyone who did not know what I normally looked like would have noticed. They would simply have thought that I was a singularly ugly person.

I never lost control in those days. The disease never took over, it just raged in me like a fever, and I was always at least partly myself. That was before we needed the cell, and before I told Helen about it. I suppose that it was wrong to marry her without telling her, but I did not expect it to get worse. And I am sure that it would have made no difference; she would have married me regardless.

On those nights when it happened I would go to bed early and turn the lights out. We had separate rooms, of course. I would tell Helen that I did not feel well and she would not bother me. She must have eventually noticed the regularity of the attacks, because once she made a very crude joke about monthly sickness, and I had to give her a stern lecture on what women did, and did not, mention, even to their husbands.

But then it continued to get worse, and finally I decided it was better to take no chances. I began to go out of town once a month. I told her that it was a business trip, and I suppose she believed me. She didn't act suspiciously, and she made no vulgar jests about it. She knew that I was not the type of creature who would keep a mistress, or go away for a gay night once a month, and so she trusted me and asked no questions.

I would go to some small town thirty or forty miles away. I went to a different town each month. I would check into some cheap little hotel (cheap, because no one would notice an unshaven man in a cheap hotel) and spend the long night in a dingy room. I would never leave that room, no matter how unpleasant it became through that night. And it certainly became unpleasant. I wanted so badly to go out. I needed . . . something. Perhaps it was the urge to run naked through the woods again. But I fought against it and conquered it and remained in the room. I always locked the door on the inside. It would have been better to have someone else lock me in, but I couldn't very well ask the clerk to do that. That would have been suspicious. So I had to rely on my willpower. Luckily I am a strong-minded man, and I managed. Although it was often very very bad, I managed.

Later, when I knew that it was getting progressively worse, it was necessary to have the cell constructed. It was a plan that I had long been considering. I had to tell my wife about the sickness then. That was the hardest part. Helen is not the most intelligent woman in the world, and at first she would not take me seriously. She would not believe me. She thought that I was joking. But then, when I had the contractor come in and build the cell and she realized that I was serious about it, she thought that I was losing my mind. Oh, she never said that, but I could tell by the way she looked at me. When we were putting the pads on the wall she kept shaking her head as though we were both being ridiculous and wasting our time. It is understandable; I cannot blame her for being dubious at first. She knows better now. She is beginning to realize, although she still makes stupid mistakes and cannot differentiate between the physical and the mental, the normal and the abnormal. It takes time.

We have had the cell for six months now. I have gone there every month and Helen has done her part without question. She is a good wife, all in all, and if she annoys me occasionally by her lack of intelligence and inability to grasp the facts, I suppose that that is only normal in most marriages when one partner is so vastly superior in mind.

I am satisfied with my wife. I shall try to be more tolerant of her faults. I would never hurt her in any way. I would never hurt anyone . . .

June 9 (Evening)
I have not been honest. It bothers me. I did not write anything untruthful, but I omitted writing about the drunkard in the hotel. I have to tell everything or else there is no point in keeping this journal, and so I must write about him. Anyway, nothing happened which I was to blame for.

It happened on the last night that I went out of town, before the cell was built. I had been thinking about making a cell, but had put it off because of Helen, because that would mean telling her all about my disease. I suppose that the episode with the drunkard was the thing that finally decided me about it. It did show me that I was liable to be dangerous, and that my control was weakening. All in all, it was just as well that it happened, since it turned out all right as far as I was concerned. I was innocent and what happened to the drunkard was his own fault completely.

It was a very poor hotel. I remember it well; it was as poor as any I had stayed at. The entrance was just a narrow doorway on the street with a sign hanging over it. The sign was crooked. There was a maroon carpet in the corridor with all the threads showing, leading to the staircase. The reception desk was just an alcove in the hall. I had to ring a bell there and wait for the clerk to come out of a room under the stairs. It took him a long time and when he came he was rubbing his eyes, and his shirt was hanging out of his trousers. He went behind the desk and shoved the book at me and yawned right in my face. He was a horrid fellow. I tell these things to show what kind of a hotel it was, and what the people who stayed there must have been like; especially the drunkard. People like that are better off dead than alive.

The desk clerk did not look the least bit disgusted when he saw that I was unshaven. I always took the precaution of not shaving for a day or two before I went to a hotel, just in case someone were to see me when I was being ill. They might think it funny that a man's beard could grow so rapidly, grow in just a few hours. It was just one of the small details that I was so careful about. I am sure that no one ever suspected. But then, it is not a thing that one tends to think about in this day and age. In the day of the psychiatrist, I am a legend.

The clerk in that place was unshaven himself, and he acted as if all the guests at the place went without a razor. Even though I had a suitcase he asked for the money in advance. I went up to my room and closed and locked the door and turned all the lights out and lay down on the bed. I kept my clothing on. The only window was small and greasy and looked out on a brick wall so that I could not see the moon. It was always harder and more painful to change when I could not see it and had to imagine it, big and yellow and round in that black sky. I wanted so much to leave that horrible little room. I remember how I waited, almost wishing for the change to come so that I could get it over with. I kept getting up and walking to the window, pacing the room, going to the filthy sink and splashing water on my face. And then I must have gone to the bed again, because the next thing I remember I had already changed. I was lying on my back, tossing and turning and groaning. I was soaked with sweat. The bed was soaked. The gray sheets were all twisted beneath me and I gripped the brass bedstead with one hand. One changed hand. It was bad. It was like having a high fever and hallucinations. But I was strong and I stuck it out and all the while I was thinking that it had never been so bad before.

And then I heard the drunkard come down the corridor. I have always despised drunkards—anyone who has to seek artificial aids to life and cannot be content and happy without stimulants and drugs. This drunkard was singing loudly and his footsteps were clumping. I lay very still as he came near the door to my room. And he must have got the rooms confused, because he stopped outside my door. He tried it. I heard the knob turn and rattle. And then he tried to fit his key into the lock and I heard it scraping and clanking. I did not move at all. I lay there with my eyes rolling and the froth on my lips. I could hear him cursing and swearing and I hated him. I have never hated anyone as much as I hated that drunkard. And I had a terrible thought . . . suppose, in this cheap hotel, his key could open my door? Suppose he were to come into the room and see me? Rage and fear moved me. I leaped from the bed and was across the room, leaning with my ear against the door. I listened. I heard his labored breathing and his muttered words. I pressed against the door so that he would not be able to open it. I am exceedingly strong when I have changed, and he could not have opened the door against me. The door felt hot and smooth against my bristly cheek and hands.

And then he began to pound on the door. He pounded very loudly, and I was afraid that he might awaken everyone, that there might be a dispute, that the night clerk might demand that I open up so that it could be settled. I waited, silently, while my insides boiled and bubbled, and he continued to bang on the door.

I think that I opened the door then.

I didn't really hurt him. But I will never forget the look on his face when he saw me! His eyes, his mouth, his skin . . . He took a step backwards, and I wanted to go after him but I knew that I must not. I possibly might have struck out at him, I do not remember. But he collapsed very suddenly. He was just a bundle of rags on the floor with the horrible smell of alcohol and the other smell of blood. I stared for a moment, my fingers hooking at the air, and then I controlled myself and slammed the door and locked it again. I remember leaning against the door and panting. I must have been very frightened. I was sure that when he awoke he would get help and they would break into my room, and I knew that I must change back to myself before they did. Perhaps the fear acted as a catalyst, because very shortly after that I lay down and when I opened my eyes I was all right once more.

In the morning the clerk was very excited. Apparently they had just taken the body away. He asked me if I had heard any noise in the night and I told him that I thought I had heard someone singing in the hall—someone intoxicated. He told me that one of the residents had been found dead in the corridor by my room. I was very surprised and asked about it. Apparently the man had died of a heart attack. That seemed the obvious solution. The clerk told me that he had been drinking and had walked up the stairs and it must have been too much for him. Drinking is very bad on the heart. The man had had a large bruise on his temple, but that must have happened when he fell down. Anyway, that is what happened with the drunkard in the hotel, and so it wasn't really my fault. I didn't hurt him.

June 11

I am afraid that the librarian is suspicious of me! It came as a terrible shock. I had never considered her intelligent enough to suspect anything, but I see now that that was my mistake ... She is one of the types that are stupid enough to believe in the things that intelligent people laugh at. That makes her very dangerous. I don't know what I should do about her. I won't go back there, of course, but if she already suspects ... I don't know. I would hate to suffer because of such a stupid woman.

I first began to distrust her when I went into the library today. I walked past her desk and nodded and she nodded back as usual, but I noticed that there was a calendar on her desk. It was right there in full view, as though she had been studying it. There had never been a calendar there before. Why should there be one now? If it was necessary in order to keep track of how long books had been out on loan she would have always had one. Anyway, the books are all stamped in the back or something. No, I am sure that she has the calendar to keep track of the full moons!

I thought that as soon as I saw it, but I wasn't sure. There was a chance that she might be innocent. I always give a person the benefit of the doubt. But then, when she followed me into the dark back room ...

It is very silent and gloomy in the back, where the big research books are. No one seems to use that room much. I was looking through an old volume and suddenly the librarian came in. She had her arms full of books, and pretended that she had come to put them on the shelves, but she didn't fool me. She was watching me. When I turned and stared at her she blushed. She said something inane, and I kept staring, and she shoved the books in at random and hurried off. She has a disgusting way of walking, so that her bottom bounces suggestively. She is overweight and unclean looking. She is an old maid, although not really so old. I have often seen young men talking to her at the desk, pretending that they are interested in some books and leaning towards her. I am sure that she has foul habits. It is no wonder that she has never married. She doesn't look like a virgin, either. But I am afraid of what she suspects. She is dangerous. I don't know what she might try to do . . .

When I left she tried to strike up a conversation. I had not stayed long and she mentioned that, just to get me talking. She was smiling and flushed, pretending to be interested in me in ways other than she is. I gave her a crisp nod and went right past the desk without saying anything. I could feel her looking at my back until I had left the building. I know that she wants to get me into a conversation so that she can find out more about me. She pretends to be flirting with me, but she has other motives. That is a pretense. But it is a mistake on her part to imagine that I am the type of man who would be interested in a flirtation.

Still, I must admit it is a possibility that she is genuinely trying to strike up an acquaintance. I know that I am appealing to women, and she is quite wretched and probably has few friends. She is much homelier than Helen. If that is the case then I have nothing to fear from her, although I must feel disgusted that any woman should attempt to start something with a happily married man. Any woman who would do that is better off dead. They are not fit to live, to corrupt our society.

Perhaps it would be better not to suddenly stop going to the library. That might simply arouse any suspicions that she has. It might be better to talk to her, and see just how much she suspects.

June 15
I went back to the library today. She tried to strike up a conversation again. I talked to her for a few minutes this time, just to see how she reacted. It is hard to tell what she is thinking, I have never had much experience with women of that sort. She appeared to be trying to tempt me. It is monstrous, but I believe it may be true. I feel relieved that she did not ask me any questions that showed she was suspicious of me, but it sickened me to see the way that she carried on. I had all I could do from letting her see how angry I was. It was hard to keep from screaming at her when she twitched

her hips and looked coy and leaned over the desk towards me. She had a disgustingly tight sweater on. It makes a man wonder what could have happened to turn a woman out that way? The calendar was still on the desk but I had a chance to look at it and saw that the stages of the moon were not marked on it. So I no longer think that I have anything to fear from her. She is more stupid than I supposed.

Afterwards I went to the poetry section and pretended to be reading some poems so that it would throw her off the trail. I hate poetry. It seems so useless. But I fooled the girl. I just hope that no one saw me talking to her and got the wrong impression.

June 24
Well, the librarian showed her hand today. It was just as I thought, she is an immoral woman. She suspected nothing of my disease, she merely lusted after me! I believe that she makes a practice of seducing men. She certainly seemed experienced.

She followed me into the back this afternoon. It was late and we were the only ones in the whole library. I didn't hear her approach, I was reading, concentrating because it was hard to see in the dim light between the high shelves, and all of a sudden she was right there beside me. When I moved, startled, she giggled. She asked if she had scared me, and then, before I could answer, she said that I needn't be frightened of her. She has very wicked eyes, they seem to reflect her soul. They gleam. I could not help but look into those terrible eyes. It was like staring at a flickering fire . . . it was hypnotic. Why is that? Why should a moral man be fascinated by evil and degradation and be unable to take his eyes away? Is the horror of seeing wickedness so strong? Try as I would I could not look away from her, and the creature mistook my loathing for interest. She moved closer to me. I forget what she said. It was meaningless, just something to say as she smiled. I think that she asked me why I was so shy and timid. I couldn't answer, I couldn't force myself to speak to her. I remember opening my mouth to tell her how I despised her, but words failed me. And then she reached out and touched my arm. Her fingers brushed my arm and it was like the touch of the Devil himself. An icy hatred moved from my arm to my heart itself, and everything faded away, the shelves and the books and the walls all vanished into a red haze and all I could see was her grue-some countenance, drawing closer and closer to mine.

I believe that she would have actually kissed me, if I had not struck her! I don't remember telling myself to slap her, so it must have been a purely reflex movement. Self-preservation works for the soul as well as the mortal life, and I had to stop her. I slapped her as hard as I could, in the face. I have never struck a woman before, but I do not regret it. That creature was less than a woman, less than a human. She was an abomination on life itself, a bloated para-site feeding on men's bodies.

After I struck her, I turned and walked away. She didn't pursue me. She did not say a word. I suppose that she was stunned by my blow. Perhaps she fell down, I did not wait to see. I just walked out of that library and came home. My hands are still trembling. It was a dreadful experience and I know that I shall never forget it. I only hope that I may have done some good; that my strength and resolve will show her that not every man can be ruined by her per-verted desires.

June 24 (Evening)
Well, I just had a shock. It was a remarkable coincidence, no doubt about that. I had just finished this afternoon's entry in this journal and gone downstairs to listen to the news on the radio. It appears that someone has murdered the librarian. The announcer said that she was found in the back room of the library, between two high bookshelves. Her neck had been broken by a tremendous blow to the side of the head. It must have happened in the very same place where she tried to work her evil designs on me. I expect that it was under much the same circumstances. She was undoubtedly in the habit of following men back there and approaching them without the slightest trace of modesty. Well, after being rebuffed by me she was most likely feeling frustrated or desperate or whatever it is that lewd women feel when they come up against a man strong enough to resist them, and I imagine that she tried harder with the next man that she managed to trap. The great coincidence of it is this man, the murderer, must have been a very moral person, the same as I, and he reacted to her foul advances with uncontrolled anger. He probably did not mean to kill her, although surely she is better off

dead, but he must have hit her the same way that I did, except he had less control over himself and struck her too hard. That is what I think has happened. I may be wrong. But whatever it was, I cannot feel sorry for that woman. I am sure that it is better she is dead.

My wife heard the broadcast too, and asked me if I had not been at the library at the approximate time of the murder. I said that it must have happened just after I left, but I didn't tell her that I was sure I knew how it had happened. That would have been too embarrassing, and I'm sure that Helen could not conceive of such a woman and would only be confused. She said that I should go to the police, that I might be able to help them. But I saw no one else, there is nothing that I can do. I don't want to get involved and, besides, I cannot help but feel sympathy for the man. Murder is a dreadful crime, of course, but under certain circumstances it is justified, and when one's morals are outraged it is very easy to lose control and to do something that would normally be out of the question. I couldn't explain this to Helen. She is not intelligent enough to understand that, in certain instances, the letter of the law is not necessarily correct. I just told her that I was sure I could not be of any assistance to the law and she agreed, although I cannot help but feel she thinks I am shirking my duty to society.

Well, the police will undoubtedly apprehend the man. It seems likely that he will give himself up after he has had time to consider and realize that it was justifiable homicide or self-defence or with extenuating circumstances, and the law should not be too harsh with him once he has told his story. I suppose he must be punished in some way, because that is the law, but for myself I think that he is more to be admired than punished. His only crime was in failing to keep himself under control, as I did in similar circumstances. But, of course, I am a remarkable man and cannot expect everyone to be as strong-willed and restrained.

June 27
I had a rather curious conversation with Helen while we were taking coffee this morning. For several minutes she seemed to want to say something, but kept hesitating. I presumed that it was about the time of month (it draws near again) or the cell or, perhaps, about seeing a doctor. But it wasn't.

"They haven't caught that murderer yet," she said.

She meant the man who killed the librarian. The police had apparently found no clues. It must be difficult to solve an unpremeditated murder, since there is no motive, and in this case the man was most likely a complete stranger to the librarian. I find myself hoping that he will escape the written law, for his actions were ordained by the higher law of morality.

I said, "Perhaps they won't."

"Don't you think that you really should go to them and tell them that you were there?" she asked.

I asked her why.

"Well . . . you must have been there at almost the same time as the killer. She was murdered before you came home, apparently. There might be something you could tell them . . ."

"I've told you. I saw nothing."

"You aren't . . . afraid to go to the police, are you?" she asked me. She looked away when she said it. I don't know what could have given her that idea. What would I be afraid of? I repeated that I knew nothing, and then I told her that I hoped the man would escape punishment because the librarian had obviously been a bad woman. I did not tell her that the woman had tried to work her ways on me, but maybe she guessed it, because she looked at me in a very strange way and then left the table and went to her room. It was a funny way for her to behave. I suppose it is her upbringing. The middle classes have such a ridiculous idea that man-made laws have some higher right than man who is behind them. I cannot understand how people can be so dense, so easily led. How can they regard the rules of society as the rules of God? They make no distinction between descriptive laws and laws that are relative to the situation; between the eternal laws of nature and God and morality, and the fluctuating and often wrong laws that men create to hinder themselves and others. It truly bothers me that this is so, that prejudice has made it so. Just think how it applies to myself . . . I would be scorned and hated and punished if anyone knew of my affliction. The authorities would most likely pass a law to make it illegal to have this disease. But what good would that do? Diseases are not governed by the laws of governments, and I would be thought a criminal although powerless to help myself. That is why no one must ever know about it. The old, almost forgotten prejudices and fears and superstitions would join forces with the new power of the authorities and destroy me. It is a terrible thing. One sees it everywhere, and can do nothing to combat it. I feel very bitter about it. If I had lived three hundred years ago I would have at least been feared and acknowledged by anyone who knew. Now I would simply be legislated against. It is a good thing that I am a well-balanced man, or there is no telling what such stupidity would drive me to.

I often feel bitter like this when the time draws near. I hate that cell so much . . .

July 1

Tomorrow I must go to the cell once more.

I have tried to avoid thinking of it. I even neglected this journal in an attempt to think of other things, but it is quite impossible. I cannot avoid the thoughts, and the thoughts torment me. I feel that I shall not be able to bear it again. Even as I write this my hands tremble and I am perspiring. It seems so unjust to punish myself because I am ill. It seems so unfair to martyr myself for the sake of an uncomprehending, uncaring society. I don't know if I am thinking this way because it is so near or because I am right. I know that my thoughts could change as the disease begins the cycle; I admit that. And yet, my reasoning is flawless.

I wonder if the cell is making the illness worse? I have not considered this before; I suppose it occurred to me, but it seemed too close to rationalization and I did not think about it. But the fact remains that it was never so bad before I started going into the cell. I always had control of myself then. Even the last time that I stayed out, the time when the drunkard had the heart attack, I was able to restrain myself. The drunkard's death was the prime factor in my decision to have the cell built, but as I look back and realize that his death had nothing to do with me I see that it was a false factor; that I acted without properly reasoning, without seeing that the cell might affect me and punish me instead of keeping me safe. Now I wonder if possibly the cell has aggravated the disease. It seems reasonable. It was always easier when I could see the sky, and since I have been shutting myself off completely it has become worse. I really don't know. I would like to see, however.

I wonder if I dare to stay out of the cell tomorrow night?

July 3 (Morning)
Nothing that I can write can possibly describe my feelings. I am in despair. I despise myself. I know that it was not my fault, but the knowledge cannot diminish the shame, the horror. I feel that the human body cannot stand this much mortification; that my heart will burst, my brain melt so that all the memories run molten together and I will die. But I am still alive. I would rather be dead. I have thought of suicide. I actually took my razor out and looked at the big blue veins in my wrists, and I think that I would have done it if it were not that the blood would remind me of what happened, and even as I felt my life drain away I would be remembering that fiendish night . . . I cannot kill myself that way. If I had sleeping pills I know that I would use them, but I have none. I have never used them. I do not approve of using drugs.

I feel a little better now. I have been lying down. I think that I see things more clearly now that I am rested. It wasn't as though I were responsible. Suicide would punish me, not the disease that turned me into the thing that committed the terrible crime. But I am still on fire with self-abasement, I hate myself. If only I had gone to the cell . . . but how was I to know? How could I have even imagined what was going to happen? I am a gentle person; it was impossible to know that my body could be used for . . . what happened. I feel as if I should take a cleaver and chop my hands off at the wrist; should have my teeth torn out at the roots. God knows, if it were possible to change the past there would be no question of it. I would surely destroy myself rather than let it happen. But there is no question of that. What is done is done. But I am so ashamed . . .

I tried to act normally when I came into the house this morning. I acted as though nothing had happened, although it was very hard. My wife didn't say anything, but I saw her look at me very closely. She didn't even ask where I had been all night, but I told her that I had been called away on business very suddenly. I don't know if she believed me. Neither of us mentioned that it had been . . . the night. Perhaps she thinks that nothing happened this month, or that I am beginning to control it better. Or perhaps . . . I hate to write this, but it is a possibility . . . perhaps she thinks that I forgot about it, and that it is my mind that causes it. I don't know. She acted as though she wanted to ask me, but she didn't. I will have to consider this . . . later, when I can think more clearly. My mind is still burning, and I can think of nothing except what happened last night . . . I keep seeing her face . . . all that I can do is to keep brushing my teeth and cleaning under my fingernails.

I have had to burn my shirt.

July 3 (Afternoon)
It was in all the newspapers!

It never occurred to me. I suppose that I was so concerned and confused, that I was thinking so much of myself, that I forgot the rest of the world. But naturally it was on the front page of all the papers, and they had it all wrong!

When I went down to lunch my wife had the papers on the table. They were all folded back so that the story about last night was on top. She did not look at me while I read them. That was a good thing, because I could not help but show my anger and pain. It was enough to make even a strong man lose restraint. I'm certain that Helen knows I am the one. I only hope that she realizes that the newspapers have it all wrong. They have made it out to be much worse than it really was, although it was certainly bad.

They called it the work of a madman! A madman! They used all the most lurid words and the worst type of sensationalism, all the most violent terms and expressions and the most ghoulish descriptions and details. And each and every paper referred to it as an insane act. Newspapers are supposed to keep to the objective facts, and not feel obligated to formulate theories about which they know nothing. But they are all so eager for sales that they must make everything sound as obscene as possible. What evil-minded fiends they must be! They have even implied that it was a sex crime! That is the worst of all. Every paper implied that the girl had been sexually assaulted! It sickens me to the very heart. They go so far as to say that her clothing was disarranged, that her thighs had been torn and bleeding and her stomach gouged and mutilated; that her blouse had been torn off and her underclothes shredded and her private parts mangled! All facts designed to make it appear that she had been sexually interfered with. Can't they see that clothing must become disarranged when one struggles as she did? Are they so sick that they can never see beyond a sexual motive for any act? Or do they ignore the truth in order to sell more papers?

I am furious! It enrages me to see that the newspapers can be so irresponsible! And the public . . . the terrible public . . . to think that the way to increase circulation is to publish such complete lies, such sensationalism. What is wrong with our society that men and women actually enjoy reading such things? How can an ill person ever hope to be cured in such a society? It is so discouraging. It makes me lose hope.

I have the papers here in my room. They are all alike. The headlines differ but the lies are the same. The headlines range from *Madman Slays Girl in Woods* to *Sex Fiend Murder* to *Mangled Corpse in Lovers' Lane.* And nowhere in any of the stories is there any suggestion of a physical illness. Are they blind? Or do they fear to look at the truth? Do they prefer the mentally ill to the innocent? What can I do about it?

I have contemplated writing letters to each of the newspapers, explaining exactly how it was, and what the disease is. They would surely publish the letters, if only to increase sales, but who knows what alterations or omissions they would make? I am sure that they would destroy any truth that I wrote them. I have learned that they are not to be trusted. I would like to have the editors of those scandalous papers locked in a room with me . . . locked in the cell with me on the night that it happens. I would like to see the way their faces change as they look upon the truth, as they realize how wrong and wicked and libelous they have been. That would be the way to show them, to teach them the truth and to teach them how to suffer for their errors at the same time. It would not be corrective punishment, but they would deserve it. They would be . . .

I should not be thinking this way. I can feel my heart begin to drum, my blood is hurtling through my veins. I suppose it must be some reaction left by last night, some after-effect of the disease. It is probably not well to let myself feel this way. It is yielding to the emotions of the sickness instead of combating it. I must never let it gain control when it is not necessary. But it is understandable why I should feel that way. I have been outraged and slandered without cause by men who care nothing for truth; men who deserve to suffer; men who would be better off dead.

I am too disgusted and angry to write any more now. Later I must write and cancel my subscriptions to those papers . . .

July 3 (Night)
I feel obligated to tell what really happened, no matter how painful the effort is. I must write it all, objectively and truthfully. It may bring me relief to purge myself this way, or it may increase the despair . . . I can only do it and see, and do it regardless. I must show that it was the act of a sick person and not the disgusting crime of a pervert. That is what hurts me most, to be labeled a pervert. A sex pervert! I, of all people, to be so misunderstood.

I hope and pray that Helen does not believe the newspapers. She is not given to thinking for herself, she has a tendency to believe whatever she reads instead of forming her own opinions, and it drives me to frenzy to imagine that she might be thinking of me in that light, by that lie. What would she feel if she believed that I had raped a young woman? The possibility of being thought capable of such a fiendish act appals me. I would hate anyone who believed that I was capable of it, hate them terribly. I have always been very pure in mind and body. Even with my wife I have tried to limit our sexual relations to a minimum. I have never been guilty of feeling any great need for sex, and usually I do it simply to satisfy Helen. I believe that she is a bit oversexed, but I have managed to regulate that, and to show her by my example that continence is the proper basis for health and purity. Overindulgence in sexual acts is every bit as heinous as taking drugs, or drinking to excess.

Perhaps the fact that it happened in that lovers' lane gave those newspapers the wrong impression. But that was merely a coincidence. I swear that I did not touch her in any unclean manner. Even after I had changed, my moral code was strong enough to resist that temptation, even if it had occurred. But it did not. There was never the slightest urge towards it. It could just as well have been a man as a girl. The fact that it was a girl, and that she was young and rather pretty, in a cheap and painted fashion, had absolutely nothing to do with what happened. I swear that I would never, under any circumstances, interfere with a woman.

I suppose that, in one way, I should be thankful that they have got it all wrong. It will throw the police off the trail. They will be searching for a madman, a sex pervert. There is no way that I could come under suspicion. My life has always been beyond reproach. The more they investigate, the further from the truth they seem to move. In the late news broadcast it was hinted that there might be a link between this crime and the librarian's murder. The poor benighted fools! How could they imagine that? It is beyond me. I suppose they are desperate to solve one crime or the other and find it less compelling if they are able to lump them together. Well, they will never find the truth, that is definite.

I see that I am still unable to write objectively. I am still a bit annoyed at the newspapers, and a little shaken by last night. Tomorrow I will write exactly how it was.

July 6
I have waited until I feel that I can explain everything calmly. I could not trust myself before. But now I am ready, and I will describe what really happened on that night, and show how wrong the newspapers were.

That afternoon I went for a long walk. I left the house just after lunch and there was plenty of time before darkness would set in. Helen did not seem to realize what night it was, or else she thought that I would only be gone a short while. She didn't question me when I went out, at any rate. I had not the faintest idea where I should spend the night, but I knew that I had to get away from that cell. I could not bear the thought of going there again. And I knew that I must get away from the town, away from people. I intended to take no chances. I thought . . . I had convinced myself . . . I truly believed that it was the confinement of the cell that had made the change so much greater in the past months. Being shut off from the air and the sky and the moon I had felt the change violently, and I believed that, since the change had to be more powerful to occur in the stifling cell, it had also been greater necessarily. I know now that that is not so, that the degree of change is not modified by the degree of struggle necessary to bring it about, but I firmly believed it then. I could not foresee any danger.

I walked around the streets aimlessly for some time, and then, in the late afternoon, I headed away from the populated areas. I walked west. I did not hurry, but I walked at a steady pace, and very soon the town was behind me and I was on the open road. It was a wide highway and motorcars roared by in clouds of dust and noise and it was very unpleasant. I have never cared for motorcars myself. I prefer to walk or to take a train. Perhaps I am somewhat old-fashioned, but I see no harm in that. I see it as a virtue in this day and age of idleness and laziness. Soon it began to grow dark and some of the cars had their headlights on. I knew that it was time to find seclusion then, and I turned up the first secondary road that I came to. This road was narrow and unpaved. It headed in a north-erly direction. There were trees on both sides and I could see more trees ahead. The noise of the highway faded behind me. There was no traffic on the small road, although there were wheel tracks in the dust. I did not know that it was too early for traffic there, you see. And I certainly did not know that it led to the local lovers' lane. Such thoughts never occur to me, and I find them disgusting. I am not naïve; I know what goes on in parked cars before people are properly married. But I did not know that I was walking towards such a place.

It was uphill. The road turned and twisted as it rose and I suppose that I walked for an hour or more without seeing another human being. Several times I saw dogs. They snarled and yelped and when I made a quick motion they ran off with their tails tucked in between their legs, looking back over their shoulders at me. Dogs are always terrified of me. Even fierce dogs that attack postmen and delivery boys run from me. I find it amusing. Their owners can never under-stand why this is so. One very large mongrel stood its ground for a moment, in the center of the road. It had very large teeth. I made a noise in my throat and moved quickly towards it and it went away very fast then, very chastened. It looked so humorous that I had to laugh.

Soon I had reached the top of the hill and the road ended in a quarry or pit of some kind. I don't know much about such things, but I believe that this one was deserted. It was growing dark by this time and I paused to rest. I sat on a flat stone and loosened my necktie. I was sweating a little from the climb but it was relaxing to

be there in the open, all alone. It brought back memories of childhood. I felt quite sure that the change would be slight and that I
would be satisfied to run through the woods as I had in the past. It
never occurred to me that I might meet another person. Everything
was so deserted and so quiet. The sounds of the woods are not like
the sounds of the cities, they are a pleasant background, almost like
music. I was content to sit there with my eyes closed, and I believe
that I would have stayed right there all night and nothing terrible
would have happened, if the car hadn't come.

I heard it when it was still a long way away. At first I thought that
it was down on the highway, but then it seemed to be getting closer.
It annoyed me. I didn't want to be disturbed and I could not see
why a car should be coming to the deserted sandpit. I waited until
I was sure that it was coming and then I left my rock and went into
the woods. I went a few yards back into the brush, where I was sure
I could not be seen, and knelt down. The ground was crisp and dry
under my knee and smelled very rich. There was still a little light
and I could see the dirt road and the pit from where I crouched.
After a while the automobile drove up in a great cloud of dust. It
drove to the end of the road and stopped. I waited, expecting the
driver to see that it was a dead end and turn around, but he did
not. He turned off the motor. That made me very angry. I felt as
though he were trespassing on my land. I stared at the car from
beneath a large clump of bushes, and that was when I realized what
was happening. There was a girl in the car. Two men and one girl.
I could not really see what was going on, but I heard a great deal
of giggling and rustling and soft voices. I knew what was going on
then. It filled me with great anger. I dug my hands into the soft
earth and made noises in my throat and hoped that they would go
away. Why wouldn't they go away? But they did not. The darkness
fell suddenly and there was the moon, shining right down on that
motorcar with all the lewd sounds coming from within. I wanted to
leave then, to run away as fast as I could, but something seemed to
hold me there. I could not leave. I could not even look away from
the motorcar. I suppose that the change must have occurred at
this time, but I was not even aware that it had started; even after I
changed I did not realize it.

And then they got out of the car! The girl was laughing and

flushed and her clothing was partially unfastened. She got out and stood beside the car and the two men got out. One of them had a blanket and he spread it on the ground. The other one kissed her. I saw his lips grind on hers, and I could tell that she liked it. She was not a good girl. I saw it all. I saw her take her undergarments off and lift her dress and lie down on the blanket, and then both of those men got down and they both . . . they took turns . . . Ah, I cannot write of that, there are some things that a normal man cannot face. But they did things to her and I crouched there in the woods and I saw everything that happened . . .

I controlled myself. Perhaps the horrible thing that I was witnessing had hypnotized me so that control was not hard. But I waited there, even though I wanted to spring at those execrable and detestable creatures, to punish them, to bring an end to their foul act. I waited and after a long time both men seemed to have sated their lust and they got up and put their clothing on. The girl was smiling. She remained on the blanket for a while. She actually seemed to be contented, as if she were satisfied with her wicked-ness! I looked at her, at that evil twisted smile on her mouth, at the way she lay with her head back and her knees raised. I looked at her throat and her arched back and her white thighs. Everything about her was flagitious and depraved. She was exposed in a beam of moonlight and made no attempt at all to cover her parts. Her legs were parted and her undergarments lay beside her on the ground. I have never imagined such base corruption.

A strange thing happened then. I do not pretend to understand it. The two men got in the motorcar. They were laughing and one of them leaned out the window and said something to the girl. She looked startled and leaped to her feet. The car started and she tried to get in. She was very distressed and the men were looking pleased with themselves. They backed around and the car turned and she pleaded with them. But they drove off. One of them waved at her from the window, and she hurled a curse at them which no gentle-man could ever repeat. She stood there, looking down the road after the car and muttering to herself. She had her hands on her hips, and the words that she mumbled were such as I have never heard before; I scarcely know the meaning of them, and I am a full-grown man. But they all had sexual reference, for even in her anger she was

depraved. I have never known a greater sinner than that woman was.
I presume that the two men, their lust satiated, had been appalled at
what they had done, and left her to punish her for her part in their
crime against nature. That is the only explanation that occurs to me,
although I do not understand why they laughed as they drove off.
There are some things that I do not understand about the relationships between men and women. But I do understand what is wrong
and that girl was wrong. That girl needed to be punished.

I didn't intend to hurt her. I don't know what I intended. I waited
until she had walked back to the blanket and then I got to my feet
and moved out into the open. She had bent down to pick up her
panties. I walked very quietly up behind her. She raised one leg and
started to draw the panties over her foot and then I must have made
some slight sound, because she turned towards me.

I don't know if she screamed. Her mouth was open but I heard
no sound. Perhaps she was too frightened to scream, or perhaps
my ears were not functioning. She staggered backwards a few
steps, her hands raised, palms out towards me. Her panties were
bundled around her ankle. The fear in her face was indescribable.
I slowly moved after her, with my hands clawed in front of me and
my teeth bared. I moved closer and she fell to the ground. Her eyes
never once left my face. Even when I crouched over her she looked
directly into my face. Her fear seemed to inspire me. I had only
meant to frighten her, I am sure. But there is something about fear
... the smell of fear ... it made me lose control. Fear and blood
have much the same smell. I could not help myself then, it was her
fault; she drove me to it just as she must have driven those two men
to that foul act. I remembered that as I saw her white thighs flash
and her painted lips move and I wanted to rip and tear and destroy;
to drive my talons into her flesh so that the blood jetted out and
that evil life was ended.

That was when I sprang on her.

And all the while she looked directly into my eyes, until her own
eyes clouded over. She seemed to remain conscious for an extraor-
dinarily long time.

I don't remember what happened afterwards. I don't know how

long I crouched over her corpse, or what I did to it. I must have been there for some time, if the newspapers have accurately reported the condition of her body. But then, they have reported nothing else correctly, and I am glad that I have been able to write this so that the truth is written somewhere.

This is the truth; this is exactly how it happened.

July 20

I have ignored this book for the past two weeks. I have not even read it. I think that I exhausted myself with my last entry, and it was a good thing to get my mind off the disease and to relax for a while. That is a serious trouble with modern civilization, it leaves so little time to relax. Luckily, I have never fallen into the habit of rushing madly after money and success and happiness. I am content to let it come to me if it will, or to do without it if it will not. I am stoical and reasonable and undoubtedly born several hundred years too late in history. But I do not complain. I have never been given to boasting, but I feel that eventually I shall be able to even reconcile myself to accepting my affliction on the same terms that I regard the other aspects of life. It is, after all, only one night per month, only twelve nights each year that I suffer. It could be so much worse. Many diseases are worse, it is just that they are common and taken for granted, whereas mine is unique and seems more horrible than it really is. It is not as bad, surely, as having cancer, or leprosy, or being blinded. Only vanity made me think it was so terrible, and I am happy to see that I have defeated such thoughts and now look at it in its true perspective. If it is a trial sent to judge me, I shall not be found lacking. I am happier now than I have been in a long while, because I am thinking clearly for the first time, thinking as clearly about my illness as I am in the habit of thinking about other things. I accept my agony in the same way as I accept my pleasures and my mild happiness. I have learned to live with the sickness just as I have learned to live with the cruelty of society, with the lesser mentality of my wife.

I have read what I wrote about that night. It is all very objective and true, and I believe it helped me to see myself more perfectly. One thing I noticed, which would have disturbed me a short time ago, but which now makes me understand better . . . In writing about what happened, I continually referred to myself as myself, instead of to the thing that I become, or to it. I see that those words were a defence, that I used them instead of facing the truth. For, of course, it and I are the same. We are the same being, with changes and differences but basically the same. I can even face up to that now, and it shows how well I am thinking. I don't know if this change in my writing happened because I was trying so hard to remember all the details, or because I am drawing nearer to it, and it to me, or purely for literary ease and convenience, but whichever caused it, I feel it is a good symptom, and shows truthfulness and lack of inhibition. It was, after all, an unusual night . . . an extraordinary night . . . it is hardly strange that I remembered it differently than I remembered those terrible nights in the cell. I will have to wait and see how things are this month, when I return to the cell again. I will bring this book with me again, and go down in plenty of time. I won't take any chances on staying outside again. I must never allow another accident to take place. But . . . I am not at all sure that, in this one instance, it was not rather a good thing. That may sound heartless, but many true thoughts do. And when one considers how many young men that woman would have debased, how many she would have led into sin and degradation and ruin . . . well, perhaps I have saved a good many. And surely the girl herself is better off dead. She had nothing whatsoever to live for. Young as she was, she was already old with sin, and she could never have been happy in her depravity . . .

To think that I actually considered suicide the day after it happened! I was so emotional, so out of character. But everything is all right now, and I have felt better for the last two weeks than I have felt for a long, long time. It is hard to give the reasons, it is almost as though I accomplished something . . . as though I have suddenly achieved something or gained something that I have wanted for a long time, without knowing it. And yet, nothing is changed. I cannot see what it is. It must be something intangible, some frustration that I never realized I had must have been removed from my mind. It may be that the shock of what happened on that night broke up whatever was blocking my mind. It does seem to have something to do with it. I cannot trace the path through my thoughts and emotions, but it is there. It is not a new feeling, but it is a new depth of satisfaction. I can remember feeling this way when I was young. It is almost the way that I felt when I destroyed my favorite toy. It is close to how I felt when I destroyed that savage dog that had attacked me. It is a very curious phenomenon. It is very peculiar that three acts which were so completely different can give such a similar feeling. I find it quite interesting . . .

July 28

The day approaches. I am quite resigned. I am in perfect physical health and my mind is clear and I live a pure life and if I must suffer one night it is hardly anything to complain of. I wish my wife would stop acting so peculiarly, however. All this month she has seemed very distant. Perhaps she actually took some stock in those false newspaper accounts, and is angry with me, but she has not mentioned it. She has never said a word about that. It is no longer front-page news, new scandals and lies have displaced it, but each day there is a small paragraph reporting the progress of the police. Each day they claim that an arrest is imminent. It makes me chuckle. I do hope that they do not arrest some innocent man. But, still, I am sure that if they do arrest someone he will be a known pervert and will be guilty of far worse crimes than mine, and so I am not worried about it. Punishment for the wrong sin is quite just, if some other sin has been committed. As far as myself . . . and the man who struck the librarian down . . . I cannot feel any guilt.

July 29

When I was coming home from my afternoon stroll today I saw a workman leave our house. There was a lorry outside, and I believe he was from the same company that built the cell for us. I asked Helen about it, and she looked startled, and then she denied that he had been there. I was curious about that at first, and for a moment I actually wondered if she might have been unfaithful to me, she acted so strange and so nervous. But that was a terrible thought and I never should have had it for a moment. It was a sin to think such a thing. I have guessed what the truth is now. She has had something done to make the cell more comfortable for me. Perhaps she has had new padding put in, or a brighter light installed. I can't imagine what else it could be. She wanted to keep it as a surprise, of course. Something that she imagines will cheer me up when I have to go to the cell. Perhaps it will, at that. I do hope, however, that she was bright enough to give a logical reason for having the padding in the cell, if the workman saw the inside. Even unintelligent construction workers sometimes have imaginations . . . I suppose they sometimes read the newspapers, too. Still, we have a right to have a padded cell if we choose, and no one can question that.

I have just wondered if perhaps the man had come to install a stronger lock on the door. Helen has been strange . . . distant. It is possible that she is frightened. Poor thing. I can understand how it is. I must make an attempt to be more pleasant, and more tolerant of her weaknesses. I should give her some little token of my affection. Perhaps I should go to her bedroom this evening. She always seems very grateful when I do that, and I have not gone for some time now. But that is her fault. She does not give any indication that she wants me to, and I only do it for her. Perhaps she has come to see that it is better to abstain as much as possible.

July 30
Helen has changed remarkably.

Who can understand the workings of the female mind? There are depths to even the simplest and most unimaginative of women that can never be probed. I feel that I have as much insight as any man, that my logic is capable of plumbing any logical depths, and yet I have no conception of what has brought about this difference in my wife. It has been coming on for some time now, I think, but last night it was the most noticeable that it has been yet. Perhaps it is simply that there is no reason for it, that the basic motions of the female atoms are erratic. I hate to think that. I prefer a well-ordered concept of life. But I am open-minded to other possibilities. I have had to be open-minded; a closed mind would not have the scope to deal with life as a man in my circumstances must do. I would not be in the least surprised to know that I am the only man who has ever suffered with my affliction and still kept his sanity. Perhaps that seems like a vain statement, but still a man must recognize his virtues in order to capitalize on them. I am humble in my pride.

Last night I went to her room. She had gone to bed early and after a while I decided to go to her. But everything was different.

When I opened her bedroom door she sat up quickly, holding the covers up to her chin and looking at me with her eyes open wide. It was almost as though she had been lying there waiting, expecting me to come. That in itself is strange. And the way that she looked ... well, it was very much like fear. She cringed when I touched her. She said nothing at all but she trembled under my hand and searched my face. I hated to see that expression, that look in her eyes. It was as though she thought last night was the night of the change. Perhaps she had lost track of the date. But surely she knows that I will never forget it? How can my own wife fear me? Is it all a result of those atrocious lies in the newspapers, or is she breaking down under the strain—suffering, perhaps, in sympathy with me? It might be that. She does seem to be different when it is getting near the night when I must go to the cell. I have heard that often one suffers for a loved one. Men are reported to have labor pains when their wives are pregnant. It might possibly be something of that nature. I prefer to think that, because it is very unpleasant to think that she fears me.

When we were first married Helen used to be very affectionate. Even passionate. Far too much so, in fact, and several times I had to ask her to please exercise a bit of restraint. It is wrong for a woman to abandon herself to carnal pleasures. I am not sure if it is wrong to feel pleasure in a carnal act, but it certainly is wrong to give oneself up to it. Once Helen tried to take the initiative in the marriage act, and several times she came right out and asked me if I would not come to her bed. I had to lecture her quite firmly about that. She was not really to blame; she was innocent and had no experience and did not realize how wrong her behaviour was. She was undoubtedly trying to please me by her overt desire and undisguised lustings. It does seem that a proper young woman should know instinctively that it is wrong, but who am I to judge? I have never attempted to set myself up as a moralist, I am simply a moral man who tries to show others the proper way to live. I had to be a bit strict with Helen, of course, but that was for her own good.

Last night it was very different, however. She was not in the least demanding, and she seemed quite pleased when we had finished and I was ready to return to my own room. All through the act she had continued to stare up at me with that strange expression.

It made me feel very uncomfortable. I am never quite comfortable while I am performing the marital duty, but this was worse. It was ... uncomfortable is not the word, but I know no word to describe it. It was an exceedingly troubling emotion. I hope that she never looks at me that way again. There is something about fear ... I don't know what it is ... it always makes me feel ... makes me imagine ... indefinite things. This is very difficult to express correctly. Vague things seem to be lurking just below the surface of my mind, unclear, clouded and dark and unsavory. Dangerous things, somehow. Shrouded images. I cannot define it more closely than this.

July 31
I am waiting for tomorrow with the usual dread and disgust, but also with a certain curiosity. I wonder how last month has affected the disease. I have been so much at peace all during July; have come to terms with myself so well, that I would not be in the least surprised to find a definite change in the sickness. Last month may have acted as a catalyst and changed the chemistry of the thing ... perhaps for the better. Whatever happens I feel that I will be able to accept it stoically.

I would tell Helen of my hopes if she did not seem so distant and unusual. But it is probably better not to, until I know. There is little benefit in raising false cheer. This morning she acted peculiarly again. I had gone out into the hall to fetch my gloves and when I turned around she was looking around the corner at me. Just her face was around the corner, and she ducked back. I went down and asked her if she wanted anything and, after mumbling for a moment, she said that she wondered whether I was going down to the basement. Why would she think that? She knows that I hate the basement, and that I never go down there until it is necessary. When I assured her of this she seemed relieved, so perhaps she is just overwrought as the day draws near. Perhaps she is afraid that it might begin sooner than usual, and that I shall have to spend more time, perhaps more than one night, in the cell. I can understand how that would bother her, and it shows her concern for me. But it also shows her complete lack of understanding of just what my disease is.

August 1
I am fairly bursting with energy today. I took a long, brisk walk after lunch. I stopped to watch some children playing in an empty lot. I seemed to share their enthusiasm for life. It made me regret the fact that I can never have children. They were so gay and carefree, that I felt sorry they must grow up and face the troubles of life. My childhood was not happy; at least it does not seem happy in my memory, except for a few outstanding occasions. But I do not envy others in this respect, because my beginnings have carried me on to a proper manhood and I am able to look back at my whole life and regret no single thing that I have ever done. Any regrets that I feel are for things not my fault, things ordained before I was created. It is surely the greatest peace that man can know when he can see his whole existence running in one continuous sequence and find that at no point has there been any shame, anything to mar his past; that his total life has been exactly as he would have willed it, considering those things in which he has a choice.

I am almost looking forward to the change tonight, I feel so certain that there will be an improvement . . . or is it that I know now that no improvement is necessary, that I understand my affliction is not nearly as bad as I believed it to be? I hope that the thing which I become can share my tranquillity.

August 1 (Night)
Well, the door is barred now. Helen has gone upstairs and I am alone in the cell. Helen tried to be very pleasant today. She cooked my favorite dinner, simple wholesome food, and she chattered away self-consciously and tried to be gay and to take my mind off what would soon happen. I appreciate her pitiful little efforts against a thing she cannot grasp. I came down quite early so that she did not have to worry about it. I was afraid that she would begin to be nervous and frightened, and wanted to spare her that ordeal . . . and spare myself witnessing it, too.

I have not noticed anything different about the cell. I was sure that she had had some improvement made, but the lock is the same and the padding is still torn in places. Perhaps she had the workman come to make an estimate and intends to have the work done next month. I wish that I had thought to put a brighter light in, however.

It is difficult to write, and the corners are in shadow. If . . .

I have just made a horrible discovery. I am at a loss to understand what it means. A cold sliver is knifing up my backbone and my flesh is like ice. I was writing before and I glanced at the wall and . . . there is a hole through the wall! It is a small hole, and I didn't notice it immediately. It is in the corner by the door, and it is large enough for someone to look through . . . to look into the cell. The hole was not there before, and there is still some concrete dust on the floor, so I know that it was made recently. That must have been why the workman was here. But why did my wife have the hole made? Whatever has possessed her? Why would she do such a fiendish thing? She must be mad! She must intend to look into the cell after the change has occurred! But why would she want to? It is beyond belief, it is monstrous. The thought that she will see me . . . see me become . . . something other than a man. I am crouching against the wall with the hole and I cannot be observed from there, but I don't know what to do about later . . . after I change. The thing is not rational, or does not care about rationality. It will not remain here against the door where it cannot be seen. I have considered trying to plug the hole with my shirt, but I fear that the shirt will become torn loose when the disease is at its frenzied pitch. Or she might poke it free with a stick. There is nothing I can do. She is going to see me!

I am sick with dread. I feel that I shall vomit. My head is spinning. Why would Helen do this to me? Is it simply morbid curiosity? Has she some perverted twist to her nature that I have never before observed? Or is it that she still doubts me, and wants proof that I am not mad, that I do not imagine it all? I do not know. The thought that she will see the change is terrible, and God knows what effect it will have on her! I can only hope that she recognizes it as an illness, and that the truth will not drive her out of her mind. But her mind is not strong and I fear . . . I have seen the look on other faces when they see me changed. The drunkard . . . the girl . . . There was a look of madness on those faces, and Helen is not strong . . . I have seen the fear in her eyes even when I am normal. After she read those lies in the newspapers, those horrible tales of mutilation and dismemberment . . . the other night in bed . . . and that fear that makes her face glow white as the moon, makes it shift and tremble until I can see only that terror and everything else fades away and I look . . . I feel . . . I feel that such fear must not be left to survive . . . How will I ever face her again after . . . when I am normal . . . then I heard the door close. I think she is coming down.

August 2?

I presume it is morning. I am all right now, although I am exhausted. My clothing is torn to shreds. Helen will be down soon to open the door. How will she face me now, after last night? I begged her to go away and she would not even answer me, she just looked into the cell and waited. My agitation brought the sickness on sooner than it should have come, and I lost all control. She saw everything. I hate her. I hate her for what she has done to me. I am on fire with rage and shame and hatred! When she opens the door I shall have to exercise great control to keep from striking her. She deserves to be struck. She deserves worse. For what she has done to me there could be no punishment too great. She made it much much worse than it has ever been before. I can clearly remember raging against the wall, trying to tear my way out, trying to rip the hole apart, and all the while she was standing there, on the other side of that indestructible barrier, looking in at everything. She is a monster, a fiend, a devil! There are no words to describe her . . .

August

I don't know the date. There is no way to tell the time. It seems an eternity. I no longer care about this record. It seems futile now. And my pen is nearly out of ink. The light seems to be growing dim too, and soon I shall be in darkness. I might be able to write with my own blood, but it hardly seems worth the effort . . . I don't like blood, it reminds me of too much. Still, trying to record something occupies my mind. It is an ally against madness. I can bear the hunger and the thirst but I could not bear to lose my mind.

I cannot understand why she has done this to me. I no longer hate her, I just cannot understand. She comes down and looks in once in a while. Once a day, once a week . . . I don't know. It is all the same here. She never says anything. She won't answer me when I speak to her. She makes a strange noise sometimes, a cackling sound. I suppose she is insane. When I plead with her she goes away . . .

?

I am so hungry.

I have tried to eat the padding from the walls, but it is no good. It makes my thirst greater. The light is nearly out now. Only by standing directly beneath it can I see to write. My vision is blurred as well. I am very weak and dizzy. I don't suppose that I will be able to write again.

I know now that I must die here. I am resigned to it. It seems proper that, if I must die, it is through no fault of my own. I have done nothing to bring this about. Like all the suffering of my life, I am innocent of the cause, I have suffered through the sins of my ancestors, and now I die through the madness of my wife. It is unjust, but proper. I must lie down now. I am sure that there will be nothing more to record.

I know it is night. I bit my arm . . .

That was the journal that I found in my aunt's drawer. There were some pages after the last entry that had been marked, but they were undecipherable. They may have been an attempt to write in the dark, or they may have been the heedless markings of something with the hand of a man. I did not look long at them. I closed the book slowly and stared out the window at the rain. A loud clap of thunder sounded and the big elm tree in the yard whipped under the wind and the wind rushed under the clouds. Somewhere a dog howled. I sat there for a long time and then I got up and put the journal in my pocket. It was getting late. I went into the hall and opened the door that led down to the basement. I had to go down there. I hesitated but I had to. The air was thick and foul and it was like walking into a grave, but I went down.

The cell was in the corner, as the book said. My footsteps were incredibly loud as I crossed the concrete floor. The door was barred and I lifted the bar quickly, without thinking about it. It groaned and rust flaked off. I tried the door but it would not move. It had been locked with a key as well. It was a large lock and the door was very strong. I stepped to the corner and after a moment found the hole. The edges had begun to crumble. I looked through it but I could see nothing within. It was black inside. I turned and walked very calmly across the basement and up the stairs. I had every intention of searching for the key to the cell. I knew that it must be somewhere in Aunt Helen's possessions. As I reached the top step it gave way under my weight. I had to leap to keep from falling. I landed off-balance in the hallway and suddenly I was running. I went out of the front door and into the storm. I am as brave as the next man, I am fit and very strong, but that day I ran and kept on running until I was far away from the house and drenched with rain. I had forgotten my coat.

That was some time ago and I have never been back to the house that I inherited from Aunt Helen. Someday I shall. I am often curious as to what is in the cell now. Surely there could be nothing there that would harm me. It all happened long ago. And Aunt Helen must have been in herself at some time, because she had the book. I have checked the old newspapers carefully, and found a report of an unsolved murder that might have been the one he wrote about. Or it might not. He was surely mad, and perhaps it was all in his mind. Of course it was all in his mind. And yet . . . I cannot help but wonder what Aunt Helen saw when she looked into the cell that night. Did she realize then, for the first time, that he was insane, and leave him for that reason? Or did she see something else? Something that drove her mad?

I shall never know, at any rate. I don't expect that she kept a journal of her own. It doesn't really trouble me. Not really. I have never been a superstitious man. But I have determined that I must never have children. Because, you see, Aunt Helen was related to me by marriage. It was her husband who was related to me by blood. I have kept the book and sometimes I read it through again, trying to find the truth. Sometimes I read it on those long white nights when the moon is bright and round and I have nothing at all to do but sit alone by my window. I live alone. I would like to have a pet, but animals don't like me. Dogs are afraid of me. It is rather boring and I shall have to start keeping a diary to occupy my time on those nights. As it is I just sit, watching the moon, watching my hands . . .

Strange Roots

ANTON PLOTNIKOV WAS INTERESTED IN WEREWOLVES.
He had been born of peasant stock in the Balkans, which undoubtedly stimulated this interest, but he had become a psychologist and therefore his interest took a scientific and rational turn, although traces of the ancient superstitions still lurked somewhere in his most primitive cells. Mainly, however, he sought scientific truth. Anton had left his unfortunate homeland after the last war and emigrated to England; took a well-paid job in research and married a passionate girl named Beta. They were reasonably happy. He bought, in due course, a fine house in the country and, with company funds, installed a small but efficient laboratory in the basement. It was understood that this laboratory would be used for the company's profit, of course, but since Anton was a valuable and brilliant scientist he was allowed a measure of freedom. This suited Anton very well, for he was a man who saw that research must not be limited, and in his spare time (and a great deal of the company's time, if truth be told) he began a comprehensive study of lycanthropy. This did not seem dishonest to Anton. His well-paid work involved investigation into the effects of chemical and glandular imbalance in mental disorders, and Anton was convinced that the phenomenon of the werewolf was based on just that—that there were scientific and medical grounds behind the legend. From time to time he reported on his work, being careful not to use the word *werewolf* but to mention only the chemical-psychological aspects in learned but vague terms. Since he was far more intelligent than the company men who read his reports, this worked out well enough. His work progressed. He began to spend more and more time in the laboratory and his wife, who was truly passionate, began to take a series of lovers. This suited her splendidly. Anton worked on a labor of love, Beta loved laboriously, and even the company, due to recent research, prospered.

There followed a series of important breakthroughs in the study of how bodily chemistry affects the behaviour of mankind. Gradually old prejudices broke down. Freud turned over ponderously in his grave. The psychoanalysts tore their hair out by the roots and moaned that Armageddon was come. Psychiatrists carried banners of protest through the streets. Shaggy students cheerfully joined the march, passionately defending the creaking knowledge that they were creatures driven by the traumas of adolescence, warped by society, inexorably motivated by events of the past. Because they had seen their mothers naked when they were three, they threw rocks at the police. Because the police had all dreamed of being marched upon by immoral women wearing boots, they arrested the students. Because the judge had once placed his penis in his sister's shoe, he fined them heavily. But through it all the research progressed. It became documented and understood that all forms of mental malfunction, save the minor fetishes, were caused by chemical imbalance. The students, no fools these, began to be converted, to throw stones at psychiatrists and plead in court that they were not guilty because their hormone secretions had ruled their behaviour. The judges took a tolerant view except when they had hangovers. Truth was beginning to conquer. But it was a long and difficult struggle. In the United States the psychiatrists lobbied in Congress, pressing for laws against this blasphemous research and finding direct relationships between glandular secretions and marijuana. The Congressmen seldom smoked marijuana but were well aware of the sluggish chemistry of their bodies, and the lobby was defeated. But only in America did the people actually believe in psychiatry and analysis, for there it had become a social thing, a status symbol. Once analysis was proven about as valid as astrology it became even more snobbish. After all, what could be more pretentious than squandering money on a myth? The analysts found a new prosperity for a time, until reverse snobbery followed and the wealthy types began to consult with their dustmen. They called them garbage collectors. The dustmen called themselves sanitary engineers, and were quite ready to lower their trash cans and take the woes of the world unto themselves. For, after all, what is it but garbage? So the dustmen became honoured and the analysts became a luxury of the middle-class. But that was America, where such things happen. The rest of the world had never believed in psychiatry anyway, and could not afford it.

*

Through it all, Anton Plotnikov worked on.

He was a physiological psychologist and understood that the functions of the mind were inseparable from those of the body. He had no desire to get wealthy clients on a couch. But eventually his work reached an impasse. He had gathered all possible data, his theories were formed, and it became necessary to advance along different lines—to observe rather than theorize, to experiment rather than gather information. For this experimentation he needed money. He needed supplies. Specifically, he needed a wolf . . .

Or rather, he required the secretions from the glands and blood of wolves. He put in a request to the company. He had not produced anything of value for some time and the company demanded further details. Anton supplied them. The company could see no possible profit motive in this line of research and turned his request down. Anton was annoyed and unhappy. He brooded. Eventually, unknown to the company and against their principles, he applied for a government grant. Complicated forms were sent to him by the appropriate agencies. He was asked to outline his work and did so. The government agencies requested further details and results and assured him his application was being considered. It was filed and forgotten. Anton waited impatiently. He continued to work as best he could and submitted, from time to time, further reports. Nothing happened. Finally Anton decided he could wait no longer. He took his own savings and determined to carry on unaided. He contacted a team of Canadian ecologists and arranged to receive the necessary secretions from wolves. They were willing to help. Their work involved knocking *canis lupus* out with tranquillizer pellets and clamping bands on the creatures' ears, and it was not difficult to take samples of blood and hormone secretions in the process. Anton met a sinister fellow named Chowder who agreed to kidnap dogs for him. This was expensive, since he felt it necessary to use the oldest breeds of dog such as greyhounds and Afghans. But, once decided, Anton gritted his teeth and paid out his hard-earned money and in due course found his laboratory stocked with caged canines. The samples arrived from Canada. He was ready to continue his work. He spent more and more time in his laboratory. The company sent him curt reminders that his work was falling behind and Beta, extremely displeased to find their savings gone, took more lovers. Anton noticed nothing, concentrating on his work. Or chose to ignore it; it was all the same to his wife. And still, from time to time, Anton sent progress reports to the various government agencies and hoped and worked and worked . . .

Anton's reports did not go entirely unnoticed. There was a bright lad named Smith in the government agency who took a certain interest and a definite amusement in the reports which trickled in. Smith had no Balkan ancestry, but was a devoted fan of Peter Cushing. He actually read the reports before filing them. Rather more improbably, he actually understood them. And, incredibly, he even took a few notes. These are a few examples:

Lycanthropy: The supposed power of a human being to transform into a wolf. Belief in werewolves.

Lycorexia: A morbid pathological condition in which one has a fixation that he is actually a wolf. He has a raging hunger for raw flesh, he mimics the movements of the animal, he howls and snarls. For practical purposes, he is the wolf. There is glandular disturbance and symptoms sometimes diagnosed as possession.

Virilism: Technically, the appearance in a female of male physical and sexual characteristics. Hirsuteness. Plotnikov believes that this term is applied only to the female because it is obviously more noticeable in them, but that a male may suffer from the same disease without attracting attention, being merely considered as exceptionally virile and masculine. There is reason to believe that this glandular disturbance may be directly related to the so-called criminal type theory. This, however, is not Plotnikov's field, and is mentioned only in passing.

Pathology: Investigation of structural and functional changes in tissue, caused by disease.

Pathomorphism: Abnormality of bodily structure.

Pathomimesis: Simulation of disease found in hysteria.

To sum up: It is Plotnikov's belief that certain chemical imbalances (substantiated by recent research into psychological disorders) were responsible for a glandular malfunction which caused the symptoms of virilism and lycorexia to appear simultaneously. This combination gave rise to the werewolf legend. Plotnikov seems to have kept an open mind here, and mentions other possible causes. For example, the last of the Neanderthal men must have seemed monstrous creatures to emerging Homo Sapiens. However, he feels that the legend is rooted in more recent times and takes the view that, due to various conditions and factors, the above mentioned glandular malfunctions were commonplace.

My viewpoint: It seems to me that his theory is valid. However, I can find no practical application for his work. His later reports indicate that he is actually doing laboratory work on certain substances derived from living wolves and hopes to isolate, or even create, the chemical which caused the disease. This is rather fascinating. However, it still seems to have no practical value, even if he succeeds. Unless he wants to create a werewolf, ha ha.

Anton's research, at first, proved negative.

He injected dog after dog with the various derivatives and serums he had created and found them unaffected. He was desolate. He could not see where he was blundering. But he pressed on. He could not use the same dog more than once, for that would destroy the experimental control, and was forced to employ Chowder once again. His funds sank to a new low. The dogs thrived with healthy (but normal) appetites. His wife thrived with healthy sexual appetites. Anton, who had always slumped, slumped more and found that his hair was rapidly departing. Chowder demanded more money. The company sent him an ultimatum which he tore up in a rare rage. He worked on doggedly with test tube and hypodermic, despairing but never quite losing hope. He was haggard and gaunt and, indeed, resembled a mad scientist in a bad film, holding a bubbling test tube up and regarding it with a red-rimmed eye; leering as he approached a dog with a dripping needle; talking to himself as he stirred and mixed his various brews.

And then, quite by accident, as often proves the case in scientific advance, a startling factor came to light . . .

Anton had just received a new greyhound from Chowder and was leading it to a cage. His mind was preoccupied and he inadvertently passed close by one of the other occupied cages, containing a vague sort of terrier which had been injected several days before and shown no effects, ill or otherwise. As he led the greyhound past, the terrier suddenly thrust its muzzle through the bars and nipped the greyhound on the flank. The greyhound spun, snarling, but Anton managed to restrain it and haul it away from the aggressor. He examined the wound and found it superficial; cleansed it and applied a disinfectant and left the greyhound in a cage. He thought little of this, at the time. He was busily at work on a new serum. This serum would not be ready for a few days and, in the meanwhile, the greyhound was not injected. It stood behind its bars and regarded Anton with a solemn and baleful eye. Then it lay down and slept. Anton worked into the night until at last, exhausted, he left the laboratory and went to bed. Beta was already asleep, smiling in her dreams. Anton crawled in carefully, so as not to disturb her. This was not because he was solicitous for her slumber as much as selfish for his own. He was well aware that his wife had rather over-developed sexual urges and knew that, if she should awaken, she would undoubtedly demand servicing. Now, Anton loved his wife, no doubt of that, but his love was not inclined towards the physical. He loved scientifically or rationally and could not stand up to the rigours of sexual relations as frequently as Beta required them. Therefore, he slipped carefully in beside her and rested his weary head on the pillow. He thought he was too exhausted to sleep, but after a while he drifted off. He tossed restlessly as his tired muscles began to relax. And then he began to dream. His dreams, as his waking thoughts, invariably centered on lycanthropy. He stood in the land of Morpheus and listened to the howlings of tormented werewolves. He trembled in delight and fear. The howling grew louder, closer. He trembled more. His delight faded and his fear increased. It occurred to the sleeping scientist that the werewolves were hungry and that he was alone. It was a dark world of twisted barren trees and deep shadows and a full white moon. Anton ran through his dreams. He fled madly, with gnarled limbs snapping at his face and tangled roots gripping his ankles. He was panting and sweating. He could not run very fast. The howling was behind him, following him and drawing ever closer. He came to a shattered ridge surmounted by a solitary, mangled tree. It was an oak tree, hideously malformed. Anton decided he must climb that tree and seek sanctuary in the high branches while the werewolves raged below. He began to climb. The rough bark scraped his hands, his feet slipped seeking purchase, gravity hauled him back. He elevated himself by scant inches. The wolves were in full cry. Dark forms shot through the shadows, he saw the gleam of a yellow eye, a flash of fangs. He screamed and drew himself upwards, knowing he was too late, too slow.

And then the werewolves were upon him . . .

Anton cried out in the grip of fang and talon.

The wolves dragged him down from the tree. He rolled in the earth, screaming, as ravenous jaws tore him asunder and savage throats gulped down his flesh. He beat with feeble arms and drew his knees up to his chest, and wondered how long it would take him to die.

Then his wife said, "Wake up!"

Anton opened his eyes.

Anton stared, unbelievingly, at the metamorphosis.

Beta was leaning over him, shaking him.

Gradually the transformation registered in his mind. Fang and claw became well-manicured fingernails, fiendish haunches were well-turned soft flanks, hairy chests were exquisite mounds capped with delightful nipples, slavering jaws were ripe red lips. And blood-lust was . . . well, just lust, he thought, with a groan.

"Wake up," she demanded.

"Not tonight, darling," Anton whimpered.

"What?"

"I'm really frightfully tired, dearest."

Beta stared at him with a pretty frown and suddenly, shockingly, the howling came again, transcending the realm of nightmare to register in his waking mind. Anton's eyes leaped wide, bewildered.

"What is it?" he asked.

Beta waited a moment, peering at him; ascertaining that he was fully awake now.

"One of those damned brutes in the laboratory, obviously," she said. "What else? You'll have to do something, Anton. I can't sleep with that horrid howling."

Anton sighed with relief.

"Of course, dearest," he said, thankful that she had awakened him for something less than carnal needs. It was far easier to descend to the laboratory and administer a sedative than to ascend his wife and administer the orgastic tranquilizer. He got up and tied his dressing gown around himself; slid his feet into well-worn slippers. He felt a chill as the perspiration of his nightmare evaporated. Beta curled up under the covers and Anton moved from the room. He was fully awake now. As he reached the top of the stairs, the howling sounded once again, and quite suddenly Anton felt another chill — a chill which had nothing to do with evaporation as it clambered up the segments of his spine.

He stood, gripping the banister, and looked down into the darkness below.

Once again the howling sounded.

It was not the howling of a dog.

Anton knew.

Anton had never heard that sound before, but somewhere deep in his primary cells he knew.

It was the cry of the wolf . . .

The savage cry faded away, seeping into the fabric of the house and running out into the night, but the fierce echo still reverberated in Anton's heart. His scientist's mind was able to baffle and channel the sound, directing it along the course of reason, but in his Balkan heart the drums of fear were beating. He stood very still. His hand gripped the railing. He was aware of a clock ticking in a recess down the hall and the slight creaking of the bed as his wife shifted her position. Then he began to tremble. This reaction was symptomatic of two emotions, far different and yet inextricably linked. There was the fear and there was also surging joy. He became a man divided, his sentience separated by the flat, calm plane of reason, dissected cleanly and sharply so that his two halves were linked only by the connecting chain between those two emotions, breaking through the calm surface of the rational division exactly as the chain of an anchor runs down from the ship to the dark anchor at the depths. Joy was the ship, riding above the deep, light and buoyant. Fear was the anchor, heavy and cold, slowly turning far below.

The sails of the ship billowed and strained as joy sought to run gaily before the wind of success but that solid anchor restrained it on the groaning chain. And Anton was restrained as these antagonistic elements waged their tug of war within the corporal shell. He stood trembling for long moments. He was well aware of the conflict but could not join in, could not take sides in the struggle. He was an objective observer, no more, and his observation was hampered, the bathysphere of reason could not descend to the depths of the anchor. The pressures were too great, the cold too severe, the amorphous submarine creatures too formidable. No light was reflected at that depth. The clock ticked on, the bed was silent now. Anton told himself that he was about to realize the fruits of his labors, the truth of his theory, the verification of his predictions, and these thoughts sent the wind at gale force behind the anchored vessel. But then the cry sounded yet again, wild and piercing, and the anchor plummeted down. The chain, fully extended, creaked and strained. The anchor was rebounding, threatening to drag the ship beneath the surface and send Anton in mad thoughtless flight.

Then the chain snapped.

Fear settled slowly into the mire and Anton was free.

Anton went very calmly down to the laboratory . . .

He opened the door very slowly, just a crack, without fear now, but with great caution. It was dark inside. The door scraped slightly and the sounds of carnage increased for a moment, horrible growlings and violent snarls. Anton waited, holding the door firmly, until the noise subsided a bit and then slipped his hand in to fumble for the light switch. The flesh crawled up his forearm, he half expected powerful jaws to close on his hand and his fingers felt like icicles in the process of melting, the drips running back down his arm. Then he pressed the switch and bright, overhead lights burst on. There was an abrupt and profound silence in the sudden glare. The silence was somehow more menacing than the sounds, with the sinister and minatory implications of soundlessness—the silent stalk, the controlled savagery awaiting prey. Anton risked an eye around the corner of the door. Then he sighed with relief.

The cages were all intact.

He opened the door further and looked about the laboratory. The dogs were cringing, every aspect of their bearing implying terror, backed in the corner of their cages, tails curled between their legs, necks bristling, all facing towards the back of the room. Anton looked along the line of their fearful vision. There was one dog which was not cringing, and Anton cringed when he looked upon it.

It was the greyhound.

And it was terrible.

The brute, frozen in sudden illumination, stared back at him. It had been fixed in the instant of a snarl, lips drawn back in a rictus. It was hideous and it was, somehow, changed. Its coat was shaggier and coarser, its eyes were wild, its fangs yellow and dripping. It poised on coiled haunches. Anton felt shelves of horror slough down his back. And then the beast sprang. It crashed against the bars and fell back. The bars were stout. They shook but held. The brute sprang again. The cage quivered. Again it fell back, snarling now, and the other dogs began to whine and whimper pitifully. Anton went into the room and closed the door behind him and for a long time he stood there looking at the thing which was no longer quite a dog . . .

Anton was not thinking logically.

He thought only that he must somehow stop that terrible howling. He moved to the workbench and prepared a powerful sedative. His hands were remarkably calm. The beast continued to throw itself against the bars, slobbering with bloodlust. Anton did not dare approach the cage. He considered, thinking carefully, and finally fastened the hypodermic to the end of a measuring stick, the needle extending beyond the end. Then he advanced, holding this makeshift weapon like a spear. The hound howled in a frenzy as he drew near, obviously seeing Anton as raw meat. Froth flew in heavy shards from its jaws. Anton approached as near as he could and extended the stick. The dog ignored it, straining its terrible muzzle through the bars, attempting to reach Anton. The needle slipped into the brute's shoulder and Anton pressed in, injecting the sedative, as the dog spun, snapping at the wound. The powerful jaws splintered the stick and the hypodermic hung for a moment from the shaggy shoulder. Then it dropped out as the beast renewed its attack on the bars. Its violence reached a new peak of fury before gradually subsiding. The drug took effect. The dog's motions became uncertain, its legs splayed. Presently it sat down, curling in a circle, and laid its head on its forepaws. Those glowing yellow eyes began to close. And all the while, even as the lids came down, it looked with hatred and hunger at Anton.

It took great courage to open that cage.

The dog was unconscious, no doubt of that, but it took great courage nonetheless for a man of Balkan peasant ancestry to enter that cage. But he did it. It was necessary, he knew, to take samples of blood and glandular secretions, and his hands were still incredibly calm and quiet as he did so. Then he locked the cage again and took his samples back to the workbench. And only then did the fact—the startling fact—strike him. He stared at the test tubes and then he turned to stare at the dog. He realized that the greyhound had not been injected with any form of serum. For an instant he was stricken with regret, thinking that the creature had gone mad with rabies or some other canine disease, and then he remembered that the dog had been bitten by the terrier. His mind very precisely followed the steps of scientific reasoning. The terrier had been injected with the serum but had not reacted as predicted. The terrier had bitten the greyhound. The greyhound had reacted exactly as predicted for the terrier. Then precise reasoning shattered and the truth struck him like an axe between the eyes.

He had discovered a chemical imbalance which was infectious.

Contagious madness . . .

And horror . . .

From that point, all further investigation fell in place exactly as Anton had predicted. He was delighted; saw himself unravelling the dark secrets through which his ancestors trembled in the Transylvanian nights. There had been a solitary oversight in his former work and, now that aleatory circumstances had bridged that gap, his work followed a logical and evident trail. The aggressive whim of a dog had founded knowledge. Anton's error was in overlooking the necessary intermediate state; in failing to see that the substance might need to mature in the living tissue of a host, combining with saliva and blood and hormones which acted as a catalyst and changed the substance from dormant to malignant. Now that problem was resolved, Anton knew, his work could continue quickly, results would be rapid, perhaps even financial aid would be forthcoming. He decided to submit a new report as soon as the next stage of investigation was completed.

In the morning, the greyhound was awake and placid. No traces of the madness were visible and the other dogs no longer regarded it with fear. Anton rubbed his hands together at this discovery, this proof that the disease waxed and ebbed in accordance with a cycle. It was predictable by inductive reasoning and explained the old legends of werewolves undergoing metamorphosis when the moon was full but, more important, it seemed to prove that his experiment was valid—that no unidentified virus had caused the madness but that it had been purely chemical. He continued with his work. He spent a great deal of time analysing the substances drawn from the greyhound and in due course discovered that it was the saliva which acted as the catalyst. He experimented with the saliva and found, further, that he was unable to create a serum which was effective in the initial injection stage—that it could only be transferred from one living organism to another in a blood-saliva-blood cycle. This complicated his work somewhat, in that he had to persuade the dogs to bite one another. But he managed. The laboratory became a bedlam, a howling house of horrors, as, from time to time, several dogs went mad simultaneously. Anton grew accustomed to it. His wife did not, but after a few days of objection seized upon the noise as an excellent excuse for spending nights away from home. Her love life prospered. And, unhindered by her protests, Anton's work advanced. He placed two infected dogs in the same cage and waited for the madness to come upon them. However, the smaller dog went mad first and tore the larger asunder. In a very short time only a few scraps of hide, shattered bones, and evil, dark stains remained to testify to the larger beast's existence. Anton saw that the cycle was affected by the animal's weight and metabolism. He constructed a double cage, separated by a sliding door which he could operate from a distance, and put an infected dog in each side. One was an Alsatian, the other a Staffordshire terrier. The terrier went berserk first and the Alsatian cringed and quivered. But several hours later the Alsatian, too, went mad. Anton drew the separation from between the cages. The two savage brutes were at one another instantly, with a ferocity both fascinating and appalling. The terrier, bred to fight, retained its inherited ability despite the madness; went low and slashed across and the Alsatian was down. The terrier tore at his opponent, ripping great mouthfuls of flesh from it while it still lived — and, while it still lived, the Alsatian continued to tear at his killer's belly. Anton winced and felt his stomach churn as he realized this was more than a fight to the death; realized that the fight was incidental to the fact; realized that the two dogs were eating each other alive!

He had to hurry from the room and vomit.

When he returned the Alsatian was dead.

The terrier was eating the body. The terrier's belly had been torn out and his entrails hung down in slippery coils and, from time to time, he mistakenly tore a mouthful from his own intestines as he fiendishly satisfied the mad hunger.

Anton went right back out and vomited again.

Two weeks after the first attack, the greyhound again underwent metamorphosis. The other infected beasts followed similar patterns, although the time cycle varied. Anton calculated and observed and made a fairly accurate chart and drew a graph correlating weight to frequency of madness. When this was done he projected the figures to include the normal weight of a man, and saw that the cycle would complete itself approximately once every month in an average-sized human being. This projection pleased him. It was in accord with the full moon cycle of the legend. He carried this line of prediction further, into unsubstantiated theory, and saw the possibility that the moon was more than a coincidence. Lunatics are a fact. A man often feels strange urges, looking at the full moon. The glandular secretions can be stimulated in many ways and, just as the adrenal glands release hormones when a creature is angry or frightened, so might the substance of madness be released by the mood of the moon. As soon as this theory had taken form, Anton was excited. He was also frustrated, for obviously he would be unable to prove it — could not deliberately inject madness into a human. But he felt it to be true and, taking it as the initial premise, he logically pursued possibilities and concluded that, in a human, the metamorphosis would be even more startling than in a dog. A man can reason and a mind can be caused to reason in twisted patterns, and the process, in man, would be psychological as well as physical. In the ability to reason lies the capacity for insanity. In the dogs the disease was purely chemical but in the mind of a man . . .

Anton shivered.

He had a distinct image, behind closed eyelids, of a peasant walking the rolling hills in the light of a full moon—a peasant who had been bitten, some time before, by a wild dog. He saw this unfortunate man pause; saw him stir restlessly, a captive of urges beyond and below his comprehension; saw him tilt his head back and gaze up at the moon. The white light washed his upthrust face. He shuddered. He frowned, wondering what illness was upon him. He was unable to take his eyes from the moon. It hung above him like a slender disc of silver, compelling, demanding . . . inexorable. The peasant sank to the ground, on all fours. His face was still thrust back. Strange sounds emanated from his tightening vocal chords, he felt his teeth, they seemed too large for his mouth; felt his fingers, crooked, the nails too long. But his mind was that of a man, and slowly he realized what was happening to him—understood the unspeakable curse upon him. And in that moment he was no longer a peasant. He was not a wolf, but he was something other than a man. And through it all his tortured mind continued to work, his reason forced into alien channels, his thoughts misshapen, mangled beyond evil, beyond human comprehension.

And then he would howl . . .

And presently another peasant would come along—a peasant who had not been savaged by a wild dog—with hurried steps through the night. And the one who was no longer quite a man would be waiting.

And a legend would be born anew.

Anton shook his head violently to clear these hideous images from his mind.

It was a thing he would never see, he told himself.

After all, he could not experiment on a man.

Could he?

Anton completed a long and detailed report and sent it off to the government agency where, eventually, it came into the hands of the bright young lad named Smith. Smith was certainly no fool. In fact, he was even more intelligent than the shaggy students who carry banners in protests. Smith realized instantly that this was an incredible discovery. He lowered the report and stared into space for a while. His lips moved. He mumbled, "Contagious glandular malfunction," several times, letting it sink in. And then he drew up a brief report of his own and sent it to the head of his department. This gentleman knew that Smith was bright and had nothing else to do anyway, and he actually read the report. He nodded and hummed and smoked his pipe, but he read it. He read it over a second time and then a third. Presently he understood what it meant. His mind was ponderous but large. It turned slowly but remorselessly and, like a millstone, ground concepts into a fine powder of their separate parts. And when his gristmill of a mind had finished, he applied himself to the all-important problem of rearranging the parts into a whole which would be profitable.

Well, men being what they are, and departmental heads of government agencies more so, he came to his decision. One assumes he was guided by patriotism. He sent Anton's report and Smith's report and an explanatory (although totally incomprehensible) covering note of his own, along to a certain unnamed research building. This building, and the agency it housed, was unnamed because the general public, not wise and patriotic like the heads of departments, is less tolerant and even inclined to stage protest marches against such agencies.

He sent it, in other words, to the biological warfare department . . .

Alvin Johnstone, who was a secret agent or spy of sorts, left his motorcar in his private parking place and entered the unnamed agency building which housed the central office. The laboratories were located elsewhere but within this edifice the decisions were taken, the judgments made, the results coordinated. Johnstone passed through the system of clearance and identification and went on up to the Chief's office. The Chief had summoned him. Johnstone did not mind working for this particular agency and knew how to calm the troubled waters of the conscience with the soothing oils of patriotism; how to rationalize that, if he did not do the job, someone else would. The Chief, on the other hand, had never felt the need for justifying his offices and knew, without really thinking about it, that expediency outweighed ethical and humanitarian ideals. He was an organizer, a practical man of the type necessary to direct scientists, whom everyone knows are impractical. He did not look practical. He looked more like an auctioneer, a jolly fellow who took snuff and wore handpainted ties. He chuckled a great deal. But beneath this façade he was pragmatic and efficient and knew the value of biological warfare—believed it superior to more conventional methods of destruction because it did not destroy the wealth of the enemy country, left the cities standing and the treasures intact and killed only living things which, after all, are only of evanescent value.

The Chief was glancing at a report when Johnstone entered. He was wearing one of his favorite ties. It had a woodpecker on it. He had a pencil in one hand and was making his own notes to add to the file. He made methodical notes. He glanced up from under a shaggy brow.

"Ah, Johnstone," he said.

"Morning, Chief."

Johnstone took a seat.

"We seem to have an interesting thing here," said the Chief. "Don't know if it will prove feasible for us or not. Not really our field. Not virology, actually. But it's a new concept and there appears to be no other agency to deal with it. We might have to set up a special branch if it proves worthwhile. In the meanwhile I think we'd better look into it thoroughly."

Johnstone waited, watching the woodpecker.

The Chief gathered the reports together and turned them; shoved them across to Johnstone. Johnstone winced at the thickness of the pile.

"Shall I read in depth?" he asked.

"Skip the technical stuff for now. Probably wouldn't understand that anyway. Just get the main idea. Rather amusing, really. Don't know if this Plotnikov fellow knows what he has here. Not sure I do, myself. But, not to put too fine a point on it, the man seems to have discovered a method of creating, well, yes, ah, werewolves..."

Johnstone looked at the Chief.

The Chief looked right back at him.

"Well, yes, really," he said.

Johnstone read the reports.

After a few pages he found his interest growing to the extent that he read more than he skimmed. The Chief took some snuff and continued to jot down ideas on his pad. He did not sneeze when he took snuff. Had he sneezed he would have used hand-painted handkerchiefs. Presently Johnstone stacked the papers neatly and looked up.

"I see," said Johnstone.

"I thought you might."

"It seems truly horrible."

"But will it be effective? That's the point. No sense in horror just for the hell of it, eh?"

Johnstone had no reply to that.

"However, if the information in these reports is correct, and if it can be adapted for use against human beings . . . well, I've been jotting down a few of the advantages which come to mind. Have a look."

He turned his pad towards Johnstone. Johnstone looked at the neat outline.

This was the list of advantages:

One: The disease can only be transferred by contact, so it eliminates the danger of feedback or blowback inherent in germ warfare. One would have to merely isolate the enemy and wait for results.

Two: Chemicals would be far safer to handle than virus. Even our laboratory boys are worried about the possibility of one of their pet germs escaping, but a chemical can't very well escape.

Three: There is likelihood that biological warfare may be outlawed by international agreement. This weapon, being chemical (like tear gas), would not fall under the outlawed definitions.

Four: There is no way to immunize a population against glandular imbalance. For every virus we create the enemy is working on antidotes and vice versa. But there can be no preventive defence against this weapon. Treatment and cure will undoubtedly be developed but can only be that — a cure, not a prophylactic.

Five: This weapon can be justified as humanitarian because it is not lethal. The enemy will kill themselves, of course, but that's hardly our fault, eh? And at first it won't even be recognized as a weapon.

Six: Perhaps the greatest advantage of all will be a side effect in the minds of the enemy. The panic, the fear, the disintegration of their culture as a legend comes alive in their streets. Especially when dealing with our Balkan friends, eh? All those superstitious Slavs . . .

Johnstone passed the notepad back.

He made no comment.

The Chief said, "You know, of course, that we've long toyed with similar ideas. LSD in the water supplies, that sort of stuff. But that's cumbersome and impractical, almost impossible to manage. This is different. If this disease proves contagious all the difficulties are removed. We would only have to inject a few prisoners of war and send them back across the lines. Or even inject a few of our own men — volunteers, one supposes — and send them in. They wouldn't develop the symptoms, but they'd carry the disease. And the fear."

"I can't imagine many men volunteering for that."

"Hum. Well, perhaps it wouldn't be necessary to let them know all the details, eh?"

Johnstone, patriotic rather than expedient, winced.

"Of course, we might use animals as carriers . . ."

Johnstone nodded.

"But an animal might well wander back across the lines, you know. I wouldn't fancy that."

Johnstone stared at the woodpecker and said, "I don't much like this idea, Chief."

The Chief chose to ignore that.

"Anyway," he said, "I want you to call on this Plotnikov. Get a general impression. I'm having a thorough checkup done on the man. He's a foreigner, you know. Have a look at some of these dogs. Find out if the serum can be taken orally. Things like that."

"Right," said Johnstone.

He stood up.

"Oh, Johnstone . . ."

Johnstone turned back.

"Better eat some garlic and carry a crucifix, eh? Ho ho ho. I can just imagine all those communist Slavs sitting in the wine cellars while a plague of werewolves howls through the streets. Scare hell out of 'em, eh?"

The Chief was chuckling. Johnstone left. The Chief took some snuff.

Anton, who would have been troubled had he known where his report had been directed, was, at the moment, troubled instead by his wife's absence. Anton had labored through the night and, by morning, completed analysis of a skin sample taken from an infected animal. The results had been enlightening. He had discovered a great amount of porphyrins in the infected cells, a substance which, in excess, caused human skin to be particularly sensitive to sunlight. In the extreme form of this condition, Gunther's disease, the victim has flesh hideously corrugated from sunburn, sprouts unnaturally coarse hair, and his teeth are discoloured to a reddish hue. The relation between such unfortunate sufferers and the appearance legend attributes to werewolves was obvious, and Anton was well pleased with his discovery. He was so pleased, in fact, that he decided to relax for the rest of the day. He left the laboratory in a fine mood. He felt like talking. He felt so fine he was not even loath to perform his marital duties, and went up to the bedroom. But Beta was not there and the bed had not been slept in. Anton stood in the doorway for a moment, disappointed and confused. It occurred to him that his wife had not been home very much at all during the last few weeks; that she had stayed out many nights without even mentioning where she had been. He frowned as he realized this, and regretted that he'd been so engrossed in his work that he hadn't fully appreciated the fact before. Anton, in his way, loved his wife. It had never occurred to him that there was any danger of losing her, and certainly he had not questioned the state of her fidelity, but now terrible doubts assailed him. He sank down on the bed and passed a hand across his brow. He fancied he could remember little danger signals, small changes in Beta which had registered and been stored below the level of actual comprehension but which came clustering to awareness now. He remembered seeing her come home several times, smiling and satisfied, her movement gracefully tired, exactly as she had appeared in the early days of their marriage, before Anton's sexual prowess had ebbed. And Beta had not even made demands on his services during the last weeks, which had seemed a relief at the time but now seemed mina-tory. Anton began to brood. He felt helpless. He had no idea of how to behave in such circumstances. He was a polite man and hated unpleasant scenes and accusations—feared to let on that he knew, let alone to issue an ultimatum. Beta might scorn an ultimatum, might leave him if he attempted to disrupt her affairs. It was very frustrating. Anton sat there on the unused bed and he brooded and he brooded. He was still brooding when Alvin Johnstone arrived . . .

Beta Plotnikov turned over languidly and kissed her current lover. He was, she thought, the best of her long line of lovers, although she always thought that about the latest one. It was a satisfying way to think. Her lover's name was Hancock and he was a robust and virile gentleman, a physical education instructor and ex-paratrooper. He was well-built and strong. He was not very intelligent. In fact, truth be known, he was slightly moronic. But that suited Beta admirably. It provided a complete contrast with her husband, who was slight and slumping but highly intelligent. It provided the best of both worlds, as far as Beta, passionate but none too bright herself, could see. Hancock grunted when she kissed him.

"I'll have to be off now, darling," she said.

"Uh," said Hancock.

"Miss me?"

"Uh."

"Love me?"

"Uh."

"Think I'm beautiful?"

"Not exactly an eyesore."

Compliments came seldom from Hancock. Beta kissed him gratefully. Then she swung her long legs over the edge of the bed and sat up. Hancock scratched his geometrically muscled belly. He watched her dress. He seemed slightly confused by the whole thing. He had never, despite his sinews and muscle, had much success with women. But Beta had responded instantly to his very first grunt and he was still, vaguely, trying to figure out why;

whether he had mysteriously become irresistible or whether there were nymphomaniac factors involved. He wondered, also, about the husband.

"Listen," he said.

Beta listened, perhaps expecting another compliment.

"What about your husband?"

"What?"

"Doesn't he wonder where you sleep?"

"Oh, he only thinks about his work."

"That's funny," said Hancock, who never thought about his own work, even while working.

"He's not suspicious, don't worry."

"Not worried. Just wondered."

"Anton doesn't even notice that I'm gone," said Beta.

But he had, he had . . .

"Then I understand," said Alvin Johnstone, as they came up from the laboratory, "that the initial attack follows within hours of being bitten and a cycle develops subsequently, but the disease is continuously infectious. Is that right?"

"Yes, that's correct," Anton said.

They moved into the library-study. Anton looked about vaguely, not accustomed to visitors and uncertain as to the etiquette involved. He shifted his meagre weight about. Johnstone leaned against a bookcase. Johnstone had been very subtle, even after discovering that Plotnikov was hardly versed enough in social intercourse to recognize the difference, and now he debated the advisability of several diverse approaches. They were silent for some time.

At last Anton said, "If I'd known you were coming, sir, I could have arranged for a demonstration. As it is, I have no uninfected canines at present . . ."

"Oh, we don't doubt the truth of your reports."

"I'm pleased that interest has been aroused in my work. I . . . I wonder . . . just which government department are you representing?"

"Oh, research. General research. We haven't actually assigned your work yet. Haven't decided in which branch it should be included. Not a common field, as you may well imagine."

Anton smiled. Then, immediately, he looked worried.

"But you do think I'll get a grant?"

"Oh, yes. Yes, I should think so. A great deal depends on my report which, I might say, will be favourable."

"Oh, thank you."

"Perhaps a grant from . . ." Johnstone paused, smiled. "Perhaps medical research. In the stricter sense. But tell me . . . how would your serum affect a human being?"

Anton, unsuspecting, said, "Well, in theory, that is just what I am seeking to prove. That the legend of the lycanthrope has pathological roots, and that, in the past, this disease was not uncommon. Now, of course, it is very rare indeed. I can't honestly claim my studies will be of medical value, you know. Oh, there are—one hears of—isolated instances from time to time. But they are seldom investigated. Prejudice and scientific incredulity and fashionable skepticism combine against truth in this case . . ."

Anton paused and peered at Johnstone. Johnstone looked very interested, tilting his head in concentration, and Anton began to lose his nervousness as he spoke of a topic close to his heart and mind.

"There are many, oh so many, cases recorded in history, of course. And in what is now thought of as mythology. Lycaon, transformed into a wolf by Zeus—that is possibly the first known example. Odysseus's men transmuted into swine. Even in the Bible we have Nebuchadnezzar thinking himself an ox and eating grass—although that is more properly termed boanthropy, it is simply a variant symptom of the disease. Oh yes, there are many instances one might quote. However, as I say, the disease is no longer common, if it exists at all. It can hardly be a medical study . . ."

"Oh, it exists," said Johnstone.

"Oh?" said Anton.

"You have created it," said Johnstone.

And he smiled politely.

In due course Anton's limited social sense sent a message to his mind. He offered his guest a seat. Johnstone took it, pulling his sharply creased trousers up, smiling all the while. Anton sat opposite. He fidgeted. He alternately smiled and frowned. It occurred to

him to offer a drink, but he did not know where, or even if, his wife
kept alcohol in the house. But Johnstone seemed perfectly at ease,
perfectly satisfied with the situation and the development of the
interview, and eventually his attitude caused Anton to relax a bit.
Johnstone smoked. Anton hastened to fetch an ashtray; could not
find one and dashed back to the laboratory to return with a culture
tray. Johnstone deposited ash with self-confidence, like a Roman
casting salt over the ruins of Carthage.

"But if your serum, as it stands, were administered to a human?
Would the effect be the same, or similar, to that with the dogs?"

Anton nodded slowly.

"In theory, yes. The adreno-salivary effect would cause hormone
secretions which, in turn, would cause the victim to undergo
mental and physical symptoms. His metabolism, growth, behaviour would all be affected and he would, I believe, think himself a
wolf . . . or a wolf man. I must confess that I shudder at the thought.
Some inherited fear passed down chemically through the genes,
perhaps." Anton looked slightly sheepish. "And yet, despite this
revulsion, I have always felt myself drawn to study such morbid
pathogenic conditions. Man has strange, perverse motivations, I
fear."

Johnstone nodded knowledgeably.

"Of course, we can't know for certain. I mean, we can't actually
experiment with a man."

"Um. I wonder."

Anton raised his brows.

"In the name of science . . ."

Anton's brows went higher and higher.

"A volunteer, of course."

"Good heavens, I couldn't do that. Why . . . why, it would be
monstrous!"

Johnstone looked placid.

"You do understand that it must be transferred via living saliva.
Surely no man would volunteer to savage another? Or, worse, to
submit to the infected bite, knowing the expected results? Surely
not . . ."

"Oh, it might be arranged. For the good of science." Johnstone
looked sharply at Anton. "And for the good of the country," he

added. "You have not, perhaps, realized the potential value of your discovery as a weapon . . ."

Anton was appalled.

"I . . . I don't know . . . I don't think I could allow myself to work on a morbific in a practical sense . . ."

"Um. It was just a thought, you understand."

Anton nodded.

"Just a casual thought. Quite natural, really. I mean, one always does think first of one's country, does one not?"

Johnstone's glance pinned Anton like a butterfly on a display board. Anton squirmed. He had never thought much of his country, or any country. But he had thought often of a government grant. Very slowly and uncertainly and tentatively, he nodded.

"What I mean," said Johnstone, softly, "in war, things are sometimes justified which normally . . . you do understand? Against an enemy, a threat to our happiness and freedom and way of life . . . You do see what I mean?"

Anton, in the grip of doubts, not fully understanding, still fixed on the pinpoints of Johnstone's gaze, continued to move his head up and down.

Then Johnstone broke the spell.

"However, we needn't discuss that for the moment. It was just an idle thought that occurred to me. Continue with your good work and I'll submit my report and we'll try to get you some money."

He stood up. Anton jumped up, relieved to be freed from the pins. He walked to the door with Johnstone and they shook hands. Johnstone left smiling. Anton looked after him. Anton was not smiling. Anton had never before known that it was acceptable to treat one's enemies outside one's moral code. It was a novel and intriguing concept. Of course, Anton had never had an enemy. He stood there in the open doorway while Johnstone got in his car and drove off. Then he stepped back and started to close the door; paused as his wife's car came down the road and turned into the drive. Anton leaned against the door. His wife was smiling behind the wheel. She looked very satisfied and happy. Anton had never had an enemy before . . .

Beta came up to the door with that leisurely long-legged stride, kissed her husband *en passant,* and walked down the hallway. Anton turned, watching the swing of her hips with an interest unusual for him and turmoil in his mind. Beta went up the stairs. Anton started to close the door, then paused once again as that sinister character named Chowder emerged from the trees fringing the drive. Chowder had orange hair and, for a moment, Anton believed that a gigantic sunflower had appeared on the scene. Chowder was facing in the other direction, rubbing his corrugated neck and staring after Johnstone's car. Then he turned with a heavy scowl and came clumping up to the door. Anton, who was never quite comfortable with Chowder in the house and who had, indeed, noted the way the man sized up the silverware, waited nervously. Chowder stopped on the steps.

"That feller a copper?" he asked.

"Who?"

Chowder jerked a thumb over his shoulder.

"Feller wot just left."

"Good heavens, no."

Chowder squinted suspiciously.

"That so? Looked like a copper to me. I can smell coppers a mile away. You sure he weren't no copper?"

"Not at all. The gentleman was from a government agency."

"Oh. Oh, that explains it. Same smell, you know. I thought maybe they were on to us."

"On to us?"

" 'Bout them nicked dogs."

Anton, who had never considered the illegal aspects of purchasing stolen dogs, and perhaps had not even realized they were stolen, looked puzzled.

Chowder said, "Huh. Well, I come to see if you were ready for another delivery. Got a new scheme worked out. Real complicated and clever. Reckon to make a raid on White City just after the dog races, get the lot. Bit expensive, but they'll be better than your run-o'-the-mill hound."

"Actually, it appears that any sort of dog will do," Anton said, and Chowder's face fell. Anton glanced back into the house. He looked to ascertain if any valuables were in the hall before inviting Chowder in, but as he did so his gaze fell on the stairway where

Beta had ascended and instantly a plan sprang upon his mind. He blinked. He turned back to Chowder. He didn't hesitate.

"I may have another job for you," Anton whispered.

"Yeah? What's that then?"

"Shhh."

Chowder looked about.

Anton bit his fingernails.

"Well?"

"My wife . . ."

"Yeah? You want her kidnapped too, huh?"

"No, no. But I . . . I wonder . . . do you think you might follow her?"

"Might. Why?"

"I fear she is . . . well, perhaps . . . being untrue to me."

"Huh?"

"That perhaps she loves another."

"Like that, is it, mate?"

"I fear so."

"Sure, I'll follow her for you. I know how it is. My own wife ran off with an Armenian. I didn't follow her, though."

Chowder nodded in sympathy. Anton nodded nervously. After they had finished nodding they made their plans.

The Chief snapped his snuffbox shut and tilted his chair back. Johnstone had just finished his verbal report. The Chief was wearing a different tie. It had a naked woman painted on it and when the Chief, as he sometimes did, pressed a bulb attached behind the tie, the naked woman's breasts ballooned. It was very clever. But he didn't press the bulb now, he shuffled through some papers.

"Initial checkup on this fellow Plotnikov. Seems a genuine type. Background okay. Company he works for did a thorough inquiry on him. Industrial secrets and such. Much more careful than our counter-intelligence boys, actually. More important, one assumes. His wife runs around with other men. But she's English, so that's all right. But you say he didn't seem keen on the idea, eh?"

"Not very."

"Pressures?"

"Well, he needs the money. Then there are the dogs, of course.

Obviously stolen. Not mongrels, good-looking dogs. Could black-mail him with that."

"Pretty weak. Perhaps we'd better have a Chinaman seduce the wife. Let Plotnikov find out about it. Well, we can work that out later."

"Do we have an Oriental operative?" Johnstone asked.

"Hell, no. But we've got some yellow paint. Same thing, isn't it?"

"I expect so."

"Anyway, we'll think of something. This is too good to miss. Werewolves! Why, this could be the start of a new Empire."

Johnstone smiled politely.

The Chief pressed the button.

Hancock sat up abruptly.

Beta slid down from his neck.

"Thought I saw something peculiar at the window," he said.

"What, darling?"

"Well, it looked like a bloody great sunflower."

"Nonsense, dearest."

"I guess you must be right."

"But it was romantic of you to think of flowers, dear."

"Huh," said Hancock.

In the cages, the dogs watched with baleful eyes and, at the table, Anton and Chowder leaned close together like Russian anarchists. Anton was pale. Chowder, whose own wife had left him for an Armenian, was gleeful.

"She's got a man, all right," he said.

"Oh dear."

"I followed her, see. Real careful. Professional. She never twigged a thing. Well, she went to this 'ere flat and used her own key to open it. It was a basement flat, so I nipped round to the side to have a dekko through the window. And let me tell you, they didn't waste no time. I'm nippy on my feet, you know. Got to be in my trade, ducking and diving. But quick as I was, they were hard at it by the time I got to the window. Hard at it, they were. I'll say. Really going to town. Not just a casual poke, like what one gets in an alley, either. Real lovey-dovey stuff. All that kissing and love-biting . . ."

"Love-biting?" asked Anton, in his grief.

"Sure. You know. Like when a bird nibbles your neck so that the blood comes oozing through the skin and then later your old lady spots the mark and gets so annoyed that she runs off with Armenians. That sorta stuff."

Anton, vaguely, had heard of such things. He even thought he recalled Beta trying to do it to him, on their honeymoon, although he couldn't be sure. Chowder was proceeding to reveal the sordid details, but Anton's mind had stuck at the words "love-biting." They played over and over again on a jammed track in his mind. Love-biting. Love-biting. Love-biting. Love-biting. And then, somehow, the words became detached from one another. They registered separately. Love. Biting. Love. Biting. His wife loved another man. His wife bit another man. The other man was Beta's lover. Therefore the other man was Anton's enemy. It was perfectly all right to bite an enemy. Johnstone had told him so. Sparks flew across gaps in Anton's mind. Anton thought and thought.

"Oh dear," said Beta. "I do believe I'm going down with a horrid cold."

She blew her nose daintily.

"Perhaps you're run down, dear," Anton said. "You've been out too much. You should relax at home."

"Yes, dear," she said, not hearing him. "I do hope it doesn't get worse. I have an important social engagement this evening."

Anton winced.

"Perhaps I'll phone Doctor Blackshaw. Dreadful nuisance, though. I can never see why, if you're a doctor, you can't give antibiotic shots and things."

"I've explained before, dear. I'm not a medical doctor. It's a different thing."

"More useful if you were."

She blew her nose again.

Anton blinked. Anton looked down at his hands. Anton pursed his lips.

"I suppose I could give you an injection of, ah, penicillin, darling," he said.

"Oh, could you? That would be convenient."

"Yes, of course I could," he said, "I could give you a shot."

And, presently, he did.

"I won't be able to come tomorrow, dear," said Beta Plotnikov.

"Why's that?" asked Hancock.

"My husband."

"Suspicious, is he?"

"Oh no, poor dear. He never suspects a thing. Not a thing. He doesn't even notice those marks you leave on my neck sometimes. That's how easy it is to deceive him. It makes me feel wicked sometimes when I think how innocent the poor dear is. So deliciously wicked."

"Well, come to think of it, you are sort of wicked. Glad you're not my wife."

"Oh, I'd never cheat against you."

"Huh."

She nuzzled him.

"But, anyway, I can't see you tomorrow. Anton has asked me to stay at home with him. Says he's been working hard and is going to take the whole day off and relax. He does work terribly hard, you know. So I guess I owe him one day of my time, after all. And he seemed so . . . well . . . almost demanding about it. Sort of worried, too. As if maybe he was afraid I'd refuse."

"Well, that's okay then."

"I won't sleep with him, of course."

"Huh? He's your husband, isn't he?"

"Why, of course. But I simply couldn't be unfaithful to you, dearest."

"Huh," said Hancock, and after a while they began to bill and coo and, because she was not going to see him for a whole day, Beta felt she should make the most of this occasion, and squirmed and moaned and, soon enough, they were gyrating in the horizontal gavotte and, in the towering heights of estral heat, they kissed and kissed . . .

Later, while dressing, Hancock paused to look in the mirror. Hancock was vain about his muscles and smiled at the deltoids. Then, abruptly, he scowled.

"What's wrong, my love?" asked Beta, from the bed.

"Huh! I don't know about your husband, but my pupils are no fools. What the hell are they going to say about these marks on my neck, huh?"

Beta giggled.

Later she went home.

Anton, for a time, suffered misgivings and regrets. He tried to convince himself that the man who had cuckolded him deserved to be punished, but found it feeble justification; tried, rather medievally, to believe that it was in the hands of the gods, like trial by combat, for he had no way of knowing whether Beta would actually kiss her lover fiercely enough to transmit the disease, nor even, other than in theory, whether it would prove effective against a human being; tried, even, to believe his actions were motivated by a desire to increase scientific knowledge. But none of these forms of rationalization were strong enough to deceive his doubts. He went through turmoils and upheavals of thought. He even worked, for a time, on the antidote he had been considering—worked desultorily, however, knowing as he turned from aspect to aspect that no antidote would be found without weeks and months of labor, and soon gave up the effort.

Then Beta came home.

She came home radiant and happy, and as he looked at her, Anton felt his doubts fade. He felt the justification which he'd been unable to find within his own mind, in his wife's obvious satisfaction. He no longer resented her infidelity, and no longer worried about it—did not know, of course, that Hancock was but one of many, and that her behaviour would not be changed by Hancock's elimination. The peace of accomplishment stilled his troubled thoughts and he came to regret but one thing—that he would not be able to take credit, in his next report, for having created—well, whatever it was that he had created. He was not absolutely sure what that would be. He waited, with interest, for the next day to pass, certain that the evening newspapers, perhaps even special editions, would bring him the results of his experiment.

That night, he made love to his wife.

He did not, however, allow her to kiss him.

There was a full moon.

Anton had not planned it that way—had not even realized that such would be the case—but when he became aware of the fact he felt a tingle. It seemed so very appropriate. It seemed to place the stamp of fate's approval upon his act. He had only to wait. He waited. The day passed slowly. Anton did not know the relevant data about Hancock's weight and metabolism, and therefore could not predict with any certainty when the madness would strike the man, but he knew it would be within twenty-four hours. The only thing necessary was to keep his wife safely at home during that period. Beta, however, had showed signs of restlessness during the day. It was the first day she had spent at home for some weeks. As the afternoon wore on Anton began to fear she might make some excuse to slip away, and he could think of no way to convince her, short of the impossible truth, that she must not be with her lover that day. Doing her best to be a dutiful wife, temporarily, Beta was determined to remain with Anton, but she was surprised by her own nervous energy, her own restless wanderings from room to room. She wondered whether her feelings for Hancock—for what else could cause her dysphoria other than the enforced separation?—were deeper than she had imagined them to be. And yet Hancock did not seem connected with her restlessness. She merely felt an overwhelming urge to leave the house—to divagate without any particular goal, even to take a long and uncharacteristic walk through the darkening countryside. This confused her. She could not understand the impulse. Presently she forced herself to take a seat by the window in the library-study, determined to fight down her restlessness.

Anton, at his desk, glanced towards his wife from time to time. He could just see the angle of her profile from behind, but it was sufficient to note the internal struggle reflected in her expression. She wants to go to him, he thought. He was worried. What if she simply got up and left? Anton did not know how to prevent this, short of physically restraining her, and even that was doubtful. Anton was not strong. Truth be known, he was exceptionally weak. Beta was a big, healthy woman. Anton felt sure she was stronger than he, and certainly fitter. He watched her hand open and close upon the arm of the chair and he worried. He thought of how it would be if she went to her lover—if she were in his arms when the disease came upon him in all its horrible fury. After a while he rose and moved very quietly to the door. He turned the key in the lock and then returned to his desk and placed the key at the very back of the drawer; locked the drawer as well. It would be very embarrassing, he knew, if she demanded the key, but any degree of unpleasantness was far better than letting her go. He felt better with that precaution taken; went over to stand behind her chair and place his hand on her shoulder. Together they looked out at the moon. It was very bright, a silver disc behind shredding clouds. There were a few stars. Anton stood quietly for a time. Beta seemed tense beneath his hand. Usually, at the slightest touch, she took it as encouragement and began to squirm. But now she was still and taut. He wondered what occupied her thoughts—told himself, with a twinge of sadness, that she must be thinking of her lover. Then anger replaced the anguish. She would think of him, perhaps, but she would never again rest in his arms. She would never again come home flushed and weary with love, her pure throat blemished with those marks of passion . . .

Anton stiffened.

Those marks of love . . .

His mouth dropped open, his heart stopped for a moment and then thundered. His terrible oversight came cascading into his mind. If Beta had infected her lover and he, in turn, had kissed her in that manner . . . afterwards . . . when his glands were already secreting the hormones . . .

Anton looked down at his wife.

She sat very still. He saw only the side of her face. But he saw her hand, as well, and her hand was hooked over the edge of the armrest. Hooked like a claw. The veins stood out in the back of her hand and ran in pronounced ridges up her forearms. Anton stepped back. Beta did not move. Beta was looking at the moon. The moonlight fell over her face. Anton walked backwards to the door, his eyes fixed upon her. She did not move at all. He reached behind his back and grasped the doorknob. But the door was locked. The key was in the desk and the desk was in the center of the room. Anton stood there for some time, unable to advance. And then, with the fibre of his body blurred by terror, he started to tiptoe towards his desk. He made no sound. But he had not yet reached the desk when his wife stood up. She stood up quickly and stiffly, facing the window. Anton halted. He had not reached the desk. He stood motionless and looked at his wife and she stood motionless and looked at the moon.

And then his wife turned around.

What had once been his wife turned around.

Anton crouched, quivering, against the locked door. His ancestry screamed in his mind. He whimpered, the sound of a small and helpless animal, transfixed by the glowing eyes of the predator.

Then Beta moved towards him.

She moved slowly. Anton looked at her burning eyes and he looked at her crooked hands and he looked at her ravenous mouth . . .

Anton was totally insane before she reached him . . .

Which was probably just as well for him . . .

Among the Wolves

THERE WAS SOMETHING ABOUT THE KILLINGS which went beyond horror. All murder is horrible enough, of course, but one recognizes contingencies, one comprehends motivations and provocations and circumstances, and can understand, objectively, how a man may be driven or guided to murder. I feel I can glimpse into the dark minds which direct murder for profit, can dismember the warped violence of hatred and revenge, can pity the remorse of a killer swept helplessly along on uncharted currents and even, with a chill of grisly perception, understand the mangled patterns of a madman's mind reflected in mutilation or the insane fear of punishment which drives a sex maniac to destroy his innocent victim in the wake of satiated lust. These things are horrible, indeed, but they are conceivable—are no more than a distortion of normal human emotion, ambition, passion, greed—a magnification of urges which all men feel and most men keep bound and imprisoned in the deepest dungeons of the subconscious, shackled by the sensibilities. Sometimes—all too often—these shadowed impulses strike off the fetters of restraint and burst ravening from the corporal cell to stalk their prey, to command their former gaolers to violence. And then the crime is done. But somehow these murders were different. They invoked a feeling beyond such motivations as rage and fear, beyond even insanity as we have come to define it. It must have been a madman, there can be little doubt of that. No sane mind could have directed such crimes, no creature of chemical balance could have committed them. And yet—how can one express it?—the specific horror of these murders was that they seemed so utterly *natural* ...

I knew rather more about these crimes than the average person, through mere circumstance—was in at the start, so to speak; for the morgue was an extension of the museum in which I was pursuing my research. The museum was attached to the university, and the morgue was in a wing of the university medical centre. One supposes it was a convenient arrangement. The medical students required cadavers, and unidentified and unclaimed bodies gravitated to the morgue; and for the good of medical progress —but I have no wish to moralize on this point. Things are done, things often are necessary, an accomplished fact is a fact, no more. I mention it only to set the scene, as it were, for my casual and superficial involvement—an involvement, I must admit, due more to morbid curiosity than any more elevated motives. I am a scientist and, quite naturally, I am curious about behaviour which does not fit the natural patterns, which floats suspended at some unexplored level of the sentient sea and defies the tides and waves of society.

I had been doing my research for some time—far longer than originally intended, for research, by its very nature, feeds upon itself and grows, extends and spreads strange and devious branches from the fundamental roots—and so, quite naturally, I came to know a number of people connected with the museum and the university and, by extension, the morgue. I became acquainted with Detective-Inspector Grant of the homicide squad and with Doctor Ramsey who performed the autopsies for the police. With Ramsey, in fact, an arrangement had developed. We found that our homes were quite close, in the same suburb, and in time we began to share the task of driving into town, alternating our motorcars to lessen the traffic and parking difficulties on the campus grounds. He proved an interesting and congenial fellow and the arrangement was very satisfactory. We became more than acquaintances, if less than friends. And it was through Ramsey, indirectly, that I came to see the first body . . .

It was my day to drive and I'd left the museum library and walked across the campus to the medical centre. It was a fine autumn day with brilliant leaves floating like colourful barques on a gentle breeze. Young couples strolled hand in hand across the lawns, and students reclined in the lee of oak and elm, talking of philosophy and love. It was a pleasant setting, slightly tinged with nostalgia— not at all the sort of time and place in which to encounter horror. I went into the medical building and down resounding corridors to Ramsey's office. He wasn't there, and his secretary told me he had been summoned to the morgue. She wrinkled her nose at the word and I didn't blame her. I had no liking for the morgue myself. It was not a place to spend an autumn day. But I went on down the stairs and along a corridor and entered the antechamber, a stark room with a tiled floor and a ramp leading up to street level and large metal doors. It was down this ramp that ambulance and hearse descended to disgorge their still burdens before rising, lightened once again, into the sunlight. It was a place of grim silence and foreshadowing. Worst of all, to me, was the smell—that sharp anti-septic scent. Does any odour smell as much of decay and corrup-tion as antiseptic? It eats at the very core of sensation, invoking the essence of death—of more than death, of that which has never known life. The scent of decay and disease is foul but natural, that of antiseptic carries the stench of sterility. It parted like morbid mist before my passage and dampened my footfalls on the tiles.

I stopped at the glass cubicle.

The attendant looked up reluctantly from a lurid paperback, recognized me and nodded. The nod served to lower his eyes once more to the novel and he was already pursuing his pleasures as he gestured me through. I passed on to the operating-room, where Doctor Ramsey was washing his hands at the sink. His white gown was splattered with dark stains and he washed his hands carefully, rubbing them together like struggling serpents in soapy froth. There was a slab in the centre of the room and a shrouded form on the slab. Ramsey looked up with a solemn face and nodded. I advanced, avoiding the slab.

"Will you be long?" I asked.

"No. The necropsy is finished. I'm waiting for Grant to arrive. Identification." The way he said it you could tell he didn't like that part of it. Maybe he didn't like any part of it. He took off the blood-stained gown and stuffed it in the hamper.

"No sense letting them see the blood, eh?" he said. "Somehow the relatives always react more to seeing blood on a gown than to seeing the corpse."

"Accident case?" I asked.

"It was no accident."

I looked at him. He shrugged.

"The man was strangled," he said.

"Oh. Hence Inspector Grant of homicide."

"Exactly."

"I'll wait outside."

Ramsey moved his head.

"Yes. An unpleasant case. The only relative is a niece. Young, I gather. I hope they weren't very close. It's always rough when they were. And pointless."

I raised my eyebrows.

"We know who the man was. No doubt of that. But legal procedure demands positive identification by a relative. It's funny how authority must always punish the innocent in the search for the guilty. Or maybe not funny."

"Indicative maybe."

"Maybe," he said, and showed a sad smile. I turned to leave, and just then Grant came through past the cubicle. A uniformed policeman and a girl followed. Grant's face was set and the cop looked stern. The girl was quite young and gazed around the room with big eyes. She seemed frightened. Of authority, perhaps. She was also rather pretty—pretty enough for the attendant to raise his attention from the vicarious thrills of his novel and regard her bottom. It struck me as a reaction perfectly suited to an attendant at a morgue. It annoyed me, too. But the man was young and had seen a good many bodies wheeled past his cubicle. Perhaps the sum total of his experience rested in the passage of death, and one must be tolerant.

Grant spoke softly to the girl, gestured to the cop and crossed the room. I noticed that his countenance was set more rigidly than normal and a lock of hair had fallen over his brow. He looked very much the way a police detective is supposed to look.

"Finished?" he asked Ramsey.

"Yes."

"Lab boys been here?"

"Yes. I sent my report round with them."

Grant seemed to notice me for the first time. We exchanged quiet greetings and he turned back to Ramsey.

"Anything that will help us?"

"I shouldn't think so. Must have been in his seventies. Hardening of the arteries, chronic . . ."

"Skip that. We know who he was, we can get those details from the reports. Not that they'll mean a goddamn thing. I mean any clue as to who did it? Or why?"

"Nothing. Nothing I could see. Not my job."

"It was strangulation, wasn't it?"

"Oh yes. Definitely."

Something in the doctor's tone caused Grant to look sharply at him.

"I mean his neck wasn't broken. He was asphyxiated. Must have been a rough death."

"They're all rough," said Grant, and his eyes shifted towards the girl. She was standing just inside the door, very pale, very frightened. The attendant was still regarding her. "This is the rough part for us. The identification. The girl's only nineteen, hardly knew the old boy, and we have to put her through this. Well . . ."

He gestured. The uniformed cop took the girl's arm and led her forward. Ramsey walked over to the head of the slab and Grant stood beside the girl. His shoulders shifted. I had the impression he wanted to put his arm around her. But he didn't. He was a policeman and he couldn't. He nodded and Ramsey drew the sheet down. He drew it down only enough to expose the face and I heard the girl draw her breath in with a sort of whimper. I looked down. I was surprised to see how old the man had been. I'd heard Ramsey say he was in his seventies, but somehow it hadn't registered—age seems irrelevant in discussing a corpse. But seeing him was different. Ramsey had obviously done his best to make the face seem relaxed and natural. But even so I could tell he'd died hard. The lips were forced upwards by the pressure of a swollen tongue and the eyes bulged beneath closed lids. The girl stared for a moment and then covered her face with both hands and turned away. Ramsey drew the sheet back over the old grey face.

"Miss?" Grant said gently.

She nodded behind her hands. It wasn't exactly a positive identification, but it satisfied the formalities, and Grant turned to the cop and said, "Take Miss Smith outside." He waited until they had left, then sighed.

"This will be a bad one," he said. "There's always so much public outrage when some old guy gets knocked off. So much interest and interference. And there seems to be no motive behind this one. Just a nice old guy. Killed in his own room. His landlady sort of took care of him, I guess. Anyway, she found the body this morning. Bringing him a pot of tea. He was on his bed and she thought he was

sleeping. Then she looked down . . . well, you know how they look
with their tongues sticking out black and their eyes popping. She
dropped the teapot, I can tell you that. The killer must have entered
by the front door. Just walked in. Had to go right past the landlady's
room, too, but she heard nothing. I think she's a bit deaf, although
she got annoyed when I asked her about her hearing. Must be deaf
or she wouldn't have been annoyed, eh? Just walked in cool as a
cucumber and strangled the old boy and walked out again. Obviously not robbery. Nothing missing. Hell, he had nothing worth
taking as far as that goes. Lived on a pension. Trimmed the hedge
in return for his meals. Had a few friends his own age and drank an
occasional glass of beer with them. No enemies as far as we know.
No opportunity to make an enemy, the way he lived. Just a quiet
old chap waiting to die . . ."

"Well, the waiting is over," Ramsey said.

"For him, yeah."

Ramsey and I both looked at Grant.

"For us, it's just beginning," he said. "A crime without motives.
Well, you know what that means. We wait for the next one."

"You think he'll kill again?" I asked.

"The mad ones always do," Grant told us. He pursed his lips;
became aware of the displaced lock over his brow and brushed it
back impatiently. "They kill and they kill again, and all we can do
is wait until a pattern develops, a general motivation rather than
a specific motive. Oh, we get them in the end. The pattern always
emerges. But it isn't a line on a graph or a pin stuck in a map. The
pattern is made by the corpses of the victims. A man can have night-
mares about that, you know. Any man. You dream of a tapestry,
and it's all vague shapes and forms and then you get closer and see
the design is made up of dead men. It isn't a tapestry then, it's a fili-
gree of intertwining limbs and arched torsos. And faces. The faces
staring out from the pattern, mouths open in silent screams of
accusation, eyes wide in sightless fear. A man . . . well, he dreams."

Grant broke off abruptly; looked rather ashamed of the intensity with which he'd been speaking and jammed a cigarette in his
mouth. It was the first time I'd ever thought of a policeman as
human, I think. He puffed on the cigarette, his cheeks sinking in,
his eyes thoughtful.

"Would you say it was the work of a madman, Doc?" he asked. "I mean, from the examination . . ."

Ramsey looked troubled.

"I'm not sure," he said. "Some aspects . . . and yet . . . Well, it's all in my report, Inspector. Black and white. It will mean more if you read it than if I talk about it. A report is always more objective and logical."

"Sure. I'll read it."

Grant turned as if to leave and then turned back, the cigarette in his teeth, his cheeks hollow.

"I'm delaying," he said. "I don't want to face that kid again. Have to, of course. But what if she asks me why the old man was killed? People ask cops things like that, you know? And will she feel better if I tell her it was a maniac? That there was no purpose, no reason; that nothing was gained by his death? Oh, I'm supposed to tell her I can't discuss it at the present time. Against regulations. Not allowed. But will that make her feel better? You drag some kid in and make her look at a dead body . . . ah, hell. It's not pleasant, Doc."

Ramsey nodded; looked at his hands thoughtfully. His hands had been scrubbed spotlessly clean, and there was nothing there to see. But he looked. I stepped back, feeling I was intruding. Grant's eyes had gone blank and his brow furrowed. The ash dropped unnoticed from his cigarette, a long ash that disintegrated when it hit the tiles and looked very improper in that sanitary and disinfected chamber. Somehow the ash looked too clean on that sterile floor.

"I hope to God it wasn't a maniac," he said very softly.

Ramsey lowered his eyes. I took another step back. Then Grant turned sharply and walked out with his shoulders square. The attendant did not look up from his book, and it was some time before Ramsey looked up from the floor . . .

We left the building and walked across to the parking lot. Most of the motorcars had gone by this time and the big concrete space looked strangely abandoned and neglected and forlorn. Ramsey hadn't spoken; he seemed to be pondering something—something both disagreeable and interesting—his expression that of a little boy using a stick to poke at the decaying carcass of a dead animal.

He was thinking about the murder, of course, and I sensed he was considering that part which was in his report and which he hadn't wanted to talk about. It had captured my interest and, by this time, we were close enough to speak openly.

"Well? Was it a madman?" I asked, when we were in the car.

Ramsey shrugged.

I made an elaborate task of fitting the keys into the ignition but did not start the engine.

"There was something—some aspect—in your report, which troubles you, wasn't there?"

"There was, yes."

"None of my business, of course . . ."

He waved a hand.

"Oh, it isn't that. It troubled me because . . . well, because it was unusual. And gruesome. I've been a doctor too long to get upset by violence and bloodshed, John. But this was different. It was . . . well, calculated. Ghastly but calculated. The fact itself implied frenzy and rage, and yet there was none of that in evidence. It was as if the killer had coldly and deliberately set about his ghoulish act . . ."

The term startled me.

"Ghoulish?" I asked.

"Oh, perhaps I'm being too dramatic. But . . . well, when behaviour normally associated with maddened impulse and blind fury is suddenly transposed to an act of rational logical expedience . . . well, it shakes a man. We are all prisoners of our own perceptions, you know. We have all learned to see things in a certain way and to interpret them in the light of our training and experience. And when a familiar object or action is suddenly glimpsed out of context . . . seen from a different angle . . . it causes turmoil within our preconceived limitations. It takes a while to get our bearings, to adjust our stance, to focus properly . . ."

"What on earth happened?" I asked.

Ramsey didn't seem to hear my question.

"When I was younger, I used to ice-skate," he said, speaking slowly. I blinked. I thought he was deliberately, and rather discourteously, changing the subject, and I reached for the ignition keys. But Ramsey continued. "I learned to skate quite well," he said. "I was never particularly adept at sports or games but in ice-skating I seemed to be more talented than most. I enjoyed it enormously. I learned to figure-skate, to cut designs across the ice. People used to watch me, admiring my abilities. But there was one strange thing. I wouldn't skate when it was dark. All the young people used to go to the rink at night, but the very thought gave me a chill. I had a vague dread—a fear even—of what lay beneath the ice at night. I visualized it—saw it in cross-section, as it were. There I was, cutting my smooth figures across the flat, predictable surface of the ice, and beneath that level there was the dark body of unfrozen water. The ice and water were related and yet they were not the same. I fashioned my designs at one plane while beneath me lay uncharted depths and inconceivable forms. So it is with life—with the human mind. We live our allotted years and carve out patterns upon a solitary level of existence, content and satisfied perhaps, and then something happens which opens a window, just for an instant, through the surface and allows us to glimpse the deeper, darker dimensions with which we share existence. We peer through this hole, we see cowled shapes and malformed concepts bloated in the waters and we shudder and look away until the ice freezes over once more and our world is smooth and flat again. Our world is as we know it, as we wish it, and we skate off and leave our pitiful little etching under our runners. And yet, from time to time, those broken areas of open waters appear to disrupt our placid world. Most men shun the glimpse, ignore the depths, pretend the ice is solid. But not all men. In the minds of a few, the hole does not freeze over quickly enough, they stare too long through the break —long enough for something to rise and crawl from that hole and take possession of the upper levels . . ."

Ramsey coughed and looked out through the windscreen.

"Madness?" I said.

"Who knows? Not sanity, surely. But madness belongs to our surface ice. After all, it is we who have defined it. It is our minds which have hardened into ice. What may come up from below, from those regions we have not labelled and named because we have not conceived of them . . ."

He shrugged and we sat in silence for a time. I began to feel uncomfortable and once more reached for the ignition. Ramsey's eyes slid sideways at the motion.

"Yes, I am surely being too dramatic," he said. "I was reacting to a personal awareness. The facts scarcely warrant such imagery. And yet they are disturbing. I expect I owe you an explanation."

I was far too curious to decline. I waited. The keys still waited in the ignition. Ramsey, who seldom smoked, asked for a cigarette. He inhaled and then studied the smoke, as if wondering whether he were doing it properly. Then, his voice very matter-of-fact now, he said, "The remarkable aspect of the murder is this: the victim was killed by human teeth." And he stared at me.

"Good Lord," I said.

Ramsey nodded.

"But you told Grant he'd been strangled ..."

"And so he had. Indeed he had. He had been strangled by the pressure of human jaws."

I shook my head.

"That is the extraordinary thing—the combination of the two. I've seen corpses who had been strangled by human hands before. I've heard—although I've never encountered it, thank God—of instances where a man, in a fit of blind rage or insane passion, had committed murder with his teeth. But the combination is quite unique. The flesh was not even broken on the throat. There had been no attempt to tear or slash, nor even any bloodshed. The pressure of those jaws had been applied slowly and carefully. Thoughtfully, even. Obviously, the killer did not want his clothing stained by blood. It appears he had used his teeth strictly for convenience. For efficiency."

"But why?" I asked.

"I can only surmise ... you see the object of my rambling talk of darkness beneath the ice? Of course. It is exactly that. It is alien to me and I can only draw conclusions within my own frame of reference. They are undoubtedly inaccurate. But this is what I assume. The killer, for some unknown reason, wished to kill this old man. He had no desire to torture the man, for every action was designed to bring death. There were no bruises or contusions to imply a beating, no signs of any attempt to cause suffering, no wounds other than the death grip. The killer, again for unknown reasons, did not use a weapon. I can reconstruct the scene within my own scheme of deduction. The victim was probably sitting or lying on his bed. It was a small furnished room with only a straight backed chair, and I think it likely he used the bed to relax. He was, after all, an old man. He would have wanted what comfort was available to him. But that is irrelevant. The murderer came in through the door. Whether he was known to the victim or not would, of course, alter the preliminary movements. But that, too, is irrelevant here. Whether already there, or forced there, the old man wound up on the bed, on his back. The killer knelt over him, one knee on either side of his chest and placed his hands on the man's throat. The man struggled—his fingernails were broken where he clawed at the killer's hands and forearms—but he was old and weak. The killer tightened his grip remorselessly. I feel sure there was no haste, no frenzy. He merely closed his hands with great deliberation. But perhaps this was the first time he'd committed murder with his bare hands. This seems likely. And it always takes a long time, relatively speaking, to choke a man to death. It must seem very long indeed to the killer . . . and to the victim. The old man's tongue came out, his eyes ballooned, and yet he did not die. It undoubtedly seemed, to the killer, that he had been strangling the man for sufficient time to kill him. And his mind was working, calculating. It occurred to him that he was not able to bring sufficient pressure to bear with his hands—that some air was still passing into those lungs. At this point, most men would surely have panicked. They would have shaken the man violently and snapped his neck, or seized a heavy object—there was a large glass ashtray beside the bed, I understand—and bludgeoned him into unconsciousness. But not our killer. There was no panic, no frenzy. He misjudged the time factor and then he sorted all the aspects out quite logically in his mind and decided that more pressure was necessary to complete the act. And when he had decided this, he followed the rational course . . ."

"Rational," I whispered.

"Absolutely rational. He lowered his head and placed his mouth upon the man's throat and proceeded to close his jaws. He didn't snap, he didn't tear, he used his teeth not as fangs but as a vice. The human jaws are very powerful. They are capable of exerting incredible strength. And so, after a while, the old man was dead and the killer unclenched his teeth and that was that."

I stared at Ramsey. I could feel the blood draining from my face, heavy and sluggish. He read the contortion of my countenance and nodded.

"Oh yes," he said. "It was horrible."

"To use his teeth for . . . *efficiency!*"

"Exactly. That was the point that disturbed me."

"It must have been a maniac," I said.

"Or a philosopher," said Ramsey, and he looked at me and I looked at him and after a while I started the motorcar and drove away. The traffic was light. The wind blew and the leaves fell and as the sun slipped down behind the afternoon angles I felt a distinct chill at my spine.

The second murder occurred several days later.

I wasn't present at the identification this time, and came to hear of the crime through a particularly sensational newspaper story—a borrowed newspaper, as it were, belonging to one of the regular visitors to the museum. Museums seem to be addictive. They each have a set of regulars who have formed the habit of frequent visits, and in the course of my research, I came to meet several of these people time and time again. One of these was a middle-aged gentleman who walked with a stiff leg and used a malacca cane, a quiet and dignified man who always nodded pleasantly, wore well-cut tweeds, and seemed a trifle lonely. I usually encountered him wandering through the natural history rooms but in this instance we met in the library. I had just finished my book and was about to go to lunch when he entered, his cane tapping through the resounding silence of leather and oak. He took a seat next to me and placed a folded newspaper on the table. I glanced over to nod and happened to notice the headlines.

"So the killer has struck again," I said.

"It would appear so."

"May I see your paper?"

"Of course."

He handed it to me and I unfolded it.

"Not the paper I usually take," he said, smiling, as if to apologize for the gutter press. It did not, in fact, seem the sort of paper this rather dignified gentleman should subscribe to, and I had always avoided it. But it carried a very detailed account of the crime, stressing the sensational aspects. The story had been written from the point of view of one of the children who had discovered the body. He was twelve years old. It was the sort of thing that sold newspapers, no doubt of that.

"It's a terrible thing," I said.

"What's that?"

"These deaths."

"Death? Oh, death is natural."

His attitude surprised me.

"Death, yes. But not murder."

He shrugged and tilted his hand in a gesture.

"Murder? But what is murder other than a form of death? It is only unnatural in legal terms, you know. Murder did not exist before we came to define it; before we made laws against it. It is law which is unnatural, not murder."

I looked at him, wondering if he were serious. He seemed so.

"I'm sure it didn't seem natural to the victims," I said.

"Oh? I should think it did. It may have seemed unjust, but certainly natural. But then, at the moment of death, one does not think in forensic terms." He smiled slightly. "Death is a jealous concept. It will not tolerate other thoughts to exist with it; it envelops the mind, it refuses to share with alien sensations."

"You seem well acquainted with the subject, sir."

He smiled again.

"Oh, I've held the concept of death," he said. "I've been very very close to dying and, I assure you, it was the most natural thing in the world."

"What manner of death?"

"By violence," he said. "By violence."

I could not picture him in conjunction with violence. I waited for him to continue, but he said no more; sat there with that slight smile. After a moment I turned to the newspaper.

The twelve-year-old boy and several other lads had been playing by the river at the old disused wharf. There was always a great deal of debris in the water at that point. The docks and pilings had collapsed over the years and timber and planks had broken away to float in the river while the pilings which still stood acted as a bottleneck, gathering the various flotsam of the river. The children had developed a game in which the debris was an enemy fleet of warships and they were a defending shore battery, using rocks and stones for ordnance. It was an exciting game. The object was to sink the enemy ships before they came into contact with the pilings and the youths were positioned along the embankment and on the dock. They were laughing and shouting and having a fine time. Their artillery was proving accurate and effective and they had already sunk an orange crate destroyer and scored several crashing hits upon an empty oil can escort vessel. Suddenly one shouted a warning. The enemy fleet was being reinforced by a new ship which came floating out from beneath the pilings in treacherous sneak attack. It appeared to be a gnarled log dripping with moss and sea weed and it floated just below the surface. The children decided it must be a nuclear submarine and posed a most serious threat; knew they had to sink it before it could release its missiles and turned the full force of their lithic ordnance on it. They bombarded it from all sides and with every calibre. Small stones cascaded around the object, and larger rocks hit the water with great splashes, causing the submarine to roll and sway in the riled waters. But all the awesome might they unleashed proved ineffective. The submarine was actually rising to the surface. In desperation three of the youths joined forces to lift a huge slab of stone and carry it out on the dock, directly above the menacing ship. The slab was an aeroplane piloted by a suicide pilot willing to give his life for his country. They took careful aim and tilted the stone from the edge of the dock. It fell, turning in the air, and scored a direct hit amidships of the submarine. The vessel seemed to crack in half. The bows and stern rose up and the children howled in victorious glee. And then, very very slowly, the log rolled over and spread out arms and it wasn't a log at all. The children fell silent. They stared in shocked disbelief. This was something unique, beyond the rules of their game, and for some time they stood lined along the dock, gaping down at the body. It was an old woman. Her body bobbled about and her grey hair spread out like moss around her bloated face, writhing on the surface. And then comprehension came and they ran for help with shouts which were not of gaiety . . .

The police were summoned and they dragged the body out. It was the old flower seller who had a stall on the embankment, not far from the wharf. Investigation showed she had been dragged to the water and immersed until she drowned. There were no injuries on her body and she must have been conscious the whole time. The time of the murder was estimated at nine o'clock the night before, about the hour she usually closed her stall. There was still light at nine o'clock. There were invariably people strolling on the embankment and along the docks and perhaps young lovers had stood, hand in hand, directly above the old woman dying beneath the pilings. It was an eerie thought. One could not help but wonder what thoughts had screamed through her mind during those eternal instants of silent struggle, while the water felt like an avalanche of hard rocks pouring into her erupting lungs. It was far easier to imagine her thoughts than to conceive of those dark concepts in the mind of her killer—the mind of a man who killed without motive, without reason, without passion.

It seemed obvious that the killer was the same man who had strangled the old pensioner a few days before. The two murders fitted the same pattern of having no pattern. The woman had no known enemies and no one could possibly have profited by her death. The killing had been cold and efficient. The police had no clues and asked anyone who might have been in the vicinity to contact them whether they had heard or seen anything or not. Anyone who had noticed a man with wet clothing anywhere in the city was asked to notify the authorities. The theory was that it was the work of a maniac. It seemed the only solution. The thought of a madman is always terrifying and this was magnified by the fact that the victims had been old and helpless and had died without reason. The police stated it was likely the man would kill again —would go on killing at regular intervals until he was captured. I had a sudden image of Detective Inspector Grant poring over all the details of the two crimes, trying desperately to project and predict and prevent, and knowing with painful frustration that he had insufficient data—and that there was only one way in which to acquire more data and that implied more victims. He would be chain-smoking cigarettes, pacing across his office, snapping at his subordinates, cross with his wife. But they would understand the great unrest of his thoughts, and would tolerate his surly behaviour. And thinking of tolerance, I found myself contrasting Grant with this gentleman whose newspaper I held—who looked at the murders in such a calm and unexpected way. I looked up from the paper; glanced sideways at him. He was turning the pages of a large volume with vague disinterest. I placed the paper on the table and he closed the book; folded the paper neatly.

"Thank you."

"Why of course," he said.

"Say what you will, it's a gruesome business."

"Oh, I daresay the papers make it seem worse than it is, you know. Circulation and all that. The human fascination with the macabre. I find myself fascinated with that strange fascination. As a scientist . . ."

"A scientist?" I said, interrupting him with an abrupt impulse to change the subject. I did not wish to hear his opinions on human failings—if indeed he thought them failings, for he had a tendency to make the unexpected statement; to view from unconsidered angles.

He nodded slowly.

"What is your field?"

"I am a naturalist."

I raised my eyebrows slightly at the old-fashioned term and he interpreted the gesture correctly; nodded and repeated the word. "Yes, a naturalist. I use the old word deliberately—to imply that I have spread myself over the natural sciences rather than specializing. A fault of modern thinking, specialization."

"But surely knowledge is accumulating too quickly for a man to encompass everything?"

"Ah, but is that valid? If all knowledge is related—and it must be, if there is any basic law to the universe—then isn't a shallow immersion in a wide subject better than penetration to blind and limited depths? I have always wished to form conclusions which draw all the branches of natural science into a tighter pattern. An ambitious goal, certainly, and yet in some ways curiously limited." He paused, peering at me sharply. I had the impression he was judging my comprehension and his glance was curious—his countenance resigned and placid on the surface, yet with sharp inquiry coming through. It was like a flash of sudden lightning exposing the inner fabric of the storm clouds for a brilliant instant. Then it faded. "Oh,

I fully understand the necessity for specialists," he continued. "Men —men of that sort of mind—must probe the depths of limited fields and form little cones of knowledge—little submerged and isolated studies from which more well rounded scholars may draw as they grope for a totality. Necessary, yes. But it seems a shame that knowledge has outpaced the evolution of the mind, does it not?" And again that keen glance probed me.

"You interest me."

"Yes? I've always believed that a man who has wide interests will prove interesting."

"And are you pursuing your interests here at the museum? I've seen you quite often and wondered if you might be doing research of some nature."

"Nothing specific. In point of fact, I come to the museum for pleasure. As some might go to the opera or the theatre. I dearly love to wander through the natural history halls. But research—no, my research is in the field. It was, at least, until my accident. Now I must content myself with less strenuous studies. Although recently I have been able to do a bit of field work. Just a bit. An application of former conclusions."

"Accident?"

"My leg. I lost my leg, as you may have noticed."

He glanced down.

"Oh, I didn't realize," I said, a trifle embarrassed.

"I've managed to adapt myself to it. One does, you know. I have an artificial limb, of course, but I'd have adapted without it. That's the story of survival. But it hinders field research, nonetheless."

This fact seemed to sadden him. He fell into a thoughtful silence. Then he looked up and smiled.

"But we've not been introduced," he said. He held out his hand. His grip was firm.

"Claymore," he said. "Edward Claymore."

I told him my name. His name had a familiar ring and after a moment I placed it; said, "I believe I've read one of your books. Dealing with ecology, was it?"

"You please me. One has vanity, of a sort. Of a sort. One hopes one's ideas are of value. And valid, of course. Yes, ecology has always been my prime study, dear to my heart. The linking of

relationships between creatures within the scope of their environ-
ment, the incredibly complex interplay between organisms, subtle,
slowly emerging as one gathers experience, and in no other way.
These relationships cannot be predicted in the laboratory nor
projected in the library. One must be there. One must observe and
record. A falsehood may be written but what one has seen is truth
—the conclusions may be wrongly drawn but one cannot argue
with the basic premise of objective fact, eh?" I nodded agreement.
A certain intensity had come into his voice as he spoke of his work
and I felt a new respect for the man. His book, as I recalled it, had
been lucid and straightforward and unpretentious; had been an
early work which, in its simplicity, had stood the test of time. It
was no longer read much, for the theory had advanced beyond its
scope, and yet the material had been proved correct and had greatly
affected later research along those lines, foreshadowing understanding. I had read it long ago, and yet found myself able to recall
certain passages of bright illumination and even simple eloquence
in his descriptions of the wild reaches of our northern forests, the
perfect balance of nature, the harmony of life and death. Seen in
the context of his work, his unusual method of looking at events
was no longer surprising. I determined to look up his book and
read it again, in the new light of our acquaintance.

Claymore was thoughtful now; seemed to be looking back into
the past, looking northward to the forests of former times. I stood
up and excused myself. He nodded absently. He was still sitting at
the table, staring at far places, as I left.

I did not encounter Claymore for the next few days, and forgot my
intention to look up a copy of his book. He may well have been at
the museum but my research had taken a sharp turn which kept
me in the library through the day and he did not appear there. I
did not, in fact, see him again until after the third crime had been
committed. This third crime was different. It did not fit the pattern
of the preceding murders and, at first, appeared to be an accident.
It was far more horrible, in its quantitative effect, than the other
crimes and yet did not excite as much public outrage because it
was impersonal. It caused anger rather than morbid fascination.
The facts were these: the home for incurables on the outskirts of

the city caught fire and, in a great inferno, burned to the ground. Twelve men and women died in the flames, including a heroic nurse who had rushed again and again through sheets of fire and saved half a dozen lives; then, making a last desperate attempt, she had been trapped as the walls collapsed and had died in the incandescent ruins. When her charred body was found she still held an old man shielded to her breast, their flesh melted and then annealed together so that the corpses were inseparable. It was some time before the embers had cooled and a proper investigation carried out and then it was discovered that the fire had been deliberately set, a case of arson; some further time before connections were made and the authorities believed it might have been the work of the same madman who had killed twice before. But it was impossible to be sure. The police were keeping an open mind and investigating the background of every patient, both victims and survivors, in an attempt to discover if anyone would have gained by the death of one of them. It was a ghastly thought, but valid in these times when bombs are placed on aeroplanes, killing dozens as a side effect of collecting insurance on a solitary passenger. Nothing came of this line of investigation, however, and I, for one, felt certain it had been the maniac.

When next I saw Claymore, I recalled his calm attitudes concerning the former murders; was interested in what he thought in this instance. I asked him whether he considered this crime natural. I'm not sure what reaction I expected, but he surprised me by screwing up his face in obvious internal conflict, a genuine attempt at decision. I was amazed. I would not have been shocked had he taken an attitude opposed to normal morality, but had not foreseen this struggle within himself. Several times he opened his mouth to speak, and then hesitated. I watched his face, my interest greatly aroused.

Our meeting had taken place in the Hall of Saurians, a great vaulted room of silence with implications of vast and imponderable time. The skeletons of brontosaurus and allosaurus loomed over us. A high skylight sent filtered illumination dropping from the dome, washing the bones and casting Jurassic shadows across the floor, articulated adumbrations of the eons. Presently, without speaking, Claymore moved on, still shrouded in thought. I followed. He moved, as it were, through the path of prehistory; came to the Cretaceous period and sank down upon the edge of a platform with a tyrannosaurus rearing above, the great jaws in the gloom of the arched roof. I sat beside him. It seemed that even the shadows of those bleached bones had a great weight—that they lay upon us with the burden of knowledge, not insight to the mind but some truth known only in our most primitive cells, long forgotten to the magnifying mind but remaining dormant in the glands, the secretions of primordial instinct. I could not understand why this strange mood had come upon me; wondered if, somehow, it could have emanated from my companion by some basic transference, as a dog senses fear in a man.

At last, he spoke.

"The nurse should not have died," he said, quite simply.

"The nurse? Why only the nurse?"

"The nurse. Her actions were so very human and so very unnatural."

"But surely noble?"

"Nobility is unnatural. That, like law, has been created outside nature. Created by man. And man stands at some undefined point between nature and logic. Only man, you know, and possibly the elephant who is mighty enough to afford it—or was until man came along—show concern and respect for the aged and infirm, tolerate the useless elements of the pack, the tribe, the species. It was quite natural for the nurse to risk—and give—her life, but only in the framework of human terms. Not natural science but philosophy. The fault lies deeper than behaviour, it is in the system itself—a system that flaunts and reverses nature and creates homes for incurables, protects the helpless, preserves the weakest units to clutter the species."

He looked sideways at me.

"You can't believe the nurse's sacrifice wrong?"

"Not by human judgments."

"Well then . . ."

"But I am speaking objectively. I am standing outside the system and wish I had a lever long enough to move it. But one man cannot, there is no fulcrum, a man can do his little part and nothing more."

"You speak objectively. But don't you feel human sentiments?"

"Of course. With my human mind, I must. But I can also look through them, penetrate the veil of emotion, and attempt to act accordingly. If man were natural, you see, he would let the useless die, as our ancestors abandoned them to the lion and the hyena. And if man were logical he would, for instance, form his armies from the ranks of the cripples, the defectives, the malformed. War is quite natural—perhaps necessary—to our species. It is a safety valve for the pressures of survival. But it would be a far more effective valve if the casualties came from the weak, allowing the strong to live. But man lies somewhere in the void, groping upwards for elusive logic while his feet are slipping from their purchase on the natural. We are driven by false instincts we term rational—instincts created within ourselves long after nature had finished imprinting her pattern. We weaken ourselves by tolerance and, at the same time, destroy other species by inverse selectivity. Only man—man, the hunter—seeks the finest trophy, the largest antlers, the beast in the prime of life. We kill the best specimens and spurn the weak; we plunder nature as we follow our own descent."

"You have strong views," I said.

Claymore nodded. His slight shadow slipped across the floor, within the dinosaur's vaulted ribcage, as he shifted his position; crossed his leg over the artificial limb.

"Yes, the dichotomy has long troubled me," he said. "As these conclusions first solidified during long winter nights in the open, I often lay awake in my sleeping bag and saw the cold starry sky as a background to my concepts. How implacable that sky seemed, how pitiless. It was then that I saw natural science cannot be isolated, can never be an enclosed sphere of knowledge, for even the non-objective sciences are inextricably linked to ecology. Man is unique. He stands above nature and imposes his half-considered concepts on the natural scheme—forces them in where they do not fit. It seems that the experiment with the big brain has taken a wrong turning—a turning nature never intended but is powerless to correct—to guide us back to the proper channel. Nature has created a Frankenstein's monster which threatens to turn upon its creator. And to destroy nature is suicidal. Far better, perhaps, if homo sapiens had been allowed to survive by virtue of thumb and upright spine, and never granted the gift and curse of vocal cord and concept; to survive like the cockroach which, I daresay, will outlast us yet."

He stretched out a hand towards the tower of bones behind us, the lesson of the extinction of the mighty, the roaring rulers of earth for millions of years reduced to skeletal silence on a platform.

"I planned a book on this subject," he said. "I never completed it, however. It would never have been published. It would merely have invited outraged attacks."

"The idea certainly invites attack," I said.

"You don't agree with me?"

"I see your logic. But surely man is above the laws of the jungle. We have mastered survival and now it is curiosity which directs us, governs us, brought us through dark ages and may yet take us to the stars."

"Curiosity? Ah yes. That will take us—somewhere . . ."

For a time we did not speak.

"However," said Claymore, at length, "all this is conjecture. I am truly sorry about that nurse . . ."

Following this remarkable conversation in the Hall of Saurians, I took the trouble to locate a copy of Claymore's book. I reread it. It was the book I had remembered and none of his anti-social ideas were expressed there. It dealt with observation and obvious conclusions and no more; implied nothing hidden beneath the level of his writing. I found it difficult to see Claymore, as I knew him, as the author of this book and decided he was not—that something had caused his outlook to alter in the interval so that the man who had written so expressively and objectively in the past was not the same man who had spoken with such intensity in the shadow of the dinosaur. I could not imagine what this might have been, what experience could have warped and embittered his mind—perhaps the loss of his leg, I wondered. And yet he'd seemed to have adjusted easily enough to that loss. I was curious and would have been most interested to know about it, but could think of no way to bring the subject up; decided to wait and hope that, in the course of our meetings, the truth would come to light.

As, indeed, it did.

But first the maniac struck again.

In many respects, the next attack was the most perplexing of all. The strangest aspect was that the victim survived—was allowed to survive the ordeal. And certainly the most horrible aspect was that the poor fellow was blind, his affliction adding to the monstrous nature of the unprovoked assault. These facts added a new twist to the emerging pattern, complicating and confusing the issue. But what really struck me was purely subjective.

I was acquainted with the victim.

His name was Bill, a big jovial sort who refused to let his blindness change his cheerful nature. He'd lost his sight in the war, spent some time in hospital, and emerged with complete self-confidence and a fierce independence. He refused even the assistance of a guide dog and was frequently seen roaming the familiar streets with a firm and steady step, behind dark glasses and a fibre-glass stick; pausing at kerbs to listen for approaching traffic or halting for a moment at a corner, head raised and senses alert as he got his bearings. I was appalled when I read of the vicious attack which had taken place in his own basement flat. It is always so much more shocking when it is someone one knows. Bill had been brutally battered and beaten and then left alive on his floor. And that was the extraordinary thing. He had not been supposed dead, for he was still conscious. The maniac had simply walked off and left him, and that behaviour was so far removed from the other attacks that the police were not ruling out the possibility of a second madman amuck in the city. However the method of attack, until it had ceased, fitted the pattern. It was calculated and efficient.

I phoned the hospital immediately and inquired about his condition; found, to my relief, that he was recovering and asked how soon he would be able to have visitors. Apparently he had already been demanding that visitors be allowed in, which was very much to be expected of Bill, and I went to see him in the morning.

He was sitting up in bed, a white bandage around his head and a cigar in his teeth. His big solid shoulders sloped down beneath the sheets, he greeted me in a loud voice and roared cheerfully at the nurse who told him he must be quiet. She turned her eyes upwards and smiled despite herself. Bill was able to make people smile that way. He was pleased to have a visitor, we chatted for a few minutes and then, without urging or suggestion from me, he told me what had happened. He seemed more angered than frightened by the attack, his self-reliance had survived and he did not, in his dark world, understand how one with sight would project and magnify the terror of his position.

"Well, Johnny boy," said Bill, "I don't know if this bastard was waiting inside my flat or if he followed me home. The coppers think he was already inside, on account of one of my neighbours, old widow down the street, got an idea she's got designs on me, you know?—well, this widow saw me come home and says there was no one following me. But I'm not so sure. Seems I would have sensed his presence if he'd been waiting there. Maybe the old gal don't see too well. Anyway, don't matter which way it was. I'd been out for my afternoon walk and I never bother to lock the door so it was a simple matter for him to get in before me or behind me, whichever. I went right into the kitchen as soon as I got home and put a pan on for coffee. I leaned my walking stick against the stove and stood there, waiting for the water to boil. Then I heard him. Just a faint sound, at first, but we blind guys get used to listening for those soft noises. I turned around real sharp and heard his foot scrape as he stepped back in surprise. 'Who's there?' I asked. Y'see, I wasn't worried at that point, I thought it might have been a friend or maybe even that old widow come to tempt me. Maybe even one of the younger gals on the street. Plenty of gals like to call on a blind guy, Johnny. Gals that don't like it known they're passionate—figure they can get me to give 'em some lovin' and never even speak, see, so I won't know who they are. Happens all the time. 'Course, once they gets to pantin' and snortin', why, straight off I can tell who it is, long's I've heard their voice before. Easy to tell by the way they pant, how long their hair is, how wide they are in the hips. But, 'course, I don't let on I know, 'cause then they won't come back. I just go along with it, askin' who they are even after I know and then they think they're on to the perfect set-up and come back again. Yeah, this bein' a blind guy got some advantages. An' if their husbands find out, why I got the perfect excuse. Ha ha. Not a bad old game. Got some real fine unfaithful wives on that street, real fine.

"Anyhow, that's what I thought—thought it was one o' them passionate wives, so I wasn't worried. Just asked who it was and sort of smiled. Then when there was no answer, I was sure it must be a gal. I stood there, waitin' for her to come up and start snugglin'. But nothing happened for quite a while. The water started to boil, still nothin' happened. I guessed the gal was shy—figured it was her first visit, see? So I said, 'Want some coffee, whoever you are?' and then I heard the bastard take a deep breath, real quick, and I thought: Oh ho, Billy boy, that ain't no gal . . . What I thought was it was an irate husband, come to rant and rave. That was when he jumped on me . . ."

Bill paused. His brow furrowed beneath the bandage and I noticed several scratches on his face and neck, parallel rows that looked like fingernail marks. His big shoulders shifted as he recalled the violence of the attack and his heavy jowled face was set. I stared at him with great respect—saw that he was reliving only the violence, not the horror. Blindness has always seemed so ultimate a handicap and I had already imagined the scene—imagined Bill cringing, asking who and why, his sightless face questing at the strange sounds, unguided hands groping before him protectively, helpless and terrified, all this in the darkness of his affliction . . . This I had imagined; had pictured with my vision. But this was not the way it had been for Bill. He remembered only his anger and rage.

"He grabbed me by the throat," Bill said. "Well, Johnny boy, that was a mistake. Pretty strong fellow, I could feel his strength in his fingers, but 'course with both his hands on me I knew just where he was. I didn't panic. I got my feet set right and then gave him a couple of good belts in the belly. Good short shovel hooks. Bang bang, just like that." His shoulders rolled, his arms moved under the sheet, the long muscles in his jaw tightened. "He let go real quick then, boy. Real quick. I heard his wind rush out hard as he stepped back. But I hadn't caught him in the solar plexus like I planned and he didn't go down. I took an almighty swipe at where I reckoned his jaw oughta be, but I misjudged it. Missed the bastard. But I followed up, pulling my shoulder around and tuckin' my chin down behind it and coiled into a hitter's crouch. I still sort of suspected it was one o' them irate husbands. Wasn't worried much. I got both fists cocked and my head down and I said, 'Come on, you bastard! You want a fight, you found the right blind fellow. Just come in here, let's see what you can do!'

"Well, he didn't do anything for a while. I could hear him gettin'
his breath back and sort of feel his eyes on me. Weird feelin', that.
I could tell he was sizing me up, plannin' his attack—could tell he
was a pretty cool fellow. He was standin' just out of reach. I thought
about lungin' for him, but figured it was better to wait—try to time
a haymaker as he came to me. So I feinted a couple of times, to get
him to make some sounds movin' but he stayed real calm. I guess
we stood like that maybe two minutes. Then I heard him move to
the side, very quiet. I thought he was leavin', that he'd had enough.
But then I heard the cupboard door open and straight off I knew
what the sonabitch was doin'. He was looking for a weapon. Well,
there were bottles and things there he could use to club me and I
didn't like that idea; tried to play on his pride; said, 'Hey, you need a
weapon against a blind fellow? What sort o' man are you?' But that
didn't work. He started movin' towards me again. Then I got a little
worried. I reached behind me and got the handle of the pan and
held the pan in front of me. The water was boilin' away real good
by then. I could feel the steam. He hesitated and I swung the pan
across my chest, waitin'. I figured if I could give 'im a face full of
steam I'd have a chance to get my hands on him. That's all I wanted.
Just to get my hands on the bastard. Should've grabbed him straight
off when he was chokin' me, 'course, but at that point I didn't know
how serious he was and figured a couple o' belly hooks would be
plenty. But he was cautious now. I couldn't hear him movin' at all.
Then somethin' hit the pan and tilted it and the hot water ran down
my forearm. I threw the pan away and missed him and somethin'
smacked me alongside the head. In the temple. The coppers told
me it was a whisky bottle. How about that? Smacks me with my
own Scotch, the swine. Anyway, it was a pretty good wallop and I
had to cover up and he hit me again, behind the neck that time and
the floor slammed against my knees. I kept trying t' get a hold on
him but he stayed out of reach and belted me a few more times in
the head and neck and then, for the first time, I realized he wanted
to kill me. Not much I could do, just kneel there and dart my hands
out in different directions hopin' to get him. He was a cool one.
No hurry at all. Wasn't even breathin' hard enough to hear now.
Couple o' times I thought he'd gone, even, and then whop! he clubs
me again. Would've killed me, I guess, 'cept I touched the handle of

my cane then as I slid to the side and I got the cane and made a great wide sweep in front of me, low down, and felt it whip against his leg. Good snappy cane, fibreglass, gave him a helluva slash. Heard him yelp. So I saw that was my only chance, and I sat there with my back against the stove and swung the stick back and forth in a low arc in front of me, fast enough so he couldn't get close without gettin' hit. I was in a bad way by then. Sort of dizzy and sick from the hammerin' I'd had. But the only thing I could think was: Grab the cane, you dirty bastard! Just waitin' for him to grab it so I'd know where he was and could lunge at him. Just wanted him in my hands, y'know. I'd have broken every bone in his body."

Bill shook his head; shrugged. Then he passed a hand along his jaw. The anger left his countenance and a look of perplexity replaced it.

"Then he left," Bill said, simply, and he shrugged once again. "Hard to figure out. I was pretty helpless by that time. And there's no doubt he wanted to kill me. Only thing I can figure is that when I hit him with the cane I hurt him pretty bad. Worse'n I thought. Took the heart out o' the bastard. I guess maybe that's what happened, 'cause he was limpin' when he left. I heard him go. Thought maybe he was trying to fool me—that he'd wait by the door an' then come sneakin' back after I stopped whippin' the cane about. But he left all right. He wasn't breathin' hard and he walked calm enough but he seemed to be favouring one leg. I heard the front door close. I sat there for a long time, holdin' the cane ready and listenin' but he was gone all right. Then I crawled out to the street and called for help. And that was that. Hard to figure. The coppers said it might have been the guy who killed a couple of other people, too, so I got to think he bit off more'n he could chew with ol' Billy, eh?"

"I expect you're right," I said.

"Guess so."

He nodded. His cigar had gone out while he spoke and he lighted it again, holding the match cupped in his hands to guide the flame. The leaf had started to uncurl and there was white ash on the bed. He held the cigar in his teeth. He was very much alive. We chatted for a few more minutes and then I left. As I was going out several other visitors came into the room. They nodded to me the quiet way one nods in a hospital and went over to Bill's bed. They were all women. Widows and unfaithful wives, no doubt. Bill greeted them cheerfully and I went out and walked to the museum.

I found it impossible to concentrate on my research.

I sat in the library and ran my eyes over the pages, again and again, without comprehension. My thoughts kept drifting back to Bill's account of the attack. The most remarkable aspect was that he had been left alive. Whether or not Bill actually believed he had driven the attacker away with his cane, it seemed obvious to me that was not the case—that Bill had been helpless at the end. He'd been terribly battered and must have been nearly unconscious. And yet, even in that brutal beating, there was an element of calculation related to the murders. The blows all appeared to have been struck with the solitary purpose of causing unconsciousness and subsequent death—not pain. There seemed no element of sadism in the method of attack. There had been pain, certainly, but not deliberate, not as an end in itself, the agony no more than a side effect of an amateur attempt at striking a mortal blow. And this created a paradox for, when the end was in sight, the maniac had broken off the attack. It had not been panic. He had not fled and, by Bill's own account, had been cool and calm. And still he had left the job unfinished. Or was it unfinished? Was there some purpose which escaped me? If the goal had been death, why should the man have settled for less? And if the goal had not been death, why had his blows been so obviously intended as lethal?

My mind spun over these disturbing questions again and again, as my eyes moved back and forth across the page and the text failed to register. At last I pushed the book away and looked at my watch. I decided that research was impossible at the time; that I might as well have an early lunch and try again in the afternoon. I replaced the volume on the shelves and left the library. At the main doors, however, a notice caught my eye and I remembered that the new natural history exhibit had been opened the day before. I'd not yet had a chance to visit it and had been eagerly awaiting the pleasure and this seemed an excellent opportunity. I turned back and took the elevator up to the new hall.

It was there I once again encountered Claymore . . .

The new exhibit was the Johnson Memorial Hall of North American Mammals and I knew it had been planned somewhat differently to the other rooms. Johnson had been a wealthy industrialist who had, in later years, found great peace and pleasure in the Canadian wilderness and had left a large sum of money for the express purpose of creating the new hall. He had also stipulated conditions. It was to be as natural as possible. The whole room was to be fashioned into a simulated forest and there were to be no straight corridors, no display cases, no guard rails. There were not even signs to identify the various flora and fauna, on the principle that the animals in the wilds did not wear labels. Johnson's desire was to create a room where one could wander at random, in simulated solitude, in the mood of the far-reaching forests. It seemed a fine idea to me, and I was anxious to see how well it had been carried out.

I was pleased as soon as I entered the hall.

The plans had been well executed. The entrance was irregularly shaped with roughly plastered walls so that one had the impression of passing through the mouth of a cave. The forest stretched away within, the walls hidden behind backdrops of distant mountains which conveyed a sense of great distance and taped music softly repeated the forest sounds, birds and breezes and vague cracklings. Water dripped rhythmically from an artificial cataract. I stood beside the entrance for a time, letting myself fall into the mood, and then advanced. It was very realistic. Narrow paths wound about between arbours and brush and rock, seemingly at random as I turned my head from side to side. At first I saw no animals. Then abruptly the vegetation opened out and I found myself looking at a colony of beaver beside a plastic pool blocked with fallen timber. The animals were there, but one had to look. I strolled on; glimpsed a lynx stretched along an overhanging limb, tufted ears laid back, snarling; turned as the path angled and stopped short as a Kodiac bear reared up. The taxidermy was excellent, the animals were realistically grouped in lifelike positions, often I caught just a flashing glance as I passed some small mammal peering from the undergrowth. I thought Johnson would have approved.

Then, turning on to a secondary trail, I found myself face to face with Claymore.

"A splendid hall, this," he said.

I nodded. Somehow, seeing Claymore, my thoughts left the artificial wilderness and returned to reality ... to the crimes we had discussed before. I mentioned I'd just come from the hospital where Bill was and Claymore appeared interested.

"Ah yes. The blind gentleman. How is he?"

"Recovering."

"Ah. The newspapers stated his condition as critical. But then, one learns never to have faith in journalism."

"He's a tough one," I said.

"Tough? Yes. Yes, I should imagine so. Obviously he had the will to survive. Admirable and natural. He will undoubtedly live until his time to die."

"Unlike the others."

"Others?"

"The other victims."

"Oh. Oh, no doubt it was their time to die."

I made no comment. Claymore nodded. "No doubt," he said again and then turned and strolled on. I followed. The path was too narrow to walk side by side and I trailed behind him. His limp seemed more noticeable and he seemed very interested in the exhibits, very alert, as if this were truly a wilderness and he were keeping an eye out for dangers or prey. From time to time he paused and used his walking stick to part the growth, revealing some secreted animal I hadn't even noticed, looking up and down. Fox and wolverine and badger lurked on every side. Presently the path opened into a clearing and Claymore halted. He sighed. A deer was bounding tangentially from us, white tail bobbed in graceful flight. At first glance I imagined the deer had been positioned as if fleeing from the visitors' approach down the path, but then I looked sideways and saw differently. Emerging from the opposite side of the clearing charged a pack of timber wolves, frozen in an instant of action, lean and fierce. I was about to point them out to Claymore when he spoke.

"Ah, it makes me long for the wilds," he said. "Books ... books can only teach what other men have learned, not what each man must learn for himself ... the sensations, the moods, the tone of nature. The totality."

He leaned on his stick.

"Well, I'm just as pleased these brutes are stuffed," I said, jokingly. "How would you like to face that lot in the flesh?"

Claymore turned, his eyebrows lifting. He saw the wolves. His reaction was startling. He cried out and took a staggering step backwards, raising his walking stick like a club. I stepped forward, afraid he would fall, but he caught his balance: lowered the stick. His face was white and he was sweating.

"Good heavens, man. What is it?" I asked.

Gradually he relaxed. The blood returned to his face and he looked embarrassed.

"Forgive me. A thoughtless reaction."

"What's wrong?"

He shook his head; moved towards the wolves and regarded them, then motioned at the pack with his stick, holding it like a fencer.

"You ask if I should like to face them," he said.

"A silly comment," I said.

"Ah, but I have," said Claymore.

I waited, hoping he would continue, sensing the past trauma in his sudden reaction. I noticed he had raised his stick more in a position of attack than defence and that even now his eyes were bright as he looked at the wolves.

He said, "They are fine specimens. Very fine. That big fellow must have weighed well over a hundred pounds, I should think. It saddens me to see a wolf which has been killed in his ferocious prime. I love wolves. I hate them but I love them for they have taught me so much. Everything is there to be learned in canis lupus. Territorial instinct, the pack urge, monogamy. And mystery. People have always thought of the wolf as different from other predators. Finer somehow, and yet inspiring fear far greater than its size and strength should warrant. Why, there is even a disease in which one believes himself to be a wolf. Lycorexia. I wonder if there is a philosophy, as well?"

He shrugged.

"You have been attacked by wolves?" I asked, hoping to hear the tale.

"No. Not attacked. But I have faced them. I faced the pack and therefore they did not attack me, you understand? And facing them, I learned to face all—to face the past as well as the future and to see myself with humility, a small part of existence, of little importance in the total scheme of life . . . and of great importance in that I learned to act as nature intended."

"You stared them down, you mean?"

He gestured vaguely.

"Oh, one might say that. But it was far more than that."

"You interest me greatly."

"Ah, it was . . . interesting. You wish to hear the story?"

"Very much. If it won't disturb you to remember . . ."

"No, not at all. I constantly remember it. You take your knowledge from books—from still lives, as it were—and perhaps you should know how my knowledge came to me."

"I should like to know."

He nodded and glanced at the wolves once more. Then he moved away with a sideward step. A fallen tree had been propped against a stump across the clearing and Claymore took a seat on the log. I sat beside him. For some time he collected his thoughts while I waited. A man passed, pausing to look at the wolves and then looking at us. Then a middle-aged woman with three children crossed the clearing. They, too, observed us for a moment. We must have looked as out of place as they did. But our ectopia was of a different nature, and I felt I belonged there, listening to Claymore as a sceptic might have listened to Socrates, knowing one need not agree to learn. The taped sounds played on and the waterfall rustled and presently Claymore spoke.

"Several months after publication of my book I returned to the north," he said. "The book—I believe you mentioned reading it?—dealt with ecology in general and now I had decided to make a study in depth on a specific relationship. For several reasons I selected that existing between wolves and moose. The most important reason was expediency, for both are territorial animals. The wolf pack sticks within its own boundaries and will tolerate no others there and the moose, in deep snow at least, remains in his own small area or yard. Well, this territorial instinct enables an observer to define the limits of the area and use the square miles within as a field laboratory with checks and controls far more accurately than if the observer had selected his own boundaries at random. I have little patience with those who set aside a tract of land without regard for the animals' own limits ... less with the modern practice of observing from aeroplanes. This may be a scientific prejudice on my part, and I've considered that sort of work since losing my leg, but cannot see it leading to accurate conclusions. However, I didn't have that problem. All my research was done on snowshoes with a pack on my back, far from the world of society. It would have been difficult to be farther. It was a world of true desolation and abandoned beauty, and my base camp was a little cabin of rough logs beside a stream which opened out, some miles below, into a river. The river was ringed by fir trees and frozen in winter. I had but one companion—my guide—a man of dubious ancestry called Charles. He had spent his life in the wilderness and was a rough, silent man with vast practical knowledge and experience. He hadn't the faintest idea what I was studying and did not care at all. He was paid and that was sufficient. That was the way I wanted it, as well, for all men are susceptible and I might well have let my conclusions be affected by a companion who understood the subject. I could ask Charles questions and he would answer from his experience, accurate and precise, not knowing what answer I sought and therefore unable to commit the common error of slanting the answer to give me satisfaction. We carried all our supplies with us and relied on Charles to provide fresh meat. I have always believed in travelling light and Charles was the sort to regard even my meagre equipment as luxury.

"We went into the wilderness in the late autumn and prepared the base camp. I made preliminary investigation and identified the wolf pack I would study—a pack some twenty strong—and the outline of their territory, where they would remain as long as the food supply permitted. Then it was necessary to wait, for wolves seldom hunt the moose until winter. In open water an adult moose can wade out so far that the pack must swim to reach him, and that is not a pleasant prospect for the wolves. But in winter the water is frozen, the beaver keep to their lodges, the snowshoe hares are insignificant meals for pack strength, and then there is the moose.

"Well, winter came.

"Charles and I followed the wolf pack. It was a time of great physical hardship and exhaustion, of dogged perseverance. Often we were away from the cabin for weeks at a time, as the pack ranged over the outer limits of their land, describing a wide and predictable circle which allowed us to anticipate them and often wait for them. This was necessary for they travelled far faster than we could follow. I learned many things but my main goal was to witness the confrontations between the pack and the moose. Seldom did I manage to be present at the actual kill, although often we arrived before the remains were devoured. This was important. It was absolutely essential that I gather data about the victims—to do an autopsy on the remains. This was no simple matter. For one thing, a healthy wolf will eat about fifteen pounds of flesh a day and, if we were far behind the kill, there was little left to examine. On the other hand, when we managed to arrive before their first hunger had been satisfied, the pack was understandably reluctant to surrender their feast to science. These were wolves of the wilds, they had not yet learned fear of man, and to shoot them would have completely ruined the natural balance existing there. The pack regarded us with curiosity and, when they sensed no fear in us, with respect. Undoubtedly they saw us as fellow carnivores, but not as rivals, as they would have another wolf pack or a fox, and territorial defence seldom extends beyond the genus. So my findings were difficult and not extensive, but I persevered and gradually certain aspects of the relationship began to take form.

"Have you ever seen a moose, full grown in the forest? The wolves had a healthy respect for their prey, and it is understandable. Seven feet tall at the shoulders, weighing a ton and a half, unpredictable in mood and often changing from docile grazing to a thundering charge without a period of transition . . . they are formidable indeed. Often a moose in deep snow can outdistance the wolves with that awkward, long-legged stride. More often they choose to stand defiantly against the pack and invariably the wolves move on in these cases, searching easier prey. I witnessed this several times and came to the conclusion that the pack tested at least ten moose for every one against which they pressed the attack. This conclusion led me to predictions which only sufficient autopsy examinations could prove and I pressed on, faithfully inspecting gnawed bones, scraps of hide, uncoiled lengths of intestine. Eventually it was enough to convince me my predictions were correct—that the wolves' depredations were essential to the moose's survival as a species; that they systematically culled the old and the infirm and left the finest specimens to benefit from limited winter food supplies. Invariably my examinations of the remains showed the same results. The victims suffered from bone disease, cysts in the lungs, tapeworm. Their teeth were worn with age and an abundance of ticks implied they suffered from a weakened condition due to innumerable other diseases. And every victim I examined, discounting calves, proved to be more than seven years old—beyond their prime. Without the wolves these old moose would have lived for a good many years yet, consuming vast amounts of food and depriving the young members of the species."

Claymore had begun to talk rapidly, warming to a subject dear to him. Now he paused, glanced sideways at me, and shrugged; smiled thinly.

"But all this is common knowledge now," he said, apologetically. "I must not bore you with this. Another aspect of vanity, eh? In my day it was just coming into acceptance and I shamelessly feel pride in my own small role in bringing it to light; in bringing it, perhaps a trifle sooner than it would have been. Still too late, of course. Too late against ignorance. I fear we shall both live to see the day when the last wolf is mangy and cowed in a zoo, when these exhibits are labelled extinct, or the museum equips an expedition to seek the last remaining pack. Perhaps. Still, they fight for survival. This is the first necessity. On the day a creature ceases to flee or to snarl, then it must die . . .

"But enough of this rambling theory. Theories hold true for all, but I must tell you my own experience."

I waited. When again he spoke his tone had changed. He still spoke with intensity, but it was a subjective quality now and there was terror lurking restrained in the timbre of his voice . . .

"There came the day when circumstances forged the links of events —events engraved in the receptive awareness of aroused sensations. There were two separate disasters, insignificant in themselves but combining to form a sum greater than the parts. The first

disaster came when Charles broke through the ice. We had travelled far from the base camp, skirting the frozen lake, and night
came. We stopped to make our camp. I regretted the delay and was
impatient to continue for the pack had not killed in several days and
they were lean with hunger. I knew they would press an attack very
soon, and hoped to be present. I was standing in the trees, looking
in the direction the pack had taken, when I heard Charles cry out. I
rushed back. A segment of the bank had collapsed beneath him and
he had crashed through the ice. I saw his head bob in the cold water,
one hand gripping the jagged splintered edge. I threw myself flat
to spread my weight and grasped him; managed to haul him from
the icy waters. He was gasping and shaking. The instant the air
touched his clothing it began to crackle and harden. Fortunately
we had already made the fire and I helped him to strip his clothing
off, wrapped him in a blanket and gave him a stiff shot of brandy.
For a long time he lay still beside the fire, shivering, his eyes pressed
closed. Finally the chill left him and I saw he was all right. But he had
a strange look in his eyes. The first words he spoke were, "My rifle
. . . I've lost my rifle." Well, I assumed he was worried about the loss
alone, and offered to replace the weapon when we returned from
the field trip, but that was not what troubled him. He had lost his
pack, including the tent, but it was the rifle which distressed him.
He said that he would have to return to the cabin—to get his other
gun before we continued on. I argued. Fate brought out my stub-
bornness, an ally of disaster. But Charles couldn't conceive of going
on without a weapon. I felt greatly frustrated. I knew the wolves
would kill soon, and could not bring myself to miss the opportunity to witness the kill. I refused to go back. He refused, at first, to
continue—did not even want to stop the night, but to go back in the
darkness. He had completely changed. It was as if he had lost a vital
organ instead of a rifle and all his taciturn confidence had vanished.
Objectively, it was more interesting, a strange twist of the person-
ality of a man who has come to rely on something apart from his
own body. But subjectively I could not tolerate it. I could not bear
to miss the opportunity ahead. I became angry and Charles, completely out of character as I'd known him, hung his head sullenly
and accepted my abuse. I even, I fear, spoke of cowardice. Even this
did not sting him to reply, other than to mutter, shaking his head,

that a man could not stay in the woods without a gun. I carried no weapon, of course. But I saw no danger. I recalled his own assurance that he'd never known wolves to attack a man. 'Not a man with a rifle,' he mumbled. 'But these wolves don't know what a rifle is, how can that make a difference?' I asked. He shrugged. 'Maybe we might smell different without a weapon,' he said. He kicked at the ground and swung his head from side to side and behaved like a spoiled child. But I was adamant and, after a long while, he reluctantly agreed to go on in the morning. Very reluctantly. And even then he continued to mutter about how impossible it was to go on without rifle and tent. I let him ramble on after he'd agreed; got into my sleeping bag beside the fire. His bag was lost but there were sufficient blankets and my groundsheet and he wrapped up in these. He was still muttering when I drifted into sleep.

"His sullen, fearful mood continued through the next day. The wolves were moving fast and far and, the farther we moved from the extra rifle at the base camp the more frequently he paused to look back over our trail, his eyes longing to retrace our steps. Still, we advanced. In the afternoon we were able to leave the pack's spoor and cut at an angle across the predictable circle, moving over rolling hills with deep snow between the slopes and stark pines on the crest. Evening was approaching. Charles was lagging and I had to urge him on, often walking well ahead of him; turning to find him gazing backwards; shouting to him, whereupon he would come forward, head down and shoulders hunched. Then sunset struck with golden shafts across the western sky and it was in this violent glow that we came upon the wolves . . .

"I topped a ridge and saw them like a string of dark slugs advancing across a rippled snowfield. I took my binoculars from their case and focused. Charles came up to stand beside me, breathing harder than usual. The wolves moved like a single segmented organism, in a perfect twisting line. Then suddenly the line broke up, the pack formed a semi-circle, sitting back on their lean haunches. Charles grunted and pointed and I turned the glasses along the line indicated, saw a copse of dark trees and, after a few moments, saw the moose.

"He was a huge fellow, completely motionless, facing the pack. He'd not yet shed his antlers and they spread like two giant hands as wide as his great height. His ears were laid back, his mane erect. The wolves rose and advanced a few paces; settled on their haunches again. The moose moved then. The bell beneath his neck swung as he turned his head. He pawed the ground with great platter feet. The wolves showed prudence despite their hunger. Their tongues lolled out and their flanks rose and fell. Finally the leader rose and advanced cautiously, turned sideways to his quarry, testing the moose's temper and resolve. The moose didn't wait. He came with a sudden rush, awkward and mighty. The wolf leaped sideways, turning in the air and the pack spun and scattered. The moose halted, snorted and pawed, and then backed into the trees again. The wolves came silently back and drew together, exactly like a conference, heads lowered, muzzles close. From time to time one raised his head to gaze at the moose. The moose pawed spurts of snow and did not look worried or reluctant . . . looked as if he would welcome an attack. I watched, fascinated. This was an important observation. I knew the wolves had not eaten in days and wondered how much hunger was necessary to override caution. A great deal, apparently, for they rose abruptly and trotted off, shoulders rising and falling in a rhythm uncannily like a human shrug in time of resignation. They crossed the snowfield and vanished from sight. The moose began to peacefully strip bark from the trees. Charles snorted and went back down the ridge, wondering what I had seen worth seeing and I stood there for some time, watching the moose in the deepening shadows. The sky had reddened, the tallest trees gathered the last light and darkness fell spreading over the ground. When I could no longer distinguish the moose I turned and started back down the incline, picking my steps carefully. Not, however, carefully enough.

"And then the second disaster struck . . ."

Claymore winced slightly.

"The definitive disaster," he said. "I had just settled my weight on my leg when something struck me just above the ankle. It didn't hurt. I thought the limb of a tree had somehow fallen on me and there was what seemed a great interval before I heard the solid clang of metal—seemed a great time lapse, although I was still suspended in the midst of falling when the sound reached my brain and as I dropped into the snow I already knew what had happened

—that I had stepped on the pan of a trap. I had fallen on my back, twisting the imprisoned leg. I sat up, brushing snow from my arms in thoughtless habit, and leaned down to inspect the damage. I still felt no pain, no feeling at all, but the moment I saw the trap I knew I was severely damaged.

"It was a huge trap made to hold a bear. The vicious jaws had sunk deeply into my leg—so deeply it seemed the toothed edges must nearly meet between torn calf and shattered shin. I inspected it very calmly; found it was old and rusted and must have lain there for years, forgotten by some long departed trapper. I looked at it from every possible angle, tilting my head this way and that, and then took the jaws in my hands and tried to open it. I could not budge it. I sat back, wondering what to do—I'd completely forgotten Charles and was undoubtedly in some form of shock. But then he called from the shadows below, asking what had happened. I felt a sense of relief as I heard his voice and shouted to him. A moment later, in a spray of snow, he was kneeling beside me.

"He winced as he saw the wound; bent over my leg and inspected the trap. His hands moved slowly at first but gradually his face darkened and he began to jerk and haul violently. His efforts twisted my leg and the first tingling of pain advanced past my knee. I clamped my teeth shut and watched him without protest, with complete confidence in his experience and ability. But then his face changed again, he cursed and squatted back. He looked sick. His forehead was glistening with sweat. He told me in slow, thoughtful tones that the release mechanism had become jammed or broken during the long untended time and that he wasn't able to open the jaws. He repeated the last several times ... 'Can't open it, won't open, can't get it to open ...' Then he cursed some more. I still felt no real panic. It seemed impossible that I was hopelessly trapped as long as I had a companion with me. I asked what we should do, quite calmly, I believe. Charles didn't answer. He wiped the back of his hand across his brow and leaned over the trap again, digging in the snow until he found the chain. He followed the chain, lifting it from the snow foot by foot, like some clanking serpent with a frozen spine; found the end secured to a large tree, encircling the bole and fastened with a stout padlock. I watched as he took the chain in both hands and hauled on it, bracing one boot against the tree and winding the links around his wrists. His shoulders heaved beneath his heavy mackinaw. Sounds came brittle on the cold air. His heel scraped the bark, he grunted and snorted, the chain rattled. At last he gave up the effort and bent to the padlock, inspecting it carefully, turning it over in his hands. His breath hung about his face like a halo. He straightened and rubbed the back of his neck, then came clumping back to where I sat. He moved behind me without a word and began fumbling with my pack; eased it from my shoulders and laid it open, searching for a tool. But there was none. Whatever we had possessed which might have proved effective had been lost through the ice. Presently he returned to the tree. He seemed to have difficulty crossing the deep snow and paused, breathing deeply, before drawing his hand axe. It was a short-handled affair, the blade flat backed, and he struck the padlock several times with it. It clanked dull but distinct and did no good at all. From his posture, the way his shoulders sloped and his head hung, I got the impression he hadn't expected the blows to be effective—had tried them for mere formality. Once more he returned to me. He knelt, cleared the snow away and struck the spring and release mechanism several sharp ringing blows. The axe rebounded and the lock refused to yield. Flakes of rust splintered from the steel and bright marks scored the metal but it would not break. Charles shook his head. The pain was increasing now. He reversed the axe and attempted to use the handle as a prying bar, but could get no leverage between the tightly clamped teeth. After a moment he chopped the axe into the earth in a gesture of frustration; grasped the jaws in his hands again and pulled. I leaned forward to help. Together we applied all our strength. But that trap was fashioned to hold a bear. We could not budge it.

" 'It's no use,' he said.

"I looked searchingly at him.

"His face clouded with anger, he scowled at me. 'Well? What do you expect? It's no use, I tell you!' He gestured at the trap. 'The big brown bears can't open these, what can I do? Eh? What can I do? Sometimes when a bear is caught like this they escape. You know how this is, eh? They escape by gnawing their foot off. That's how. The big bear chews his own paw through, so what do you expect me to do?' I said nothing. Gradually his anger lessened. He glanced

towards the tree. 'I might chop the tree down,' he said, but even as
he spoke we both knew it was impossible. He had only the hand
axe, the tree was large, even if it were possible it would take far
too long. 'Even then, you would still be trapped. I would have to
carry you, dragging the trap and chain. Or build a litter and haul
you behind me. If one had a rifle, the spring could be shot apart,
of course. But one does not have the rifle.' He looked sharply at
me as he said this. Despite the growing pain, I felt indignant at this
reproach; said, 'That's right. We haven't the rifle. So what shall we
do?' He didn't answer for a while. Then he shrugged. 'I will need
tools. The hacksaw, the crowbar. Also the first aid kit. The spare
first aid kit . . .' He nodded to me, to himself. 'Yes, that will be necessary, your leg must be treated before you can be moved.'

" 'But those things are at the cabin,' I said.

"Charles looked away.

"Then I felt the first awful weight of panic . . ."

Claymore looked at me almost with challenge. I was staring,
open mouthed, completely absorbed in his tale, caught up in the
complex mood behind the words.

"He left you?" I asked.

Claymore nodded.

"Yes. He left me. It was the fact of not having his rifle, you see. I
feel certain that, had he not lost the weapon, he would have found
some other solution; wouldn't have abandoned me. But he had lost
the gun and, with it, his courage, his confidence. All his experience
was related to the possession of a firearm, and without it he could
not function, he could not relate circumstances to past experience.
Standing over me he seemed to have no more substance than his
shadow; could no more direct his own behaviour than that shadow
could defy the commands of the fading light. And then, of course,
there were the wolves . . .

"All our efforts, although they seemed to have lasted a long time,
had passed quickly. Time had been suspended by stress. The sky
was still violent with gold and fire behind strato-cumulus formations. I distinctly remember turning to look at this flaming sunset;
noticing it without relation to my plight, as my mind turned away
from reality in self-defence. I thought quite composedly how
beautiful the colours were with the dark pines thrusting up like

a palisade. And then, gradually, I became aware of other broken silhouettes above the ridge. It was as if the tournure of the land had shifted subtly, as if during our suspended period of time the world had continued to age and upheavals had altered the contours. I shielded my eyes and stared into the incandescent sunset and gradually the objects took form and became the wolves.

"The pack sat on top of the ridge and regarded us in silent hunger. I spoke—I used my voice, although the syllables were broken and did not take verbal form—and Charles turned to look; jerked up sharply, his face mangled by fear. The wolves followed his motion with their yellow eyes. 'They never attack humans,' I said. And Charles knew this as well as I, but he did not have his gun. He whispered, 'They have no fear of us. You would not let me kill them . . .' Trying to shift the responsibility on to me, of course; to justify his act even before he committed it. And then I knew, definitely, that he would leave me.

"Charles began making preparations then, without another word. I watched him in silence with the fires of agony spreading through my thigh and hip, eager for fuel. He made a fire. He gathered all the wood in the immediate vicinity and stacked it beside me. He took the blankets and sleeping bag from my pack and wrapped them carefully—tenderly even—around me. His actions were stiff and jerky and he could not look at me; could not bring himself to tell me he was leaving. Strangely enough, I felt I should make it easier for him, since it was an irrevocable decision. I asked, 'How soon can you be back?' He looked at me then; seemed relieved that I was not pleading or arguing; that I accepted the necessity. He assured me he could travel very fast alone and unencumbered; that he could be back in two days, maybe less, no more. 'All right,' I told him. 'Obviously you must have tools to free me.' 'And the other rifle,' he added, quickly. The axe was still jammed in the ground and he drew it out; looked at it for a moment, reluctant to part with his only weapon. Then he handed it to me. He held it out by the handle, as if still undecided—as if he might snatch it away at the last moment. But when I grasped the blade he let it go. He tied his snowshoes on, fumbling with the laces and glancing sideways at the ridge. Then he stood up and nodded. 'It is the only way,' he said. 'Yes,' I said, 'it is how it must be.' 'I will hurry. I will return with the rifle.' The way he said it, I could tell he believed he would be returning not for rescue, but revenge. Then he moved off, swinging the big snowshoes wide and moving fast. I watched him until he had passed into the trees. Then I turned and watched the wolves and they watched me . . ."

"My God," I said, the exclamation forced from me as Claymore paused. He was looking at the mounted wolves across the clearing. It was lunchtime now and no one else had passed through the hall for some time. We seemed very much alone and, somehow, I got the impression that Claymore was talking more to himself than to me. I had no wish to destroy the mood with which he spoke, and stilled the urge to comment. He lowered his eyes and regarded his legs then looked at the wolves once again. They stared back with glass eyes.

"I took stock of the situation," he said. "I felt, at first, that I would be able to survive until Charles returned. I kept telling myself that there are few, if any, recorded instances of wolves attacking humans in North America. I had the axe and my sheath knife and the fire. I had a plentiful supply of firewood. I tried to look upon my plight as an experiment, a chance at first hand observation, and actually managed to feel almost cheerful for a short while. But it could not last. I don't suppose I'd expected it to, really. There was the pain and there were the wolves. The pain had become unbearable and the wolves were hungry. I told myself the wolves would not approach the fire and fashioned a tourniquet for my leg, using one of the groundsheets and turning it tight with the axe handle. I was able to cut off the pain this way, but was afraid of stopping circulation too long and each time I released the pressure the agony flooded back worse than before, increasing with each turn of the axe. Time passed with incredible slowness. The sunset lingered, the wolves waited. Then, at last, it was night. I shifted another length of wood on the fire, raising the flames and increasing the circle of light. I could no longer see the wolves, but I could hear them panting. And then, suddenly, I could see them. They had come down the slope to the very rim of the firelight, formless grey shapes with glowing eyes. I threw small flaming sticks at them and they backed away calmly. I held the axe in one hand and the knife in the other, turned my back to the fire and waited. Panic faded into a stupor. I blacked out.

"I couldn't have been unconscious long, only minutes perhaps, certainly less than an hour. The fire still burned brightly. But when I awoke it was with a cold and certain resolve, as if my mind had fashioned a formula while my consciousness was gone. The situation was very clear. I knew that if I remained there I would die. The pain, the cold, the wolves—by one or all I would die. And I was determined not to die; thought of the moose driving the pack away with his charge and then thought of the bear for whom this trap had been designed—the bear who would devour his own leg to escape, governed by a natural instinct far deeper than pain could delve. I saw the only possibility of survival quite objectively.

"I had the axe.

"I had to remove my leg.

"It was decided. I considered no other course of action; refused to contemplate the blinding agony and the unspeakable horror of the act. I used only one rationalization—telling myself my leg was hopelessly mangled already and would never be of use to me again; that I would be cutting away a thing already dead. But I didn't really need to convince myself of this, for I was merely an animal in a trap. Very carefully I began to plan the operation.

"I placed the blade of my knife in the hottest embers of the fire. It was a large triangular blade, very keen, which I used to dissect the remains of the wolf pack's kills. I tested the blade of the axe with my thumb. It seemed sharp—it had to be sharp enough, for I had no way to hone it. Then I waited for the knife to heat. I was very calm. I took out my pipe and tobacco and lighted it with a burning twig. I smoked slowly and contemplatively, watching the smoke rise against the flames. I timed it just right, so that when the pipe had burned out the knife had begun to glow. I knocked the ash out and put my pipe in my pocket, then tightened the tourniquet just above the knee. I raised the axe with both hands and marked an imaginary line across my shin; lifted my torso, threw my shoulders back, and brought the axe down.

"But my nerve failed.

"At the last instant, involuntarily, I twisted the stroke to the side.

The blade bit into the earth beside my leg and the concussion leaped at my elbows and shoulder sockets. I cursed myself for a coward. And, as if the wolves could sense the failure of my courage, they moved nearer. One wolf advanced ahead of the pack—the same, I thought, that had advanced to test the moose. Anger surged up in me. I screamed loudly and the wolf retreated, lowering his muzzle. The anger helped. It purified my perceptions. I took one of the blankets and draped it over my leg, smoothing it around the calf so that the contour could be seen. I was very annoyed with my leg. But, covered with the blanket, it ceased to be a leg, it was a lump beneath a blanket, no more. I drew the axe edge across this lump at the proper spot, wrinkling the blanket to leave a visible line. I raised the axe once more. I looked at a wrinkle in a blanket. Just a wrinkle in a blanket in the wavering light of a fire. And then, very accurately and very hard, I chopped down.

"This time I did not fail.

"The blow did not sever the leg, but it broke through the slender shin bone and cut deeply into the flesh. I stared at it. I tried to raise the axe but it was stuck. I had to heave with all my strength to withdraw it, and the blood spurted behind. There was more blood than I had imagined and it rose with incredible force, towering above me and then splattering in all directions. The blanket turned instantly dark. I was seized by frenzy. My mind rushed from my body and I saw myself from above, a wild madman broken in dancing flames, spewing heavy blood in wide arcs, roaring and jerking and lifting the axe. I had but one thought: I had to finish the task. I fell upon my leg, hacking savagely time and again, no longer capable of accurate strokes but chopping and slashing with insane fury, sawing the blade back and forth across parting tendons and pounding the edge through convulsing muscle.

"I have no recollection of when the leg finally parted. I did not know at the time. But it did and I found myself pounding the earth, digging great furrows in the soaked ground, separated from the trap and from the grisly burden it held.

"A semblance of sanity snapped taut in my brain then. I dropped the axe and grasped the glowing knife; clamped the flat blade against the ghastly stump. The odour of charred tissue and boiling blood sprang up in overpowering waves. I held my breath and held the knife and the bleeding stopped. The pain, too, had stopped. My nerves could not convey this message of horror, this agony beyond sensation's scope. I sat there, gasping and gaping. I stared at the trap. Blood bubbled and coiled from the shapeless, lifeless lump in the clamped jaws. It was hideous. I did not want this monstrous object near me. I leaned forward and raised the trap, swung it and threw it from me with all my might. It flew, the chain clanking, and the blanket dropped away. The trap bounced twice when it landed.

"Again I blacked out.

"And again awoke.

"I awoke with a sense of relief and with the wolves making sounds very near. I gripped the gory axe and surged upwards. Every trace of fear had left me, severed as surely as my leg, and I rose to fight. But the pack were not attacking me. They were clustered about the trap. They snarled and growled and their powerful jaws snapped. The wolves were devouring that useless scrap I had abandoned, and somehow that fact was more terrible than the amputation. I shifted back, my arm brushed a burning log and the flames leaped higher. A wolf raised his jowls, his muzzle dark with blood, his eye reflecting the flames. His jaws worked slowly, crunching down, and the flesh disappeared. Some part of my mind insisted it was just flesh and some other part knew it had been my leg and I vomited into the fire . . ."

Claymore's head jerked.

"And so it was," he said, and spread his hands.

I stared at him. I felt like vomiting myself. He turned and ran that searching glance across my face.

"You do understand?"

"I . . . My God . . . I don't know what to say . . ."

"Oh, the horror of it, yes. But you do understand why I did not die . . . why I am alive to tell you this macabre little tale?"

I didn't answer.

"The wolves did not attack, of course. I was too . . . aroused . . . for fear. They tested me and I waited with the axe and they drew back and squatted and then they moved off to seek easier prey. I did not shout at them, did not depend on the fire; I drove them off by the instincts they sensed within me. I daresay they would have found the moose better quarry that night. I was more than a man, because I had become less and it was more than a leg that I cut away. I waited until dawn. I remember little of that time. I believe I ate a bit of food from my pack and systematically loosened the tourniquet. At any rate, I did whatever survival demanded. In the morning I began to crawl. I hardly thought about directions; knew my instincts would guide me. As they did. My mind was free for other thoughts, for concepts. I envisioned revenge upon Charles for a time, but not seriously, for I realized he had acted in accord with nature. The pack does not wait for the injured individual, the species does not risk survival for the organism, the body does not pause for the loss of a cell. Hatred and rage dried up in the basin of my brain, emotion evaporated and laid bare the true fabric of the mind. And in this dry bed all my experience flowed together, all branches met and shared the same natural roots. Some might say I went mad in the long hours of my ordeal, but whatever I lost it was not sanity . . .

"And that was that.

"Charles found me later that day, the next day, whenever. He had his rifle and his confidence and, when the first shock had passed he respected me greatly for what I had done. He did not understand, as a man reasons, but he sensed, as a man should. And do you?"

I could not answer.

I don't believe Claymore expected an answer, beyond what he saw in my face. That was sufficient. Presently he stood up; leaned on his stick for a moment, then nodded pleasantly and moved away. I remained on the log and he went down the trail between the trees. I wondered where he was going. He had told me that lately he'd been doing a bit of field work. Just a bit, he'd said. An application of former knowledge. But that could mean anything. I watched him as he came to a bend. His limp was more noticeable as he turned. The man who had attacked Bill had favoured one leg when he left. But Bill might have injured him. And Bill, of course, had survived. He had been tested and he survived. Then Claymore was gone and I sat there for some time. Presently, just as if this had been a real forest, a chill seemed to move through the trees and caused me to shiver, there among the wolves . . .

A Cross to Bear

THEY WERE THREE MEN, not young, who shared the habit of walking in the park on pleasant afternoons. At first they politely avoided one another, as strangers do, but in time they began to nod as they passed, and then to exchange greetings, and eventually to speak together and become acquainted. They had little in common. Their backgrounds were not at all similar and such philosophies of life as they possessed were widely separated. But they shared one thing. They had time. And so they met and discovered that different backgrounds did not prevent friendship, and came to look forward to the casual meetings beside the placid river. Their respective pasts diverged rapidly, but at this point they met, in space and time, if nothing else, and that was sufficient. Gradually, without forcing it, they came to know a great deal about one another.

Andrews was a historian, well thought of by his bookish colleagues but without the creative spark which would have made him known to the public. A learned and passive man, he had led a sedentary life and asked no more. He had a long and sober face, wore spectacles, and used a walking stick.

Barlow was a self-made businessman. He had risen from a lowly job as a tourist escort (he preferred to say courier) to become the managing director of a large and prosperous firm of travel agents, and was fond of relating episodes which indirectly implied how he had risen by his bootstraps. He was never obnoxious or obvious about this, however, and was often amusing. He had a florid complexion and wore a watch chain across his waistcoat.

Carter had been a jack-of-all-trades who, in his time, had dabbled in many strange things and many strange places and was content that the adventures were behind him. He had leathery skin and wore a red scarf knotted at his neck in lieu of a necktie. Neither Andrews nor Barlow were at all snobbish, and did not object to this affection—realized it was more than affectation since the scarf had formerly been functional in keeping perspiration from running beneath his collar in warmer lands and had become quite natural to Carter, although he no longer had cause to sweat.

Usually they met by expected accident in the park, although several times in the early stages of their friendship they had met elsewhere, by arrangement. But these occasions had never been quite satisfying. The differences between them became more pronounced in social situations. They met once in a public house near the park, but Andrews, who never took alcoholic drinks, seemed uncomfortable. They had dinner at Barlow's spacious and grand, if somewhat hollow, home and found that Carter did not fit into the surroundings in a strangely physical sense, like a slightly warped segment of a jigsaw puzzle. Carter himself was at ease, but certain aspects of his appearance affected the other two. The brandy glass was too symmetrical in his large horny hand, his clothing too casual in the leather and wood of the library, his seamed skin more suited to cover the old volumes on the shelves behind him than to bind a human skull. They stopped at Andrews's club and were profoundly bored by the members and the atmosphere. And so, by tacit agreement, they came to limit their meetings to the comfortable common ground of the park. It was on such an occasion that Barlow told of his experiences in the Spanish morgue and, indirectly, reminded Carter of the curious affair of the jaguar-man.

The three men sat on a bench beside the river, beneath the overhanging trees. It was late afternoon and there were not many others in the park. A few courting couples passed, a few children ran and shouted on the opposite bank, someone was flying a kite in the distance. No one paid any notice to the men on the bench. They were not very noticeable, just three conventional men passing the time, and Carter's red neckerchief was hardly remarkable in the relaxed atmosphere of the park. Barlow was smoking a cigar and Carter was smoking a stubby black pipe. Andrews did not smoke. Andrews had been telling an anecdote concerned with an anachronism which had slipped into one of his early books which had magnified in the developing text until it became a preposterous distortion causing him great embarrassment. His narrative flowed as slowly as the river, neither interesting nor obtrusive, mild and rather pointless. Like many historians, he could not get beyond the facts and dates, could not fashion a meaningful theme behind his words. However, the reference to Spain served to remind Barlow of his adventure there, and when Andrews had finished, and they had waited a proper length of time to make certain he actually was finished, since the conclusion had been as pointless as the development, Barlow studied the even white ash on his cigar and spoke.

"Spain," he said. "I've been there. I don't know much about Spanish history, but of course I know what all the landmarks and famous buildings are from my days as a courier. Had to memorize all that. Always liked Spain, it was a good place to relax. And yet, I had one of the most disturbing incidents of my life there."

He paused and regarded the ash once more. Andrews and Carter waited patiently for his tale, and Barlow waited to make sure they wanted to hear it. Barlow had a great fear of boring his companions, possibly stemming from the days when he had to strive to make a tour interesting and meaningful. After a suitable pause, he began again.

"It was when I was young and impressionable," he said. "I expect that things far more frightening have occurred since, but one invariably remembers the first time things happen. They are more disturbing because they are unique and unknown. This particular incident occurred just after I'd started guiding the travelling sheep around Europe and it was the first time I'd encountered the courier's nightmare—a death in the party. It happened in Granada. I had a group of ancient tourists with me and had just got checked into our hotel. We were only scheduled for one day there, and the plan was to have lunch in the hotel and look at the Alhambra in the afternoon. I was in my room, reading a guidebook so I'd know what to tell them when they asked the invariable questions, when all of a sudden I heard a great weeping and wailing and then someone pounded on my door. I opened it, fearing the worst, and there was one of the wives who had suddenly become a widow. Only she couldn't believe it. She kept insisting that he was asleep and that someone should wake him up in time for lunch. I went down to their room and there he was, stretched out fully clothed on the bed, dead as could be. I tried to console her but she just kept shaking her head and asking him to wake up and saying how it would be a shame to miss lunch, since it was already paid for. That seemed very important to her. I suppose it was a defence mechanism, transferring the importance of his death to an insignificant fact. I tried to reason with her, but she didn't seem to hear me. She sat down at the foot of the bed and began taking his shoes off. Well, there was nothing I could do there, so I went downstairs and sent a clerk for the authorities. But this was during siesta, you see, and the police and the coroner were all sleeping, so no one could come for several hours. It was very unpleasant. I went back up to the room and the woman was still sitting beside the body, still trying to wake him. Gave me an eerie feeling, that. His eyes were wide open, you see, and I had the strangest sensation that any minute he was going to sit up and ask for his lunch. That was the most significant fact, somehow — that damn lunch. And she kept repeating, 'It would be a crime to waste it, since it's paid for.' It got me so frustrated that eventually I told her she could have a refund. I wasn't sure what company procedure was in such a case, but I would have been willing to give her the whole price out of my own pocket, just to make her stop talking about it. But even that didn't calm her down. It wasn't the money at all, of course. So finally I left her there and went back to my own room and waited for the authorities. Eventually they arrived. They came to my room and I took them down the hall and when we went in the dead man's room, I had a shock. There was the widow, still sitting on the bed, and what had she done but had lunch — for two — sent up to their room. And, calm as could be, she was eating her own food and trying to spoon the other portion into the dead man's mouth. It really shook me, I'll confess. Made me feel physically sick. There were food stains on his lips and chin and the front of his shirt, and I think she'd actually pried his mouth open and got some of the stuff into his throat. Well, it even bothered the cops. They didn't know what to do. Spaniards don't give much of a damn about death, but we were afraid that the woman had gone mad. That's the second worst courier's nightmare, insanity. It might even be the worst, I don't know. Never had it happen, thank God. Because as soon as they'd carted the body away, the woman relaxed and seemed quite undisturbed. She was so calm that she even came out to the Alhambra with the rest of the party, and took a great interest in the Moorish architecture. So I thought it was all over. But the really horrid part was still to come . . ."

Barlow puffed on his cigar and looked at his companions; nodded slightly, seeing that he held their interest, puffed again and continued.

"Well, the widow decided to remain in Granada to make arrangements, of course, and we had to leave in the morning. I don't mind telling you I was glad I'd be gone . . . couldn't forget how she'd forced that food into his dead mouth. But then, just as I was getting ready for bed, she came down to my room again, all flustered. All their money and both passports were in her husband's wallet, and where was the wallet but in his trousers, and where were the trousers but on the deceased, and where was he but in the morgue? Naturally, I had to take care of it. I didn't want to, but the poor woman spoke no Spanish and, anyway, if we tried to get the wallet returned through legal channels I figured Spanish indolence and inefficiency and red tape might take weeks. I just couldn't leave her there with no money or passport. So I had to go to the morgue.

"I expected it would be just like home, you know, but it wasn't. First of all, the morgue wasn't in the city. It was an isolated building outside the city limits, in the foothills of the Sierra Nevada. By the time I got there, it was dark. I mean, it was night. It wasn't really dark because there was a full moon. Everything was silver and black, and those mountains were looming up behind the building. They were very ominous. How do I describe them? Even in daylight they are sort of foreboding. The colours . . . they seem to be formed of modelling clay. Different colours of clay that some impatient child has moulded into one lump, you know. And dotted with poppies so red that they didn't seem real—like the paper flowers one sees on flag day. But at night, with the sky all bright around that disc of a moon, and the last dregs of sunset very murky on the opposite side of the sky—well, it gave me goose flesh. I kept thinking of the Spanish gypsy superstitions about those things they call mantequeros—wild creatures that look like men from a distance and when you get close to them you see they aren't really men at all, only then it's too late because they roam the hills looking for men to eat. Lot of nonsense, of course. But still . . . well, I wanted to get it over with as fast as possible. I walked up to the entrance and found that the door was open. I knocked and called but no one came. There was no attendant at night. Can't say I blame anyone for not wanting such a job, at that. But what could I do? We were leaving early in the morning and I had to get that wallet. I went in. There was only one room. The moonlight poured in the doorway and there were big flat shelves along the walls, in the shadows. I took a step forward and my foot rang out loudly on the tiled floor. I took another step, looking from side to side, wondering how I could find the body. And then I saw it. There was a slab in the middle of the room, directly in the path of the moonlight, and the body was on the slab. Right there in plain sight. I went over and stood beside the slab, looking down at the corpse. I stared at it. The eyes had been closed, but the mouth was wide open. He seemed to be waiting to be fed. There were unchewed food particles in his mouth and on his lips, and his false teeth had slipped out of position. I must have stood there for a good ten minutes trying to get my courage up. Every time I started to reach out a wave of revulsion passed through me and I jerked my hands away. Finally, I closed my eyes and grabbed him by the shoulders very suddenly, not allowing myself time to think, and heaved him into a sitting position. Once I touched him most of my dread vanished. It was only a corpse, after all. It couldn't hurt me. I told myself my fear had been ridiculous and felt so relieved—forced relief into my feelings—that I was able to very calmly draw his wallet from his hip pocket. I had to unbutton the pocket first, and then work it out carefully. I put it in my own pocket and then—so very very calm now—I decided I had better close his mouth. Some vague concept of respect for the dead, you know. I placed the heel of my hand under his jaw and pushed it shut. His lips were forced out by the false teeth. It made him look as if he were pouting. Then I started to lower the body again, and all of a sudden his mouth dropped wide open. The jaw slammed down like a guillotine, with a distinct little click, against his chest. I guess his wife had dislocated his jaw when she pried it open with the spoon. But it scared hell out of me. I let the body go and ran—actually ran—to the door. Then I looked back. The body hadn't fallen, he was still in a sitting position and the moonlight was full on his face. His mouth lolled open like a hungry wolf, unbelievably wide and dark, just as if he were soundlessly screaming. Screaming for me to return and straighten his body out on the slab. But I'm damned if I did. I went away and left him sitting there. Often wondered what they thought when they found him like that in the morning . . ."

Barlow shrugged and smiled faintly. It was growing dark and the river made soft sounds against the bank. The children had stopped playing and the kite no longer drifted above the trees.

"Perhaps it doesn't seem so terrible to you," he said. "It doesn't seem so bad to me, either, thinking back on it. But at the time it affected me greatly. It was the setting which frightened me, of course. Not the corpse. After all, they can't rise from the dead, can they?"

"Well," said Carter, "there are those who say differently."

"Oh?"

His two companions looked at Carter and he knocked the ash from his pipe; began to fill it again, pressing the tobacco down with his thumb. He struck a match and lighted it; pressed it down and lighted it a second time, then puffed until it was burning evenly. His eyes were distant.

"Well?" Barlow asked.

"All this happened a long time ago, you know. Things were different then. One thought differently. Just as you were disturbed by the setting in the morgue, by the strange surroundings. Sitting here, we recognize the variety of natural phenomena, but in other circumstances one tends to credit the supernatural—to ascribe a cause beyond the definitions of natural law. Oh, I wasn't superstitious. Not a bit. Never have been. And yet . . . well, I vowed I'd never transport another missionary up that river . . ."

He puffed away contentedly. The stubby pipe hissed, light gray smoke billowed up in the dusk.

"Well?" Barlow repeated.

"I've never told the story before. It might take some time . . ."

"Time is what we have, my friend," said Andrews.

"Have you ever heard of a jaguar-man?"

"Isn't that something like a werewolf?" Barlow asked.

"Something like that."

Andrews coughed. He had a very pedantic way of coughing.

"Excuse me," he said, "I believe that is the South American

equivalent of the werewolf. The legend of lycanthropy is almost universal, you know. Quite remarkably similar in all continents. But in countries where they do not have wolves, the most fearsome carnivore is substituted. In China and Japan they ascribed the powers of metamorphosis to the tiger or fox. In Greece and Turkey they used the boar. Africa has the hyena, leopard, and crocodile. But the basic legend is very similar everywhere."

"Well, I wouldn't know about all that," said Carter. "But I knew about the jaguar-man. Lot of nonsense. But the point is, the natives believed in it. They thought that certain sorcerers could turn into jaguars, or maybe that their spirits could leave the bodies and take over a real jaguar's form. I'm not quite sure which . . ."

"Both theories usually exist together," Andrews said. "It's the classic legend. Funny how it spread throughout the world."

"Funny? Oh, maybe. And yet, if a thing is universally believed . . ." Carter shrugged.

"Of course, in many cases this legend was used by the witchdoctors and sorcerers. They played upon primitive fears to further their own ends, deliberately spreading superstition to strengthen their positions. Sometimes they even dressed in the skin of these animals to inspire terror or even to commit a crime."

"Oh, I'm not saying there isn't a scientific explanation for such things," Carter told him. "I'm just saying that the people believed it, that's the thing. Not that I did, certainly. I've never had any superstition at all."

"Superstition is another historical concept," Andrews said. He was about to continue when Barlow gestured impatiently.

"Never mind the theories. Let's hear Bill's story."

"Oh, of course. Forgive me."

"Ever seen a jaguar-man, Bill?"

Barlow laughed as he asked this, but Carter looked serious. "I've seen the work of one. A nasty business."

"Tell us about it."

Carter nodded. He was collecting his thoughts.

"You must understand that this was a long time ago, gentlemen," he said, almost apologetically.

Then he began to speak.

"It was when Sam and I were running a private trading outfit. I guess I've mentioned that before. We had an old steamship and used to trade up and down the river and the tributaries and sometimes we'd take a passenger, although there weren't many that wanted to go into those wilds. We also had a long-term contract to supply the mission. It was just a small place quite a ways inland, and we only went there two or three times a year. Old boy name of Wright ran it, all on his own. Nice old fella. Got to know him quite well over the years. Then one day, when we were due to take the usual shipload to the mission, another missionary turned up in town. He was the replacement for Wright, a young man, very zealous and impatient to be started. Quite an impressive figure of a man he was, too. A big, rangy type with a sharp glance, a way of turning his head to suddenly look at a man with that keen glance, like the blade of an axe. He came down to the ship the first time we met, striding along the wharf for all the world like Christ walking on the waters, full of confidence, you know, and right off he began telling me about his duty to save souls. I didn't pay much attention because I've never been superstitious and didn't have much religion to speak of. But I sort of humored him and made out I agreed and believed what he was saying, because I figured it would be easier that way. Otherwise he'd have been trying to convert me. And, of course, I had to be polite since he was a passenger and we needed the money. I didn't have any idea what trouble there would be, in the end. The strange paradox in the man's thoughts. There the savages were chucking spears at the ship and he was standing in plain sight commanding us to put down our weapons and preaching about how they were benighted unfortunates who must not be killed, and then a bit later he does an about-face and pleaded with us to use our guns to stop a harmless burial rite. Never could understand such reasoning. Didn't want us to kill in self-defence, but thought killing justified to stop a mere ceremony. Oh, I can see how it was offensive to him, with his religious convictions. I never minded the headhunters much, myself. I mean, you know just where you stand with a headhunter. But with him it was different. Superstition was his greatest enemy. Other sorts of superstition, things he'd never encountered. I can't see what the harm is in burning a man's heart after he's dead. Can't see how God would mind much, either. But not that missionary. He got so excited he was frothing at the mouth.

"But I'm getting ahead of my story. Never was much good at telling a story. Can't remember jokes, either, although I guess maybe that's a different thing."

Carter deliberated for some minutes, his brow furrowed and his pipe smoldering in his teeth.

"Well, there was Sam and I and this missionary fella and our three native crewmen. That was all. The missionary's name was Stanford. I forget what the blacks were called, but that isn't important. They were useful enough. They could run the boat as well as Sam or I, although they hadn't the faintest idea of the principles behind it. Didn't understand about steam and such. They thought the boiler was a sort of minor god that drank water and breathed steam. Good enough chaps, for all that. Ignorance never hurt a man. But we hadn't gone more than a few miles upstream before this Stanford had them lined up, telling them all about God and keeping them from their duties. I had to ask him not to interfere with their work and he began ranting at me about how it was a sin to leave them in ignorance and I got a little heated and told him it was better ignorant than holed on a sandbank, and that shut him up. I don't think he was afraid of drowning so much as falling into the muck on the riverbank. That was on account of he was so clean, you see. Cleanest man I ever knew. Used to wash himself five or six times a day. Always looking at the grease and oil on Sam and me as well, not to mention the blacks on whom the dirt didn't show up so much because they were black anyhow. Mind you, the load of blankets and clothing he'd brought to cover the natives' nakedness didn't look all that clean, either. Secondhand, came from the hospital I think. But no one knew much about germs and sterilization and such in those days. He just liked to wash, I guess. Thought it was what God wanted.

"Cut quite a figure, he did, standing at the rail sniffing the jungle. Looked like a prophet. You could see he was a man with a mission just by looking at his eyes. Sort of deep and fiery, with flared nostrils and a thrusting jaw. Good looking fella, too. Couldn't see why on earth he wanted to bury himself in that jungle. Could have had the girls chasing after him in any city in the world, I should think. Didn't seem quite real, somehow, in his black suit and white linen, on that river. You know that river? No? The jungle comes right down to the banks, real wild rain forest, no trails at all. At some points where the stream narrowed the trees met right overhead so we were steaming through a green corridor with vines looping down above. And hot! My God, it was hot. Hot and sticky. But Stanford didn't seem to sweat much, he was so clean, even in his heavy suit. Sam and I wore shirts because of the mosquitoes but the blacks were half-naked and glistening. The mosquitoes didn't trouble them any. Stanford didn't like them to expose their bare torsos, thought it was indecent, but after I told him not to bother them he didn't say much, just wiggled his fine nose in disgust and muttered some prayers.

"We were well upriver, only a few days from the mission, when the attack came.

"There was a spot where we had to pass to one side of a sandbank in the middle of the stream. Quite a large bank, long and thin, with grassy humps appearing first and then a shallow yellow sandbar. The trees overhang the banks at that point. To get by we had to follow a course very close to the verge of the jungle and when we were about halfway past the sandbank they began shouting and screeching in the trees. Sam and I looked at one another and then, without a word, we got our carbines and got up on top of the wheelhouse and lay down flat. One of the boys was inside the house, steering, and the other two got their knives out and crouched down behind the packing crates. But that fool missionary just stood at the rail, looking noble. He didn't seem to understand that this was hostile territory. I called down to him to take cover, but he didn't seem to hear. He seemed confused by it all.

"Then they started shooting arrows and throwing spears. The arrows looked like little twigs that couldn't hurt anyone, although I don't know but that they were poisoned, but the spears were big and heavy. One struck into the wall of the wheelhouse and split the planking wide open. Another hit the deck right beside Stanford's foot and bounced across and into the water on the far side. He just looked down at the spot and scowled disdainfully. I shouted to him again and he looked up. He started shouting back, but I couldn't hear what he said because just then Sam started firing. We couldn't see a thing, of course. Just jungle. But we figured we might have a lucky hit, or that maybe the noise would frighten them off. So we banged away as fast as we could. The bullets snapped through the foliage and ferns and smacked against the boles of trees. Well, the screaming stopped then. But we kept firing. And suddenly Stanford's face appeared right at my elbow, black with rage. What he'd done, he'd hooked his fingers over the top of the wheelhouse and drew himself up that way, so that only his head and fingers were above the roof and he was shouting into my ear—shouting about how it was a great sin to kill, and especially to kill a fella who hadn't been baptized. And it struck me so funny that I had to laugh. I guess it was a reaction, now that the danger seemed to have passed, and I just guffawed right in his disembodied face, while Sam continued to fire. Then we had drawn clear of the sandbank and the boy took us back into the center of the current. It was safe enough in midstream, and we came down from the wheelhouse. Stanford was waiting to berate us. He was very angry, gesturing and pointing at us with his index finger, his hair all wild and his eyes bright. The boys stared at him and rolled their eyes and grinned nervously. Sam tried to explain that they had meant to kill us, but it didn't seem to make any difference at all. He just couldn't understand. After a while he quieted down, but for the rest of the trip he brooded glumly and hardly spoke at all. Just washed his hands and brooded . . .

"Well, then we came to the mission.

"We nudged up to the shore where there was a sort of crude platform serving as a wharf and Wright came limping down to greet us. He was a nice old fella that the natives fed pretty well because he doctored them and didn't interfere where he wasn't wanted. He looked disappointed when he saw Stanford. Not surprised, just disappointed. I guess he'd been expecting to be replaced soon. They shook hands and I got the boys started unloading the supplies while they talked, then we went up to Wright's hut. It was just like all the other huts, a fact which startled Stanford. He wrinkled his nose and stood by the door, turning his head about as though looking for something. He didn't look pleased. It was a small, dusty village with a bamboo stockade running in a semi-circle back from the water. Some of the huts were supported on poles over the bank of the river. Stanford looked at all this and, from time to time, he blinked and flushed and lowered his eyes. I tried to follow his line of vision. There were naked children running about, and he winced at that, but what really got to him was that some of the women had bare breasts. A couple were grinding some sort of grain in a wooden mortar, looking shyly at the missionary and grinning. Their breasts swung back and forth over the bowl, and Stanford's eyes seemed to pivot as he stared at them, and then he shook his head violently. I could see the muscles of his jaw grow tight, determined.

" 'Why is this permitted?' he asked.

"Wright tried to explain that it was not immodesty, that it was just the natural mode of dress for these people, but Stanford just kept shaking his head.

"Then he asked where the church was.

"Well, there was no church. When Wright admitted this, Stanford looked in disbelief down his long nose. He said, 'I don't understand you.' Then he shook his head some more. Wright said he figured there were things more important than a church, that he was trying to establish a hospital of sorts and instruct them in medical procedures and sanitary methods. Stanford wasn't impressed. 'But what of their souls?' he demanded. Wright told him he was instructing them in the tenets of Christianity, and that it was important to get a sound background of theory established before one imposed a church upon them—that otherwise they would fail to understand the significance of the church. But he couldn't get through to Stanford at all. The younger missionary became very quiet and angry. We went into the hut. Wright got out a bottle of brandy and Sam and I took a drink with him. But this made Stanford more furious. He looked at us and then, very coldly, asked if Wright was in the habit of such incontinence. Wright blushed and talked about aiding the digestion and such, and Stanford talked about invalid excuses. There was more. Pretty soon they were arguing heatedly. I can't remember all they argued about. Couldn't follow all the arguments at the time, as I recall. But the gist of it was that Stanford considered that Wright had made a complete failure of the mission—that he had committed a positive sin by letting the savages carry on naturally.

" 'You have failed miserably,' he said. 'You have failed to be strict enough, strong enough!'

" 'I didn't come here to be strict,' Wright said, growing angry himself by this time. 'I came to help them.'

" 'You were sent here to save them, and you have failed. I can only thank providence that I have come to this place, where the laws of God have been ignored, and that the harm you have caused by your neglect will not prove irreparable.'

"And then Stanford turned and stood staring at the wall, very straight and stiff, shoulders squared, muttering to himself. His fingers clenched and unclenched at his sides. Poor Wright looked at Sam and I and sighed. That was that.

"Well, after a while Stanford calmed down somewhat. The boys had brought the crates up and stacked them around the missionary's hut and he sat on one of the boxes and tried to look tolerant and resigned. Wright was encouraged enough to volunteer to show him the hospital and the school. He showed little interest. In truth, neither was very interesting, although one couldn't expect much. The hospital was a large bamboo enclosure with a thatched sunshade and grass pallets on the ground. Two or three old people were groaning on the pallets, wasted and wizened, and Stanford averted his eyes as if he found physical infirmity distasteful. The school was even less impressive, without desks or books, except for a Bible. Stanford nodded approval about the Bible, however. Then it was time to meet the headman. There was a bit of indecision over whether they should go to the headman's hut, or summon him to the missionary's hut, and in the end they met in the center of the clearing. The headman was a proud fellow with plenty of scars on his face and chest and an aristocratic bearing. He didn't understand what was going on. Stanford raised his hand and blessed the man, quickly and disinterestedly, and the headman, thinking it was some form of greeting, emulated the gesture. This was when we discovered that Stanford didn't speak a word of the local dialect. Not a word. He seemed to think it wasn't very important; had expected that Wright would have taught them all to speak English or Latin by this time. Wright just looked confused. And then another nasty moment occurred. The village witch doctor came marching up to meet the new missionary. Well, as you may imagine, witch doctors and missionaries are not all that compatible. Wright had managed to get along with the old boy all right, because he didn't try to interfere in his business—went out of his way to make their spheres of influence seem separate, so that there was no question of superior magic between them, and didn't object to the old rites being celebrated. In return, the witch doctor had rather grudgingly come to respect Wright. But we could all see instantly that this wouldn't be the case with Stanford. It would have been humorous, that meeting, if it hadn't foreshadowed trouble in the future. The witch doctor was an ancient fella, his skin as dry and aged as parchment—not parchment made from papyrus, but from the pulp of mahogany. He had long, greasy hair and dark, furtive eyes. His eyes seemed to reflect a certain wisdom, and to be much younger than his face, and they were set very deeply. One had the impression that his eye sockets were so deep that he could not look sideways without turning his head—that if he turned his eyes, he would look only at the shelf of his own skull. He wore a filthy old skin over his shoulders, a rag around his loins and a brilliant headdress of feathers. He did not smell very well. Stanford, in fact, recoiled from the man's odour. But the witch doctor didn't realize what had caused that retreat, and perhaps assumed that Stanford had recognized the power of his magic, for he actually smiled—a remarkable thing, to see that old toothless face smile. Then came the part which was almost humorous. Stanford raised his hand and blessed the man. He held a small silver crucifix and made the gesture perfunctorily. And the witch doctor, in return, held up some old dried bones and made gestures of his own. There they stood, blessing one another. I saw a hint of amusement pass over Wright's face. Then it disappeared as Stanford turned to him.

" 'Who is this man?' he asked.

"Wright hemmed and hawed. He was embarrassed again. Stanford repeated the question and, finally, Wright blurted it out. Stanford's eyes grew very very wide. He said, 'A witch doctor? A witch doctor? Am I going mad? Is everyone totally mad? A witch doctor?' And the old witch doctor looked from one to the other—I guess I was right about the eye sockets, because he swivelled his whole head on the scrawny pivot of his neck—and then, quite distinctly, in English, he repeated the words. 'Witch doctor,' he said, and pointed to his chest with the handful of dry bones and looked very proud of his title.

"Stanford turned abruptly and walked back to the missionary's hut, and the witch doctor rattled his bones and, funny as it was, we could all see that there was going to be difficulty.

"What else was there? It's not easy to recall details, after this length of time—to decide which facts have bearing on the ultimate disaster. Let's see . . . there was the thing of the stockade, yes. Yes, that was important. Wright had tried to establish a plantation outside the palisade. Bananas aren't indigenous to that country, but they grow well enough if they are imported, and one of his favorite projects had always been to teach the natives to cultivate the fields, to afford them some sort of security. Well, they hadn't quite grasped the idea and it wasn't much of a plantation. A bit overgrown and untended. But the bananas themselves were flourishing, perfectly suited to the soil and climate and not really requiring much attention. Wright felt he had to explain this project to Stanford. Stanford was still dazed by the fact that there was a witch doctor in the same village as the mission, and he followed along in a sort of stupor. Wright pointed out the fields and mentioned some of the things that had to be done, to keep the jungle back. Stanford paid no attention. We came back into the village and, noticing that the bamboo stockade was not very sturdy, I mentioned that we'd been attacked down river. I wondered if it might not be wise to strengthen the fortifications. But Wright, speaking to me and perhaps not thinking that his replacement was listening, said that the headhunters had never attacked this village and seldom came up this far into the headwaters. The stockade, he said, was just to make the village feel secure against the evil spirits about which Ooma—that was the witch doctor's name—kept them terrified. It was standard procedure, of course, and Wright thought nothing of it, but suddenly Stanford wheeled and faced him.

" 'Am I to assume that those walls are to keep the devil without?' he asked, coldly.

" 'Well, devils, yes,' Wright said.

" 'The devil. Satan. The fallen angel.'

"Wright lowered his head nervously. He wouldn't look at Stanford, and maybe he had begun to feel that he had, indeed, been a failure. Staring at the ground, he mumbled about how these people still believed in evil spirits of the forest—water demons, tree spirits, wind devils. And, I believe, it was at this point when mention of the jaguar-men was first made, although at the time, of course, it made no particular impression on me. No more than any of the other things he spoke of. Stanford had gone white in the face again, his lips trembled. The whole affair had been a series of crests of anger followed by depressions of resignation. He didn't speak. Wright, now that he had begun, felt he should explain further, and mentioned that Ooma performed certain precautionary rites and sacrifices to ward off these evil spirits; suggested that it was just as well to let him continue to do so. 'It can do no harm,' he said, by way of offering an excuse, and this caused even greater anger in Stanford. At length Wright fell silent. Stanford said, 'We have nothing further to say to one another.' He walked away. He was quite serious about that, and did not speak another word to the old missionary.

"Wright was to return with us.

"We stayed the night to give him a chance to get his possessions packed and loaded. Sam and I slept on the boat and Wright stayed in the hut with Stanford, but all that night not a word passed between them. Early in the morning, Wright gathered his meagre belongings. While he packed, Stanford was unpacking the crates which we had brought with us—the usual consignment and also the boxes which he'd brought himself. Sam and I offered to help, but he refused with a gesture; tore violently at the packing cases, as if taking his annoyance out on the wood and nails. We had the boys load Wright's possessions on the boat while the missionary said good-bye to the villagers. They couldn't seem to understand that he was leaving forever, or why. This parting took some time, as he wished to speak to each villager individually, and in the meanwhile Stanford had unloaded a crate of cheap cotton dresses and begun to distribute them among the women, gesturing and averting his eyes. The women were pleased and excited about the colourful cotton cloth, although they did not understand about modesty at all. They didn't know how to put a dress on. Most of them merely tied them about their waists, like sarongs, leaving their breasts bare. Then they strutted about in their new finery, adding the sin of vanity to that of indecency in Stanford's eyes—averted eyes, of course. Eventually he gave up on this and walked away, leaving them to fight and tussle over the remaining cloth, and even old Ooma seized a dress for himself and strutted as proud as any of the women.

"Stanford returned to the unpacking, and the next crate he opened happened to be Wright's regular consignment of brandy. We'd forgotten all about this in the tension of the circumstances and the desire to be away, and the first we recalled it was when Stanford came striding down to the ship with the crate in his arms. He was very powerful. He carried it as if it had no weight at all, holding it well away from his chest, almost at arm's length, as if it were liable to contaminate him. Without a word, he threw the crate over the ship rail. It smacked heavily on the deck and the wood splintered, but fortunately it had been well packed in wood shavings and none of the bottles shattered. Sam, rather impertinently, thanked him. He just glared at us and turned back. Wright had finished with his farewells and they passed close by each other as he came down to the boat, but Stanford refused to notice his predecessor. A great crowd of villagers followed Wright to the water and stood about, smiling and kicking up dust, as he clambered aboard. He looked very old and sad. He sat on deck and from time to time raised his hand, in a sort of feeble wave, which the natives enthusiastically copied. He was looking beyond them, at the dusty little village which had so long been his home.

"We had to wait a bit longer to get the steam up.

"Pretty soon the crowd lost interest in Wright's departure—I expect they still believed he would return—and wandered back to the village. The women began grinding with their mortars and pestles of hard wood, the men were squatting about greasing their bows and sharpening flint-tipped arrows and spears, preparing for a hunt. Ooma, very fine in his new dress—it was bright yellow—was chanting and rolling bones to ensure that the hunters were successful. Then the sound of hammering came from amidst the buildings. We could hear Stanford shout from time to time and the hammering rang out, a strangely alien sound in that village, too regular, too sharp. I noticed some of the men wander towards the sound. They undoubtedly thought the new white witch doctor was making his own spell to aid their hunt. I went into the bows and from there could see what he was up to. He'd taken the packing crates apart, straightened out the nails and was using them to build an altar beside his hut. I watched him for a while, fascinated by his energy. He had no hammer, and was using the flat of an axe to drive the nails, striking violently. I had the impression that he was striking these blows against more than wood—was striking at sin itself, at ignorance—whose ignorance, Ooma's or his own, I could not say—at the ideas he wished to destroy; that he was, with each blow, committing the deicide of false gods. He hadn't even removed his coat. I had never yet seen him without his coat and tie. His hair flew about wildly and he was sweating for the first time. A group had gathered around him, watching with great interest, and between strokes he spoke to them. They jabbered back. No one understood. Sparks glinted from the axe and some of the planks split. Then Sam called to me. The steam was up. We were ready to depart.

"As the village slipped away, Stanford was hidden from sight for a moment, and then he appeared again, viewed between hut and palisade. He had managed to get half a dozen of the women kneeling at the altar. They were grinning and giggling. The men stood behind and nodded, perhaps pleased that this new man had chosen to help them in the hunt. He thought they were worshipping, and they thought the crucifix represented some wood spirit, I suppose. Perhaps it was just as well they had no common language.

"Then we moved into midstream and he was lost to sight.

"The last sound we heard, as we steamed away, was the ringing of a small bell."

Carter broke off his narrative and looked at the little stream gurgling peacefully at his feet; frowned, as if he saw a different stream, from a different time, reflected in the darkening waters. Andrews and Barlow waited patiently for him to begin again and presently he did so.

"That was the last I saw of Stanford or the village for some six months. That little bell was the last impression I had. Somehow the tinkling seemed as out of place as the hammering had been, muffled in the thick jungle growth. I suppose, in a way, I had been impressed by the man—not favourably, you know, but an indelible impression nonetheless. Or perhaps, at that time, I felt only relief at being finished of him, and the impression came later because of the events—well, no matter. I retain a distinct visual image of Stanford along with a memory of distaste and, of course, pity. I have spoken about him a great deal—too much, possibly—but I felt it was necessary to try to show you what sort of man he was at the beginning. He was strong, very strong. He proved how strong he was, and that caused his ultimate downfall. But that came later. During the interim, neither Sam nor I thought much about him, other than occasionally wondering how he was getting along—not caring, just out of curiosity, you know. And I'm sure old Wright thought a great deal about it, wondering if his own works had been carried on or abolished. I remember how tremendously defeated he looked when we steamed away, as he gazed back at the village and the plantation without. He had moisture at the eyes. I assumed that his sorrow was at leaving, but later—we had drunk some of the brandy by that time—he asked me, very seriously, whether I considered him a failure. I assured him he had been absolutely right, but he wasn't very convinced. I suppose he was getting too old, at that, and had lost the courage of his convictions. Now that he had no duties to occupy his time, he began to tear apart the things he had done, and wonder if they had been worthy. I suppose we all do, gentlemen, when that time of life is upon us, eh?"

Carter glanced at his companions. Neither replied, although thoughts flowed behind their eyes, and they knew perfectly well what he meant. Andrews poked at the ground with his stick and Barlow fingered his gold watch chain and Carter loosened his gay red bandana before he continued.

"Time passed," he said. "Time passes. Soon enough, it was necessary to take a new load of supplies to the mission and the consignment was delivered to the ship. It was the same as usual, even to the case of brandy. We knew that Stanford would not want the brandy and figured there was no sense in loading it. We also saw no sense in returning it. Sam and I divided half the bottles, and took the other half around to Wright. He was still in the town, living in a cheap hotel, absolutely at loose ends. He was too old to go home and had nothing to do there but wander through the streets. He had aged considerably. His eyes were vague. We stopped to have a drink with him and found his conversation point-less and wandering. He couldn't understand where the brandy had come from and we didn't press the point. He seemed grateful to have it and the church could afford it—owed him that much—and it seemed proper and right. Finally, when we were leaving, he came to understand that we were going back to the mission. He couldn't believe that six months had passed, and kept asking us if there had been trouble. We explained it was a routine journey but he shook his head and mumbled about evil spirits and how he had failed and asked us to do everything we could for his villagers. He had forgotten all about Stanford, it seems. That was just as well. We left him with his brandy and went back to the ship.

"The trip was uneventful.

"We had managed to retain the same three boys and, by this time, they had become quite capable of running the ship on their own, although they still believed the boiler was a water demon. We had to pass close to the shore to avoid the same sandbar, and took the precaution of getting on the wheelhouse with the carbines and stacking crates around us, but we weren't attacked and saw no sign of savages. It was a very smooth passage and, of course, we should have suspected that this was merely the lull before the trouble we were to encounter at the mission. Curious how the events of life invariably move with an undulating rhythm. It seems to be a descriptive law of life. But there was no foreshadowing of the evil until the night before we reached the village. We did not move at night, of course, because of the danger of snags and floating trees and newly formed sandbars, and had just anchored in midstream and settled down to the evening meal. Then we heard the jaguar cry. It is impossible to attribute direction to sound in a rain forest, but it seemed to come from ahead, in the vicinity of the mission. It was not remarkable to hear a jaguar, of course, and neither Sam nor I would have thought anything of it but for the exceptional behaviour of the crew. They stopped eating and rolled their eyes about, food dropping from their open mouths. They made signs with their hands. When we asked them what was troubling them, they wouldn't answer. The cry came again and they cocked their heads, listening intently and shivering. Then, simultaneously but without a word, all three got up and took their food below. We looked at one another and followed; found them squatting around the still hot boiler, which was, of course, the most powerful demon on board. They were somewhat calmer then. One of them had begun to stuff food into his mouth again. But they all glistened with rivulets of sweat and they all had wide eyes. Sam asked one of them what had disturbed them.

"One—the one who had started eating, a broad-chested young brute who'd always seemed quite fearless—said, 'The cry.' The others nodded.

" 'But it was only a jaguar,' Sam said.

" 'No. Different.'

" 'What was it then?'

" 'It was the cry of a jaguar-man,' he said, and at that instant the howl sounded a third time and they huddled against the boiler with complete disregard for the heat of the metal. Sam and I shook our heads and went back on deck. We knew it was futile to tell them otherwise and didn't try. Of course, we thought it was perfect nonsense. But they had been right. That was exactly what it was . . ."

Barlow turned on the bench and looked sharply at Carter. It was quite dark now and he could barely make out the profile of Carter's face. Andrews frowned at the ground, where he had chopped it up with the end of his walking stick. The stick felt damp in his hands. After a moment Carter faced Barlow and twitched his shoulders in a gesture which failed, somehow, to be a shrug.

"I mean, of course," he said softly, "that was exactly what it was to them. To Sam and me . . . well, neither of us was superstitious. What we may have thought is unimportant and it's better if I continue with the facts of the matter.

"As soon as we drew up to the wharf, we could tell that there was trouble. It was a tense scene—so tense that no one had even seen us approach. The villagers were banded together in a sullen group with the headman at the front and Stanford was facing them, obviously furious and gesturing at heaven and hell. He was shouting in English and stamping his foot to accent the incomprehensible words. Sam and I stood at the rail and we were both struck by various small changes in the village. The plantation was almost completely overgrown now and tentacles of jungle reached to the palisade. A roof had been erected over the altar Stanford had made, much sturdier than any of the other buildings, and the bell was suspended over this roof in a little wooden tower. All the women wore cotton dresses, and wore them correctly, covering their breasts. But these impressions registered superficially in our minds, for we were concentrating on the strange tableau in the clearing. We didn't know what to do. The boat nudged and bumped against the makeshift platform, causing us to sway and grip the rail. I don't know how long we remained there but at length someone saw us and pointed. The headman looked in our direction and then Stanford turned, his face dark with rage. He squinted for a moment, then seemed to realize who we were and with a final violent gesture directed at the natives he came running towards us. His face was streaked with sweat and dust, the first time I'd seen him less than clean, and his features were contorted. He pounded over the planks and grasped the rail with one hand.

" 'Thank God you've come,' he gasped, tilting his head back to look up at us. 'You're just in time.'

" 'In time for what?' Sam asked.

" 'To prevent sacrilege.'

"I told him to calm down and explain, but he wouldn't listen. He kept saying that we must hurry and that we were to bring our firearms. Well, that surprised us. We remembered, you see, how he hadn't wanted us to use our rifles even in self-defence and so we assumed this must be something very bad indeed. He had both hands on the rail now and was shaking the boat frantically, and shouting for us to hurry before it was too late. Well, we didn't like to take the rifles into the village, but what could we do? It was all so sudden, and we hadn't any idea what it was all about. So finally we got the two carbines and followed Stanford up to the village. We were very careful to keep the weapons pointed at the ground but all the natives moved away, looking at the guns with big eyes. They knew what guns could do . . . knew they were the militant arm of Christianity. As the crowd broke up we saw the old witch doctor, squatting over some bones and feathers in front of his hut. He glanced up at us and glowered, then dropped his face and spat fiercely and concentrated on his incantations and charms.

"Stanford led us past the makeshift church and paused at the door of his own hut. He looked in and took a deep breath, then stepped back and pointed into the interior. I moved to the door and looked in. Sam looked over my shoulder and I heard his breath rasp sharply. It was not a pretty sight. A mangled body never is.

"It was a young fella, quite dead of course. The body was stretched out on the floor and someone — obviously Stanford — had made an attempt to position the limbs in a peaceful attitude. The hands were folded over the chest and the eyes had been closed. But somehow this attitude only added to the horror. It seemed a mockery to have positioned such a horribly mutilated body in that manner. The throat had been torn out, the torso was shredded with ghastly wounds and I saw the white arch of his ribcage — unbelievably white — through the gashes in the dark flesh.

"Stanford was facing us, but still pointed sideways at the body with a righteous forefinger.

" 'Jaguar?' I asked.

"He nodded.

" 'Well? It's gruesome enough but what's the trouble?'

"Stanford had to make several attempts before he was able to control his voice. At last he said, 'They wish to desecrate the dead.' I raised my eyebrows. 'They intend to . . . were going to . . . to cut the heart from this corpse and burn it!'

" 'Oh, that,' Sam said.

"We sighed and put our carbines down, leaning them against the wall. It was the first time we'd encountered this thing, but we'd heard about it and we knew what it meant. We didn't know how to explain it to Stanford, however, and his eyes were pouncing back and forth between us. Finally Sam said, 'I guess you haven't mastered the dialect yet, huh?' and Stanford said, 'What do you mean? I understand what they intend to do all right.' Sam nodded. 'Yes, but you have to understand why. It's a rite they have.' Stanford's lip curled up like a cat's. 'A rite? An abomination, a blasphemy!' 'No,' Sam said, sort of slow and weary. 'No, just a rite. A ritual. They have a superstition about these things. For some reason they must believe this fella was killed by a jaguar-man and they believe that you got to burn the victim's heart before his soul can be released. Don't know why they think that, but that's the way they see it. It's harmless enough and it keeps them happy.'

"Stanford fairly howled then. He hopped up and down as if he were throwing a tantrum, but somehow it wasn't very funny. 'Harmless?' he repeated. 'Harmless? To defile the dead? And a Christian, at that. I baptized this man myself. He was my most faithful convert, perhaps the only one who truly believed. I will not allow his body to be defiled. He will go whole to a hallowed grave. No matter what the consequences! You understand? No matter what, I say! I will prevent this fiendish act!' He was foaming at the mouth as he shouted these words. The cords stood out in his neck, his face was thrust forwards, his arms moved. He seemed on the verge of violence. But then, quite suddenly, he lowered his head. His shoulders seemed to slide down. 'He died in the church, you know,' he said, in a soft voice. 'I found him dead at the altar. He was kneeling there and at first I thought he was praying and then I saw the blood. I . . . I don't know if he dragged himself there with his last breath, hauling his poor torn body along the ground . . . or perhaps he had been worshipping when the beast attacked him. I don't know. If only I'd been able to erect walls . . . my fault . . . the church is open, you see. And yet a church should be open for all good men . . .' He looked up, his eyes hollow with suffering. 'Please understand me. He was a good man, a true Christian. He took a Christian name. Joseph. He was so proud—not vanity, you understand—so pleased with his new name. Like a child, really. So you can see why you must not—cannot—let them do this thing. You must talk to them, reason with them. Perhaps if you explain that he was of the white man's religion it will make a difference . . . make them see that they cannot use his body for a ceremony offensive to his God. Yes, they might understand that. Somehow. Please . . .'

"How did I feel? Stanford's thinking was alien to me, and yet I saw his point of view well enough. I could even feel a sympathetic vibration of his turmoil and pain. I felt sorry for the man, that's the thing. And, too, he had this strength. It was difficult to refuse him . . . difficult even to look at him, pitiful and powerful at the same time, incapable of comprehending any dogma but his own and yet absolutely incorruptible within his limits. He placed his hand on my shoulder and stared at me. Sam moved nervously beside us, and I could tell he felt the same as I. There seemed to be no choice. I agreed to talk to the headman. We wouldn't use the guns, of course, but there seemed little harm in trying to reason with the man, even if I were reasoning with arguments which were not mine. Simply to be a translator, the mouthpiece for Stanford. He squeezed my shoulder gently, as one does to a companion, a friend, a comrade. 'Thank you and God bless you,' he said. Well, I had to help him if I could, that was all there was to it.

"The headman was standing by the palisade, half-turned towards the open gates, ready for flight. He was afraid of the guns. The rest of the village had scattered. Some hid in their huts, some had gone into the overgrown plantation. They were not a warlike people, of course. That was why the mission existed there, amidst a peaceful village surrounded by stronger tribes. So we had no fear of them. We left the carbines leaning against the hut and walked towards the headman. He made one quick movement towards the gates, like a feint, and then paused. He saw we had no firearms and after a moment was able to resume his proud bearing. He advanced to meet us. The villagers came drifting up cautiously behind him from their huts and through the gates and Stanford stood in the doorway of his own hut, as if barring the entrance. His expression was hopeful and determined. Sam and I greeted the headman solemnly and respectfully and then we squatted in the dust to talk. The villagers formed a silent semi-circle behind him. They looked timid and curious. But the headman himself — it was strange — he looked exactly like Stanford. He looked hopeful and determined. It is hard to conceive of two men whose features were more dissimilar, and yet at that moment the headman might have been a reflection of Stanford, glimpsed in a black looking glass. Even the scars on his countenance seemed no more than faults in the glass. We spoke for some moments to no consequence, fulfilling the formalities of the meeting and then, gradually, the story emerged . . .

"The dead man had, indeed, been converted.

"To the headman, the villagers, even, one supposes, to the witch doctor, there was no paradox between Stanford's religion and their own superstitions. They believed in many gods, and were quite willing to admit the existence of Stanford's god — even to pay him respect and to believe, because he was the god of the white man, that he was a most powerful being. They were willing to worship as Stanford demonstrated they should — more than willing, they were quite eager to appease this new deity. It seemed quite proper. But it was inconceivable that they should cease to pay homage to their former beliefs. They were not, you see, as narrow-minded as Stanford. And that was where the trouble began — with his narrow-minded attitudes. You can imagine how frustrating it was for him. He would believe he'd converted one of the villagers because the man had been to his church and then he'd discover this same man participating in one of the pagan ceremonies, sacrificing a cock, consulting the witch doctor. He'd become enraged. I can picture the scenes all right. It must have been like Christ driving the moneychangers from the temple. The headman mentioned some of this, how he'd broken fertility idols, interrupted sacrifices, scattered the feathers and bones used to predict the future, torn the sacred periapts from their necks. They resented this, and yet tolerated his interference. Perhaps they feared him as a man—he was powerfully built, constructed on a larger scale than the natives, and must have appeared truly dangerous with his flashing anger and his black coat-tails flying like wings behind him as he advanced, face thrust forwards, index finger pointing towards the object of his wrath—or perhaps they feared his god. Possibly both. The very fact that he could disrupt their worship and come to no harm, of course, protected him from them. They reasoned that, if he were powerful enough to avoid punishment from the devils and spirits of their religion, he must be protected by his own god—that his god was more powerful than theirs. For him. That's the point. They thought his god was personal to him, not that he was more potent in any objective sense. And, after all, they could see the manifestations of the ancient deities for themselves. The storm and the swamp and the carnivore. It seems to me they would have had to be braver—and more simple—than they were to neglect the old religion. Nor did they. They practiced the old ceremonies in secrecy and the new in his presence and the compromise satisfied them. The witch doctor may have resented sharing his domain but made no attempt to disrupt it. He, too, feared the white god. So this uneasy balance was maintained for some months.

"Then Joseph tilted the scales.

"He was a young man, no more than a boy really. It is impossible to tell the age of these people. They mature quickly and age rapidly. But he hadn't yet participated in the ceremony of manhood so he couldn't have been more than a youth. And he'd come to awareness since Stanford had arrived. He hadn't been indoctrinated and wasn't steeped in the old fears, recognized Stanford's power and became, as Stanford told us, a true convert. He even learned a bit of English. Not much. More, I daresay, than Stanford had learned of his own language. They became very close and, eventually, Stanford took the boy to live in his own hut. I expect he was lonely and certainly he was delighted at finally achieving success. Probably the youth was more intelligent than most of the villagers. But under Stanford's influence, he became arrogant. He refused to participate in the old rites and treated the witch doctor with insolence. He wore a cross at his neck and carried it like a shield. Even the headman had no influence over him. His parents—the whole village—despaired of him, were scandalized by him. His very presence became an outrage as he strutted about the village with the cross on his chest, sneering at the elders. He announced that he would, when the time came, refuse the ceremony of manhood. This could not be tolerated. The elders consulted and decided he must be banished. But he lived with Stanford. They did not know how to exile him. How do you banish a man who refuses to recognize your authority? And then they went to the witch doctor, seeking his advice. He was well aware of the situation, of course, but had remained aloof from it, to avoid direct confrontation with Stanford. But once they went to him he had no choice. He lighted his sacred pots and scattered the bones on the ground. He studied the pattern in which they fell. The pots smoldered and smoked and he went into a trance. His voice became a high-pitched wail, his old body trembled. I expect he was stalling, trying to find a solution without losing face. Perhaps he would have, for he was a clever old devil. But at this point Stanford made his gravest blunder. He had never directly interfered with Ooma before, and now he did.

"Joseph knew that his future was being decided in the throwing of the bones, and told Stanford. He was a trifle nervous. Stanford gave him confidence. Stanford was not about to lose his solitary follower. They went together to the hut of the witch doctor. Stanford ranted and raged, Ooma took no notice—took refuge, as it were, in his trance. And this indifference, real or feigned, drove Stanford's anger beyond control. He lashed out with his foot and tilted one of the burning pots. The elders crouched away in terror. Stanford was determined to show what nonsense this ceremony was, and gestured to the boy to help him. Joseph hesitated for a moment. Stanford overturned another pot. And then, in a passion of enthusiasm, Joseph joined in the desecration. He kicked at the pots and the bones. He stamped on the embers and crushed the bones underfoot. Stanford stood back, arms crossed over his chest, and looked on with full approval as the boy destroyed the religious objects. Then they turned away. Stanford put his arm around the boy's shoulder and they walked back to their hut. And, at that point, Ooma came out of his trance. He regarded the scattered objects before him and then, slowly, raised his eyes to look at Joseph. His eyes ... the headman, as he told this, shuddered, and behind him the villagers nodded and whispered to themselves. 'He possessed the eyes of the jaguar,' he told us. And they all knew, then, that Joseph would die.

"And they all knew how ...

"And he did ...

"Well, it might have been a coincidence, you know. It is conceivable that a man-eating jaguar, through pure chance, happened to strike that night. But it seemed far more likely that the witch doctor had been directly responsible ... had killed the boy himself and made it look like the work of a beast. Sam and I suggested this, in a roundabout way, not wishing to be offensive. But the headman failed to see our point—understood the inference, but saw no paradox. These people did not draw a sharp line between spiritual and physical entities, between the natural and the supernatural. A jaguar-man was not exactly a deity, but was feared more than most of the gods. When the headman understood what we were saying, he nodded agreement. Certainly it might have been the witch doctor, he admitted. He suspected as much himself. And it was common knowledge that many witch doctors possessed the power of transformation. It seemed perfectly logical that Ooma had used this power to avenge himself against Joseph ... to instil fear and prevent others from acting as the boy had. But what difference did it make? Whether it was the witch doctor in the form of a beast, or whether he had sent his spirit out to control a beast, or if it had been another jaguar-man entirely, it was all the same in the result. The boy had been killed by a jaguar-man, and therefore his heart must burn ...

"The headman rocked back on his heels and nodded, as if his

explanation had solved everything—as if it had been no more than a problem of translation. And, still standing in his doorway, Stanford saw that the talk had ended and assumed an expectant expression. He, too, counted on the translation. But no translator was going to reconcile that difficulty. We hadn't really expected to. We thanked the headman and walked back to Stanford. 'Well?' he asked. We started to tell him what the headman had said. We didn't get far. Stanford's face began to change, to darken and sort of contort. He interrupted us. He whispered and he shouted and the whispers were worse, somehow, than the outcries. He spoke of demonology and the work of the devil. He even, as I recall, threatened us with eternal damnation. Then he became quiet again. 'Will you prevent it, gentlemen?' he asked, very calmly. 'In the name of God, will you prevent it?' 'There is nothing we can do,' I told him. 'The guns,' he said. I shook my head. He was staring intently at me, and then suddenly he wasn't. He didn't shift his eyes, but he looked through me. Lord knows what he was looking at, or into. The headman and some of the villagers had advanced behind us, depending on our ability to reason with him, and perhaps he was looking at them. Then he roared. A positive roar. He spun about and seized one of the carbines which were still leaning against the wall. He moved very quickly, knocking Sam to one side and snatching up the weapon in one motion. Then he turned on the villagers and thrust the gun at them. He didn't know how to hold it property—didn't even have his finger on the trigger—but he prodded it at them as if it were a spear and they knew nothing about triggers, of course. They fled, howling. In the space of seconds there was not a native left in sight. Even old Ooma had vanished. There was no one there but Sam and I and Stanford and the corpse.

"He looked down at the carbine in his hands. He seemed surprised to see it there, and leaned it very cautiously against the wall once more. Had he threatened us with it, I think we should have overpowered him without hesitation, but he didn't. He just set it down. He looked embarrassed. He shrugged. Sam said, 'Well, I expect you'll be coming back with us now.' He blinked. 'What's that? Of course not. My work here has not even begun, as this day's evil testifies.' 'I wouldn't advise you to stay here after this,' Sam said. 'You've threatened them with a gun and you've offended their beliefs.' 'I'll destroy those beliefs before I'm finished,' Stanford said, through his teeth. 'Suit yourself,' said Sam.

"Stanford leaned against the wall, beside the rifles. Then, slowly, he descended into a sitting position, and looked up at us. 'I wonder, gentlemen, if you would be so kind as to prepare a burial place for the departed?' he asked. 'I fear I am too weary.'

"He certainly looked it. His physical appearance seemed to change as often and as dramatically as his moods. He towered with anger and shrunk with resignation. A trick of perception, no doubt. We didn't want to be a part of this thing, but it was a bit late to halt it and we figured it would be best to get the body out of sight before we left. There was a chance—just a chance—that they might forgive him with the physical symbol of the confrontation removed. It was the least we could do, and all we could do. And if it meant we could never again come to this village, well we only came there to supply the mission, anyway. So we agreed to dig the grave.

"It was late afternoon by this time. The shadows of the stockade extended to the river. It would have been wiser to dig the grave in the morning, of course, but somehow we couldn't have postponed it. It was a task to be done without taking time to think about it. Sam suggested that we measure the body so that we didn't make the grave larger than necessary, and this seemed a logical, if unpleasant, idea. We entered the hut. We had nothing to measure with, nor did Stanford, and in the end we laid the carbine alongside the body, marked the spot and shifted it up. Joseph was not very tall. The carbines were short, the sort of rifle which is useful in heavy bush, and even so he measured only one and a half barrel lengths. He was young and slender and the cross was still around his neck. Somehow it made me more fully aware of his death, seeing that cross—the same amplification of the horror I'd felt when I saw that his hands had been folded in repose. Worse, in a way. It was only a crude wooden cross—perhaps he'd made it himself—and it rested on his breast just over one of the gruesome wounds where the skin had peeled away. I wanted to move it, but couldn't bring myself to touch him ... drew my hand back and, at the movement, several heavy-bodied flies rose from the corpse, gorged with blood, hovered in the air for a moment and then settled again to the feast.

One alighted on his face and began to crawl about, looking for a wound. I hadn't the energy to brush them away. What did it matter? Sam and I went back out and Stanford handed us spades. He said he would stay with the body, to watch over it. When he entered the hut we heard the flies buzz. We took the carbines and the spades and walked without speaking to the graveyard . . .

"It was eerie. It was silent and there was moonlight. The village seemed strangely two-dimensional, flat blacks and silver patches, and the jungle was plastered against the sky. We knew where the graveyard was, for Wright had proudly pointed it out to us once, long before. The natives had been accustomed to leaving their dead out for the scavengers to deal with, but Wright had seen this as a possible means of creating man-eaters — of giving the large carnivores the taste for human flesh — and the villagers had understood him when he explained this. That was the difference between Wright and Stanford. Wright wanted to improve their lives and Stanford wished to improve their deaths. We went through the gate and followed a narrow path back from the palisades. There was heavy jungle on our right and, from time to time, I thought I saw dark movements and assumed the villagers were watching us from the trees. We carried the rifles so that they could not help but see them and we walked quickly. Soon enough we came to the graveyard. It was very neat. The graves were laid out in precise rows and over each mound a black wooden cross raised its crosspiece like the wings of a vulture descending. We went directly to the end of one of these rows and, without a word, began to dig. The earth was soft and moist and rich. It turned over easily and the spades bit deeply. It required little effort and we both looked, with every rise, towards the trees. But no one attempted to stop us. My senses must have been particularly alert, for I remember that scene in great visual detail. Our shadows fell into the pit we were opening in the earth. To the left, through a slender gap between black growth, there was moonlight on the river and overhead the sky was the colour of pewter, an inverted bowl from which the moon was slipping, the moonlight pouring. The jungle was still. Only Sam and I moved in that scene and our spades made the only sound. That was remarkable. The jungle is seldom silent. And then, abruptly, the silence was torn apart by Stanford's scream. He screamed once — just once. For a moment we were frozen. Sam was bent over, his spade half in the earth, and I had straightened to let the loose soil slide behind me. Sam looked up at me and I looked down at him. We were waiting for a second scream, but it did not come. He only screamed one time. Then, still without speaking, we took up the rifles and went back. We didn't hurry. We knew it was too late for haste, for when a man screams only once it is always too late.

"Stanford was dead.

"He lay across the doorway, his feet sticking out and his head inside. His toes pointed upwards. His boots gleamed. He had always been immaculate and it was proper that his boots were well polished. We moved in from opposite sides of the doorway. Sam's face was taut. Mine must have looked the same. We carried the guns out before us as we converged and I thrust the muzzle into the hut ahead of me. But there was nothing inside—nothing but the top half of Stanford's body. His throat was torn open and heavy ropes of blood writhed from the wound. Blood had splattered around the room. But there was nothing else. Nothing. You see, Joseph's body was no longer there.

"The villagers came back in silent groups, as if they felt that danger had passed—that the white god had departed with his mortal representative. They did not fear us and we no longer had cause to fear them. What we feared—well, it was a fearsome thing. Yes, we were afraid. I had to force myself to kneel beside the body. He was dead, that was quite obvious, and yet it was so natural to feel for his heartbeat or pulse, such habits are so strong. Yet I could not bring myself to place my ear against that gory breast. I took his wrist instead. There was no pulse. His fist was clenched and a leather thong hung from between his fingers. I stared at this thong for some time and I set my teeth. Then I pried his hand open. It took considerable strength to draw those fingers back, but I managed it and there in his palm, clenched so tightly that the edges had broken through the skin, was the object I had expected to find. He had grasped it with all his strength and with the last effort of his life. It was Joseph's cross . . ."

"What a ghastly experience," Andrews said. He was visibly shaken and the blood had drained from his long scholarly face. There were elements of horror in his expression.

"Ghastly? Yes, it was that," said Carter.

"How do you explain it?" Barlow asked.

"I don't know that I do. I've tried, of course. Several possibilities come to mind. It could have been an actual jaguar, you know. A remarkable coincidence but possible. The beast might have returned for his kill, found Stanford there and struck him down and dragged Joseph's body off. I doubt it, though. There were no paw marks around the hut, for one thing. Or, I suppose, the witch doctor could have killed him. But he was such a frail old fellow and Stanford was large and powerful. Or it could have been Joseph . . ."

"But the man was dead," Barlow said.

"So we thought. But we could have been wrong. Many of those primitive people have a tendency to go into a self-induced trance in times of stress. Something akin to what we think of as suspended animation. Perhaps Joseph was not so far removed from the superstitions of his tribe after all. He may have regretted his actions, half believing the jaguar-man must come for him and driving himself to an agony of suspense and anxiety. So that, when the witch doctor appeared in the skin of a jaguar, he fell into a trance . . . or was mesmerized. His wounds looked mortal enough, God knows, but possibly they were more superficial than it seemed. And then, when he awoke on the death mat—I find this every bit as horrible as what the natives believed—he actually believed himself to be a jaguar-man and, believing it, acted accordingly and attacked the only man in sight. He should have been no match for Stanford. And yet with the violence of madness, and with Stanford petrified as he saw a dead man rise . . . well, who knows?"

Carter shrugged.

"At least it's an explanation," Barlow said.

"It's an attempt at a scientific explanation. But what is that, really, but a semantic difference? What does the terminology matter if the effect is the same? If a man awakes from a trance or rises from the dead, it's all the same to those who admit to both possibilities. At the time—well, as I've said, one's thoughts can be changed by the setting. I was not in civilization. I was not a savage but I was in a savage land . . ."

Carter's face was troubled.

"Then that was the end of it?" Barlow asked.

"Just about. There was only the one thing left to do. We did it. We never went back to that village."

"What thing was that?" Barlow asked.

Carter turned to face him.

"Why, we had to bury Stanford. The villagers were afraid to touch the body. They still had too much respect for his god. He might not have been as powerful as a jaguar-man, but he was not to be trifled with. And we couldn't just leave his body there. We'd already started digging the grave for Joseph and figured it would do just as well for Stanford. They were both Christians, after all. It was too late that night. We slept on the boat and, with the first light, finished the grave and buried Stanford. Neither Sam nor I knew the proper words to say over a grave, especially a missionary's grave, but we buried him with his prayer book and put a wooden cross up and bent our heads in silence for a while. Then we walked back. Sam went directly to the boat. There was no need to unload the supplies now, and he wanted to get the steam up. But I went back through the village. I don't know why. I crossed the clearing and stopped in front of the little makeshift church. The shadow of the belfry fell into the clearing. Two slender posts and, between them, the distorted shadow of the bell. There was a breeze from the river and the shadow of the bell swayed back and forth. But it was a gentle breeze and the bell did not ring. I remember thinking how strange it was that a bell was swinging without a sound. Then I walked on past the fire. The charred smell still hung on the saturated air. It made my stomach heave. I didn't know it would linger so long, that stench. I didn't know the human breast was so resistant, either, nor that it would be so spongy in my hands. But the savages were afraid to touch him and someone had to do it. I had to. Because I wasn't superstitious, you see . . ."

The Hunter

IT WAS A FINE BRIGHT MORNING.

Ralph Conrad came out of the Bridge Hotel and shrugged his knapsack into a more comfortable position across his shoulders; smiled at the low sun and mopped his florid brow with a red polka-dot handkerchief. There were several motor-cars in the parking lot, but no traffic on the road at this early hour, and Ralph was very much at peace with himself. He felt especially peaceful because the hotel clerk, befuddled and sleepy, had made a ten-shilling error in Ralph's favour, and Ralph was of a thrifty nature. That was why he was on a walking tour of Dartmoor. When he had first retired several years before, he had contemplated taking up golf for exercise, but the expense of that game had troubled him more than his inability to predict the direction the ball would travel, and since the exercise gained by walking through open country was certainly equal to that gained by pursuing an elusive little white ball through various frustrating hazards and roughs, Ralph had forsaken golf in favour of leisurely walking tours. He had walked through the Lake District and Northern Wales and this was the third day of his tour of Dartmoor. He planned, vaguely, to walk on the Continent some day, but that wasn't definite or immediate; it was a thing to think about rather than do, because Ralph liked the English life he was accustomed to, liked to have a destination where he would find a hot meal and a comfortable bed, familiar food and conversation in a familiar language beside an open fire when he relaxed after a long day's tramp. He had also heard that the Continent was frightfully expensive.

Ralph walked up to the highway and along the shoulder for several hundred yards, anxious to progress some distance before the clerk discovered his error. He wore stout shoes and carried a walking stick with an electric torch built into the handle; he had an Ordnance survey map and knew how to cross rough country without

getting lost, impressing the landscape upon his mind and using his
wristwatch and the sun to estimate the points of the compass. This
ability pleased him, since it had saved him the expense of purchasing a compass. He carried a light lunch and a Thermos of coffee and
had planned to arrive comfortably at his next stop around dinner-
time. His route had been meticulously laid out on the map, and
presently he turned from the road and set out across the moors.

The sun was hot. Ralph thought that perhaps it would be un-
pleasantly warm later in the day, and he walked rather more quickly
than usual so that he could slow down later, if the heat made it
necessary. His route took him along the crest of a hill. A narrow
stream wound through the marshy land below on the left, and a
higher ridge of land studded with rocky tors bordered his path on
the right. The tors were individually marked on his excellent map
and he judged his progress by them, admiring the formations as he
studied the terrain. This was some of the loveliest and most desolate country in England, and Ralph appreciated it greatly. He was
all alone. There was no noise of motor-car or factory to disturb
his tranquillity, no scent of petrol or fumes of industry to over-
whelm the dry perfume of the heather, no black smoke twisted
against the fluffy white clouds. The stream twinkled through the
mossy ground and his heavy shoes crunched on the coarse tufts
of grass, squelching occasionally when he moved too low on the
slope. Ralph drew deep breaths of clean air into his lungs. He had
stopped smoking years before, when the rising tax on tobacco had
made the expense greater than the satisfaction, but this pure air was
even better than nicotine, and he complimented himself on the
willpower it had taken to forsake cigarettes, not even considering
the economies of the sacrifice.

When he had been walking for nearly an hour, Ralph came to
a low, flat rock and sat down to rest. He scraped some mud from
his shoes with the tip of his stick and unscrewed the cap from his
Thermos jug, poured some coffee into the cap and was about to
drink when he noticed something in the reeds near the stream. He
lowered the cup and looked harder. He couldn't quite make out
what it was. The sun was bright and he had to squint and shield
his eyes. He wished that he had sunglasses, but didn't think the
frequency of sunlight justified buying them; he thought that he

really should have a pair of field-glasses and wondered what they might cost in a pawn shop.

Ralph didn't want to move down the hill because the land was damp and marshy there and he hated to get his feet wet, but he was basically a curious man, and who knew but what the object might be something valuable? He knew he would never forgive himself if he walked on without investigating.

He climbed up on the rock to get a higher angle, but still couldn't make out what it was. It looked almost like a man, he thought, but that could hardly be possible. A man wouldn't be lying in that swampy ground, surely. Not with the exorbitant prices that dry cleaners charged these days.

He climbed down again and finished his coffee, still undecided whether he should risk the dampness, replaced the Thermos jug in his pack, looked ahead, then shrugged and started cautiously down the incline.

The lower he went, the softer the ground became. His feet squished as the mud sucked at them, his stick sank deeply and gave little support. Reeds replaced the coarse grass, and he found it more difficult to keep the object in sight since, although he was closer to it, he no longer had the advantage of elevation. He was just about to deny his curiosity and return to the high ground when he came upon a shoe.

His eyes narrowed as he looked at it. It was quite definitely a shoe, sunk well down in the muck. He crouched and pried it up with his stick; lifted it between thumb and forefinger. It had apparently been sucked off as its owner walked or ran through the mud and abandoned there. Ralph turned it about and saw that it was in fairly good condition, a bit run down at the heel but with a great deal of wear left in it; measured it beside his own shoe and decided it would be too small for him. He couldn't understand this. Someone had recently passed this way in a hurry—such a great hurry that he had not paused to retrieve his shoe. Such reckless abandoning of a useful article was beyond Ralph's comprehension. He looked around, hoping perhaps to find the other shoe. They might fit him, after all. There was no other shoe, but he noticed an indentation in the ground and moved to it. It looked like a foot-print. Water had seeped into it and the edge had crumbled. There was another similar indentation beyond, and Ralph moved in that direction, the shoe still gripped gingerly in his fingers. He was very curious indeed now. After all, one shoe was useless to its owner, and there seemed a reasonably good chance that the mate had also been abandoned.

Then he saw the object that had first caught his attention. The footprints led in that direction, and it looked like a bundle of rags glimpsed through the reeds. Perhaps, he thought, a complete outfit of clothing cast off in some moment of insanity.

Ralph approached warily; halted abruptly.

It was certainly a pile of clothing, and from one end protruded a human foot. Ralph stared at the foot. It wore a sock but no shoe. Ralph looked at the shoe he held and then back at the foot. He felt confused and dazed. He had never come upon a situation like this before in all his rambles; he felt that he should do something but had no precedent to help him decide what steps were called for. After a few moments he took a firmer grip on his stick and advanced with resolution and determination, until he was standing beside the body. One arm was outflung, the other hidden in the shredded rags. The rags were darkly stained with blood and the coat had been pulled above the shoulders so that it covered the man's head.

"I say there," Ralph said.

There was no reply.

"I say, my man. Are you all right?"

The rags were silent.

Ralph took a deep breath. He hated to get involved in difficulties that didn't concern him, but saw that he had no choice. He crouched and drew the coat down so he could see the man's face.

And then the peaceful countryside was shattered by his scream.

The man had no head.

And Ralph had never encountered such a thing before . . .

2

John Wetherby was in the habit of dining several times a week at his club in St James's. He invariably ate the same well-balanced meal, drank the same full-bodied burgundy, and then went into the bar for the same excellent brandy and Havana cigar. But Wetherby was not a creature of thoughtless habit. He simply found this a comfortable and satisfying routine, and saw no reason to alter it, any more than he would have changed his tailor or the rather outdated cut of his suits.

Wetherby's club was The Venturers. He had been a member for many years, and, not being plagued by a compulsion to join and belong, he subscribed to no other club. The Venturers had, however, changed considerably over the years. It had become fashionable rather than purposeful and the requirements for membership were based more on social standing than accomplishment. It was no longer the sort of club that Wetherby would have selected for himself, but he didn't contemplate a change; he doubted if any new club would prove more suitable and thought, if he thought of it at all, that it was more likely the tempo of the world rather than the tone of his club which had changed. Or perhaps, he sighed at the idea that he himself had changed with age, and failed to keep up with life.

There were times when he regretted this, such as when he walked into the bar and saw the younger members lounging about in well-cut suits and seldom-cut hair, with pretence and affectation. Wetherby was a tolerant man. He could regret without resenting. But he felt a definite longing for former days, when there had been mutual interest among the members—adventures to be recalled over the brandy or, better still, further adventures to be planned and anticipated. But this was in the past. It had been a long time since Wetherby had had an adventure, and even if some of the old members had been present, the conversation would of necessity have dwelt on the past; it would have been a sad pleasure, recalling things that could no longer be.

Wetherby glanced around the dining-room. There was no one there he knew. There seldom was now. Of all the friends and companions he could recall from better days, only Byron had not succumbed to the advance of age; only Byron, timelessly pursuing his curious theories of life and death, might have had some new tale to tell. But Byron never came to London now. He still lived a life of adventure, and had no need to reminisce about the past. Wetherby admired Byron without envying him, approved of the man without approving of his methods. It had been nearly ten years since he had last seen Byron and Wetherby vividly recalled that evening.

They had been drinking brandy at the bar. Byron had just returned from Africa and Wetherby had just decided it was time for him to give up big-game hunting. They had talked for a while about the last expedition they'd been on together, in north-west Canada, and then Wetherby had mentioned his decision to retire. Byron had been annoyed, almost angry, about it. Wetherby himself was rather sad, but the decision was unalterable. He was no longer young, his eyes and his reflexes had lost the sharpness required. He had spent his youth practising a passion for hunting; but now his youth was over, and Wetherby did not care to pursue danger when he might not enjoy it, might prove a liability rather than an asset to his companions.

But hunting, to Byron, was far more than a pleasure or a pastime; it was more than a passion, it was a philosophy of life. Byron had become excited, trying to convince Wetherby he was making a grave mistake in deciding to live a life of comfort in London. Byron's voice was resonant and deep, and with the fervour of his words, he began speaking loudly, gesturing widely.

Several of the younger members had been standing beside them at the bar, and they looked on with interest, obviously amused by the intensity of Byron's speech, undoubtedly considering him an anachronism in their modern world. One of them, a large young man with an insolent face, drew closer. A leader of the liberal new aristocracy. He winked at his companions and hovered beside Byron. He was so close that Byron, despite his impassioned mono-logue, could not fail to notice him.

Byron paused in the middle of a sentence and turned towards the young man; stared at him. Byron's eyes were piercing, he did not stare the way a man stares in a city, he stared as one does, with full concentration and awareness, in the jungle. He said nothing. The young man tried to return the gaze but his civilized eyes faltered, and he sought refuge in words.

"I couldn't help but overhear you, sir," he said. He had a cultured voice and emphasized the "sir".

Byron didn't seem to hear.

"You are, I understand, a big-game hunter?"

Byron said nothing. Wetherby said, "That is correct, young man. We both are."

But the man wasn't interested in Wetherby. His face had become flushed under Byron's eyes.

"Perhaps you can tell me—something I've always wondered—what on earth is the pleasure that full-grown and presumably intelligent men get out of murdering defenceless animals?"

It was not the thing to say to Byron.

Wetherby was angry himself. Tolerance has limits. The young man's cohorts moved closer, grinning behind their champion. But Byron still said nothing. He continued to stare but, slowly, his expression shifted until he was regarding the man in precisely the same manner as one might some foul object upon which one has inadvertently trod.

The young man became intensely uncomfortable. His friends were expecting him to make some brilliant comment which would terminate the encounter, and yet he could not force himself to look at Byron's eyes.

"I don't mean to intrude, of course," he said. "But tell me—" Encouraged by the sound of his own educated voice, he smiled again. "Tell me, is it a sense of power? Of accomplishment? Some regression to the past, when killing was an honourable and necessary thing?"

"I cannot tell you," Byron said.

"I thought not," the man said. He started to turn away, his lips smirking. His friends grinned at their clever comrade.

"However, I could show you," Byron said.

The young man turned back, surprised. Byron had moved out from the bar. He was smiling, too. They say a tiger smiles and a hyena laughs, but perhaps they are mistaken.

"I beg your pardon?" the young man said.

"The pleasure I get from killing," Byron said. "I could show you just what it is. I think it would be a very great pleasure, showing you, although I doubt you would die with the nobility of an animal."

Everyone was very quiet. The young man's lips parted, but he said nothing. His friends no longer smiled. They had seen something very dark in Byron's eyes, something they would never comprehend. After a moment the young man turned away; Byron shrugged and leaned on the bar again. Wetherby let his breath out slowly. He had seen Byron kill, and he knew that face very well. It was not a face one could forget. The young men left very soon.

"I thought, for a moment—" Wetherby said.

Byron nodded.

"It would have been so easy," he said.

Wetherby didn't doubt it.

That was Byron . . .

The waiter brought the bill, knowing from long experience that Wetherby would not take brandy at the table. Wetherby signed it and stood up; headed for the bar, through the solid, oak-panelled rooms. He was a tall man with steel-grey hair and angular features, wearing a new suit which was tailored so well that it looked old. Middle age may have dulled his vision and blunted his reflexes, but a life of civilized comfort had not harmed him noticeably. He was lean and hard and straight, and weighed exactly the same as he had on his last hunting trip, with Byron in Canada. Wetherby was thinking about Byron as he entered the bar.

It was a strange coincidence.

Detective Superintendent Justin Bell was drinking a pint of beer at the bar. He had a brick-red face and a nondescript grey suit and looked very much like a policeman. He raised his glass and Wetherby joined him. He was pleased to see him; Bell was one of the older members, and Wetherby had seconded his application, following a tongue-in-cheek discussion over whether police work qualified as adventurous endeavour and, therefore, met the requirements of membership. That was before the rules had been changed, when The Venturers had a purpose. Bell was well liked and had the proper outlook and temperament for the club, and so he had been admitted to the rolls, even though his occupation was suspect.

"Hello, John," Bell said.

"How are you, Justin?"

"Tired."

"You haven't been here for quite a while."

"No time. I envy your life of ease. Always have. It's a fortunate man who can retire from a life of pleasure to a life of relaxation without a period of work in between."

Wetherby laughed. He had always felt the same way; had, without the slightest taint of snobbery, considered himself very lucky to have been born wealthy.

"Drink?" he asked.

Bell finished his beer and slid the glass across the bar. The barman wore a wine-coloured jacket and was very efficient and polite; although young, he was able to distinguish between the old-established Venturers and the fashionable new members; knew the difference between dignity and familiarity. Wetherby had a brandy and Bell had another pint of beer. His preference for beer had begun to extend his waistline slightly, but that merely made him look more like an efficient lawman.

"It's good to see you," Wetherby said.

"As a matter of fact, I came here to see you. Thought you'd be here."

"Good Lord. Not about that parking ticket?"

They laughed at the private reference to a slight bending of a minor law.

After a moment, Bell said, "I need your advice, John."

"Whatever for?"

"Possibly a murder."

Wetherby blinked. Bell drank.

"At least, we're treating it as murder. I don't really know that it is."

"Surely there's no advice I can give you on that?"

"Perhaps not. Not if it actually is murder."

"This sounds very mysterious," Wetherby said. He began to fill his pipe very carefully. He hadn't tasted the brandy yet.

"Well, it is, in a way. I expect you've read something about it. The headless body on Dartmoor. I believe that was how the newspapers billed it."

"Oh yes. Yes, I did see something about that. A bit out of your territory, isn't it?"

"Well, there are curious aspects. It baffled the chief constable down there and he asked for assistance. Good judge, I'd say. It baffles me, too. Anyway, the commissioner assigned Thurlow and me to the case. I've just come back from there. Came back to see you specifically."

Wetherby had the briar filled; he lighted it, tamped it down and touched the flame again. He smoked Afrikander and, like most good tobaccos, it didn't smell as good as it tasted. Bell lit a cigarette.

"Well?" Wetherby asked.

"There's a very distinct possibility that this killing was the work of some animal. Everything, bar one curious fact, points to that. And I can't think of anyone who would be more qualified to advise me on that. One way or the other."

"I see," Wetherby said. He tasted the brandy. "What sort of animal did you have in mind?"

"None. I don't know a damn thing about animals and Thurlow knows less. My wife had a cat once, but it ran away. And I think there's a mole in my garden. That's the lot."

Wetherby smiled.

"I thought maybe you could tell me by examining the marks on the body and the plaster casts of the tracks."

Wetherby nodded. "Yes, I should think I could," he said. "Were the tracks plain?"

"Not very."

"Well, I can certainly get an idea what sort of animal it was, if nothing else. A carnivore, I assume?"

"I don't know. The body wasn't devoured, if that's anything to go on. But it was savaged. Mangled. The police doctor swears that only a wild and savage animal could have done it. In fact, we would have been definite on that, except for the one curious fact—the one the papers all stressed, of course—the remarkable incident of the decapitation, as Doyle might have said. That was what confused the local police. The chief is a doddery old sort anyhow, all vintage port and confusion." Bell gestured with his pint.

"We never did find the head," he added.

Wetherby thought for a few moments, drawing on his pipe. It was rather like old times, pondering a problem at this bar, although the conversation on all sides dealt more with fashion and art than life and death.

"So this animal—if it was an animal—was something powerful enough to tear a man's head off, eh?"

Bell shrugged.

"In England? It seems doubtful. Possibly a pack of wild dogs, but I shouldn't think so. You've checked with all the zoos and circuses about an escaped carnivore, of course?"

Bell looked pained.

Wetherby said, "Of course. Sorry, Justin."

"It's a bit more confusing than that, actually," Bell said. "The head wasn't torn off. Not the way an animal would tear a body. The body was ripped and clawed, almost shredded, but the head was severed quite neatly."

Wetherby frowned through the tobacco haze.

"That would mean enormous strength. Some animal powerful enough to take the skull in its jaws and yank it off with one explosive jerk. And hold the body down at the same time."

"As clean as a knife or a guillotine," Bell said. His face was clouded as he recalled the corpse. "What animal could have done that?"

"I don't know. Perhaps if I saw the tracks. A buffalo, for instance, might be able to hook a man's head off with one stroke of its horns. But if the body was clawed—I don't know, Justin. Perhaps some madman with a weapon that inflicted wounds like talons?"

"No. They were claw marks, all right. Fangs, too. No man could have done that."

"Well, I'll be glad to help you in any way I can."

"Could you come down to Dartmoor with me? On expenses, of course. The ground was soft and we've got some fair casts of the prints. You might recognize them."

Bell remembered that he, too, was on expenses. He signalled for another round.

"It's been a long time since I've done any tracking. Still, I suppose that knowledge doesn't leave entirely. I could give it a try."

Bell was unfolding a map. He spread it out on the bar, holding one corner down with his beer glass. Several of the young members looked over in interest. It had been a long time since a map had been studied at that bar. Wetherby leaned over and Bell pointed with a thick finger.

"The body was found—" The finger described a circle, then jabbed on to the map. "Here. Beside this stream."

Wetherby nodded, automatically forming an image of the terrain as he studied the contour map. Then, as his area of interest widened, he looked surprised; he took the pipe from his mouth, frowning.

"You knew Byron, didn't you?"

"Oh yes."

"Why, he lives there." Wetherby looked at the map again. It was remarkably detailed. "His house can't be more than a mile from where the body was discovered."

"Yes, I know."

"You could have saved yourself a trip by asking his advice. Or isn't he in the country?"

Bell looked uncomfortable.

"Actually, I did go to Byron," he said. "He wasn't interested in helping me. Always was a strange sort. The whole damn thing seemed to amuse him and he said something about it being just as well to kill people off, to counterbalance the population explosion. Said there were too damn many people in the world as it was."

"Yes, that's Byron. But surely he would have been interested in a challenge of this nature?"

"He was interested in the plaster casts, all right. Looked at them for quite a while, and I thought he had an idea what might have made them. But then he just shrugged and wouldn't venture an opinion. In fact, he suggested that I see you. Said you'd be more interested and concerned about what happened to humanity." Bell paused. "Of course, I intended to see you anyway. I only went to Byron's first because it was closer."

Wetherby grinned.

"Rather like hunting tigers in Africa," he said. "Are you sure you checked the zoo?"

They laughed and Wetherby bought a round of drinks.

"It certainly isn't like Byron to pass up an opportunity like this," Wetherby said. "Not that he ever had much regard for life, human or otherwise—he was more concerned with death—but if he thought this was a dangerous animal he'd be out with his gun. The more dangerous, the faster he'd be out. Last time I saw him he cursed me for giving up danger and living in town. Either he doesn't think it's an animal or, perhaps, he didn't want to help the authorities. That seems more likely. He might be out looking for the killer on his own. And, knowing Byron, he'll find it. Still, as you say, he's a strange fellow and I don't pretend to understand him."

"Will you come down with me, John?"

"You could have brought the casts with you."

"Yes, I considered it. But I'd like you down there. This is one of those killings without apparent motive which may never be solved. And the worst thing about them is they are so often repeated. Whether it was a man or a beast, there seems a good chance it will kill again."

"And you'd like me there if it does."

"Exactly. If anyone could track the killer, it would be you. And if, God forbid, it kills again, it would be better if you had a fresh trail. If we ever solve this, I think it more likely to be by physical means, rather than deduction. As Doyle surely never said."

Wetherby nodded. There was nothing to keep him in London, and the thought of getting into the open again was pleasant. He thought it might be nice to see Byron again, too. Byron and he had shared danger many times, and if that was the sole bond between them, it was a strong bond.

"All right, Justin. I'll come."

Bell folded the map and stuffed it in his pocket. His suit bulged with the encumbrance of such stuffings, and Wetherby wondered, smiling, if there was a magnifying glass somewhere in those drooping pockets. They sat at a table in the corner and had a last drink, making their plans to go down to Dartmoor in the morning. More through habits of conversation, than because Wetherby needed the information, Bell filled in the details of the killing. There was a great deal and yet there wasn't enough. The man who discovered the body was certainly not connected in any way other than circumstance. The body, with some difficulty, had been identified. It was an old fellow named Randal who had lived a hermitic life in the area, and who had been arrested for poaching several times. It seemed likely that he'd been doing just that when his death found him. The tracks made it obvious that Randal had been walking along the firm ground higher up the hill, and had fled towards the stream when he had seen his killer. He had almost reached the water when it overtook him, and he had died at the same spot where his body had been found. There was no sign that he had been injured as he ran, as might have been the case had an animal worried him, snapping at his heels until he was brought down. As soon as his killer caught him, it killed him. There were some signs of short but violent struggle, Randal had rolled over several times and his fingernails were splintered. His clothing had been torn to shreds, but his pockets hadn't been emptied, and contained four shillings and half an ounce of rolling tobacco. Randal had been an amusing local character, an eccentric with no known enemies, and the killing seemed entirely pointless.

Bell stopped talking; shook his head.

"It was a particularly ugly death," he said. "I don't suppose it was any worse for poor old Randal than any number of deaths might have been, but I'll tell you, John—I don't relish the thought of seeing another corpse like this."

Bell shook his head again.

He was going to.

3

Damn me, thought Brian Hammond. Damn me for a fool.

He leaned forward, both hands clamped on the steering wheel, and peered out through the rain-washed windscreen. It was hard to see the road. The wipers left curved blurs across the glass and the headlights shot pale beams futilely against the trees. Hammond's dark-jowled face, illuminated in the green glow of the dashlights, was angry and worried. He was a salesman but he looked like a merchant seaman. He had, in fact, been a merchant seaman when he was younger, but then he had looked more like a salesman. It was the type of face destined to foil enterprise. Brian sat rigidly in the seat, a cigar clamped in his teeth, as he steered along the dark and winding country lane.

How did I manage to miss that turning? he wondered. And why don't they put signposts on these blasted roads? How do they expect a man to find his way without any signs? All the taxes I pay, and I can't even find a road sign. Not to mention a petrol station.

His eyes turned down to the fuel gauge. The needle was hovering on the empty mark.

Damn this God-forsaken area, he thought. All the local country bumpkins are asleep, no one to ask directions, haven't even seen a house. Can't see anything anyway in this damn rain. Don't think I've got petrol for more than another mile or so. Damn car drinks petrol. Ought to get a smaller car, except then I wouldn't have any room for all these damn samples. Not that it would matter much. Haven't sold a damn thing all day. The boss will squawk like a stuck pig, too, damn him. How does he expect me to sell electronic equipment in this bloody area? Nothing here but sheep. These yokels probably never even heard of electricity and I'm supposed to sell them equipment. Ought to give Cornwall independence, and then give them Dartmoor. Get rid of the damn place.

He turned a sharp corner and the lane rose ahead, dark and deserted.

That damn Ed Davis is working in London, too, he thought. Probably made plenty of sales today and now he's celebrating in the West End. Lucky bastard. Probably drinking champagne. Damn him, anyway. Why should he get all the choice territory just because he's been with the company longer? It isn't fair.

The car banged against the high shoulder of the road and Hammond snarled as he turned the wheel. He felt very sorry for himself. If there was any justice in the world he would be home by his fireside watching television while his wife made him a nice cup of tea. I wonder what my wife is doing now? he thought. She hates it when I have to travel. 'Course, she knows I can't get into any trouble down here. I guess she just hates to have me be away. Real passionate, that wife of mine. I wonder if she went up to the pub tonight? He bit hard on the cigar. Ah, she wouldn't go to the pub alone. She's not like that. Faithful, my wife. But that damn Humphries is always trying to flirt with her in the pub. Caught her smiling back at him once, too. I'll bet she's gone up to the pub to flirt with Humphries.

Hammond looked at his watch. It was past closing time.

No, she isn't in the pub, he thought. Must be home. I'd phone her if this damn place had any phone boxes. All the taxes I pay and I can't even find a phone box when I want one. But if I phoned and she wasn't home— Ah, she'd be home. I wonder if that damn

Humphries is home with her? If I thought for one minute that
she—

Hammond shook his head and squinted into the black night.
The wipers skimmed ineffectively over a film of water and the car
veered from side to side. The samples slid around on the back seat,
the tyres hummed, the foul cigar smoke hung heavy in the air. He
had to drive slowly and it seemed he'd been driving for a very long
time. And then the motor coughed and sputtered.

Oh no, Hammond thought.

The motor gulped the last ounce of petrol and the car glided to
a silent stop. Brian sat scowling behind the wheel, thinking of the
futility of joining the AA when he couldn't phone for aid. His mood
was black. He felt sure that his wife was with that rogue Humphries
and that he was going to lose his job because he'd sold nothing. He
relighted his cigar and puffed away, wondering what to do. He had
no idea where he was, and saw little sense in trying to walk somewhere in the dark. The rain was falling heavily. Hammond sighed
and resigned himself to a cramped night in the car. The battery
wasn't new, and he turned the lights off. But the road was narrow
and dark, and it was dangerous without lights in the remote possibility that another car might come along. He opened the glove
box and took out the flasher, pulled his collar up and opened the
door. The rain singled him out, finding chinks in the armour of his
clothing, and he swore to himself as he walked back a few yards
and placed the flasher on its tripod behind the car. He snapped it
on and the red light began to blink. It lighted the trees with an eerie
effect. It was very unreal. He stood there for a moment, watching
the trees appear red and black, red and black. His cigar had gone
out again and a loose leaf curled down. He was looking at the trees
and then he was looking at something else that came out from
the trees. For a moment he merely looked surprised, then his eyes
widened and the cigar dropped as his mouth opened to scream. But
only a whimper of fear came out.

Hammond turned and ran, without thinking where he was
heading. He ran past his car, blind and dumb with terror. He ran for
perhaps fifty yards before it caught him . . .

4

John Wetherby sat by the dying embers of his fire, drinking a last brandy and considering the things that Bell had told him. It was a comfortable room. The grandfather clock ticked with soothing regularity in the corner, the pendulum catching flashes of reflection through the arc. The walls were lined with beautifully bound books, the carpet was deep and soft, heavy tapestries were drawn across the wide windows. But, Wetherby, in his thoughts, was dissociated from this room; was back in a former way of life, with a different pattern of reason. He was trying to anticipate what he would learn in Dartmoor, to predict before seeing them what the tracks might be, what animal could be responsible for the unusual aspects of the case. And, not the least remarkable aspect, to one who knew Byron, was the man's failure to rise to a challenge of this nature, even for purely selfish reasons. That was a mystery in itself, quite apart from the killing. Byron was a man who had always gone out of his way to find a challenge; he invariably did things in the most risky and dangerous fashion simply to create a challenge against his life itself. And, the older he got, the greater this need became. As Wetherby began to feel himself slowing down and relied on his experience to do things the safest and easiest way, Byron had seemed compelled to increase the difficulties of the tasks he took in hand. Wetherby had hunted with Byron many times, in India and Africa and once, the last time, in the wilderness of northern Canada. He vividly recalled that Canada expedition. Never had Byron taken a risk that seemed more pointless—danger for the pure sake of danger. Byron wanted a Kodiak bear, and he wanted it alone, insisted that Wetherby wait at a distance too great to be of any possible aid. And, although he had splendid guns, he had borrowed a .30–06 from their guide, a good gun but much too light for the job; a gun he had not even fired before. Wetherby had protested in vain. Byron was not a man to listen to reason, much less argument, and so Wetherby had waited. He could still recall the tenseness he had felt on that memorable day. He had been waiting on a hill, surrounded by evergreens. It was autumn. The forest was burning with colour, trees ablaze in reds and yellows. The ground was crisp with early frost and a chill wind stirred from the north. Wetherby had watched Byron's figure diminish as he strode away moving towards where they knew the bear was waiting. Byron looked very casual, but that was deceptive. His red and black plaid shooting coat blended against the background of leaves. He looked very small, drawing farther away, towards the dense thicket where his quarry waited. He was already out of effective range, Wetherby would be helpless from where he stood. He gripped his rifle, but knew it was useless. Byron was completely on his own.

Byron was almost at the thicket when the bear reared up. Even at that distance, Wetherby was astounded at the monster's size. He saw Byron raise the rifle, a tiny manikin only a few yards from those fourteen hundred pounds of power and fury. The bear's head seemed larger than Byron, towering three feet above him as the beast rose on its hind legs. And then the bear was off balance, twisting around and down, thrashing in death, and it seemed a long time later that the sharp crack of the rifle reached Wetherby's ears. Byron had turned and raised the gun, motioning for Wetherby to advance. Wetherby had advanced.

Byron was smiling, looking down at the bear. It was a smile of pure pleasure. He had fired once, as the bear roared in warning, and the slug had gone up through the roof of that terrible mouth and into the brain. It had not emerged. There was no mark on the trophy.

"A fine shot," Wetherby said.

"I couldn't very well have missed at that range. Couldn't afford to, either."

"Not with that," Wetherby said, looking at the rifle.

"Oh, a .30–06 will kill a bear if the shot is placed right."

"Obviously."

Byron was amused. "Why should I use a heavier weapon than I need? That just makes a man sloppy. That .402 you carry, for instance. You could have dropped it even with a bad shot, broken its shoulder or shattered its leg and then finished it at your leisure. That isn't hunting, John. That isn't living. That's not the way to keep life and give death. You're a fine hunter and a splendid shot, but your values are wrong."

"Perhaps," Wetherby said with a mixture of admiration and annoyance, half understanding what Byron meant, and resenting an understanding he did not follow.

"Not perhaps. A categorical fact. An objective truth."

"But if you hadn't made a perfect shot—if something had happened, if the bear had shifted just a few inches as you fired— you couldn't have stopped a wounded charge with a rifle that light. Even if your second shot had been perfect, it would have killed you through sheer impetus and reflex."

Byron smiled again. This was a different smile.

"No," he said. "But that's a moot point."

Wetherby raised his eyebrows.

Byron tossed the rifle to him. Wetherby caught it. He knew, absolutely, what Byron meant then. He worked the lever. The empty shell ejected. There had been only one bullet in the rifle.

"You're mad," Wetherby said.

And Byron laughed in mad delight . . .

Later, by the campfire, Byron had been in a thoughtful, philosophi- cal mood. His immediate pleasure had faded, and he seemed pos- sessed with a need to share his attitudes with Wetherby. They were alone. Their guide was skinning the bear where it had fallen; it was too huge to move. Wetherby was still greatly disturbed by the enor- mous risk Byron had taken; a risk that seemed to border on the unbalance of madness.

"Can't you understand, John?" Byron said. He was almost plead- ing for understanding.

"I don't know. I see the emotion of it—even the accomplish- ment. But it's suicidal, Byron. Some day—"

Byron silenced him with a gesture. His eyes were bright in the firelight.

"Danger, John. Only in danger are we alive. Only by risking our lives can we appreciate them. How much fuller our existence is than that of a city man, castrated by civilization, emasculated by society and safety. There is no life there, no danger and no joy, no risk and, therefore, nothing to risk. And we give life as we take it, John. That bear was never more alive than the instant before the bullet entered his brain. If we, the hunters, are more alive and aware, then it must work even more so for the hunted. I love the things I kill, John. The things that would kill me if I was too slow, if I failed to observe, if my shot failed. I love them, I say. I could have been the world's greatest animal tamer, you know. I have a rapport with wild creatures. I can sense their thoughts, their feelings, and meet them on their own level. There is no animal I could not manage, no bestial level upon which I couldn't meet them. If I chose to befriend a beast, instead of killing it—" His voice softened, he looked off into the distance, across the darkening hills of an endless wilderness. He did not look at Wetherby when he spoke again. Perhaps he was not speaking to Wetherby.

"But I like to kill," he said. "I think, perhaps, I might even like to be killed—in the proper fashion . . ."

Their guide returned, dragging the skin behind him on a travois, and they talked no more of such things. That was the last time they hunted together.

Wetherby felt a vague uneasiness, recalling these strange words from that faraway place. Byron had often made him uneasy, in some indefinite way, in much the same way that he felt uneasy about an animal that was acting peculiar—when he couldn't tell if it intended to charge or to flee. There were many traits of the animal in Byron, at that. A strange man. Wetherby wondered if he had changed at all with the years, and looked forward to seeing him again. And that reminded him that it was late, and that he must rise early. He had arranged to meet Bell at eight o'clock in the morning, and didn't want to oversleep. Wetherby refused to have a telephone or an alarm clock, and depended on a method he had developed of setting his mind to awake at a given hour, but it had been some time since he had been forced to use this ability. He wasn't sure if it would still be effective; he decided that he had better go to bed.

Wetherby stood up and finished his nightcap, regarding the glowing embers. The door knocker clanked disturbingly through the quiet rooms.

Wetherby frowned, looking at the clock. It was a strange hour for visitors, and he didn't welcome unexpected visits at any hour. Then he shrugged, went into the hall and walked down to the door.

Bell stood on the threshold, looking flustered.

"Sorry to disturb you," he said.

"Quite all right. Come in."

Bell entered, holding his hat in both hands. He seemed uncertain, preoccupied, no longer the same man who had recently been with Wetherby at the club.

"Was there something you forgot to tell me?"

Bell shook his head.

"Come on into the study. There's a fire there. Will you have a drink?"

"I haven't time, John. I'll have to go down to Dartmoor immediately. I'd like you to come with me."

"Tonight?" Wetherby said. He didn't relish the idea. "Can't it wait until morning? I can take a train down and meet you there."

"I want you to have a look at the tracks while they're still fresh."

Wetherby blinked.

"What?" he asked.

Bell seemed to snap out of the mood that blanketed his thoughts then. He looked sheepish.

"Sorry, John. I guess I'm not thinking. I didn't tell you."

"Tell me what?" Wetherby asked.

"The killer, whatever it is, has killed again."

5

The police driver was expert, the motor-car was fast, and the roads were empty. Wetherby and Bell rode in the back seat. Wetherby had brought one of his sporting rifles and wore an old bush jacket. He felt a touch of the familiar old thrill at the start of the hunt, although it was greatly modified by circumstance. It was more like going after a man-eating tiger than a trophy. It was very much like going after a man-eater, in fact. They didn't talk much. Bell looked weary, his hard red face drawn and tense, chain-smoking cigarettes. It was a black night. The lights of London were behind, and on Salisbury Plain they ran into the storm that was sweeping the West Country. The slippery road didn't seem to trouble the driver, and they shot on through the rain without reducing the speed. Dawn had just begun to pale the sky behind them when they pulled into the parking lot at The Bridge Hotel.

The driver consulted a map with the quick efficiency of long practice, pulled out of the parking lot and turned on to a secondary road leading north. He had to go slower now. They ran through hedgerows and trees, flickering shadows in the headlights, and then they cornered into a blinding glare of white light.

The area was cordoned off and arc lamps had been rigged. The narrow lane was starkly flooded in the powerful crossbeams and uniformed policemen moved in the shadows of the trees on either side. Several police cars were drawn up along the shoulder of the road and Hammond's warning flasher was still blinking weakly against the greater light.

Detective Sergeant Thurlow came over and opened the door. His face was grim. He carried an electric torch and his shoes were thick with mud.

"I've left the body where it was," he said.

"Identity?" Bell asked. He got out of the car. Wetherby got out the other side.

"Yes," Thurlow said. "Driver's licence and credit cards in the glove box. Man named Hammond. A salesman from London. Apparently he'd run out of petrol and went behind the car to set up a flasher." He glanced at the winking light. It was a sad little effort, overwhelmed in the glare.

"Turn it off, for God's sake," Bell said, irritably.

Someone snapped the flasher off.

"The killer came out from the trees there, and Hammond ran some fifty yards up the road before it got him," Thurlow said. Bell looked up the road.

"He ran past his car, eh?"

Thurlow nodded.

"You'd think he would have tried to get back in the car and lock the door, wouldn't you?" Bell said, more to himself than anything else.

Thurlow nodded. "The locks worked on all the doors," he said. "I considered that. I suppose he didn't have time to open the door, or was too frightened to think of it."

Wetherby had come around the front of the police car. He was carrying his rifle. Thurlow raised an eyebrow and Bell introduced them. They shook hands and Thurlow's palm was damp.

"Anything else?" Bell asked.

"The same things. Plenty of tracks. They look like the same ones. The same thing that got Randal."

"Who found the body?"

"Young fellow bicycling home from his girl's house. He's waiting in my car. Must have come along just a few minutes after it happened. The body was still warm when I got here. Gave him one hell of a jolt."

"He's lucky he didn't come a bit sooner," Bell said. "I'll speak to him later. Let's have a look at the body."

They walked on past Hammond's car. Wetherby still carried the rifle. The body had been covered with a rubber sheet, and blood had seeped out at the sides in thick coils along the road. A young constable with a very white face stood to attention.

"Pull it down," Bell said.

The constable squatted and pulled the sheet down. Wetherby winced. The body was horribly mangled, the belly was torn open and the intestines trailed out in twisted loops. Wetherby had seen death like this before, and his first thought was that it looked like the mauling of a leopard. The young constable stood up quickly and walked to the side of the road; he leaned over and made noises.

"Did you find the head?" Bell asked.

"No. It's gone," Thurlow said.

No leopard did that, Wetherby thought.

"Well, John?" Bell asked.

Wetherby was kneeling on the wet earth, looking at the tracks. Farther into the trees a detective was taking plaster casts and another was photographing them. Behind them a group was fingerprinting the car inside and out and measuring distances and positions. They all worked with quick skill, and would miss nothing, if anything was there. Wetherby looked up, frowning. Bell's face was suddenly etched in the flash of the photographer's camera.

"I don't know. I have an idea I've seen tracks like these before. But damned if I can place them. They're almost like a gigantic weasel at this point, but notice how deep the claw marks are. And farther back they're different."

"Different?" Bell asked sharply.

Wetherby nodded.

"You mean there may have been two animals? Different animals?"

"Perhaps. More likely, the tracks changed when the creature began to run. The different stride, you see."

Bell nodded. Wetherby stood up, brushing at his knees.

"It was walking up to this point," Wetherby said. He glanced back at the road. "It walked to here, and then it ran after its prey. That's when the tracks change. But Justin—when it walked—it walked on two legs."

And they were silent for some time.

"Can you trail it?" Bell asked.

They were standing back at his car. The rain was still slashing through the light and black clouds had become visible as the sky paled above them. Thurlow stood beside them, nervously looking from side to side.

"Maybe. In the morning, perhaps. I'll need daylight."

Bell nodded.

"There's nothing more we can do here now, then. We may as well go back to The Bridge Hotel and wait for daylight. We can get an early start from there."

"If only we knew what the hell we were looking for," Thurlow said. "A man or an animal?"

"Something that walks on two legs and runs on four," Bell added. "A man or an animal?"

"Or some combination of the two?" Thurlow said.

Bell looked at him and Thurlow shrugged sheepishly.

"You don't believe in such things?" Bell asked.

"No. Of course not."

But he looked very strange.

It foreshadowed the dark fear to come.

6

Wetherby and Bell returned to The Bridge Hotel in the morning. The rain had stopped but the day was grim with fog. They went into the lounge and sat by the window, their shoes caked with mud and their faces dark with the stubble of beards. They were both tired. It had been a night long with futility. Wetherby had attempted to follow the killer's tracks in the early light, had followed the spoor easily enough for several hundred feet beyond the road, and then lost the trail. The trail had simply vanished abruptly, as though deliberately obliterated, with no period of transition. There was a spoor, and then there was no spoor. Bell had followed, silent and dependent in this aspect of the hunt, while Wetherby sought a continuation of the tracks farther on. They had walked in a wide circle around the point where the tracks ended, but had found nothing; repeated the circle farther back, thinking that the killer might have backtracked and left the original trail on a tangent; followed a long arc on the opposite side of the lane from the visible trail, in case it had backtracked all the way with the instinct of the cunning beast knowing it will be pursued. But there was no further trace. It walked like a man, and ran like a beast, and Wetherby's tired mind wondered if it also flew like a bird.

They had returned to the lane after that. A police car was waiting for them, the driver leaning on the wing smoking a cigarette. Hammond's body had been removed but the dark stain of his blood still marked the spot where he had died. Bell stopped by the car but Wetherby had one more check to make. He squatted in the muddy lane and, using his fountain pen as a makeshift ruler, measured the depth of the animal's tracks; he also measured Hammond's tracks and then his own. Bell stood scratching his head. Wetherby had moved from the lane and taken a fourth measurement at the point where the killer had been walking. His forehead had corrugated as he looked at the fountain pen and struggled with his conclusions, and then he had walked slowly back to the car and they had been driven to the hotel.

*

"Sorry, Justin." Wetherby sat, looking out of the window. The fog was drifting in long streams across the moors, a few motorcars passed on the road.

"You did your best, John. If any man could have followed the trail, it would have been you."

Wetherby shrugged; he didn't deny it.

"What now?" he asked.

"I don't know. I'm worried, John. I'm having some dogs brought down, but I wouldn't count on them. You still have no opinion on what it might be?"

"Less than before. None of the facts fit together. The marks on the body, for instance. I should say they were the work of a cat. Particularly the disembowelment. Not something as powerful as a lion or tiger. A powerful beast, mauling the body that way, would have crushed the bones, whereas these wounds were comparatively superficial ... the ribs weren't broken, even though the stomach was ripped out. More like the work of a leopard. Something fairly light and completely ferocious, tearing with sharp talons rather than crushing. But that doesn't tie in with the strength necessary to sever the neck so cleanly. That would take unbelievable force."

Bell nodded, crossing his legs. A shard of mud dropped on to the carpet and he regarded it thoughtfully.

"And the tracks?" he asked.

"They're vaguely familiar to me, but damned if I can remember where I saw them before."

"There can't be many animals that walk on their hind legs and run on all fours," Bell said.

"Possibly an ape of some sort ... a bear for a short distance, although it's not likely. But there's another thing about the prints that I find even more confusing. The way they change when this animal begins to run. They become more shallow. Naturally, with the animal's weight distributed on four feet, the tracks wouldn't be as deep, but the difference was much greater than it should have been. I measured the depth of the prints, using my own footprints to test the resistance of the soil, and using Hammond's prints to make sure the rain hadn't affected the quality of the ground to any great degree. The conclusion was rather startling."

Bell waited, leaning on his elbow. A waiter looked in the door, then withdrew. They could hear voices at the desk as someone registered.

"When the creature was walking," Wetherby said, "it weighed somewhat more than I do. Presumably it was balanced on its hind legs, and the print it left was roughly the same in area as my own print, but it was deeper. I should say it weighed somewhere around fourteen stone ... the weight of a leopard, possibly, nothing larger. But when it ran, the prints were much more shallow than the double distribution of that weight can account for. They were no deeper than a smallish animal would have made. Something around forty pounds."

Bell considered this without expression and said, "What would account for that?"

"It seems as though this creature just skimmed over the ground ... as if it were a large bird, an ostrich perhaps, not actually flying but using its wings to take most of its weight from the ground. And if it also had the power of flight, this could account for the way the trail vanished."

"A gigantic man-eating bird?" Bell said, rather louder than he'd intended.

Wetherby's smile was weary.

"No, that isn't possible. I was just toying with some of the conflicting facts. No bird runs on four legs and has five distinctly clawed toes."

"Well then?"

"The only alternative seems to be that it was fairly bowling along ... running so fast that it just skimmed the surface of the ground. Incredible speed from a standing start."

Bell's eyes flickered as he added another meagre grain to his knowledge of the killer.

"So we know it must be exceptionally fast," he said.

"But that raises another paradox."

"Oh?"

"The victim ... Hammond ... ran for some fifty yards ..."

"Fifty-three and some inches," Bell said.

"Yes. And how could a man have run so far if his pursuer was so fast? It didn't overtake him immediately, it followed him at an apparently great speed, and yet it didn't catch him for some fifty yards. Probably six or seven seconds. And they must have been terrible seconds for Hammond."

"It must have allowed him a head start . . . toyed with him . . . that would be like a cat, wouldn't it?"

"Possibly. I don't know what to think. It almost seems as though there were two different animals. A large, two-legged one and a smaller four-legged one. But there weren't two sets of tracks, only one set that changed form."

There was a considerable silence, although Bell's mind was roaring with activity.

"An animal . . . a creature . . . a being that can change its form at will?" Bell asked the window. Or perhaps he asked the dark fog beyond. He was thinking of what Thurlow had hinted, and Wetherby knew what was in his mind. But that was too monstrous for serious consideration. Too preposterous for belief. At this stage . . .

"There must be some explanation," Wetherby said. "Some fact eludes us or some simple point that we have failed to see, or to understand."

"Of course," Bell said.

He continued to stare at the fog.

The waiter looked in again. He was a nervous little man, overawed by the presence of a law enforcement officer, and suffering the guilt that all totally innocent men feel when confronted by an agent of the superstructure—fearing law far more than crime.

Bell signalled to him and the waiter came over slowly.

"Sir?"

"Coffee," Bell said.

"Right away, sir."

"And bring me some paper."

"Paper, sir?"

"Paper, for God's sake. Something to write on."

"Yes, sir."

The waiter retreated with squared shoulders.

"Obviously a man who has never broken a law," Bell said, showing remarkable insight considering his trade. He smiled slightly, perfunctorily, a man who would not hesitate to bend the law to achieve justice.

"We know so little," he said. "So many various facts without a pattern. The only way to get a killer like this is to wait until a pattern is established, and that is obviously not a satisfying method. How many deaths must occur before it links up? Do beasts conform to a pattern, too, John?"

"Definitely. More than man, I'd say. In their fashion."

"Will this killer conform?"

"Yes. If only in the territory and the time when it kills ... the frequency of its kills. But it doesn't devour its victims, so we can't very well anticipate it by a hunger cycle. It will be strictly a blood-lust cycle, and to form a pattern from that we must know what the killer is ... or wait, as you say, until it establishes its own pattern."

Bell winced. The waiter returned with a tray, coffee and a pad of writing paper, placed the objects carefully on the table and stood at attention. Bell waved and he departed. Bell tore a sheet of paper from the pad and squared it before him.

"Both deaths occurred within a mile or so of each other," he said. "Maybe that narrows the field, maybe not." He began marking the paper with a ball-point pen. "If it's an animal, it must have a lair somewhere in this area ... a cave, a burrow, a tree ... some place it regards as home. All animals have a well-developed sense of territorial possession, I believe." Wetherby nodded, but Bell was looking at the paper and talking to himself. His pen moved swiftly. He was sketching a crude map. Wetherby watched the lines take form and context, and saw that Bell had committed the terrain to memory. He made a dark cross against a vertical line and the tip of the pen lingered over it for a moment, then moved on to inscribe a second cross. He regarded it for a moment, nodded, and printed a few words on the map, nodded again and turned it around. He tapped his pen against the paper as Wetherby looked at it and saw, with his trained eye, that Bell had incorporated all the significant points, and that the rough map nicely outlined the area and placed the territory he had seen in context.

The highway ran diagonally across the paper in a gradual south-westerly arc from top right to bottom left and this line was divided by a stream twisting horizontally across the centre of the sheet. The stream passed under the highway, and the hotel—named for the bridge over the water—was at the junction. The hotel was

south of the highway, and opposite another line, representing a
secondary road, made a right angle to the north. Beside the stream,
west of the hotel, was the cross where Randal had died, and on
the secondary road north of the hotel was Hammond's cross. The
hotel and the two morbid crosses formed a triangle.

Bell's pen moved between the crosses.

"You can see that there isn't much distance between the kills,
cross-country," he said.

"What is it, about two miles?"

"About that."

"Where is Byron's house?"

"Byron's?"

"I'd like to have a word with him."

Bell drew the paper back and added another line and a square.
The line represented a narrow lane running west from the secondary road and Byron's house was at the end.

"The lane leaves the secondary road quite near where Hammond
was killed," Bell said. "Runs through the hedgerows for a mile or so
and ends at Byron's. His place was the manor house at one time,
but that was before motor-cars and the lane is quite narrow."

Wetherby was judging distances, thinking he might walk to
Byron's. He realized that adding Byron's house to the three points
of the triangle formed a rough square. But that meant nothing.
Bell was marking the paper again, just doodling now; he added the
ridge lined with tors that ran parallel between the stream and the
lane. There are no great distances in England, and the confined
area gave Wetherby an idea. He looked out of the window and
raised his eyebrows.

"Any ideas?" Bell asked.

"Possibly. I think we might treat this the same way we'd treat a
man-eating tiger. I've done that before. Instead of trying to track it
or anticipate it, we might attract it."

"Set a trap for it?"

Wetherby nodded.

"How?" Bell asked.

"We could stake out a goat or something, I suppose. But obviously it prefers human prey . . ."

"And obviously we can't stake out a man."

"If we could leave the corpse where it was . . ."

"This isn't India, John. You know I can't do that. There'd be hell to pay."

"Of course. Suppose I were to wait myself. Not in one spot particularly, just wander around the moors and roads at night? It's a remote possibility, but not all that far-fetched. There can't be many people on the moors at night, and if the territory is limited, then the killer's opportunities are limited as well. If I made my presence obvious . . ."

Bell scowled.

"Make yourself a potential victim? I didn't bring you down here for that."

"It's been done before."

Bell shook his head, considering more than refusing. Wetherby, now that he had had the idea, was rather excited by the prospect. It had been a long time . . .

"I couldn't let you go alone," Bell said.

"It would have to be alone, Justin. This is work for a solitary hunter, not a posse. Too many people would simply give it warning. And, of course, it's not a question of you giving permission. I have every right to walk on the moors at night. Nothing official. No repercussions at all."

"Well, I can't stop you."

"It might work, Justin. I think it's well worth a try."

Bell was still scowling. He sipped his coffee.

"What can we lose?" Wetherby asked.

"Your head," Bell told him.

They finished the coffee in silence.

"I might be able to persuade Byron to join me," Wetherby said. He glanced at the map again. "We've worked together on man-eaters. I'll go out to his place this afternoon. But I'd like to try, with or without Byron."

"As I said, I can't stop you. Officially. You still have your gun permits?"

"Yes. It shouldn't be dangerous, really. We're letting the confusing aspects of this affect our thinking. Justin. It can certainly be no more dangerous than any big-game hunting. It's not a ghost, nothing uncanny, just a beast that has to be killed—something I've done often enough for pleasure. Just because this is England the facts have made greater impact on us, the contrast has fired our imagination. But if I keep away from the rocks and trees, keep well in the open where it can't surprise me, it should be safe enough. Both the victims were surprised and unarmed, and both had a chance to run for a considerable distance before it brought them down. But even if it is as fast as those tracks imply, I'll be ready for it. I won't be running."

"You sound as if you like the idea."

"Ah, the old thrill, eh?"

"Any help you want . . ."

"Unofficial?"

"I never impose limits," Bell said.

Wetherby said, "I'll let you know."

"More coffee?" Bell asked.

He had seen the waiter's eye appear around the corner. The eye disappeared again and they heard whispering in the hallway. Bell scowled at the door.

"No, I think not. I'd like to get cleaned up now and then go over to Byron's."

"I'll leave the car and driver at your disposal."

"Want to come along?"

Bell shook his head. He had no desire to see Byron again; he had an irritating idea that Byron had been laughing at him when he had requested an opinion on his former visit. He wanted more coffee and looked fiercely towards the door, willing the waiter to appear. Another man appeared. Wetherby stood up and the man walked directly over to the table. He was a small fellow, prematurely bald with soft eyes and a disreputably rumpled jacket. He looked like a rookie reporter and had a notebook and pens in his breast pocket.

"Oh God, the Press," Bell said.

The reporter stuck his hand out at Wetherby.

"Detective Superintendent Bell?" he asked.

"Do I look like a detective?" Wetherby said, in a tone of horror that was only half assumed.

"Aaron Rose," the reporter said, and mentioned the name of his newspaper. It was a Sunday scandal sheet. He moved past Wetherby and pointed his handshake across the table. Bell looked up morosely.

"Detective Superintendent Bell?" Rose asked.

"Do I look like a detective?" Bell snarled.

Bell sounded like a detective. Wetherby moved smiling towards the door and reporter Aaron Rose stood scratching his scalp and considering the deception of appearances.

7

The driver knew where Byron's was. Wetherby sat beside him, filling his pipe, as they drove from the hotel parking lot and turned across the highway. It was the same way they had gone before, when they first went to the scene of the killing and later, in the daylight, when Wetherby had attempted to follow the trail. This time they didn't travel so far up the secondary road but turned off on a lane to the left. Wetherby remembered noticing the turning before. They ran along smoothly, following the winding lane through hedgerows and sudden glimpses of open, rolling land. It was still foggy. The fog hugged the open land and Wetherby regarded it thoughtfully; he imagined how the moors would be at night and thought that, despite what he had told Bell, a night alone on the moors might well prove more terrifying than any jungle. It was a question of the unexpected, the startling contrast between danger and the placid everyday reality of this mild country. But this realization only served to increase his eagerness, and he looked forward to the hunt as he would have in the past.

Half a mile down the lane they passed a public house, a little thatched building which the driver eyed with a thirsty eye. It was called, with a nice twist on the traditional, The King's Torso. But in the light of recent events, it was an ominous name.

"You won't have to wait for me at Byron's," Wetherby said.

The driver looked delighted. They drove on and after another half-mile came to Byron's. Wetherby got out and the driver reversed into the drive and headed back down the lane, where The King's Torso waited. Wetherby stood for a moment, his pipe in his teeth, surveying the manor house of former years. It was impressive. The building was well back from the lane, a timeless structure of different centuries and different architectural styles, with gables and turrets and stone chimneys, grey and grim against the windswept moors. From the back came the steady thump of someone cutting wood. The sound stopped as Wetherby walked up the drive, and Byron came around the side of the house, an axe over his shoulder. He smiled and walked down to meet Wetherby.

"I thought you'd be around," Byron said.

His grip was as firm as ever. Byron hadn't changed at all, he was as timeless as his home. He was tall and lean, an immensely powerful man with the long muscles of endurance defined without bulk. His face was weathered leather and his eyes were bright with life; his hair was clipped short and his clothing was ancient. He rested the axe against the ground and leaned on the handle.

"So Bell has persuaded you to join the witch hunt, eh?"

Wetherby smiled and shrugged.

"I rather thought you might. I'm pleased to see you haven't lost the urge to action."

Byron's eyes moved up and down, and Wetherby had the uncomfortable thought that he was being critically inspected. He puffed on his pipe and stared back. Then Byron laughed and clapped a big hand on Wetherby's shoulder and they walked back up to the house.

"I'm surprised you declined the offer," Wetherby said.

"Oh, I have other interests. I haven't stopped living yet, John. I'm planning a South American trip early next year, as a matter of fact. Interested?"

"No, I'm still retired."

Byron shook his head. They went into the house and down a cold and impersonal hallway with an atmosphere like a National Trust castle. They turned into a huge room hung with trophies. A wood fire was burning fiercely and the comfortable leather chairs drew the light deeply below the polished surface. They sat by the fire. Wetherby noticed the Kodiak bear he had watched Byron bring down with a single shot from a gun which was far too light for the job. It was mounted upright in the corner, its gigantic head snarling some nine feet above the floor, and Wetherby felt again that awe of a man facing that monster with one bullet in a .30-06.

"Drink?" Byron asked.

"I'd like some coffee."

"Grant!" Byron barked.

A man appeared at the doorway. His clothing was, if anything, more ancient than Byron's, his hands large and gnarled and his face etched with deep lines. He had a twisted leg.

"Bring some coffee," Byron said.

The man nodded sullenly and moved off, his leg wheeling after him.

"My servant," Byron said.

"I thought you disapproved of servants?"

Byron shook his head.

"No, I disapprove of servile men. Grant is a most inefficient servant, but he isn't servile. He used to be a Cornish tin miner, a man who has experienced life to the limits. Restricted within those limits, of course. I hired him because he almost beat me hand wrestling."

"What?"

"You remember the game, surely?"

Byron raised his forearm, hand open and fingers extended upwards, and made a pressing motion across his chest. Wetherby nodded.

"Oh, that. Yes, I remember."

"We had a contest once."

"You beat me."

"Yes. It's not a game I lose. But it took seven minutes by the stop watch before I put your arm down, and I gained a great respect for you, John. I put Grant down in five minutes, by the way. Can you still hold your own?"

Byron placed his elbow on the table; he looked expectant, almost hopeful. But Wetherby laughed and shook his head, and Byron sighed.

"You look fit enough."

"I'm all right," Wetherby said.

"A pity you've given up life."

"Just moved on to a different life."

"Oh, it's the same thing," Byron said.

"You can't expect everyone to agree with your ideas."

"Never mind. What of this man-killer? What do you think?"

"I don't really know. You've heard that it killed again last night?"

"Yes. I heard."

"I came down from London with Bell just afterwards."

"You saw the tracks?"

"Yes. They looked vaguely familiar."

Byron leaned back in his chair.

"Couldn't you identify them?" he asked.

"No, I believe I've seen similar tracks before, but I couldn't place them."

"You should have been able to, John. Ten years ago you would have."

Wetherby didn't like that.

"Bell told me you didn't recognize the casts," he said.

Byron smiled, started to speak and then shrugged.

"Well? Did you?"

"Oh, casts are a different thing," he said. "I dare say I would have recognized the tracks themselves."

"But you couldn't be bothered."

"Exactly."

Wetherby wanted to say more. Instead he refilled his pipe. It was hard to know just how much to say to Byron. Grant returned with the coffee on a silver tray, swaying from good leg to bad with a curiously rapid gait. He banged the tray down on the table. The coffee spilled into the saucers, hands accustomed to ravaging the earth were not suited to the more delicate tasks of a servant. He swivelled about and clumped out of the room without speaking.

"I'm sure you'll be able to track this animal, anyway, John," Byron said. "You won't have lost all your skill."

"I didn't this morning."

"Oh, you'll probably have another chance."

Wetherby stared at him.

"Well, if an animal kills twice, it's a good bet it will kill again, eh? I'm just being practical."

"You think it is an animal, then?"

"Undoubtedly."

"I suppose so. But what animal could have severed the heads that way?"

"It should prove interesting, finding out."

"Interesting? My God, Byron. Two men have been brutally killed. This isn't a pleasure trip."

Byron sipped his coffee placidly.

"Hunting should always be a pleasure, John. You know that. If it's necessary, that should merely add to the pleasure. And if it's dangerous, all the better."

"I am rather excited about it," Wetherby admitted.

"And it could be dangerous," Byron said.

"Well, it certainly has the ability to kill a man."

"What gun are you using?"

"I have the Winchester with me."

"Too much gun," Byron said. He sighed and sipped his coffee. "You've seen the tracks, it isn't a large animal. You always did tend to carry too much firepower. It makes a man careless about his shooting."

"But it will stop it," Wetherby said.

"Oh, it will do that. If efficiency is what you look for. And if you hit it, of course."

"I'll hit it. I haven't lost everything."

"That's good. How do you propose to find it?"

Byron sounded interested and Wetherby leaned forward, hoping to get his old companion enthused enough to join the hunt.

"I expect I'll apply the usual methods. Treat it as a hunt. Try to follow a fresh trail if it kills again. Or try to anticipate it . . . wait for it, let it find me."

"On the moors at night?" Byron's eyes gleamed. "That would be like the old days, John. Remember the man-eater of Sunda?"

Byron gestured at the wall. Wetherby turned. The tiger's head snarled viciously at them. Wetherby remembered, all right. They had left the half-devoured corpse of a Hindu villager and waited for the tiger to return to its kill. The man's widow had howled heart-rendingly at such a misuse of her late husband, but the headman had showed more sense, or less emotion, which amounted to the same thing.

"You waited in a tree, John," Byron said.

"And you waited on the ground by the body. Yes, I remember it. It was a near thing for you."

"You never did see the beauty of that . . . that the risk had to be positive to make it worthwhile, that the man-eater had to have his chance to live or die the same as I did."

Wetherby looked at the tiger's head again. He remembered the sudden blur of orange and black through the jungle night, that quick rush of death that had carried the cat's dead body past its executioner. Byron had fired from a crouch and hurled himself to one side as the tiger, already dead, stormed past to collapse at the base of the tree where Wetherby waited, where Wetherby had no time to fire.

"That fellow had already killed over two hundred human beings, Byron. It wasn't—it shouldn't have been—a question of the thrill. Killing it was a worthwhile end no matter how we'd managed it."

Byron was looking at the trophy, too.

"Do you really believe that the lives of two hundred primitive and ignorant savages are equal to the life of that magnificent killer? Yes, I expect you do. Don't you see that the life of the killer is invariably superior to the life of the victim?"

Wetherby stared, not quite sure how serious Byron was. Even in the old days, his curious attitudes had never extended this far.

"You had all the ability a man could need, John. If only you'd had the philosophy. You could have been as good as I was. You were as fast, you shot as well, your instincts were as fine. But you waited in a tree, John." The scorn was evident. It might not have been intentional, but Byron could not keep it from his tone. "I could no more have waited in safety than I could use a weapon so heavy that even a poor shot would bring the quarry down. That was where we differed, and where you failed."

Wetherby was stung. He sat rigidly on the end of his chair.

"Wasn't I as good as you?" he asked.

"Oh, perhaps. In your way. That's not what I'm talking about, John. Not ability, not achievement. Understanding. A way of life. Did I tell you I'm writing a book?" He stood up. Wetherby followed him across the room. A battered old typewriter was surrounded by disordered paper on a table in the corner. Byron picked up several sheets and looked at them; put them down again. "A book about my philosophy," he said. "I'd like you to read it some day. You might understand, then. But not until it's finished."

He turned and looked out of the window. The land rolled away behind the house, mist and cloud merging in the distance.

"Or perhaps out there at night," Byron said.

"What?"

"On the moors at night. Perhaps you might learn to understand then, John."

"But you won't come with me?"

"This—this is more to my taste, I will say. You are doing the proper thing when you make yourself the bait. It appeals to me. If I thought you were still the man I once knew I might join you —I might give you this beast. But you're soft now, John. We aren't compatible."

"I'm not soft," Wetherby said.

"Oh? Well, perhaps not. Perhaps I have misjudged you. But I'm seldom wrong about man or beast."

"I'll be going now," Wetherby said.

"You're quite welcome to stay here."

"I've already booked at the hotel."

They walked back across the room. The bear loomed up above them, the tiger grimaced in its eternal snarl. But these things were dead.

"You're angry, John," Byron said.

Wetherby shrugged.

"Perhaps I was wrong. If I was wrong, I'll join your hunt. Will you prove me wrong?"

"I can't prove anything," Wetherby said.

"You can, you know."

Byron sat. He placed his elbow on the table and smiled up at Wetherby.

"You lasted seven minutes once, John. Can you last seven now? Five? If you can hold me for one minute I'll join you?"

"This is childish."

"Childish? Basic, possibly. But how then are we to judge our fellow men? Come, John."

Stung to anger, Wetherby sat opposite Byron. He flexed his arm several times and placed his elbow on the table level with Byron's. They locked hands. Wetherby wanted very much to beat Byron at this game. It was no longer childish to him, he was taut with that need. Byron was still smiling. His hand felt rough and dry, and he was relaxed. They stared at each other across their hands.

"Are you ready, John?"

Wetherby nodded.

Byron placed his left hand on the table and looked at his wrist-watch.

"Proceed," he said.

Wetherby drew a deep breath and snapped into sudden pressure, using all his strength in the first surge, trying to gain an initial advantage. It was like pressing against a concrete slab. Byron's hand did not move, it did not quiver. His long bicep seemed hardly to tense, but his forearm was a bar of steel that would not bend. His smile was unchanged.

"Ten seconds," he said. "I'm waiting, John."

Wetherby pressed with all the power he possessed. His arm leaped with the effort, his chest swelled as the pressure ran along his muscles. He knew his face was flushed and his hand began to falter. Byron hardly seemed aware of the energy summoned against him. He looked at his watch again, and then he applied his own strength. Wetherby's hand began to move back through a steady arc. He was powerless to resist. His forearm drew towards the level, his wrist bent back, he felt as though his bones were bending.

And then his arm was down.

"Fifty seconds," Byron said.

Wetherby shook his hand. It was limp and lifeless. All his energy had seeped away, even his anger had gone.

"Yes, I am seldom wrong about a man," Byron said. "But good luck in your quest, John."

Wetherby walked back along the narrow lane. His arm ached. The police car was parked outside The King's Torso, but he walked on past without taking much notice. He was preoccupied with a sense of failure, a self-doubt and a troubling idea that Byron had, after all, been right.

8

The wind billowed across the rolling moors, shredding the fog in its wake. Wetherby walked through ribbons of grey mist against a black night. He made no attempt at stealth. His pipe crackled as he drew on it and trailed smoke lighter than the fog, a warm companion on a cold night. He was wrapped in a heavy cloak and had a hip flask of brandy and an electric torch. The torch was unlighted, and his rifle was loaded, the safety catch under his thumb. He was following the course of the stream westward from the highway and south of the ridge. The tors were black against a dark sky and the water made a rippling background noise punctuated by the regular croaking of frogs along the bank. His rubber boots squelched in the soft mud and reeds bent beneath his stride. Wetherby was enjoying this solitary trek; he hadn't realized how much he had missed the tingle of danger and the sharp sense of readiness. In that much, at least, Byron had been right.

Wetherby had left the hotel as soon as it was dark. The lights were still on in the bar, traffic moved along the highway and cars pulled in and out of the parking lot. But as soon as he had left the road he was alone. It wasn't a case of distance, he hadn't come more than a mile along the bank of the stream, and yet the feeling of solitude was absolute. He could just as easily have been in the darkest heart of a forest. It was the feeling he wanted, the situation he had looked for. He planned to follow the stream to the point where Randal had been killed, and then cut back across country, over the ridge and the open land beyond, across the lane that led to Byron's and on to the secondary road somewhere near where Hammond had been killed. From there he could follow the secondary road back to the highway and the hotel. It wasn't any great distance and he had all night. It was, he decided, the likeliest way to find his quarry. Since he was offering himself as the hunted as well as the hunter, there was little sense in waiting in a static blind. Concealing himself would have defeated his purpose, and there was little chance of seeing anything moving on the moors unless it came to him.

Wetherby walked on at a regular pace, carefully avoiding the large rocks and occasional trees which might have offered concealment, both to expose himself and to limit the danger of a sudden, unexpected attack. He moved in a zig-zag pattern, alternately heading upwards towards the ridge and then back down towards the stream. When his pipe had burned out he whistled tunelessly for a while, the innocent sound of a man who expects nothing, who is unaware of danger. Presently he filled the pipe again, and lighted it with the match cupped in one hand so that it did not dazzle his eyes.

He was very near the spot where Randal's body had been found when he stopped and took some brandy from his flask. It seemed a peaceful place, the stream bubbling along beside him and the moon attempting to get through the clouds. It was hard to imagine sudden death here. But Wetherby didn't allow himself to be lulled into false security. He remembered the mangled body in the road as he turned up towards the ridge. There were more rocks as he drew higher and he circled around the larger ones, knowing that whatever the thing was he hunted, it had to get at him to kill him, and as long as he could see it coming he would be all right. All he needed was a few yards in which to bring his gun on to it. He came to the crest and paused, outlined against the sky from all directions. He could see the headlights of a motor-car moving along the highway and the land was a black gulf between. Somewhere in that gulf, it might be waiting, and he hoped so. He walked on.

But he didn't find it.

Or, perhaps, it didn't find him.

The King's Torso was owned by a retired naval man named Bruce Newton. Bruce was a dapper fellow with a clipped moustache and brightly checked shirts who didn't much care if he had many customers. That was why he had retired to this little pub on the seldom-travelled lane between Byron's house and the secondary road. One of the few regulars at The King's Torso was a young man named Ronald Lake, who lived with his young and recent bride in a pleasant cottage on the moors, a brisk ten minutes' walk north from the lane. Lake always walked. He had no motor-car, and there was no road leading to his cottage anyway, so he had to walk even had he not wanted to. But Lake liked walking. He had renounced the conveniences of the modern world after a few years of hectic endeavour in London, and was fortunate enough to have a wife who agreed completely with his desire for simplicity, and was perfectly happy to lead an uncomplicated life. They were both very lazy in a fine fashion. Lake had a small private income which maintained them in an economic and sufficient manner and left their time free. Lake dabbled at painting. He wasn't a good painter and knew he wasn't and didn't really care. He might have preferred to be good, given the choice, but didn't think much about it; he simply enjoyed painting and had no aspirations to fame or art. His wife was content to spend her time reading *Wuthering Heights*. They were pleasant people without pretence. Bruce liked Lake. It was the sort of customer he had visualized when deciding to become a country publican, and Lake was in the habit of strolling down to the pub four or five nights a week for a pint or two of beer. He always bought Bruce a drink on the first round and Bruce always bought the second. If he stayed for a third they played darts for it. Quite frequently, Lake was the only customer in The King's Torso, and that suited them both very nicely.

Lake stood up and stretched.

He had been working on a still life with flowers and an aubergine, and his clothes were smudged with bright reds and yellows and purple. When he pushed a fallen lock of hair back from his forehead, he left a smear of colour on his brow. Lake didn't concern himself with such trifles. His wife was reading in an armchair by the fire, a pretty young woman who might be overweight in later years.

"Well, that's enough for tonight," Lake said.

"Ummm."

"I think maybe I'll toddle on down to Bruce's for half an hour, dear."

"Ummm."

"Want to come?"

"Oh, I think not. I'll just read for a while, darling. I'll wait up for you." She smiled and turned back to her book. Lake looked admiringly at the clean line of her neck. He loved her very much and considered himself a very fortunate man; often he wished he were able to express his love more intensely, but he knew it wasn't necessary. He bent over and kissed her neck and she smiled without looking up.

"I'll be back soon, dear," Lake said.

He pulled a corduroy jacket on and tied a woollen scarf around his neck as he went out. He closed the door behind him and heard the latch drop into place. There was no lock on the door—in keeping with a simple life. After all, they had no enemies and nothing of much value, and locks had no place in such a way of life.

Lake walked quite rapidly for one of such a lackadaisical nature, swinging his arms vigorously. He could see the lights of the pub ahead and, to his right and somewhat farther away, the lights of Byron's big house. He had never met Byron, and thought without envy that it might be pleasant to live in such a grand home. But it was only a fleeting idea. He came out on the lane and walked on down to the pub. There were no customers. Bruce was leaning on the bar chewing a toothpick and a cosy fire jumped in the grate.

"Didn't expect to see you tonight," Bruce said.

"Oh?"

Bruce was filling a pint mug without asking.

"I thought you wouldn't be walking around at night with this killer on the prowl."

"Killer?" Lake asked. He scratched his head.

"Haven't you seen the papers?"

"Well, I never take the papers. Since I renounced the hurly-burly of life I find no interest in the affairs of the world."

"Yeah. Well this happened right near here. Two men have been killed in the last few days. Did you know old Randal?"

"Randal? The odd old fellow? Sure, I've seen him around."

"Well, he was the first victim."

"Good Lord."

"Then there was some salesman fella last night. Got done right up the road."

"A maniac?"

Bruce shrugged.

"They say it's some kind of animal. Must have escaped from a zoo somewhere. I had a copper in here this afternoon, told me all about it. Said he was driving some big-game hunter around, someone they brought down from London. So I guess it's an animal, all right."

Lake glanced towards the window.

"So I wouldn't be all that keen on walking around after dark," Bruce said.

"Oh, I'll be all right."

They each took a drink.

"I don't suppose I should leave Hazel home alone, though. She doesn't know anything about this, if she heard something prowling about outside she might go out to have a look."

"That wouldn't do," Bruce said.

"What sort of animal do they figure it is?"

"Well, this copper that was here wouldn't say. Claimed he didn't know. But I figure they know all right, it's just that coppers never tell you anything. The way I see it, if they brought this geezer down from London, they must have a pretty fair idea what he's supposed to shoot. That figures, doesn't it?"

Lake nodded doubtfully. He was troubled, not so much by death itself, but by the concept that death could intrude on his peaceful existence. He finished his pint.

"Have one with me," Bruce said.

"Well . . . maybe I'd better get back home. Just in case. I wouldn't want Hazel to be frightened."

"Yeah. You'd better be careful yourself. If I were you I'd move a bit lively across the moor. They say it tore old Randal to pieces." Bruce nodded then, as an afterthought of less importance, said, "The salesman bloke, too."

Lake looked a trifle uneasy.

"Well, thanks for warning me," he said. He moved to the door and hesitated. The night was dark and the idea of another pint attractive. But he couldn't very well leave Hazel alone. He waved to Bruce and went out. He walked down the lane more rapidly than usual, his shoulders hunched. The cold was very noticeable and he shivered, wishing that he had worn a warmer coat. He left the lane through a gap in the hedgerow and started across the familiar route to his cottage, following the contour of the land rather than a definite footpath. He noticed that the lights were out at the manor house and glanced at his wristwatch, squinting in the dark; he had only been gone twenty-five minutes. He told himself there was nothing to worry about and smiled at himself as he looked nervously over his shoulder. He wondered if Bruce had been pulling his leg. The idea of some man-killing animal stalking these civilized lands was absurd . . . as absurd as the eerie feeling he had of being watched or followed. But he walked even faster, so that he was breathing quite heavily by the time he could see the lights from his cottage. Some of his tenseness left him then, and he slowed down for a moment, then frowned. He saw the little square of illumination from the window, but he saw another pillar of light beside it, a narrow ledge cast out on the ground which could only have come from the doorway. The door was ajar. He looked around quickly and stumbled as his pace increased once more.

The door was open a few inches and Lake was shivering as he walked into the geometric rectangle of light that dropped from the opening. He pushed the door before him and went in, then smiled. His fear had been ridiculous, the dark night had seized his imagination. Everything was as it had been when he left. He could see his wife's arm on the chair.

"I'm home, dear," he said.

There was no reply.

Lake wandered towards his easel. The bright reds and yellows flooded his vision. There seemed to be too much red. Lake noticed that he had been more careless than usual with his paint, there were heavy red smears on the carpet and red paint was dripping from the bookcase. His face clouded. It looked as if he had absent-mindedly squirted the oil from the tube in all directions. There was even a long red smear across the back of Hazel's chair. That must have happened when he'd bent over to kiss her neck, Lake thought. He remembered standing in this same spot, looking at the line of his wife's neck and thinking how fortunate he was. He looked now, but he could not see her neck. Only the red smear. He hoped she had not leaned back and got the paint in her hair.

"Are you awake, dear?"

There was no reply.

"Bruce was telling me a rather disturbing thing . . ."

His wife was silent.

She must have fallen asleep, Lake thought. He moved towards her chair. He thought he'd better wipe that paint away before she straightened up and rubbed her head across it. It didn't seem the right colour, somehow. It was a darker red than he had been using on the canvas. He looked back towards the painting, wondering about that, and reached down to touch his wife on the shoulder. His hand was on her left shoulder and he was looking back at the canvas. The red seemed to be lighter there. He let his hand slide over to stroke Hazel's hair. It slid on to her right shoulder. There seemed to be a great deal of slippery oil paint all over her shoulders.

Lake turned, very slowly, and looked down into the chair . . .

Wetherby had the reflexes of the hunter.

He was crouched, the rifle levelled, before the sound registered in his conscious brain. His finger caressed the trigger and his nerves vibrated with the jangling surge of adrenalin, the heart-stopping song of action. And then the magic of readiness was gone, and he cursed silently.

"Wetherby!" Thurlow called.

Thurlow's torch turned in an arc across the heather.

Wetherby pushed the safety catch back on and came out of his crouch. Thurlow jumped, startled, and Wetherby saw that the detective carried a shotgun in nervous hands.

"It's all right," he called.

He advanced. Thurlow stood waiting. Wetherby had just descended from the line of tors and Thurlow had come from the lane.

"Here you are," Thurlow said. He pointed the shotgun away.

"Damn! If the killer was around, you've certainly given him warning," Wetherby said. "I told Bell I didn't want any interference."

"Bell sent me to find you, sir."

"Did you have to be so obvious?"

"Sorry if I startled you," Thurlow said. He didn't sound apologetic.

"Apart from the fact I might have shot you, you've ruined any chance of finding this beast."

"It's too late for stealth tonight."

Wetherby started to reply, then paused. He looked at Thurlow's eyes and saw the truth adumbrated there.

"It's killed again," he said. It wasn't a question, and Thurlow nodded, pointing back towards the lane.

"Just on the other side of the lane," he said.

They headed back together.

The bright flash of bulbs whitened the little room; whitened the pale faces of the detectives who were dusting for prints, and blackened the streams of blood. Lake sat in the corner, staring at his red hands with the wide eyes of shock and horror. The full reality had not yet pierced the defences of his sanity. Bell said nothing. He pointed towards the chair and Wetherby crossed the room and looked into it. He winced. He hadn't expected it to be a woman. *Wuthering Heights* was in her lap, one page half torn out, her lifeless hand drooped over the arm of the chair and her legs were extended towards the dying fire. Her shoulders met in a dark mass of gore. The chair was torn with the marks of bloody claws.

"Well?" Bell asked.

Wetherby felt his vocal cords rebel as he started to speak. He closed his eyes against the surge of nausea.

"An animal?" Bell asked.

"It has to be. An animal or some dark fiend from hell itself."

"But how did it get in?"

Lake moaned.

"I closed the door," he said.

"Get him out of here," Bell said.

Thurlow moved towards Lake. Lake would not move. His limbs were solid and would not bend.

"It was closed," he said.

Wetherby looked at Bell. Bell grimaced. They moved back behind the chair, but they could still see her hand hanging over the arm; saw a heavy drop of blood move sluggishly down her middle finger and dangle for a moment before it dropped to the carpet. It made a remarkably wet sound as it merged with the blood beneath. Thurlow and a constable were attempting to get Lake to his feet.

"Whatever it was, it opened the door," Bell said.

"Locked?"

"No. There isn't a lock. But it's on a latch, it has to be lifted from the outside." They moved to the door. A detective was dusting the latch and they waited until he had finished. A photographer flashed a photo of it. There was no blood on the door. Wetherby squatted, judging the distance from the ground to the latch.

"What creature that left those claw marks could have opened a door?" Bell asked. It was obviously rhetorical. They stepped aside as Thurlow led Lake out. Lake was still looking at his hands.

"I thought it was paint," he said.

He laughed suddenly, an abrupt burst of laughter followed by a hysterical giggling which choked into a sob. Thurlow guided him towards a police van which had come bumping across the moors. He got in willingly enough, sitting rigidly in the seat. The constable got in beside him and Thurlow came back.

"There's something here we don't understand," he said.

"That's a goddamn brilliant statement," Bell snapped.

"No, I don't mean that." He looked at Bell, a searching glance, and Bell turned his eyes away. "Something we may never know," Thurlow said. "Something beyond the comprehension of man, perhaps . . . I think I believe that, sir. Something of ancient legend and derided superstition is stalking these moors at night. If it were . . . anything . . . it wouldn't surprise me."

"Shut up, Thurlow."

Thurlow shook his head.

"I can't help what I feel, sir," he said. "You can't alter that."

"You're tired. You aren't being rational."

Thurlow shrugged. He clamped his mouth closed, but he looked at the chair, and then he looked at the latch on the door.

9

The body had been removed, the police experts had made a thorough search which revealed nothing, and Wetherby and Bell remained in the cottage. Wetherby didn't expect to find anything that had escaped the keen and practised eyes of the police, but he hoped he might possibly see something in a different light, place a new interpretation on something already noticed and passed over. But there was nothing. Not a single hair had the animal shed, which was surprising considering the ferocity of its attack. There were plenty of claw marks etched in blood, but only around and on the chair. No bloody trail led to the door. It seemed almost as if the killer had wiped his bloody talons clean on the carpet before slinking off.

"You don't recognize those marks?" Bell asked, without hope.

"No. This is more difficult than prints on the ground. They were long, sharp claws but it isn't possible to tell more than that. There may be some prints outside, though. Although, as you've undoubtedly noticed the blood trail doesn't return to the door. Unless this beast can leap a considerable distance from a standstill, or fly, it appears that it has quite deliberately covered its tracks."

"Shall we look outside?"

"We can try, although I think we'll have a better chance in the morning."

They moved to the door. The lights of a motor vehicle came bobbing towards them, rising and falling over the uncertain terrain. Wetherby crouched and inspected the ground beside the door in the beam of his torch. He found nothing. The ground was fairly firm, but some track should have been left. The vehicle drew nearer, the twin beams flashed on the cottage wall and stopped moving. A door closed and a confused, howling din arose. The headlights went out and a single torch beam moved towards the cottage, bringing the noise with it. Thurlow came over.

"The dogs are here, sir," he said.

"I have ears," Bell said.

"There's nothing here," Wetherby said, standing up. The dogs were straining and baying on their leads and the handler had difficulty in restraining them. Bell snapped quick instructions to the handler. He didn't like using dogs, they had no part in his way of detection ... an element from the past, before scientific methods, and he had summoned them as a last resort when science was baffled. But he didn't like it. There was nothing about this case that he liked.

"You'd better wait," he said to Wetherby. "If these brutes can pick up the scent I'd like you to come."

"Of course."

"If there is a scent, they'll find it," the handler said, his loyalty stung by the reference to brutes.

"Well, get on with it then."

The handler took the dogs into the cottage. Wetherby and Bell waited outside. A cold wind was dipping across the land, singing a background mood below the excited cries of the dogs. Both men were struck by a feeling of displacement, as if this scene were occurring in the past, was somehow not real, as if they stood apart and observed but had no part in it. Thurlow's face reflected his own thoughts, and he said nothing. The dogs came crowding en masse through the door, tugging against their leads and digging at the ground.

"There's a scent in there, all right," the handler said. "I can smell it myself."

Wetherby nodded.

"You noticed it?" Bell asked.

"Vaguely. It must have been quite strong before the room was filled with cigarette smoke and sweating men. But it was still noticeable. Like the prints, it's somehow familiar to me but I just can't place it."

"An animal smell?"

"Certainly not a human smell."

"This killer must be some animal," Bell said. "Some frightfully clever animal that can open doors and cover its tracks behind it . . . so clever that it leads us to believe it must be human, even. But why in hell does it kill? The other two . . . it might have suddenly been disturbed by them, been frightened or attacked through instinct when they fled . . . but this . . . it came into this cottage. It opened the door and deliberately entered to kill. Purely for the love of killing, the desire to destroy. If it is an animal—and it seems it must be—we can forget about a pattern, of course. But there must be some motive; even animals act for some reason. But why? We can eliminate hunger, it doesn't eat its victims . . ." Bell paused. His face twisted in a terrible grimace.

"Unless," he said. "Unless it eats only the heads."

Somehow, for some reason which was strictly emotional and strictly human, it was a terrible concept.

The dogs set out in a determined fashion, as if they knew their job and were proceeding to do it well. Ten minutes later they were as baffled as their masters. They didn't seem to know what was expected of them, what trail to follow. They tried to branch off in various directions, snapping at each other in their frustration. Wetherby took careful note of their actions. He had worked with dogs before, and he understood them. He knew that they were defeated before the dogs themselves knew it. He remembered how the tracks had changed as they left the road on the previous trail, and wondered if this was what was throwing them off the scent somehow. It seemed unlikely, far more unlikely than the changing tracks themselves. It was not inconceivable that a beast would run on four feet and walk on two, but the idea that it could also change its scent was a different matter. And yet the fact remained that the dogs could not follow it over open ground. There was no water to hide the trail, no tree into which it could have climbed, but the scent abruptly halted a few hundred feet from the cottage door. The handler was leading the dogs in a circle around the cottage in an attempt to pick up a second trail, in case the killer had backtracked, and Wetherby looked up at the sky. It was preposterous to imagine a creature with those other characteristics flying, and he didn't believe it possible, but he looked upwards. He didn't know what he expected to see moving across that dark sky, but all he saw were clouds.

"Apparently it has obliterated its scent, somehow," the handler said. He looked annoyed. "The dogs can't seem to follow it beyond this point."

"Then get those howling fiends away from here," Bell snapped. And they were indeed howling, not in the excitement they had showed upon arrival, but in a tone that showed their absolute frustration, their tails lowered and their eyes baleful. They followed their handler back to the van willingly, whining now. The door slammed after them.

"Want to try in the morning?" Bell asked.

"I'll try. But I wouldn't hope for much, Justin. If it can lose a pack of trained dogs so easily—"

"Dogs!" he snorted.

"Don't underestimate the dogs," Wetherby said. "I would have thought they could follow it. Not very far, perhaps, but certainly until it had reached water or trees, some means of breaking the scent."

"I honestly don't know what else to do," Bell said. He gestured with open palms upwards. "Maybe this isn't a police matter at all, I don't know. Maybe I should put you in charge. Our methods don't seem very effective. How do you apply modern detection against something that kills without motive? Without a common denominator among the victims? Even with a madman, some pattern emerges. We could catch Jack the Ripper if he were still around, his murders had a pattern. His victims were prostitutes. But this thing . . . it doesn't kill whores, or poachers or salesmen or housewives.

It merely kills. It seems to leave an abundance of evidence at the scene, but no way to follow it or deduce where it has gone. What in hell do I do, John?"

Wetherby didn't know.

10

They returned in the morning, dull with the anticipation of futility. The driver pulled over to the edge of the lane just beyond The King's Torso. They couldn't quite see the cottage from there because the land rolled up between. Bell told the driver to stay with the car and they got out. The driver lighted a cigarette and settled for the wait. A man came down the lane, wearing a belted trench-coat and a felt hat and walking with a bouncy step. He had been standing outside The King's Torso, waiting for them. Bell scowled. It was Aaron Rose, the reporter, looking exceptionally eager as he approached. Another man followed behind him with a camera slung over his shoulder.

"Any comments for the Press?" he asked.

"None."

"Can you predict when you'll be making an arrest?"

He had his notebook out.

"How in hell can I? I don't even know what we're going to arrest, let alone when."

"May I quote that?"

"For Christ's sake no."

"You didn't make any comments to the reporters back at the hotel, did you?" Rose asked, suddenly afraid that he'd blundered by anticipation, by arriving here ahead of the police.

Bell didn't answer. He moved towards the break in the hedgerow and Wetherby followed.

"Mind if I tag along?" Rose asked.

"Yes," Bell said, with neither sarcasm nor anger.

"Oh. Well, is it all right to take some pictures at the cottage? The constable there wouldn't let us in earlier."

"Yes, I do mind. Especially for that rag you work for."

Rose winced at such reference to the Press.

"Listen, you wait here. Perhaps I'll have a statement when I get back. All right?"

"Yeah. Sure."

Rose watched the two men walk away. The photographer fingered his camera eagerly. All he had photographed so far was the exterior of the cottage, and he was feeling slighted. But Rose suddenly blinked; his expression changed. He had just realized what line his story should take. Murders were one a hundred, man-killing beasts a novelty but not unheard of. What he needed was a completely different approach, a means of capitalizing on the shock and horror of human torment in the greatest possible manner. This was Rose's first big assignment and he desperately wanted to make it a success for sensational journalism.

"I think I've got it," he said.

"Huh?"

"The angle. I think I have an idea."

The photographer grunted. He resented ideas. They could not be captured on film. Rose began to walk slowly back towards the pub, his mind leaping violently. He didn't for a moment believe what he intended to write, but that was of no importance whatsoever. Few of the readers would believe it, either. But they would see the startling headline, and they would buy the paper, and Aaron Rose would be a success. He was impatient to begin his story, and annoyed that he knew so little background material; he wished he were in London so he could go to the library and gather knowledge of lycanthropy, to add a touch of learning as a sober background for the sensational headline. He visualized how that headline would look in print . . . how it would scream from the front page.

Does a werewolf stalk the moors?

Surprisingly, there were tracks.

The ground was firm, and Wetherby had not expected to find tracks, but they were there and they were obvious, deep and plain. They came from the house, but did not begin at the house. The ground hadn't changed, it was as firm as it was by the door, but the tracks began some distance away and continued in a straight line heading roughly north, and then they stopped. They went in the same direction that the dogs had attempted to follow the scent, and they began just about where the dogs had lost the scent. It was as if the trail had been deliberately left at this point, or deliberately erased on both sides, and the inconsistency was baffling. A creature able to move without trace wouldn't have blundered at random points, unless it was a deliberate attempt to lead its pursuers in a false direction. But then it seemed that the trail would have been left from the cottage itself, not beginning at a point some hundred yards beyond.

"It walked here," Wetherby said.

"On two legs?"

Wetherby nodded.

Bell looked back towards the cottage. A uniformed policeman stood by the door.

"Nothing could have jumped this far," he said.

"Nothing we know about."

"Could it have run to here, and only left the trail when it began to walk?"

Wetherby shrugged.

"I'm beginning to think this creature can do anything."

"The dogs . . ."

Wetherby nodded grimly.

The dogs had followed the scent to the point where the tracks began. No farther. They had not followed where the tracks were obvious in the ground, where the scent, if it existed at all, should certainly have been. Even Bell understood that there were implications to that—implications that led to far-fetched and mind-staggering conclusions.

"But an animal—or a man—can't simply cease to leave a scent," Bell said. "Certainly not where it has left an obvious trail."

"That's right. But if the dogs had followed a certain scent to this point—the scent that they had followed from the cottage, a strong and noticeable scent—and that specific scent suddenly changed—"

Wetherby paused, not sure what he wanted to say, knowing what he thought, but hesitating to voice it.

"When the creature began to walk on two legs—"

Bell was watching him closely.

"If some change occurred—if it was, in some way, no longer the same creature that had run on all fours—"

"It's possible," Bell whispered. He hadn't meant to whisper.

"I know," Wetherby said.

But there were the tracks, commencing where the scent had ceased—where the dogs had lost the trail of the creature that had killed at the cottage, and where that creature had begun to walk like a man . . .

Wetherby could find no further tracks in that general direction, and once more he attempted to pick up the trail by following a circle with the cottage as the centre. Bell walked behind him in silence. The first circle was completed without finding anything, and Wetherby suggested that they move farther from the cabin and make another attempt. They both realized that it was futile, but there was nothing else to do, and they felt a great need to be doing something. They walked north from the cabin for perhaps half a mile, then turned in an arc to the west, circling and keeping the cottage as equidistant as unaided judgement could manage. The circumference of this path was thus about three miles, and they moved slowly. Wetherby paused to inspect the ground from time to time, spreading the grass and heather and pushing with his finger to test the resistance. They left no tracks themselves, and found none. The circle passed within a few hundred yards of Byron's house, turned back towards the east and skirted the lane, went on behind The King's Torso as far as the trees that bordered the secondary road and then curved back towards the starting point. They arrived back where they had begun and had found nothing. The sky was darkening and there was a smell of impending rain. They stood and looked helplessly at one another, then headed back towards the lane without speaking.

This course brought them to the line of tracks once more.

"I expect I'd better send a team out here to take casts," Bell said.

"Purely for routine," Wetherby said. "These tracks are the same as the others, the casts won't be different."

"I've been thinking about what you said," Bell said, looking towards the cottage. "If—if such a change were possible, how would it account for these tracks being plain here and then abruptly stopping?"

Wetherby, too, had been thinking. They were not thoughts that he liked, conclusions that fitted the facts but were alien to all his beliefs . . . more, they were alien to his disbeliefs. He pondered for a few moments before he spoke.

"Granting such a metamorphosis, which I don't . . . it seems obvious. A creature, a beast running on all fours suddenly undergoes a transformation. It becomes a creature that walks on two legs. Such a change would certainly have the strongest possible side effects. Perhaps even unconsciousness. And then, after a while, the creature, the changed creature, would stagger off in a stupor, perhaps not remembering how he had come to this place or suffering unbelievable horror and remorse. It might stagger away for a short distance in this half-conscious state before it realized the possible consequences of what it had done in its previous form. That would be when it might begin to cover its tracks, through instinctive self-preservation. This is all idle conjecture, of course. It isn't possible . . ."

"Not the remorse, anyway," Bell said.

Wetherby looked at him. Granted the initial premise, that had seemed valid enough.

"If it felt remorse it would want to get as far away as possible and try to forget what it had been responsible for, wouldn't it?"

Wetherby nodded.

"It wouldn't take the head with it, as a gruesome reminder."

"I guess not," Wetherby said, and they continued back to the lane. They came through the hedgerow by the police car. The driver had his hat pulled down and was sleeping. He snored slightly.

"I need a drink," Bell said.

Wetherby nodded. They walked past the car towards The King's Torso. They both needed a drink, although neither was thirsty.

Aaron Rose was suffering a conflict of conscience and ambition. He sat at the bar of The King's Torso with his notebook open beside his beer. The photographer sat beside him. He had his camera beside his beer, but had no conscience outside the frame of a lens. He drank quickly but Rose sipped at his beer and considered his plight. Not that he had any choice in the matter, there was no decision he had to make and no way he could influence the results. But Rose was a man who worried about everything, and at the moment he was worried because his hopes were divided. It was quite simple, really, although nothing is simple to a man who worries. As a man, a man with a conscience, Rose hoped that the killer would be captured or slain before he killed again. The last killing had particularly influenced him in this, because it seemed far worse than the others, there was something so tragic about a young woman dying helplessly and horribly in her own home. But, as a junior reporter on his first big assignment, he hoped that the killer would not be found before the weekend, so that his story would not be obsolete for the Sunday edition. The report of a capture would not be nearly as thrilling and sensational as the story of these terrible unsolved crimes, especially the story he intended to write. Even any hint that the police were on the trail of the killer would dampen the shock value, for that depended totally on the terror of the unknown. Rose had the proper instinct and knew what sold newspapers. But, because he was a worrier with a conscience, and despite the fact that he could affect the result in no way, Rose was suffering with his hopes, and because he was basically an honest man he admitted his hopes even to himself. He admitted that he hoped the killer would not be uncovered before the weekend, provided of course that it did not kill again. Of course. And his face twisted in anxiety as he realized that a further killing would greatly enhance the value of his story. That provided a new conflict, far more terrible than the first, and his face provided the battleground of his emotions.

Rose turned as the door opened. Wetherby and Bell went up to the bar and Bruce moved down to serve them.

"You cops?" he asked. He looked very sad.

"I am," Bell said.

"I'm a reporter," Rose said, and mentioned his paper.

"Any luck?" Bruce asked.

Bell said, "I'll have a pint."

"No luck, eh? Can't you follow this animal's tracks or something? I mean, you got to do something. You can't have something like this running around killing people, can you? Why aren't you out looking for clues or evidence or something?"

Rose slid his notebook up the bar, sensing a local colour angle.

"We'll get it. In time," Bell said.

"Time? And what about the meantime? You gonna let it kill more innocent people?"

"Don't you feel the police are doing enough?" Rose asked. "As a local citizen, I mean?"

Bruce ignored him.

"Give me a beer, will you," Bell said.

Bruce shrugged and began filling a pint. He said, "Guess I didn't mean to snap at you, but Mrs Lake was a fine person. Her husband is a regular here. It was a terrible thing." He shook his head and shoved the pint over the bar. "Can't you get the Army down here or something? Organize a search? They'd find it all right."

"I'll consider your advice," Bell said.

"You ought to."

"Brandy," Wetherby said.

"Can I quote you? About the Army?"

"You can just shut up, for God's sake."

"My readers have a right to know."

"Readers? You think people read that rag you work for? They just buy it for the pictures of naked women and the juicier divorce cases."

Rose looked hurt.

"He's right, you know," Bruce said. "That's the only reason I ever buy it."

"Can I quote that?" Rose asked, then frowned and thought better of it. He leaned sullenly on the bar beside Bell. Bruce set Wetherby's brandy down and Wetherby took a long drink, discarding the ritual of smell and taste. It went down well. Some of the tenseness left him, the mental construction of fact without belief. He took a second swallow and the door opened. Byron came in.

"Saw the car down the road," he said. He had a heavy walking stick and a tweed cap. He walked over to the bar and stood beside Wetherby. Bell turned slightly away.

"Are you pursuing your investigations here?" Byron asked.

Wetherby saw Bell tense. He said, "I suppose you've heard about last night?"

Byron nodded. Bell doused his anger with beer.

"Any tracks?" Byron asked.

"Some. Not enough to follow."

"No? That's a shame. I thought that by now your old skill might have returned."

"No one could have followed that trail," Wetherby said.

Byron smiled. He ordered a beer and leaned his stick against the bar. Bruce slid the beer over.

"You're welcome to try," Bell said.

Byron shook his head.

"But you're the man who's always right, aren't you? Well, this is a challenge for you. Wetherby says that no man could follow that trail. What about it?"

"Oh, doubtless he's right," Byron said, smiling again.

Bruce said, "Didn't you used to be a big-game hunter, Mr Byron?"

"I am a hunter. Yes. You misuse the past tense, my man."

"Can't you maybe find the killer?"

"I haven't tried."

Bruce looked from Byron to Bell.

"If you cops didn't want all the glory for yourselves—"

Bell said, "Mr Byron has declined to assist us. I asked him."

Bruce looked at Byron again.

"It's no concern of mine," Byron said.

"No concern—are you crazy? Don't you care that these people were killed?" He leaned on the bar, his thin face pointing at Byron. Byron placidly sipped his beer. "Hazel Lake was killed last night," Bruce said. "Did you know her? She never harmed a soul, never did a bad thing in her life—"

"I expect she never did a thing. Full stop."

Bruce blinked. He looked like an angry badger. Blood flushed darkly into his face. "I don't want your custom," he said. "Drink up and get out of here."

Byron paused, the mug half raised. He was balanced between anger and amusement. Confronted by a man who did not understand his concepts, Byron hovered between scorn and rage for a moment. And then he laughed.

"Ah, you are angry," he said. He set the mug down on the bar. "That's good. I like to see a man in anger, with the courage to speak . . . courage in his beliefs, stupid as they may be. It is, at least, a living emotion."

"If I come over this bar, these cops will have to pull me off you," Bruce said. He was half Byron's size and he trembled with his sudden hatred.

"And what about you, Justin?" Byron asked. "Are you feeling anything? Does any semblance of activity begin to surge sluggishly behind that policeman's face? Or is it a policeman's mind that vegetates there?"

"What in hell is wrong with you?" Wetherby asked.

"Wrong? Nothing. Perhaps I'm a trifle outspoken. But don't you see? If people feel anything, even anger, or fear, even doubt, then at least they are alive." He stared at Wetherby for a moment. "If you are alive enough, then you will find your killer," he said.

Byron turned and walked out, tapping his stick along the floor. He didn't hurry. Bruce's eyes bulged after him, as though he wanted to send his eyeballs like bullets into Byron's back.

"That heartless bastard," he muttered.

Rose was gaping.

"Who was that?" he asked.

No one answered him. Byron was gone, and he had left a vacuum of black silence behind him . . . a vacuum which only their own thoughts could fill, and they were not pleasant thoughts and they led towards unspeakable conclusions.

II

Fear stood over the land.

It was a blanket of fear, invisible but oppressive and intense, and it covered the moors like an overcast sky, more ominous than an impending storm. The fear was all the greater because the people did not know what it was they feared, what the monstrous being was that had three times struck so terribly. They no longer spoke of it often, as they had at first, for the fear had increased with each killing and reached absolute intensity with the death of Hazel Lake, peacefully reading by her fireside. This was a people who had long regarded their home as their castle, sanctuary inviolate, and a new dimension was added to their terror. Nowhere was safe, this fiend might come at any time, to any place, and anyone might be his next victim. It wasn't death itself that brought such consuming fear, it was the unknown quality of that death, the method of dying and the agony of wondering if the creature would strike again . . .

where it would strike ... whom it would kill. Superstition, never far below the surface of civilized minds, came bubbling up in globules of terror, bursting and enflaming the brain.

The national newspapers played up the horror, capitalizing on shock, and sensationalism sold papers throughout the rest of the country. But in those few square miles where the creature had struck, it was pure fear that sold papers, and trembling hands that held them opened to the headlines of horror. The majority of the papers played with the angle of doubt, the uncertainty whether it was man or beast, but Aaron Rose's scandal sheet pulled out all the stops on the lycanthrope line. The editor was immensely pleased with Rose's story, and ran a companion piece dealing with the supposedly recorded instances of werewolves, and ghouls in the Balkans and, killing two birds with one stone, hinted that the killer was obviously an immigrant or at least of foreign extraction, since Englishmen were never werewolves. The editorial questioned police efficiency in no uncertain terms, asking whether any attempt had been made to establish a lunar cycle and whether the amount of blood remaining in the corpses had been measured, on the chance that it might be a vampire. No one connected with the paper believed the story line, certainly, but that didn't matter at all.

Aaron Rose was not as pleased with his success as he might have been, however. He was closer to the killings and farther from the editorial offices, and he felt the fear surrounding him. He worried, thinking that his story might have added to that fear, but justified himself by thinking that it was just as well that the people were afraid, that it would make them more cautious. When he was not worrying, he was planning his next story, intending to focus it around local comment and opinion, but he found that more difficult than he had imagined. People who would normally have jumped at a chance to be quoted in a national newspaper looked at him solemnly and said nothing; they resented being asked to comment about something so overwhelming, so tragic and so close to home. It was far beyond the point of being a topic of conversation. Rose abandoned the direct approach and went into the nearest market town to mingle with the populace and overhear their private words. It was a small village on the moors with narrow cobbled streets and several cheerful-looking pubs, but when he entered the pubs the pervading sense of gloom was severe. Faces were pale in the gloomy interior and conversation was hushed and solemn. Rose settled himself in a dark corner and listened. He heard one bold fellow announce that this killer was a fiend and should be tortured to death, but heard several whisper the question that plagued them all: what is this thing that walks among us in the night? And when Aaron Rose looked into their eyes, he knew that everyone shared the common thought: who is next? Who is next? And Rose felt a sympathetic twinge of the freezing fear that closed its fetid talons on these people; he felt it reach out to grasp at his own heart . . .

The police were helpless, and Justin Bell underwent agonies of indecision, not knowing whether to concentrate his search on man or beast, and beleaguered by dark concepts he hadn't known lurked in his mind—unspoken and vague primordial fears that had been carried through the aeons since man's ancestors crawled out of the slime and began their ascent. He told himself that it was an anamorphosis, a deformed figure which would appear in proportion if only he could view it correctly, but at the same time he feared it was something that could never be shaped by human logic, something beyond the understanding of man because it was more than man and less than man, some monstrous combination of man and beast from a dimension apart from ours. At times, in the light of day, he ridiculed himself for such fanciful thoughts, but in the night the facts came tumbling back—it walked as a man and ran as a beast, it possessed talons that could shred human flesh and still open doors, the strength to tear a man's head off and the grisly desire to carry that head away to its lair. It could change its tracks and alter its scent, and was transmogrification beyond such a being?

Bell began to place more and more faith in Wetherby, perhaps with a subconscious desire to relieve himself of some of the terrible burden of helplessness and absolve himself of some of the guilt if it killed again . . .

And Wetherby failed.

Each night he walked the windswept moors and each morning he returned tired and drawn with more than physical fatigue. It had ceased to be a pleasure. Alone in the night, his shoulder-blades drew together across the icy bridge of his backbone, and he had a constant and terrible sensation that he was being watched; that the creature followed him and waited for him; that it had the ability to differentiate between a helpless victim and a dangerous opponent, and was waiting for Wetherby to make the fatal slip, the sudden irrevocable blunder through lack of concentration or failure of awareness which would transform him from hunter to hunted, opponent to victim. At times this feeling of being watched was so powerful that Wetherby halted abruptly and spun about, crouched and ready, positive that the creature was behind him. But he saw nothing. At other moments, loathing his own fear, he would shout aloud as a challenge to the unseen beast and stand tense and strained, listening for an answer that did not come, listening to silence on those anechoic moors.

Wetherby was not a man of fear.

He had never taken deliberate chances as Byron did, but he had never declined a necessary risk. He had followed wounded lions into thick bush and faced charging buffalo with steady nerves, but this uncertainty ate at his courage, the sensation of being watched from the dark devoured his confidence, and he knew he would soon begin to make mistakes; knew he could afford no mistakes; began to believe that Byron had been right, that he had lost his skill and grown soft. It was necessary to force himself away from the warmth of the hotel as night fell, and he had no willing determination left—only the lever of pride to keep him at his quest. And when another night's vigil was over, he had to admit the relief he felt at returning to his comfortable bedroom once more . . . the desire to crawl into his bed and sleep which went far beyond physical tiredness.

But he did not sleep well.

He drew the blinds against the dawn and went to bed, but when sleep came it was disturbed. He dreamed. Confused images danced through his mind, snatches from the past mingled with some uncertain future, a jumbled connexion between the two binding them together. He saw the dream image of himself, felt the heaviness of his limbs and knew he could not move quickly; heard a howling wind and felt a cold solitude, and then there was a rush, sudden and blinding, and he moved very slowly to face it, his rifle stiff and unmanageable in his hands. The creature was upon him, he felt its foul breath flow over his face, felt fangs sink into his flesh and fiendish haunches draw up for the fatal stroke. He looked into the creature's face—and awoke, sweating and writhing in his bed, with only a nightmare hint of what the creature had been, only a half-remembered glimpse of a near-human countenance; and half-awake, Wetherby wondered where he could have a silver bullet moulded . . .

Wetherby was sitting in the hotel lounge with Aaron Rose when Byron walked in. Wetherby had become rather fond of Rose. He realized that the reporter had depths beyond ambition, and found him pleasant company when he was not inscribing the conversation in his notebook. Ambition was not the same thing to Wetherby as it was to Rose, because he had never needed success in the same fashion, but he could sympathize with it, and tolerate it. Rose noticed Byron first, and remembered him from that rather violent conversation at The King's Torso. Byron was memorable. Wetherby was surprised to see him there, and for some reason could not remember whether he was angry with Byron or not. It was some paradox of the emotions that Byron inspired in him.

"Good morning," Byron said.

He smiled pleasantly. He was wearing shabby tweeds and had a fine pair of field-glasses slung over his shoulder. A metal badge hung from his lapel.

"I'm on my way to the races," he said. "Newton Abbot. Thought you might care to join me."

For a moment, Wetherby was tempted to agree. He would have liked to get away from this place, to forget all about the killings and his fruitless hunt. But he knew that the thoughts would accompany him.

"No. Thanks for asking, but I don't much feel like it now."

Byron pulled a chair up and sat down. Rose was watching him closely, with marked interest.

"You look worried, John."

"Certainly I'm worried."

"No results as yet, I take it?"

"No, nothing. I've been out there every night without a glimpse or a sound. Nothing at all. And yet I get the feeling that I've been very close to it many times. You know the sensation, Byron. The eerie feeling that I'm being watched. That it is waiting for me to blunder. The same way you feel when you're after a wounded buffalo and you know damn well that it has doubled back and is waiting beside the trail."

"Yes, I know the feeling," Byron said. He made it sound like a great pleasure, a sensation in which he took delight.

"If only I could be sure . . ."

"Sure? Sure of what?"

"If I knew for certain it was waiting for me, it would be better. I would be calmer. But I can't tell, I don't know if my sense is reliable or if my mind is playing tricks."

"Ah, John. You may lose your reflexes but you never lose your intuition. If you feel it is there, it is there. Uncertainty is a civilized trait, don't let self-doubt take command. When you stalked a wounded buffalo, you had no doubts. You knew it was waiting. You didn't know when it would come, or where it would come from, but you knew positively that it would come. And it did. You didn't have much time, John. A buffalo comes with its head lowered and the boss protecting its head and you had to shoot fast and well the first time. You did, of course, because you are sitting here alive. But in those days you knew it was coming. And now you tell me that you can't be sure, that you can't trust your sensations?" He looked into Wetherby's eyes and cold fingers walked up Wetherby's vertebrae.

"You've lost it all, John," he said, softly. "When this thing wants you, it will take you. It will wait and you will be too slow and it will take you. When it wants."

Wetherby and Byron looked at each other, and Rose looked from one to the other with his mouth open. Then Wetherby lowered his eyes. A thought that he didn't like at all had stirred in his mind.

"Perhaps," he said.

They didn't speak for a while. Then Byron, his tone matter-of-fact now, said: "The trouble is that you are too involved, John. You feel too strongly, your mind has centred upon what this creature has done, rather than what you intend to do. This isn't a hunt, as far as you're concerned, you feel you must kill this thing before it strikes again. But, you know, these killings may not be a bad thing."

Byron looked out the window.

"I've seen people alive with fear. Seen farmers carrying guns on their way to the barn, housewives looking over their shoulders in crowded streets. They are alert, they are alive because the possibility of death hangs over their minds."

"And that isn't a bad thing?"

"I think not. When is a man more alive than on his way to the gallows? What cigarette tastes as good as the last one, when the firing squad is waiting? These deaths may well turn out to be a benefit, in the end. When they can be viewed with proper distance and objectivity. A few useless lives snuffed out, and ten thousand people granted the awareness of their existence, the joy of their survival."

"You can't believe that, Byron," Wetherby said, but he knew that Byron did.

Byron shrugged.

"Oh, it's one point of view," he said. "Are you sure you won't come with me? Steeplechasing. A dangerous game and a fine sport. A National Hunt jockey has an awareness of life which is arcane in our jaded society. I would have liked to be a steeplechase jockey. Ride in the Grand National. Think of the fullness of feeling as Becher's looms up before you and horses are thundering on all sides..." Byron's mind had wandered, he shifted in his chair as though in a saddle, then returned to reality and laughed at his daydream.

"No, I won't go," Wetherby said.

Byron shrugged. Bell appeared at the doorway, saw Byron and screwed his face up in distaste as he crossed the room. Byron stood up.

"Well, I'll be off then," he said.

He moved away, passing Bell. They didn't speak.

"Is he mad?" Rose asked.

"I often wonder."

"There's something about his voice—his tone of voice—when he speaks of danger of death. I wonder..."

Bell sat down. He showed distaste for Rose, too, but not as greatly as he had for Byron.

"Any news?" Rose asked.

"I've decided to request a massive search by the Army," Bell said. He spoke to Wetherby, but Rose got his notebook out.

"And what will they be told to look for?" Wetherby asked.

"God knows," Bell said.

Rose wrote it down faithfully.

12

Wetherby had followed the same pattern in his nightly searches, following the stream at first and then cutting back over the ridge and across the lane towards the secondary road. He saw no reason to expand this area, since it encompassed the three places where the killer had struck, but he decided to vary it by starting from the other direction. He had no hopes that this would bring results, but it was at least a variation and might make him feel less helpless and, too, if the creature had indeed been watching him he might well surprise it by approaching from the opposite direction. But he had few hopes of this, either; he felt that the creature knew exactly where he was at all times, and would make no mistakes—an eerie certainty that he would never encounter it until the creature wished him to. Wetherby hated these thoughts, for they seemed to sum up all the failure of nerve and instinct that Byron had accused him of, but they dogged his mind relentlessly, ready to pounce the moment his conscious will relaxed for a moment, clinging despite his efforts to shake them away.

Wetherby was feeling the strain of his vigil.

He came out of the hotel at dusk. It was a pleasant evening, remarkably warm and cloudless and the moors rolled away in a patchwork of moonlight. Wetherby rather wished that he had gone to the races with Byron, that he had nothing more important on his mind than to study a form book and search for a decent-priced winner. He waited at the verge of the highway for a motor-car to pass, and Aaron Rose came running after him.

"Mind if I walk along with you for a ways?"

"Of course."

They crossed the highway and headed up the secondary road.

"That's a nice-looking weapon," Rose said.

"It will do the job. If I ever get a chance to use it."

"You sound discouraged."

Wetherby shrugged.

"Listen, any chance I could come with you tonight?"

"Absolutely none."

"I'm not frightened."

"It isn't that," Wetherby said. He was almost tempted to grant the request. It would have been much easier if he had a companion. But he knew that would defeat his purpose; that the beast would never show if he were not alone, and that he would be sacrificing whatever chance he had to his failure of nerve, his growing dread of being alone. He said, "I don't want to be responsible for anyone else, and this creature would be wary if I weren't alone."

"Yeah. I guess. I admire you, going after it alone. It takes courage, Wetherby. I'd like to do an article about it. Later, of course. When it's over."

Wetherby smiled faintly. They had come to the turning on to the lane, and followed it along between the hedgerows. An old man on a bicycle pedalled past, going home earlier than usual from the pub. No one stayed out late now. They walked on in silence until they were at The King's Torso.

"Want a drink before you start?" Rose asked.

Wetherby looked at the sky. There was still some light low in the east—as good an excuse as any for delaying.

"All right," he said.

There was only one customer in the pub—Grant the ex-miner, sitting in the corner with a pint of beer. He didn't look at them as they entered, his eyes were turned to the past, towards the bowels of the earth. Rose had a whisky and Wetherby drank a brandy. It tasted good, and he wanted another, but he knew that would not be wise. There was no light left in the east and he set out with forced determination.

"Good man, that," Rose said.

"Hasn't done Hazel Lake much good," Bruce said.

"Who has? He's trying."

"Yeah, I guess that's right. If I had a gun, I'd get out after it myself. Don't have a gun. Read your story in the paper on Sunday. Load of old rubbish, you ask me."

Rose didn't argue.

"Werewolves! Ain't no werewolves. Leastwise, not in England. Might be an immigrant, though, you can't never tell. Or some animal that was sneaked in to avoid quarantine."

Grant looked up. His eyes were deep set in curiously hollow sockets, as if he had come to resemble the holes he had gouged in the earth.

"It's no animal," he said.

His voice was hollow, too, as though he carried his own echoes in his throat.

"What do you think it is, then?" Bruce asked.

"They're making a mistake, looking for it above the ground. That's all I'll say."

"You think it lives in a cave?" Rose asked, looking for an angle.

"Not a cave. In the earth. None of you ever been down in the earth. You don't know. No one knows, if he's never been down in the earth. There are strange things there."

"Like what?" Rose asked.

Grant looked at his empty mug.

"Will you have a drink with me?"

Grant nodded sullenly, taking no favours. He came up to the bar. Bruce filled his mug.

"You were saying?" Rose prompted, jotting the price of a pint on his expense account.

"Eh?"

"These subterranean creatures?"

"Oh, aye. Strange things. You can hear them moving in the shafts and tunnels. And in the rocks, too. They know how to move along the veins. Strange, slimy creatures, oozing through the earth. And stink! You can smell 'em for days after they've been in a tunnel."

"Have you ever seen one?"

"Not me. Once a man's seen one . . . they got him!"

He grasped Rose's jacket suddenly, pulling his face close and hissing the final words. Rose leaped in his strong hands.

"Once they got a man in their slimy claws, you never see him again. They suck him back into the rocks. Just like that. Slurp and he's gone. They hate men, because men have come down to their home, you see. Men disturb them with explosions and drills, and they get even by causing cave-ins. We wake them up, tunnelling through their level, and they don't like it. Oh, we know all about them. We know."

"Why haven't the miners told anyone about these things?"

"We have. But it's all hushed up, you see. The mine owners won't let it get out. They're all in league with the politicians. If people knew what lurks down there, well pretty soon no one would become a miner, see. They're bloody clever, those mine owners. They don't give a damn how many men get slurped into the rock."

Grant stared intensely at Rose. Rose wriggled free from his hands.

"You think this killer comes from under the ground, then?"

"Where else could it come from? Eh? Where else? It figures, don't it? We dig down there, and pretty soon they were bound to start coming up here. And there are thousands of 'em, too. Millions, maybe."

"Are there any recorded instances?"

Grant smiled crookedly. He had said enough for one beer. He went back to his table without reply.

"You don't want to take no notice of him," Bruce said. "Crazy. Works for that mad bastard Byron, so I guess he's crazy, too. Contagious, maybe."

"Byron is surely unbalanced."

"Yeah. The bastard."

Rose sipped his drink contemplatively, his narrow shoulders twitching. He contemplated a subterranean approach in his next article, looked absently towards the window and started. He had suddenly realized that it was dark, and it startled him. It was a considerable walk back to the hotel, and Rose was a man who had never taken a chance in his life, who worried about the statistical chance of being struck by meteors as much as he did motor-cars. He was amazed that his preoccupation, even with the pursuit of success, had left him in his position.

"I'd better be off now," he said, sliding from the stool.

"Say, you on foot?" Bruce asked.

Rose nodded unhappily.

"Well, you better be careful."

"Yeah. I'll hurry."

"Don't do no good to be careful," Grant said.

Rose looked at him nervously.

"You won't see it coming. That's 'cause it don't come at you on the ground, see. It can suddenly pop up right under your feet. That's the way they get you. Pop! Just like that. One minute you're all alone, the next it's got you. Slurp! And down into the ground you go. It's a horrible death."

Rose shuddered as he went out.

Grant moved to the bar to get a refill.

"Say, are there really things like that under the ground?" Bruce asked, looking towards his beer cellar entrance.

"Don't be daft. A beer's a beer."

Rose walked quickly down the lane. He kept his eyes forwards, resisting a temptation to peer back over his shoulder and even to glance suspiciously at the ground beneath his feet, and he told himself that his nervousness was absurd; that the likelihood of anything (a vague anything, he refused to make his dread concrete by giving it a name) happening to him was so remote that it was unimaginable. He worried, of course, but managed to limit his worry to the statistical averages that had always plagued him, as if he were worrying about being struck by a motor-car. The night seemed remarkably dark, although there was a bright moon and no clouds, and the moon cast shadows along the hedgerows and did not benefit failing nerves. Rose began to play a game, fixing his eyes on some point a little distance ahead and concentrating on it as it drew nearer, until he had passed it and then fixing on a new point, breaking the walk up by dividing it into a multitude of short walks. It preoccupied his mind and lessened the tension.

A huge shadow loomed up before him.

Rose gasped and jumped. The shadow jumped with him. He turned in terror, and let his breath out in relief as his heart began to beat once more. It had been his own shadow, thrown before him by the headlights of a silently approaching motorcar. He stepped aside to let the car pass, his heart still pounding, but already calming himself with the thought that there was certainly more danger from motor-cars on this unlighted lane than there could be from his nameless dread.

The motor-car drew past him very slowly. It was a police car.

The driver looked closely at Rose, scrutinizing him with hard eyes, and Rose felt much better knowing that the police were patrolling the area. The car speeded up a bit, winked red brake lights as it came to the junction of the secondary road, then wheeled around the turning. Rose wondered why he hadn't asked for a lift; he supposed that he'd been too startled by that looming shadow to think properly. He began to walk again. He looked ahead, seeking his next point of division, and noticed the red phone box at the junction some hundred yards ahead. That was a convenient point and he stared at it. It seemed to be moving away from him as his eyes played games of their own in the moonlight. He began walking faster. And then, gradually, he realized that whatever was walking on the other side of the hedgerow was walking faster, keeping abreast of him. He had so carefully shut his mind against his fear that the knowledge didn't register as a whole, but seeped into his mind in disintegrated bits. The terror did not come until he had actually turned and looked at the hedgerow; stared as the hedge parted, and he looked into the grotesque face of death.

Rose ran.

He ran as fast as madness could propel him down the narrow lane. He had looked into the face of the killer, but it made no impression on his mind. His mind did not function, he did not feel anything as his instincts took possession of his functions. Perhaps the soundwaves of the feet that padded behind him reached his ears, but his ears sent no impression to his brain. His brain was screaming too loud to hear. He stumbled, but was running too fast to fall; came crashing up against the phone box and yanked the door open; hurled himself inside this cubicle sanctuary of society and pulled the door closed behind him. Something slammed against the closing door with violent fury. Rose was still controlled by his instincts, and they were the instincts of civilized man. He had already jammed his finger in the dial and lifted the receiver to call for impossible salvation, when the door sprang open behind him, and Aaron Rose was drawn down with his finger still hooked in the dial . . .

Wetherby came to the top of the ridge beside a mound of rocks and stood there, looking down. The stream wound through the moonlight like the slimy track of a snail and the open land between was silver-filigreed by the slender shadows of the reeds. Wetherby stood very still and looked. If anything was moving down there, he would have seen its shadow beneath it. This was the first night that the moon had been his ally. But nothing moved, and he saw little sense in proceeding farther in that direction. He decided he would follow the crest of the ridge back to the secondary road, carefully circling each rocky mound ...

Wetherby jumped with realization.

For a moment he quivered, taut and tight, and then he relaxed, cursing his stupidity. He had made his first blunder. He had climbed the ridge and stood beside that high peak of stone, hardly noticing it. He had stood there for several minutes. If the killer had been lurking in those rocks, Wetherby would have died beside them. It was unbelievable carelessness, a mistake he would never have made in the past, a routine that had been second nature to him—until now.

Wetherby was sweating. He mopped his brow and drew his brandy flask out. Byron had been right, he knew, and the knowledge brought Wetherby as close as he had ever been to self-pity. The tension had got to him, and the blunders had begun. He took a large swallow and felt the heat of alcohol along his cold spine. He thought, deeply and objectively, weighing the possibilities and loathing the conclusions. Then he sighed. He knew that he should not be there, that his day was past and his skill was gone. If he continued, he was going to die, and Wetherby did not want to die.

Wetherby turned slowly and started walking back the way he had come. His shoulders felt heavy, he was tired. He was finished. He wondered how he would tell Bell ...

Wetherby came out on the lane just east of The King's Torso. The pub had closed, the lights were off. It was just as well, because Wetherby did not want to see anyone; he felt that his failure was inscribed on his face, that any man could decipher the runes of his defeat. He walked slowly down the lane, keeping in the centre and looking to both sides. He intended to make no more mistakes now, and thought how ironic it would be if he were to die now that he had given up the quest. All he wanted to do was to return to the warm safety of his room, return to London in the morning and close his mind to recrimination. But, to a man like Wetherby, a man like Wetherby had been, the knowledge of this was a torment far greater than death, and his emotions began to rebel against his mind.

Because he was watching the hedgerows with his eyes, and because his senses were directed against his mind, Wetherby did not notice the phone box until he was quite near to it—near enough to see the heap inside, to see that the door was slightly open. The door was open because a leg protruded from the booth. The receiver dangled at the end of its cord. Wetherby opened the door and looked in. A shaft of wind blew past him and the receiver began to revolve very slowly, turning just where the man's head should have been. Wetherby recognized the man's blood-spattered clothing with a cold lack of feeling.

It would make a splendid headline for the newspaper which had employed Aaron Rose.

Wetherby's hand had already stretched out to lift the receiver and telephone for the police when the savage hatred sank a shaft into his brain. It was hatred of himself. He stared at that hand that was so willing to seek help, and he hated himself so much that it was unbearable, that the hatred had to be transferred to save his mind. He stepped out of the booth and let the door swing gently closed on Rose's leg, moved away from the lane and looked at the ground. The tracks were there. He followed them. He was not being cautious now. He was possessed, and caution was there because it was part of his possession; not because he was afraid, but because he must live to kill. He would make no mistake this time. The hunter did not blunder when he did not think.

The tracks ran beside the hedgerow, back the way Wetherby had come. He wondered, without caring, if the creature had been crouched there when he walked past. The trail was plain for some distance before it stopped. But Wetherby paused for only a moment at the end of the tracks. Then he moved on. There was a broken stalk of grass, a crumpled shard of moss, the faintest imprint of a foot. There were all the things that he knew now, as a certainty, but he had failed to see before. He scarcely bothered to look at

them now. His course was direct, and he knew with cold precision
exactly where he was going . . .

13

Byron was waiting.

He was waiting beside the house, but Wetherby did not come up
the walk. He came from behind the woodshed and the moonlight
was running up the barrel of his rifle. Byron stood up and smiled.
His smile formed a curious pattern on his face; he looked in some
strange way relieved.

"You came silently," he said.

He carefully leaned his axe against the house.

"I thought you would never come," he said.

Wetherby said nothing.

"The races were excellent. A pity you missed them. There was
a pile-up at one fence. Two horses killed and a jockey fractured his
collar-bone. One horse had a broken back and they let it suffer until
they could erect a tent around it, so that the people wouldn't see
them kill it. That says something for our world, eh?"

"Where is it, Byron?"

"What, John?"

"I don't know what it is. I want it. I'm absolutely cold, Byron,
and I can kill you if I must."

"That's good. You really should have recognized the tracks long
ago, John. You should have followed it. I know, because I very carefully laid the trail. Did you follow it tonight, or did you guess?"

"I suppose I knew all the time," Wetherby said. His gun was
pointed at the ground but the safety catch was off. "But tonight I
realized something—perhaps it was something you tried to tell me.
It was like a magnet, drawing me here tonight."

"No. It was a touch of your old skill. That's all. The hunter's
instinct." There was respect and genuine affection in his expression. "Do you understand why I did it?"

"I know the purpose in your deranged mind."

"You still think I'm insane? But clever, you must admit. And
I succeeded in giving these rustic clods a reason to live. Perhaps

more than they deserve." Byron leaned against the house. His hand played over the axe handle. "If they had been brave, I might have let them live. Perhaps not. But John, the fear! You should have seen the fear in their eyes . . ."

"Was Hazel Lake supposed to be brave?"

"Oh, what does it matter? Her death made it more terrible for the others, that was all."

Wetherby's finger caressed the trigger. But he couldn't kill yet, it was not resolved. He did not know himself yet.

"What do you think it was?" Byron asked.

"Which?"

"Ah, you'd realized that much. That's good. I made the two-legged tracks, of course. A simple matter of borrowing the claws from several different trophies and fastening them to an old pair of boots. Quite simple, but clever. You were certainly taken in by it. Half bear, half lion. But have you forgotten seeing those other tracks?"

Wetherby was forgetting nothing now, because he was not consciously thinking.

"Wolverine?" he said.

"Excellent, John. Excellent. Remember when we studied those tracks together. Must have been ten years ago now. You mentioned that a wolverine could never be tamed, I believe. It wasn't easy. I was forced to breed one in captivity to get any semblance of control. But then, I always did have a rapport with wild animals. I didn't really tame it, of course. I reduced myself and met it on its own level. It knows I am necessary for its survival, and we hunt together as equals."

"My God," Wetherby said.

"It gets in the cage willingly enough now," Byron said. "It's a bit more difficult after the kill, but I manage. See how simple it was, really? How effective?" Byron's hand had closed on the axe handle. Wetherby ignored it.

"But now, the question, John . . . what are you going to do?"

Byron was balanced, his knees bent. He was enjoying it immensely.

"You haven't a chance," Wetherby said.

"That isn't what I mean. You know I am immune to fear. In that respect, perhaps I am mad. A pleasant madness. But I've longed for you to come, John. You were perhaps the only man alive who had a chance with me. A slight chance. I was so disappointed when I saw how you had changed. How easy you would be. Are you going to try to kill me, John? Or will you try to inform the police? How much is left of the man I knew?"

"I don't know," Wetherby said. Then he said, "Enough."

"Come, I'll show you my bloodthirsty little friend," Byron said, moving suddenly away from the wall. He left the axe where it was, and the quick movement did not cause any reaction in Wetherby. Byron walked past him, close, and Wetherby regarded the space between his shoulders where the bullet would kill. He followed Byron. Byron swung open the angled doors that led to the cellar and went down into the dark. Wetherby went in behind him. It was very dark and for a moment he couldn't see Byron. Then Byron turned the lights on. The wolverine snarled from its cage, its stink filled the close room. Thirty pounds of claws and fangs and pure hatred, it turned its terrible eyes on Wetherby. He stared at it, a small monster that could inspire terror in a grizzly bear or put a pack of wolves to flight. Byron stood beside the cage. He smiled again. Wetherby raised his eyes reluctantly from the hypnotic gaze of the beast and looked at Byron. He looked beyond Byron and felt his stomach turn.

There on the wall, very effectively mounted on oak plaques, three human heads looked with glass eyes across the room. The lips were drawn back in snarls. And hanging from the ceiling, supported by a hook through the scalp, swung a face that Wetherby knew, a man that Wetherby had liked. Aaron Rose's head turned through a slow revolution, until the countenance was full to Wetherby, the face twisted in unspeakable horror and gore dripping from the severed neck. A white glint of bone parted the flesh at the throat. Byron made a sweeping gesture of presentation.

"My trophies," he said.

Then he was not smiling. He was crouched beside the cage, his hand on the lock. The wolverine reached out with curled claws, instinctively, then drew them back with slow reluctance as Byron's fingers scratched its bristling neck.

"Well?" Byron asked.

Wetherby did not move.

"He comes fast, John. There will be time for one shot, perhaps. But I come fast, too."

"Not here," Wetherby said.

Byron's brow arched.

Wetherby knew what he had to do. What he absolutely had to do, beyond right and wrong, beyond hatred and fear ... beyond self-preservation, if need be.

Wetherby worked the lever. The shells spun from the chamber and clattered on the concrete floor. He counted the clicks. Byron too, was counting. Wetherby worked a bullet into the chamber and stopped ejecting.

"Two bullets, John?" Byron asked.

"Bring your friend."

"Ah. Quite so. I judged you badly, John."

Byron was still stroking the wolverine. It was impossible to stroke a wolverine, uncanny and inhuman. But Byron was more than a man. Or less than human. The wolverine rubbed against him, but its eyes were on Wetherby and its fiendish jaws dripped in anticipation.

"If I was wrong, John," Byron said. "If men are beyond salvation, I have at least saved you." Again he smiled.

"Here?" he asked.

"No. Out there."

"Much better."

"I'll walk towards the tors."

"Excellent."

"Don't be long, Byron."

"No. Of course not."

Wetherby moved backwards to the stairs. Then he turned and went up with his back towards Byron. Byron nodded in approval.

"I'll see you soon," Byron said.

Wetherby was afraid.

But it was a healthy fear. It was not the strained tension of the nights before, his senses were alive and tingling, his blood pounded but his muscles were calm. He was smiling in the dark at the crest of the ridge. Every detail of the land was impressed effortlessly on his mind. A solitary cloud was drifting towards the moon, slipping through the sky. It was going to bring black night when it blocked that moonlight, and Wetherby welcomed the shadows because he had no need for light. He wanted very much to live, and he understood Byron at last. In that much, at least, Byron had known. He wanted to live because he was alive, and because the wind was blowing across the moors, and because he had two bullets in his rifle . . .

AFTERWORD
Scream of the Wolf

"You find it fascinating that four human beings have been slaughtered?"

– Scream of the Wolf

I N THE EARLY TEENS of the series, there was some joking that *The Pan Book of Horror Stories* ought to be renamed *The Pan Book of David Case* . . . since editor Herbert van Thal got in the habit of including novella-length Case stories that sometimes ran to half the wordage of his annual collections.

Case in point: "The Hunter", from Case's collection *The Cell: Three Tales of Horror*, which takes up pages 9-92 of the 190-page *Twelfth Pan Book of Horror Stories*, issued in 1971 (with a skull-in-a-snowman cover).

Most of van Thal's selections were simple set-up-and-payoff gruesome jokes—*Tales from the Crypt* retold in a slightly fussy British literary clubman's manner. "The Hunter" is a short mystery novel, which riffs on classic werewolf stories (a frequent Case theme), *The Hound of the Baskervilles* (something is howling on Dartmoor) and Richard Connell's classic, much-imitated short story "The Most Dangerous Game".

It has a good puzzle, gruesome horror and a strong theme in its deconstruction of Hemingwayesque manliness as embodied by the antagonists—big-game hunters who get involved when a series of mauling deaths takes place in the West of England, evoking 1960s tabloid tales of "the Beast of Bodmin" or sundry phantom pumas and leopards reputed to roam the wilder stretches of the countryside.

In 1974, "The Hunter" turned up as *Scream of the Wolf*, a TV movie scripted by novelist Richard Matheson and directed by producer Dan Curtis which relocates the action from Devon to California. *The Pan Book of Horror Stories* always seemed a deeply

British institution, and there was seldom any crossover with what was going on in American horror through its run. Van Thal occasionally reprinted an American writer (Patricia Highsmith's "The Terrapin" is also in the *Twelfth Pan Book of Horror Stories*), but rarely looked to Matheson, Robert Bloch, Ray Bradbury or the other mainstays of August Derleth's anthologies or Rod Serling's TV shows.

However, American eyes were drawn to the anthologies—in need of material for his horror series *Night Gallery* (1969-73), Serling found a few good 'uns in van Thal's backlist, leading to odd US TV credits for R. Chetwynd-Hayes, Basil Copper, Dulcie Grey, Christianna Brand and Oscar Cook.

Curtis, who had cut his teeth on horror with the *Dark Shadows* soap (1966-71), busily set about a two-pronged assault on the TV movie, with adaptations of classic texts (*Strange Case of Dr Jekyll and Mr Hyde*, 1968; *Frankenstein*, 1973; *The Picture of Dorian Gray*, 1973; *The Turn of the Screw*, 1974) and more modern horrors, usually scripted by Matheson (or William F. Nolan) and adapted from more recent fiction. Like Serling, he was voracious enough in his search for material to come across van Thal and, therefore, David Case.

Curtis's contemporary TV movie horrors broke big with *The Night Stalker* (1972), scripted by Matheson (from an unpublished novel by Jeff Rice) and directed by John Llewellyn Moxey, in which washed-up, wise-cracking journo Carl Kolchak (Darren McGavin) investigates a series of murders in Las Vegas and discovers that the culprit is a real-life, dangerous, super-human vampire.

A huge ratings success, *The Night Stalker* inspired Curtis to follow up with a sequel, *The Night Strangler* (1973), and an imitation obviously intended as a series pilot, *The Norliss Tapes* (1973)—though it was Kolchak who spun off into a (short-lived) series.

Scream of the Wolf, which the prolific Curtis and Matheson seemingly dashed off in tea-breaks while they were working on the more elaborate Jack Palance version of *Dracula* (1974), is a faithful adaptation of Case's story, to the extent of lifting whole passages of dialogue, but it also fits the template of *The Night Stalker*.

Again, we get a series of mystery mutilation deaths—more or less, one every act break—and the official cops, represented by Sheriff Vernon Bell (Philip Carey), are baffled while a lone burned-out writer, John Wetherby (Peter Graves), works out the truth and sets out alone to face the monster.

Tracks suggest the killer is an animal which changes weight and scent and runs on four legs but walks on two. In a reversal of the Kolchak format, Wetherby's girlfriend Sandy (Jo Ann Pflug, who'd played Kolchak's girlfriend in *The Night Strangler*) tries to sell him on the werewolf theory, but the protagonist insists (rightly) on a non-supernatural explanation.

It's a whodunit with few suspects—though there's a feint late in the day when obvious culprit Byron Douglas (Clint Walker), who has all but boasted of his guilt, is found ripped to shreds by the mystery monster. The survivor of a wolf-mauling on safari, Byron is oddly reticent about joining in the hunt for the killer beast and claims that all these murders are good for the community, giving the "rustic clods" a sense of being alive even as death threatens them. Sandy isn't the only one to suspect that he might be a were-wolf—which, given the number of shape-shifter TV movies (*Moon of the Wolf*, 1972; *Death Moon*, 1978) around at the time, wasn't too far-fetched a suggestion.

1970s TV movies often cast actors like Graves and Walker (or Darren McGavin), veterans of series TV who got to flex acting muscles in one-off dramas. Graves, of course, had done six seasons of *Mission: Impossible* (1967-73) as IMF master-planner Jim Phelps, and spent the '70s in the likes of *Where Have All the People Gone* (1974) and *Death Car on the Freeway* (1979) before turning to deadpan comedy as the pilot in *Airplane!* (1980).

Walker had done 108 episodes of *Cheyenne* (1955-62) as big, tall Western adventurer Cheyenne Bodie, served as one of *The Dirty Dozen* (1967) and found good TV terror roles in *Killdozer!* (1974) and *Snowbeast* (1977), tackling an alien-possessed bulldozer and a skiing Bigfoot respectively.

Case and Matheson give the leading men quite a bit of dialogue to chew on, and the relationship between the two big-game hunters—Wetherby has lost his nerve and now just writes books while Byron needles him about his masculinity and takes his love of the chase to horrific extremes—is an update of that between Rainsford and Zaroff in "The Most Dangerous Game". Without offending network standards and practices by making it blatant,

Walker also plays Byron as weirdly (and subtly) gay, fixating on his former hunting partner—and doing his best to scare off his heterosexual love interest—and inviting him into a homoerotic dance of manly death which starts with arm-wrestling and winds up with a stalk in the night and a gun loaded with only two bullets.

As in the story, the police procedural elements fall away in the third act, which is all about the confrontation between the two hunters. Like Connell, Case builds up to the titanic fight but then leaves it to the reader's imagination . . . like everyone who's ever made a film of "The Most Dangerous Game", Curtis and Matheson show us what happens and how it all pans out.

1970s TV movies have a particular look and pacing that's engaging and almost comforting—and, courtesy of *Dark Shadows* composer Robert Cobert, *Scream of the Wolf* also has a distinctive jazzy yet sinister sound. Curtis gives us overhead shots of the Californian coast and foggy wooded areas, though Case's original story makes better use of Dartmoor. It's almost a shame the rights weren't snapped up for an episode of the BBC's *Menace* (1970-73) or ITV's *Thriller* (1973-76) . . . imagine William Gaunt (of *Menace*'s wilderness tale "Judas Goat", 1973) and Peter O'Toole (of the BBC's *Rogue Male*, 1977) as Wetherby and Byron in a shot-on-location 1970s British TV adaptation of "The Hunter".

We took films like *Scream of the Wolf* for granted when they were regularly airing on late-night TV, because they're tamer than the theatrically-released horrors of the era . . . but they now have a concise, creepy appeal which shouldn't be overlooked.

Kim Newman
London
September 2015

DAVID F. CASE was born in upstate New York in 1937. Since the early 1960s he has lived in London, as well as spending time in Greece and Spain. His acclaimed collection *The Cell: Three Tales of Horror* appeared in 1969, and it was followed by the novels *Fengriffen: A Chilling Tale*, *Wolf Tracks* and *The Third Grave*. His other collections include *Brotherly Love and Other Tales of Trust and Knowledge*, *Pelican Cay & Other Disquieting Tales*, and an omnibus volume in the *Masters of the Weird Tale* series from Centipede Press. A regular contributor to the legendary *Pan Book of Horror Stories* during the early 1970s, his powerful zombie novella "Pelican Cay" in *Dark Terrors 5* was nominated for a World Fantasy Award in 2001.

STEPHEN JONES lives in London, England. A Hugo Award nominee, he is the winner of three World Fantasy Awards, three International Horror Guild Awards, four Bram Stoker Awards, twenty-one British Fantasy Awards and a Lifetime Achievement Award from the Horror Writers Association. One of Britain's most acclaimed horror and dark fantasy writers and editors, he has more than 135 books to his credit, including *The Art of Horror: An Illustrated History*, *Horrorology: The Lexicon of Fear*, the *Zombie Apocalypse!* series and twenty-six volumes of *Best New Horror*. You can visit his website at www.stephenjoneseditor.com or follow him on Facebook at Stephen Jones–Editor.

KIM NEWMAN is a novelist, critic and broadcaster. His most recent publications include the non-fiction studies *Kim Newman's Movie Dungeon* and *Quatermass and the Pit*, the mini-series *Witchfinder: The Mysteries of Unland* (a spin-off from Mike Mignola's *Hellboy* series with Maura McHugh) for Dark Horse Comics, the expanded reissues of his acclaimed *Anno Dracula* series, and his latest novel, *Secrets of Drearcliff Grange School*. He is a contributing editor to *Sight & Sound* and *Empire* magazines, has written and broadcast widely, and scripted radio and television documentaries. His official website is at www.johnnyalucard.com and he is on Twitter as @AnnoDracula.